# THE
# HERETIC
# ROYAL

Also by G. A. Aiken

NEW YORK TIMES BESTSELLING AUTHOR

# G.A. AIKEN

# THE
# HERETIC
# ROYAL

KENSINGTON
PUBLISHING CORP.

www.kensingtonbooks.com

KENSINGTON BOOKS are published by

Kensington Publishing Corp.
119 West 40th Street
New York, NY 10018

All Kensington titles, imprints, and distributed lines are available at special quantity discounts for bulk purchases for sales promotion, premiums, fundraising, educational, or institutional use.

Special book excerpts or customized printings can also be created to fit specific needs. For details, write or phone the office of the Kensington Sales Manager: Kensington Publishing Corp., 119 West 40th Street, New York, NY 10018. Attn. Sales Department. Phone: 1-800-221-2647.

Kensington and the K logo Reg. U.S. Pat. & TM Off.

ISBN-13: 978-1-4967-3510-2 (ebook)

ISBN-13: 978-1-4967-3508-9

First Kensington Trade Paperback Printing: January 2023

10 9 8 7 6 5 4 3 2 1

Printed in the United States of America

# CHAPTER 1

"*Deal with them.*"

He could not actually hear those words over the sound of all the thundering hooves crashing against the ground—his queen's battalion charging into the town the false ruler had built for herself and her friends—but he could hear the unknown woman's words whispering through the wind, could *see* her in his mind, standing tall and gesturing toward their riders with a toss of her hand.

He tried to yell a warning to the soldiers he was forced to ride with. He himself was no soldier, of course. He shouldn't even be here! But King Marius, the Wielder of Hate, had ordered him to go, and his master had not opposed the command. He was there, apparently, to "help" the soldiers in this attack, and then bring back news of what he'd witnessed. He knew his king didn't expect most of these soldiers to survive; what he really wanted was an idea of how many troops the false queen had left after her battle with the king's half brother. Cyrus the Honored had a powerful and hateful god on his side, but this false queen had still defeated him.

As the battalion had approached early that morning, racing toward the massive gates surrounding the false queen's tower, he truly thought this would not be much of a battle. More like a slaughter. Something the soldiers' true queen, Beatrix, loved to indulge in. But then the chattering wind around them had picked up and, suddenly, the ground beneath their feet shook. Again and again and again. Like something heavy hitting the earth. He tried to stop the soldiers. He warned the commander that they must turn back, but he was summarily dismissed. Ignored. These soldiers had no time for magicks or those who wielded them, when bloodshed and undefended females were on the horizon. So the battalion rode on toward the gates of the false queen's kingdom. They rode on, even as he screamed at them to stop. His caution was no longer due to the moving ground but to what he saw on the other side of those massive gates. Or, rather, looming above them.

Heads and shoulders. Giant heads and shoulders that were encased in armor with openings that allowed scaled wings to freely unfurl from their backs.

He screamed and screamed to the soldiers, but either they continued to ignore him or they couldn't hear him over the sounds of all those hooves. Or maybe their lust for destruction was simply too high for them to see the danger right in front of them. They rode on and he was by their side even after they took the gate down. But then an enormous head—wearing a helm so large a small family could happily live in it with a few pet dogs—appeared in the space between the now-open gates. It drew in breath and almost all the soldiers' horses came to a crashing halt. Prey always knew predators, so the horses that hadn't crashed into each other and fallen to the ground, attempted to turn and run away, despite their riders' snarling demands to keep going forward.

He didn't wait for his horse to react; he turned it away and was charging off when flames, powerful and unforgiving, ripped apart the battalion he'd just left behind. He heard the screams of the men and their horses. At least the ones who weren't immediately disintegrated by the inferno, like the commander and those he'd hand-picked to ride by his side as they led the charge. They were wiped out before they even knew what was happening. But the rest of the battalion . . . they screamed. And screamed. He knew some would try to roll on the ground to put out the flames, but it would be of no use. These weren't the flames of an out-of-control wildfire burning in a forest. No buckets of water or helpful animal skins thrown over writhing bodies were going to help.

He kept riding, even as he used his mind and magicks to call out to his master to warn him. To beg his master to use his strong powers to open a doorway and yank him back to the safety of the true queen's palace.

But as he felt his master respond to his panicked call, asking him what was wrong, the horse he rode abruptly stopped at the sound of a low whistle.

A calm, low whistle he didn't have time to think about before the horse went up on its hind legs, tossing him off in the same moment. He wasn't much of a rider, and the horse had been given to him by one of the soldiers. Meaning the beast had no loyalty to him whatsoever. So when called to stop . . . it stopped.

He fell hard, barely able to wrap himself in a protection spell before he hit the ground. He'd saved himself a broken spine, which was the most he could ask. It still took him time to get back to his feet because the wind was knocked out of him. But, to his triumph, he did get up. He did stand on his shaky legs.

Then a voice behind him asked, "And what are you doing, wizard?"

He froze, piss running down his leg even before he looked behind him. That's how great was the fear their kind caused. Just *knowing* they were around made a man or wizard soil himself.

Even the fact that it sounded like a female voice gave him no comfort. The females were known to be more ferocious than any of the males.

He forced himself to face the thing that had spoken to him. Like the others he'd seen, this one was covered in armor and weapons. A helm on its head; chainmail and plate protecting the important parts of its body. It stood over him like the false queen's tower, but he'd felt no dread looking at that tower. It was just something to be brought down, hopefully with the false queen's family inside. That would bring the true queen great joy!

But his chance to prove himself to his queen and master were now gone.

The creature gazed at him for what felt like forever until the tall, ancient forest trees behind it began to move and another one of those things appeared.

"What are you doing?" the new one asked, its voice male.

"Found this one trying to escape the fate of that army over there," the other replied, gesturing with a black talon.

"Ooooh," the male said. "Breakfast."

"You can eat later. Should we take this one back to Annwyl?"

Even though the dragon was not speaking to him, he opened his mouth to insist that, "Yes, you should take me back to whomever you want," in the hopes of garnering a few more seconds of life. But something tore through his chest with such force, he felt his heart tear from its moorings. With only a few seconds of life left, he looked down to see that it wasn't a spear that had gone through his body but a . . . tail?

A tail covered in scales with a sharp point at the end. A point that now held his still-beating heart. The attack had been that swift.

"Keep the horse," the owner of the tail ordered. "He's good stock. But no mercy for anyone who would abandon their own army to run away."

He felt his body floating away from the ground and assumed his god had come for him. But as his sight dimmed and the last of his breath and blood left his body, he realized that it was the tail still stuck in his chest that was lifting him.

"And," the male said from the enveloping darkness, "if you're hungry, have this one's heart. It seems quite juicy."

*"Kill all of them!"*

Ainsley closed her eyes and waited to be wiped out by flames just as the attacking army had been wiped out a few moments before. But after nearly a minute of waiting . . . she realized she was still alive. Maybe.

She forced herself to open one eye to see if she was still alive or on the next plane of existence. Maybe with her ancestors waiting for her. Or maybe she would be floating in space, waiting for her soul to be called back to earth for a newborn.

But no, none of that was happening. Instead, she was still in the middle of the fortress training ring, behind her sisters, with a crazed warrior woman standing in front of them . . . and dragons. She was surrounded by gargantuan dragons.

Dragons that could speak. Just like she spoke. They could also smile, laugh, and appear annoyed. All the things that Ainsley considered uniquely human, they could do.

Of course, they could also fly, breathe fire, and crush any human merely by stepping on them.

And yet, despite the many things they could do to destroy all life around them, it wasn't the dragons that made Ainsley the most afraid.

Although terrifying, the dragons seemed restrained in their immaculate armor and polite conversation. She could almost imagine some of them offering a "beg your pardon" before treating a defenseless human like a pastry treat shoved into one of those horrifying maws.

No. Her fear and, she was guessing, the fear of her sisters, was centered on the woman. The human woman standing before them in a sleeveless chainmail shirt and leather leggings and boots. She had big, strong arms covered in scars; two short swords strapped to her back; and long, loose, dark brown hair with golden streaks that looked as if it hadn't seen a comb in years. But even with that hair covering most of her face, Ainsley could still see multiple scars going from one side to the other. Some were long and jagged, going from her forehead down to her jaw. Other scars were short but deep. All proving that the woman had been in more than one battle and had survived.

It was her eyes, though. Those dark, gray-green eyes that made Ainsley shudder.

Because they were the eyes of a madwoman.

A madwoman with control of dragons. A lot of dragons that could talk and use weapons beyond their ability to breathe fire.

The suns weren't even up, and it was already a shitty day!

The madwoman pointed at her eldest sister, Keeley, and demanded, "Is it you? Are you the enslaver?"

Keeley opened her mouth to speak, but only an odd squeak came out. Ainsley leaned around her to see her face, and Keeley cleared her throat before trying once more. She didn't even manage a squeak on her second try. All that came out was a weird grunt.

Eyes wide, Ainsley's second oldest sister, Gemma, looked back and up at Keeley.

"What are you doing?" she hissed between gritted teeth.

But all Keeley could manage was a panicked fluttering of her hands and a shake of her head.

Gemma crossed her eyes and looked back at the madwoman. "I—" was all she got out before the madwoman pointed at the rune embroidered on Gemma's surcoat and snarled, "Are you a monk?"

"Uh . . ." Maybe it was the way the question was asked that disturbed Gemma. Or the crazed look in the madwoman's eyes. But whatever it was, "uh" was the only thing Ainsley's sister, a war monk who had destroyed enemies without even a moment of regret or fear, could manage at the moment.

Putting all of them in a precarious position. Since their silence seemed to enrage the madwoman.

"Well?" the madwoman pushed. "*ANSWER ME!*"

He sensed her fear through the wind; the breeze touching the tips of his ears. He sat up and let his gaze examine the lands around him. He saw nothing, but knew something was wrong. Not just from her fear but . . .

The wind. It was the wind that told him something was wrong. There should be no wind on this early morning. It should be still. Calm. But there was a strong wind, making the trees sway wildly back and forth. The younger, weaker trunks appeared ready to snap from the force.

He stood and his pack stood with him. She needed him. He could feel it through the ground beneath his paws. Could smell it in the wild wind that whipped around him. Could hear it in the silence of the early-morning birds and the crows that didn't caw and croak and complain.

Wasting no more time, he ran. He ran with everything he had. Ran as if the demons of his hell spurred him on with their whips of chain and fire. Because she needed him and nothing, absolutely nothing would stop him from going to her and protecting the human female who had protected him as a pup and cared for him until he was old enough and strong enough to care for himself.

He charged over hills and through villages, past lakes and through rivers, into forests and out of caves until he reached her territory. He and his pack dashed through the destroyed gates, spotting warrior monks and witches and priests standing outside the town walls with their weapons at the ready but none of them making a decisive move to protect the queen who had protected them. He sneered at their weakness, leaping over the burned bodies of soldiers and guards.

He noticed the dragons in the training ring, standing tall and proud in their battle armor, but that didn't stop him or his pack. Every hell had its own dragons, and they were more terrifying than these mortal ones with their long, shiny hair and rules of etiquette. Hells' dragons had no etiquette.

He jumped over the clawed feet and charged around the threatening tails so he could reach the human woman he adored. He saw her, standing with two of her sisters. Before them all stood a woman. She yelled at the one he protected and her sisters. He picked up speed, preparing to leap onto the female intruder's back and take her down to the ground, where he could destroy her before any harm came to his human.

But as he readied his body to leap the last few feet, the woman turned her head. When he saw her profile, he braced all four paws in front of himself to stop his full-speed run. The rest of his pack tumbled over one another in their attempt to stop as well, for they'd recognized the woman too, even though they'd never seen her in person. Had never stood before her. Had never heard her voice. They all still knew her. Everyone in every hell knew her.

Finally spotting the pack, the woman turned to face them fully, and that's when he spun around and sprinted out the way he'd come.

The children, he realized. He should sneak up to the high tower floors and protect the children. That's what his human would want him to do. Right? At least that's what he convinced himself of as he led his pack as far away from the crazed female as he could get.

Ainsley watched the demon wolf that her eldest sister adored—and that adored her back—awkwardly spin around with his entire demon wolf pack and run away.

She blinked. Stunned.

Every one of those beasts had looked right at the dragons and continued to charge in to help Ainsley's sister, but as soon as this madwoman turned to look at them . . . they ran away?

Over the years, Ainsley had seen those wolves and the lead wolf in particular, put themselves in the most dangerous of situations simply to protect Keeley. But one look at this woman and . . .

They ran away.

Even more frightening than the demon wolves running away

was the realization that Ainsley had yet to see any of the centaurs. They had a whole army's worth of centaurs roaming these lands to help Queen Keeley keep the crown from her sister. Meaning that Keeley couldn't burp without a centaur rushing to her side to make sure she was safe. And yet the queen and her two royal sisters were surrounded by dragons and not one centaur had shown up?

Had they truly heard nothing? Seen nothing of the many dragons flying overhead? Had they not even smelled the burning flesh?

How was that possible . . . ?

Unless the mighty centaurs were already dead.

Gods, if that was true . . .

It was time to go. With the centaurs burned to ash—most likely—and the demon wolves making a mad escape, Ainsley was not about to stand here and wait to be torn apart by the claws and fangs of dragons. Did this madwoman have claws and fangs, too? She might! There was nothing Ainsley wouldn't believe at this moment.

So she would remove herself and get to higher ground. She just needed a bow and arrow to pierce this female through the heart and, hopefully, be done with her. Or, at the very least, weaken her so that all the fanatic monks and priests waiting on the other side of the town wall could attack.

What Ainsley was *not* going to do, however, was stand here, waiting to die.

Ainsley took one small step back but, without turning, Gemma reached around their eldest sister and grabbed hold of Ainsley's hand.

She yanked her close so that Ainsley now stood in front of Keeley as well. A position she did not enjoy. Then Gemma pressed her booted foot against Ainsley's to hold her in place.

"You're not going anywhere," Gemma whispered, ignoring her sister's pained whimper.

"Aren't *I* the baby?" Ainsley demanded. "You two have always insisted on protecting me."

"Your baby days are officially over, and that means we protect the *queen*. And that's not you!"

"After you two are killed by that crazy woman and eaten by the dragons, I'll be queen and—*oww!* You cow!" she gasped after Gemma rammed that foot down onto hers.

"You will stay here with us and we will all die together!" Gemma angrily hissed. "Like a *family.*"

"Stop muttering!" the madwoman barked out.

"Sorry," Gemma quickly replied, her foot again pinning Ainsley's to the ground.

The madwoman waved Gemma away and replied, "I'm not talking to you."

Ainsley glanced back at Keeley, but her eldest sister could do nothing but shrug. Because if the madwoman wasn't talking to Ainsley and Gemma, then who was she . . . ?

"Who the hells are you talking to?" a dragon asked, removing its helm to reveal shiny black hair tied into a braid that went down its back. But a short lock of that hair fell across its dark eyes, somehow making it appear much less monstrous.

The madwoman faced the dragon, boldly staring at it.

"Does who I'm talking to matter right now?" the madwoman asked.

Frowning, the dragon simply replied, "Yes. Yes, it does matter."

He hated this.

Hated it with everything in him.

And because of the treacherous behavior of blood kin more than seven thousand years ago . . . he was now forced to endure it, had been enduring it every week for more than a year now.

This predawn meeting was particularly bad because there was nothing to discuss. One large battle had ended not too long ago, but there were more battles to come. Something they were all prepared and trained for. Why they were here in the first place to go over and over things they already knew, he had no idea.

He looked around at all the centaurs in the apple grove, forced to waste their time, while Her Royal Highness—Princess Laila of the Scarred Earth Clan and future Ruling Mare of the Amichai—rambled on about the most mundane things on this good earth.

If it were any other day, he would grunt and stomp his hind legs until he annoyed the two brothers of Her Royal Highness so much, she told him and his tribe to leave in order to keep her kin from starting a fight they could never possibly win. Like her mother, Princess Laila wisely avoided any fights with his tribe. Her ancestors may have won the throne seven thousand years ago, but they'd never win it now. So she permitted no opening that would allow such a thing. See? Wise.

But today, he did nothing to force Her Royal Highness to end this ridiculous meeting of centaurs. Because today something was actually *happening*.

It had started just minutes before this waste-of-time event, when Gruffyn of the Torn Moon Clan had felt the power of ancient magicks flow over him like a warm blanket. He'd immediately snapped awake and looked around him, expecting to find some master wizard standing directly before him. But he'd only found Sarff, the female who had trained him in the way of magicks and mystical powers and beheadings. She gazed up at the sky but Gruff saw nothing. That, of course, only meant that whoever wielded this power was much stronger than he could ever dream.

"Good," Sarff had muttered when he'd come to stand beside her; her gaze still locked on the sky. "I was worried you'd sleep through all this like the rest of our pitiful tribe." She'd gestured to his sleeping sister and the team members handpicked by his father. Their orders a year ago had been simple: join the other centaur warrior clans chosen to protect and assist the new human queen. Something that made none of the clans happy. Why were they protecting a *human* queen? The humans had never done anything to protect them. But the ruling mare would hear no dissent. So Gruff and the others had followed orders, as they'd been trained to do.

It wasn't easy, though. Being around all these humans. The new royals—Queen Keeley and her lot—had no problem with Gruff's kind, accepting them easily and without concern. But the others, from peasants to those of royal blood who could trace their lineage back centuries, were much less comfortable with those born with two arms and four legs. Some centaurs attempted to ease the concerns of these people by spending most days in their human form. But that had become less effective now that everyone understood centaurs wore chainmail kilts. The kilts, created by their best centaur blacksmiths and enhanced by their strongest shamans, allowed their kind to shift between their natural and human forms as often as necessary because the mail changed with them. As humans, the kilts hid their nakedness. But as centaurs, the chainmail protected their flanks during battle, adjusting to the size of the wearer as needed. It was ingenious armor and, for millennia, had successfully hidden Gruff's kind from human eyes. Centaurs could walk around the humans of this land and be thought of as nothing more than "those strange Amichai folk." But now it seemed that everyone knew most of the Amichai folk were centaurs. Not all of them, of course. There were a few tribes that lived at the base of the Amichai Mountains that were humans whose families had been part of those lands for eons.

Unfortunately, everything had changed because of a fight for power between two sisters: Queen Keeley and Queen Beatrix. It was believed that if Queen Keeley won this war, the Amichai could go back to their mountains and live a mostly peaceful life. But if Queen Beatrix and her massive armies won, there would be no peace for anyone. When the war started, Gruff thought the ruling mare and her mate were being overdramatic about it all, but after two years of Beatrix's rule, he'd come to realize that her reign would be a nightmare from which no one would ever wake.

So here they all were, attempting to help, even though many of them really didn't want to.

Nor did their common purpose make them a close, friendly bunch. In fact, the other centaur tribes found Gruff's kin "a lot to take," as a fellow centaur had put it less than two days after they'd set off for Queen Keeley's lands. There were several reasons for that general opinion.

First, it was the Torn Moon Clan's attitude. They were known for being difficult, terse, and extremely unfriendly. Not one or two members of their clan but *all* of them. From the oldest stallion to the youngest foal. Most of Gruff's kin found mates who were un-friendly and difficult simply to ensure they kept their bloodline strong.

Then, of course, there was the clan's insatiable lust for vengeance. But if vengeance could not be quickly obtained, that wasn't a problem, because the Torn Moon Clan loved holding a grudge.

That wasn't all that set Gruff's clan apart from his fellow Amichai.

It was their warrior centaur form—the form they shifted into during battle—that disturbed the others most. Their battle antlers were different. Their eyes. Even their size was considered unnatural. But whether centaur or warrior centaur, the Torn Moon Clan's hooves always set them apart from the others. For while most centaurs roamed the lower and mid-levels of the Amichai Mountain range, Gruff's people made the highest mountaintops their home. Close to snow and ice, with the big-horned sheep and goats nearby. Those born directly into the Torn Moon bloodline not only tolerated—and thrived in—the brutal cold of those high-up terrains but they also had hooves that allowed them to climb hills and mountainsides the way other centaurs could race across open fields. It was a skill many complained was "strange" or "disturbing," but Gruff knew they were simply jealous of the Torn Moon's agility. Especially during brutal battles when the high ground gave them such a massive advantage.

Gruff enjoyed being up high. It gave him a clear view of *all* his enemies, which was good, because as his clan's appointed Grudge Holder, it was important to know his enemies' locations in case any grudge-debts had to be paid.

Turning his head this way and that, Gruff hoped to hear something that would give him an idea of what was going on. No one unleashed such powerful magicks without reason. But he'd heard nothing. Something that bothered him more than if he'd heard the sounds of a brutal battle.

"Yes," Sarff had agreed, noting his movements. "You're right. No snow wolves slinking back to their dens for day-sleep. No birds. No ice sheep. Everything is quiet." She'd closed her eyes and lifted her face to the sky. "And the magicks are so strong. I haven't felt anything like this before."

That was truly something, because there wasn't much Sarff had not "felt" before; the battle witch was renowned for her brutal skills with a spell or a mace.

Like Sarff, Gruff had a way with the steel and a kinship to the gods that allowed him to call on the powers of air, earth, and fire during battle. He doubted he'd ever have Sarff's powers, but he was not sure he'd want them. Communicating with gods directly didn't sound like something he'd enjoy at all.

"This could be bad, ya know." Sarff had briefly glanced at him before turning her gaze back to the sky. "Magicks like that ain't here by accident. We should prepare ourselves for battle."

The Torn Moon Clan was always prepared for battle. They slept standing up with their weapons strapped to their bodies. And when they chose their mates, they didn't give a piece of jewelry as a sign of lifelong commitment but a small, sharpened blade with a jewel-encrusted handle.

Gruff let his senses reach out and they immediately hit a mystical wall that was so strong it might as well be physical. It might as well be made of steel or the mountain he stood on. His gaze had searched the horizon before him while he'd let his senses feel along the mystical wall.

To untrained eyes nothing would look wrong or out of place, but that wall that hid something mighty from his and Sarff's view.

Now, that was real power. A power he could only dream of possessing.

What truly concerned him, though, was that he didn't understand what was being hidden. The prey inside him sensed danger nearby, but he sensed that every moment he was awake. What he didn't feel, however, was a need to run. When he wanted to run, he knew something truly terrifying was coming; his prey animal told him to escape before it was too late. It was a need that, as a warrior, he had been trained since birth to control and manage so he never brought shame on his clan.

"I don't understand," Sarff had said softly, echoing his thoughts. "What are we *not* supposed to see?"

That's what worried Gruff then and now, during this ridiculous meeting. It took an immense amount of power to hide the true world from the view of many. A power that would drain the one who unleashed it and leave the earth they stood upon, bleeding. Why would any magickal being risk so much?

"Are you hearing voices again?" a silver dragon barked.

"I don't hear voices," the madwoman snapped back before adding, "Anymore."

"Is that supposed to make us feel better?" the silver demanded. "Because it does *not*."

"If you don't hear voices, then who are you speaking to?" the black dragon softly asked.

She pointed to a spot behind a gold dragon. "Them."

"Oh, gods," Ainsley heard Gemma breathe out. "Those idiots."

It was a unit of war monks. Gemma was the leader of her order, but some of the other orders had yet to accept her control of their armies. For instance, the small unit moving slowly across the courtyard had refused to have anything to do with Gemma because they believed their primary war god hated the one her order followed. Just remembering that had Ainsley rolling her eyes.

And it was this same, ridiculous order that was heading toward the madwoman, not for any logical reason, she was sure, but because of some religious rule that no one with sense would understand or obey. Especially since these particular war monks were known for being a fanatical order that wore all black and abstained from any sex. Even with each other. Ainsley found them endlessly fascinating because she couldn't imagine anyone willingly taking on such a restriction. Even for a god.

Gemma motioned the monks away with a wide wave of her arm, but she was ignored. Ainsley hoped that Gemma would start waving with both arms because that would finally force her to release Ainsley's hand, but no.

A gold dragon watched the monks move around him but didn't make any defensive moves.

Once the group was mostly in front of the dragon, the monk leading the way aimed a damning finger at the madwoman and announced, "We know who you are, vile female! We know what you've done!"

Ainsley gawked, fascinated by the unfolding drama, while the dragons did nothing more than roll their eyes or toss their front claws up in obvious frustration and disbelief.

The madwoman's eyes narrowed on the monks, and Ainsley cringed a little. Because she looked even more terrifying when she seemed to lock onto a target. And right now, all those strident monks were the madwoman's target.

"*We will not let you do your deadly work here, Annwyl the Bloody!*" the monk yelled.

Ainsley saw Gemma's entire body stiffen and her grip on Ainsley's hand tightened so much, she finally had to yank it away before her sister broke all the bones.

"What's wrong?" Ainsley demanded, rubbing her hand.

"That woman is Annwyl the Bloody."

"It can't be," Keeley gasped out. "It can't be Annwyl the Bloody. It can't!"

Ainsley pulled her foot out from under Gemma's, took a step back, and asked the only thing she could think of: "Who?"

# CHAPTER 2

Sister Olga peeked from under her lashes and watched as her fellow novitiate sister stood and turned away from the blessed object of devotion dedicated to their god.

As her tall sister-in-training headed toward the door of their quarters, Olga continued to watch. Although she knew she should be focused on her prayers—her prayers would help keep her and her sisters safe—she could never turn away from Sister Hilda. Because no one ever knew what Hilda was about to do next.

"And where do you think you are going, Sister Hilda?" Mother Superior demanded as soon as Hilda's hand landed on the door handle.

"I'm going to find out what's going on outside." Hilda always spoke with absolute confidence, no matter the situation. Olga envied her such confidence. None of the other novitiates had anything like it.

"There's nothing going on outside, Sister."

"Really?" Hilda replied. "The screaming suggests there is."

"Let me rephrase, then. There's nothing going on outside that you need to see."

"The screams of 'Dragon! Dear gods! It's dragons! We're all going to die!' suggests there is something out there for me to see."

"There's no such thing as dragons."

"So everyone in town is simply having a mass delusion?"

"Well, let's say there are dragons. What—exactly—will *you* do?"

"Not sure. Perhaps warn you if they are about to burn this *wooden* hut down."

Mother Superior tucked her hands inside the sleeves of her robes. "Sister Hilda, you will stay here and pray with your sisters. Now get back over to the—"

"No," Hilda boldly cut in, as was her way. "I will go outside and find out what's going on and help if necessary."

"You were given an order, Sister. Now follow it."

Hilda let out a breath. A clear sign she was barely holding on to her patience. She had very little as it was. After a moment, she faced Mother Superior. Hilda towered over their spiritual leader as she towered over most of the novitiates. She wasn't merely tall, though. She was wide of shoulder and powerful of thigh. Some of the older nuns joked amongst themselves that she was secretly one of the centaurs in human form, but Olga felt certain Hilda wasn't. Mostly because Hilda didn't pay any attention to the centaurs. If she was trying to pretend *not* to be a centaur, she would probably try harder to distance herself from them. But she didn't seem to care about them or for them and if she had to talk to them for some reason, she did. If she needed something from them, she asked. And if they managed to get on her nerves for some reason, she told them to . . . well . . . "fuck off." An incident that would set back Hilda's novitiate training at least another year as punishment.

And, Olga feared, whatever was about to happen might put Hilda's novitiate training back for a lifetime.

"You do understand," Hilda said in that cool way she had, "my role here is not merely to pray. I am not here to be an inactive devotee to our god. I am to be a battle nun. I am to protect the religious sisters of all orders to the best of my ability. I can't do that if I'm locked away . . . *praying*."

"The Abbess will protect us," Mother Superior insisted. "She is fully trained and a full battle nun. You, however, are nothing more than a novitiate. And will do as you are told. Now . . . back in line, and pray."

"No," Hilda said, turning again to the door.

Mother Superior, finally losing patience with one of her nuns ignoring her orders, grabbed Hilda's upper arm.

No longer able to discreetly watch from under her lashes, Olga opened her eyes wide and almost called out for Mother Superior to stop and let Hilda go. But it was too late for any of that.

Hilda turned and, with her free hand, grabbed Mother Superior by the throat, forcing her back as she choked her.

What was frightening . . . terrifying, really, was that the expression on Hilda's face never changed. She didn't look angry. She didn't explode in rage. Although, in truth, she never did. But everyone knew that Hilda didn't like to be touched. Unlike the rest of them, who felt that their vow of chastity was a painful, hard sacrifice they would only make for the god they loved, Hilda felt no such loss. She enjoyed remaining untouched by anyone and everyone, and she had never been shy about announcing it to the universe.

So putting a hand on her had been foolhardy at best, downright stupid at worst.

The strong, hearty nuns who used to work the fields of their old convent before it had been burned down rushed to Mother Superior's side, doing their best to pull Hilda's hand off their leader's throat. But while the nuns might be strong, a battle nun was stronger.

"I've made it so clear, for so long, what my calling is," Hilda calmly explained while continuing to choke Mother Superior, "and you continue to ignore me. But when I hear the screams of others and I know that my order is in grave danger, then I believe *my* god wants me to do all I can to protect everyone. That is my true calling. That is the role I have been given to perform. And I will not let anyone stop me."

Hilda neared the sacred altar where the blessed object of the order's devotion lay, surrounded by a multitude of candles that must be kept lit at all times. Before one candle could go out, a new one would be placed down and lit. Nuns surrounded the altar all day and night, their only duty at that time to manage the many candles.

When Hilda had marched Mother Superior up to the sacred altar, she stopped. Olga was sure Mother Superior could feel the heat from all those candles so close to her highly flammable robes. No one knew Hilda well enough to be sure she would not purposely set their Mother Superior on fire.

"Do we now understand each other, Mother Superior?"

But Mother Superior didn't answer. She, like the other nuns, was too busy trying to pull Hilda's hand away from her throat.

That's when Hilda shoved Mother Superior hard into the sacred altar, knocking over many of the candles. Thankfully, instead of setting Mother Superior's robes on fire, they simply fell over and went out, but that seemed to panic the older nuns more than if their leader had instead burst into flames. There were screams of, "Noooo!" and most of the sisters jumped into action, rushing to reposition and relight all the candles that had fallen.

Hilda released Mother Superior then, watching the woman drop to her knees and gasp desperately for air. Then she turned and walked out the door. Only Olga and Mother Superior noticed her exit. Only Olga and Mother Superior cared about it.

The once-every-new-moon meeting continued as planned, but neither Her Royal Highness nor her two brothers seemed to notice that something extraordinary was happening at this very moment. All around them power and danger flowed like rushing waters off a cliff. And yet, other than his own clan, the centaurs noticed nothing. Felt nothing. To them it was like any other day. How could they all be so blind to what every other animal had noticed?

Usually, when they had these meetings, herds of wild horses showed up because they knew the centaurs would share their apples with them. Horses knew they were safe around Gruff's people. Yet no herd had come and, even worse, none of the Amichai had noticed.

How these "royal" centaurs had lasted as long as they had, confounded him. Could his clan have really lost the reins of power to *these* centaurs? Really?

It was a story known by every centaur. How seven thousand and three years ago, the members of Torn Moon Clan were the leaders of the Amichai. His ancestors had brought the many centaur clans together and led them into the Amichai Mountains with a plan to make centaurs the rulers of a world gone mad. It was a world with out-of-control humans murdering anything and everything in their way; dragons eating anything that crossed their path; minotaur tribes constantly at war with each other and not caring who or what got trampled during those bloody battles; dwarves carelessly building their cities under the ground and ignoring the occasional sink-holes they created—entire villages and cities sometimes disappearing due to accidental explosions and unplanned rock slides; and the mad elves using other beings in their "experiments."

The Torn Moon Clan had intended to put a stop to the insanity and get control of all the land on both sides of the Amichai Mountains. Gruff had no idea how they'd hoped to achieve their plans—it was so long ago—but he had complete faith in his war-loving ancestors. He doubted their ideas would have been pleasant, but he was sure they would have been effective.

What happened next had mostly been lost to history, but the gist of it was that the Torn Moon's cousins, the Scarred Earth tribe, worked behind their own blood kins' collective backs to put truces and alliances in place. Lands were divided. As the border between the dragons' lands and everyone else, the Amichai Mountains were important territory. The only ones not involved in any of the negotiations were the Torn Moon Clan and the humans. Apparently neither could be trusted not to "start the killing." The humans out of sheer panic at seeing all the different species that lived among them, and the Torn Moon Clan because . . . well . . . because they seemed to just enjoy killing.

Although that wasn't true. It was really that the Torn Moon Clan didn't shy away from war and, sometimes, war was the only way out of bad situations. And splitting up their lands so that humans could feel safe seemed like a bad decision to his tribe. Too bad the Ruling Mare never got her chance to explain that. Instead, her cousins decided to betray her and the Torn Moon Clan.

By the time the Ruling Mare found out what was going on, the other clans had been turned against her, and binding agreements had already been signed in blood. When the Ruling Mare refused to relinquish her crown, a vicious honor fight ended the reign of Gruff's clan and firmly put the Scarred Earth on the throne from then until now.

It wasn't knowing their ancestor had lost the single combat contest that bothered the Torn Moon Clan so much. A loss was a loss. If you couldn't win a fight, you shouldn't be in command. If his ancestor's eldest daughter had been old enough, she would have most likely fought her mother for that crown herself one day. Maybe even killed her if necessary. And done it with no remorse.

Instead, what bothered Gruff's clan was what the Scarred Earth had done beforehand. Going behind the Ruling Mare's back, arranging alliances with dragons, minotaurs, elves, and dwarves without even telling her. Turning the other clans against their own cousins before challenging them for the throne.

As far as Gruff's clan was concerned—then and now—the Scarred Earth didn't *deserve* their throne. They were too disloyal. Too untrustworthy. Too human.

And although it had been more than seven thousand years since those events had transpired, the trait the Torn Moon Clan was best known for—then and now—was holding a grudge.

In fact, Gruff's official title was Holder of the Grudge. It meant that one day he would lead his clan. Not because his father was the Ruling Stallion but because his grudge holding had become infamous before he'd even hit his tenth winter. As his mother had said at the time, "How can a brood mare *not* be proud?"

"Do you see something, Cousin?"

Without moving his head, Gruff shifted his gaze to the royal who'd asked the question. One of Her Royal Highness's brothers. The dark-haired one. He was smarter than the light-haired one. But both were idiots.

Even now they were just standing there . . . staring at him . . . their tails slapping the flies away from their useless asses.

"Well?" the dark-haired one pushed. "Are you going to answer me?"

"My brother did answer you," Briallen flatly told the royals.

"He did?"

"He did. When he grunted."

Smirking, the light-haired one asked, "Your brother *grunted* his answer at us?"

"You're lucky he did that . . . Cousin. If it were me, I'd let you all burn," Briallen retorted.

"Such a charming mare!" the light-haired one cheered.

"Let us all burn?" the smarter one asked. "What the fuck does that even mean?"

"Don't you royals feel it at all?" Sarff sneered. "The power that fills the air?"

"He's staring at power filling the air?" the dark-haired one shot back.

"No." The healer pointed deeper into the copse of trees. "He's staring at her."

As one, the other tribes all turned toward the tall, white-haired female dressed in pristine white robes. She leaned comfortably against one of the trees and ate an apple.

"Who?" the dark-haired one asked.

"See how blind they are, Gruffyn? To the danger?" the battle witch asked.

"What danger, Sarff?" Her Royal Highness responded, moving past her useless brothers. "I don't see anyone."

Sarff glanced at him, and Gruff grunted at her silent question.

"You see nothing, but Gruffyn and I see a tall female with white hair and a scar on her face. She is watching us."

"A spy?" Her Royal Highness asked, narrowing her eyes on a spot a few feet away from where the woman stood, trying to search for what Gruff and Sarff saw.

"No. Not a spy. She looks like a human woman . . . but she's not."

"Then what is she?"

Sarff shrugged her small shoulders and calmly replied, "A dragon."

Her Royal Highness frowned, confused. The dark-haired one sighed and turned to walk away. The light-haired one crossed his eyes like an annoyed yearling and chuckled.

"You two see a . . . dragon?" Her Royal Highness haltingly asked.

"No. We see a woman."

"A woman. Doing what?"

"Eating an apple. Yes, Gruff?" Sarff checked with him. And he grunted in response because Sarff understood his grunts.

"But it's not a woman eating an apple . . . it's a *dragon*?"

"Right. She's a dragon eating an apple. Guess they like apples, too."

"Can we just get back to the meeting?" the dark-haired one barked over his shoulder, refusing even to look at them.

"Perhaps my brother has a point—" Her Royal Highness gently remarked, beginning to turn away.

"But," Sarff cut in, "we smell the flame. Feel the beat of the wings. It took some time to get through the magicks, but Gruffyn and I are starting to feel their presence."

Sarff was correct. Gruff was starting to feel the beasts all around him. That's why the other animals were gone. That's why they were all hiding. They didn't want to end up as ashes. Or a quick meal.

"Dragons," the light-haired one said, already bored with the conversation. "Uh-huh."

"*Their* presence?" Her Highness asked.

"Even now," Sarff said, a small smile on her lips, "they invade your queen's tower."

Gruff's treacherous cousins turned in the direction of the tower. It rose up from the town walls and battlements that encircled it, the two suns beginning to light the stonemason dwarves' creation. And, Gruff was sure, it appeared completely fine to those who could not see or feel the powerful magicks of the dragons.

They proved Gruff's point by turning back to him and his tribemates and saying in unison, "Huh."

Brother Batsheva, a novitiate from the Order of Righteous Valor, watched in fascination as the monks of a different—and entirely foolish—order moved closer to the dragons so they could challenge a crazed warrior. These were not small dragons, either, but the really big ones she'd always heard about growing up. It wasn't that they were simply dragons, though that was terrifying. Or that they could unleash flame and fly. All of which was horrifying on its own. But she hunted bear when she could, and they were big and terrifying too. No, it wasn't the size of the dragons or their power. All wild animals were powerful but could be handled when necessary. What concerned her was that one didn't find many bears wearing chainmail and wielding swords. Or chatting with each other like they were at a bloody tea party. Bears didn't do that, which made bears much easier to kill.

These dragons, however, were . . . thoughtful? Yes. Thoughtful and rational. Reasonable, even. Meaning they would be much harder to kill than if they were instinctive killing machines burning everything in sight.

That's why she was staying back here, behind one of the barracks that allowed her to watch what was going on without actually being seen. Because unlike the other monks, she had no intention of challenging dragons or the insane woman leading them.

Of course, Sheva's attitude was probably why, after joining the monkhood as a young child, she was still a novitiate after nearly two decades among the Order of Righteous Valor. As she'd informed an elder once, "I said I'd *fight* for our god. I never said I'd die for him."

Just the look in the old bastard's eyes had told her that he was going to do his best to keep her right where she was . . . cleaning up horse shit and other brothers' weapons. Fun!

A hand grazed Sheva's back and she unsheathed her short sword, turning quickly before she could be struck down first. But her wrist was caught mid-swing and her arm held in place. She immediately recognized the cold, calculating eyes of her favorite novice nun and, laughing, said, "I can't believe they let you out, good Sister! Don't you have candles to light?"

"I carefully explained I had more important things to do."

Sheva pulled her arm away and resheathed her weapon. "How many did you kill?"

"None, of course." Hilda leaned around the barracks wall so she could see what was happening in the courtyard.

"Really?"

"I'm not a wolf, Sheva. Therefore, I have no need to slaughter the sheep."

Sheva smiled and teased, "I have no idea why you became a nun, Sister Death."

"I was called by my god. Just like you."

Except Sheva had never been called. No gods spoke to her. No emissaries of greater powers asked for her to join their ranks. But she didn't bother to mention any of that at the moment.

"Should we rescue her?" Hilda asked. And Sheva knew the nun spoke of Ainsley. The only other person Hilda could tolerate. Barely.

"I wanted to try, but her sister has such a tight grip on her, I'm sure our favorite princess's limb has been starved for blood. Every time she tries to move away, Brother Gemma drags her back with that healthy blacksmith strength they all got from their mother." Sheva leaned around Hilda so she could also see the action in the courtyard. "Perhaps there is a family suicide pact."

"The cranky princess lives in trees and actively avoids her two elder sisters. So I doubt she'd agreed to die along with them unless she has no choice. Besides, no one wants to die by dragon fire. I've heard you burn slowly. Like a roasting. So that you're cooked properly to their taste. They don't like their food overdone."

Sheva glanced up at the nun. "What a lovely bit of information."

"Of course, we could just go over there, grab her, and make a run for it."

"After what you just told me about dragon fire? I think not, woman."

"Our gods will protect us, I'm sure."

"War gods are not fans of those who are stupid. And jumping between the royals and giant dragons feels, in this moment, decidedly stupid."

"But isn't that what those other war monks are doing?"

Sheva leaned out a bit to get a wider view and saw that the other war monks were now calling out to the crazed woman who traveled with dragons. Dragons! And they were yelling at her like a whore on the street.

"They," Sheva replied, "are doing something decidedly stupid."

"Perhaps *their* war gods will protect them."

Sheva shook her head sadly and sighed. "No. When it comes to intense stupidity—war gods are all the same."

It was said that those who crossed the Amichai Mountains into the dark, unknown lands on the other side never returned. It was said they were lost to the mists of dark magicks and the claws of vile beasts. The ruler of these lands, it was said . . . was one called Annwyl the Bloody.

A dark, monstrous female born of both man and demon. She could suck the souls of men from their bodies and would murder babies in front of their wailing mothers. The traveling bards said the female was nine feet tall and had hooves instead of feet; a gold and diamond-encrusted crown, smeared in the blood of her millions of victims, had been permanently seared to her skull by one of the many dark gods she worshipped.

To enter her corrupt palace was to know that you would die, but not until Annwyl the Bloody had finished sucking the marrow from your bones while demon troubadours played instruments made of human flesh and sinew.

Remembering all that, Ainsley frowned a bit and looked at Annwyl the Bloody.

This Annwyl boldly stared at the order of monks through the light brown hair blowing across her face as the still morning air picked up a bit into a light wind. She wore dark brown leather breeches and boots, a chainmail shirt with no sleeves, and steel bands around her wrists. She appeared to be about six feet tall or so. Taller than Gemma but not as tall as Keeley. Nor were her shoulders as large as Keeley's. But nearly every part of the foreign queen showed strong, well-used muscle.

What Ainsley didn't see was a baby-devouring demon beast. She saw a warrior woman. An insane warrior woman appearing to be seconds from losing her reason entirely, but still . . .

"Go, Mad Queen!" the monk yelled out. "Go from these sacred, precious lands and *never* return!"

There was a long pause after that command. Then the silver dragon finally asked the monk, "Or what . . . exactly?"

"Or we will do to her what she has done to the innocent *babies* of her people!"

The Mad Queen's head turned ever so slightly as her gaze locked onto the monk. Ainsley also managed to catch the tail end of a dramatic grimace from the black dragon. He grimaced. Then he sighed. Then he put his steel helm back on, which Ainsley did not take as a good sign.

It was as if the words the monk had used were the worst possible things he could have said.

Ainsley held her breath, waiting to see what the Mad Queen would—

The insane, almost hysterical scream the Mad Queen unleashed had Gemma pushing Ainsley and Keeley back several feet before she unsheathed her own weapon to protect them all.

Instead of retreating, the black-clad monks all charged forward, sprinting onto the dragons and using the beasts' tails to run up their backs and onto their heads. Once on their heads, each monk launched himself off the dragon's snout, sword at the ready, many of them letting out a war cry as they landed on the ground to face this threat head-on.

Yet despite the nearness of the attacking monks, not one dragon unleashed their natural weapon—the mighty dragon fire. Instead, one of the dragons—the bright gold one—raised a talon and said with what sounded like true kindness, "Dear lads, I wouldn't do that if I were you."

But it was too late, the monks rushed toward the Mad Queen, who just stood there, breathing deeply and—from what Ainsley could tell—seething with rage. She stood there until the first monk was close enough. Then the two swords strapped to the Mad Queen's back were drawn and she swung.

It was that scream. That horrible, human scream ringing out through the land just as the two suns rose over the hills and the skies lightened.

A scream that startled everyone, including the white-haired female watching them.

Whatever magicks the female had been using to blind all the centaurs to the truth surrounding them immediately dropped, and his brethren began to blink and look around them in confusion. Because now they could see everything.

Sarff gave a small cough and Gruff turned his gaze back to the female. She'd stepped away from the tree she'd been leaning against, her eyes locked on the skies.

"Your Royal Highness . . ." Sarff finally prompted, and Princess

Laila turned in time to see the white-haired female suddenly engulfed in flames. Flames that only lasted a few seconds and burned none of the trees or ground nearby her. When those flames disappeared, it was a dragon that stood there. An enormous, white-scaled dragon with long white hair, still clad in pristine white robes. But robes that fit her dragon form as well as they had her human one. And with a toss of all that white hair, she unfurled her wings and took to the skies, sending a wave of wind and debris at the centaurs watching her.

While all the others coughed and covered their eyes, trying not to fall on their asses from the power of the beast flying away, Gruff managed to keep his focus as the dragon soared higher and higher into the air. He was glad he kept that focus, too. Because what he eventually saw told him a lot.

Gruff grunted at the princess's royal brothers, and after glaring at him for such rudeness—he assumed—they followed his gaze to the sky . . . and the many dragons flying over their heads.

"Fuuuuuuuck," the light-haired brother breathed out, prompting the rest of the herd to turn their gazes skyward.

Knowing that many of them wanted to make a run for it, Gruff was impressed that only a few took several panicked steps away or reared up on their hind legs. But none of his people ran. His kind never did, no matter the horror of what awaited them.

"Do your best to save the queen and the children," Princess Laila gently ordered her army. "Now go. And may our strongest of gods be with all of you."

The first sword blow took a leg. The next a hand. Another attack had her burying one sword in a monk's chest, before she yanked it out and spun away from the piercing power of a pike.

Her blade moved fast and her body easily followed. She slashed and cut and spun and slashed and cut some more, splattering pieces of monk all over the training ring.

The lead monk silently charged toward the Mad Queen when her back was turned as she dispatched three others with her two blades and a brutal blow to a chest with her foot.

The lead monk was moments from burying his blade in the queen's spine when she turned to face him and brought her two swords together, taking his head in one brutal strike. The Mad Queen watched impassively as the head dropped to the ground and rolled across her foot, the lead monk's blood splashing from his open neck and across the foreign royal's face and chest.

Two more monks wisely stopped short of Annwyl the Bloody and, instead, combined their magickal powers and unleashed them at the Mad Queen. A bright, powerful light slammed into and *through* her, causing her to stop mid-swing. She closed her eyes and took in a short, surprised breath. That's when the scars that covered her body suddenly blazed to life, dark red light pulsating from each one, growing in intensity until it all abruptly stopped and Queen Annwyl's eyes opened.

Holding the gazes of the remaining monks she hadn't hacked or slashed to death, the Mad Queen moved back a few feet before suddenly letting out an earth-shaking roar that had most of the dragons taking a step or two away from her.

Annwyl the Bloody brought her swords up and back down, slashing the air across her body, before she bolted with incredible speed toward the remaining and now-terrified monks.

Wisely those monks fled, running around and under the dragons. Running as fast as their human legs could carry them. But the Mad Queen continued on . . . until Keeley darted out in front of her, stopping the crazed woman's attempt to finish off her enemies.

Realizing Keeley had gotten past her, Gemma started to go after their sister, but Ainsley grabbed the monk's chainmail cowl and dragged her back. It was a fight, too, and Gemma was much stronger than Ainsley. Thankfully Ainsley suddenly had help. A novice monk on one side took a good grip on Gemma's right arm and a battle-nun-in-training took firm hold of the left. With Ainsley's arm around Gemma's neck, the three of them managed to keep a firm grip on her.

Ainsley briefly wondered if she should release Gemma so she could go and defend their queen—something Gemma had committed to do in a very recent and unnecessary blood ritual in front of her entire Order—but Ainsley had faith in Keeley. She always had, which meant holding on to a struggling and cursing Gemma while hoping for the best.

* * *

Keeley yanked her hammer from her back and swung it. The foreign queen ducked the head of the weapon but came up with her two swords swinging, aimed right for Keeley's neck.

She knew she could have jumped out of the way and struck Annwyl the Bloody down from behind. But what would that get her in the long run with the dragons still standing by, at the ready? No, she had to trust herself and block out everything else. Especially Gemma, who was screaming at her to "*Kill the crazy cunt!*"

Because Keeley wasn't just "in a fight." Nor was she only fighting for herself. For *her* life. She had an entire town of men, women, and children depending on her.

Understanding this, Keeley placed one hand by the head of her hammer and used the other to grip the end of the handle. Then she brought up her weapon and prayed . . .

Ainsley's breath caught in her throat just as the steel of two swords slammed into the steel of Keeley's hammer, the sound of that impact ringing out over the morning air. The hammer's handle blocked the Mad Queen's swords and Keeley's strength held the Mad Queen at bay.

"All of you, *out!*" Keeley ordered over her shoulder at the scattering of black-clad monks that hadn't been smart enough to exit the courtyard completely. Keeley—like everyone else, it seemed—was ignoring the dragons since they seemed to have no intention of interfering at the moment.

"*Now!*" Keeley bellowed when the monks took their sweet time following their queen's orders.

"Keeley, no!" Gemma barked, still struggling to break free of Ainsley's grip.

"I mean it!" Keeley insisted. "Everyone back behind the gates. Go!"

The few remaining monks finally did as they were told, returning to their positions behind the walls. Once they were gone, Keeley looked into the face of the Mad Queen and said, "I am *not* the one you are looking for, Queen Annwyl. Does this *look* like the Palace of the Old King? A palace that has been around for more centuries than anyone can count? Do you see a king by my side, who *thinks* he runs things? Or a court with everyone bowing and scraping? Most importantly . . . do you see slaves? Adult or children? You don't, because I am not Beatrix. I am Keeley. And this is *my* queendom."

"I—" the Mad Queen began, but something white and extremely large landed on the walls directly above them, cutting off the queen's next words.

It was another dragon, but this one was different. It wasn't simply that its hair and scales were bright white or the eyes a stunning blue. It wasn't that it was bigger than some of the other dragons. What Ainsley truly noticed was this dragon lacked armor and weapons. And yet, despite that, it had no qualms about snapping at the Mad Queen, "What have you done, Annwyl?" A female dragon, Ainsley realized.

"I—" the Mad Queen began again.

"Don't lie to me. I know you've done something." The She-dragon glanced down, gasped, and landed on the ground. But unlike the other dragons, her landing did not shake the earth when her claws touched down. Despite her size, the She-dragon moved as if she weighed no more than a bird. "What is this?" she demanded, lifting up a torso by the cowl it was still wearing. "You're killing *monks* now?"

Pushing Keeley away by shoving her swords against Keeley's hammer, the royal moved around Ainsley's sister and snarled at the She-dragon, "*They started it!*"

"Oh . . . Annwyl." And the She-dragon sounded *so* disappointed that Ainsley actually felt guilty, and she hadn't done *anything*!

"Oh, Annwyl?" the Mad Queen snarled back. "You're 'oh, Annwyl-ing' *me?*"

"This is *your* fault, you know," the She-dragon announced, and a long silence followed that statement until she looked over at the black dragon, resplendent in his armor, pitiless black eyes glaring out from under his helm.

"What now?" the black dragon snapped.

"This is also your fault. She's like this because of you."

"How is any of this *my* fault?"

"It's your job to keep an eye on her."

"It's my job to keep her from razing a queendom to the ground and dancing on the ashes, which—so far—I've done."

"Then what's this?" the She-dragon barked, shaking an armless monk torso with one talon. "Eh? What is this?"

"A foolish human who thought he could take on Annwyl the Bloody. How's that my fault? It's not like we didn't warn them."

"I did warn them," the gold dragon piped in. "Very clearly. They ignored me."

"See?" the black dragon said, leaning back on his haunches and crossing his forearms over his chest. Something that looked utterly bizarre to Ainsley. Because who knew dragons could do that?

The She-dragon sighed. "I'm so disappointed in all of you." And, again, Ainsley felt that guilt for no apparent reason. Her life had been invaded by these things and yet, she felt guilty simply because this female had that inflection in her voice. Her tone was just so damning!

"Disappointed in *me?*" a silver dragon exclaimed. "What the battle fuck did *I* do?"

"Nothing! You did *nothing*. As usual."

"Why is this deranged female *my* responsibility? If you'd all listened to me, we could have killed her a long time ago and been done with her!"

The Mad Queen lifted one of her swords, pointing it directly at the silver dragon.

"Come, then!" Annwyl the Bloody yelled up to him. "And take your chances, useless prick!"

The silver gave a ferocious but short roar, and the Mad Queen began to march toward him. But the She-dragon was having none of it.

"*That is enough!*" she bellowed. "More than enough!" But the silver dragon and Annwyl the Bloody began to yell at each other *and* the She-dragon about who was right and who was wrong and who should die, ignoring the She-dragon's command to "Stop it! Stop it now!"

Finally, the She-dragon moved her blue gaze to the black dragon and practically begged, "Aren't you going to *do* anything? *Say* anything?"

"Well . . ." He gave a small shrug. "Mum will be disappointed if we come back without Briec, but we can always tell her he fell during the heat of battle."

"A lie I'm sure she'll happily accept," the gold dragon giddily added.

The She-dragon stomped her back claw and, for the first time, the earth and buildings shook around them.

"That is not what I mean, Fearghus the Destroyer! *And you know it!*"

# CHAPTER 3

They finally reached the massive walls of the queen's tower, and although there were battalions-worth of war monks and battle priests yelling at them to stop, Gruff's people kept going through the open gates.

The sight of all those dragons standing around in full armor while the remains of dead humans littered the ground did nothing to deter Gruff or his clan. All of them were trained warriors, ready to battle anything that came their way. Even giant lizards with wings.

The centaurs already had their weapons drawn and battle cries falling from their lips, when Queen Keeley suddenly rushed forward and raised her hands high in the air.

*"Laila, no!"*

Princess Laila came to an abrupt stop at the queen's screamed order, her front legs rising in the air, her hind legs dancing in a small circle. The rest of them did their best not to collide with the centaur in front or behind them. Some also reared, others were able to swerve or quickly trot away before crashing into one of their own.

Once they had managed to stop their attack, though the entire group kept their weapons raised just in case, Gruff took a moment to examine the area and determine what they'd just rushed into. And even he had to admit . . . it was weird.

Just one or two of the dragons standing in the middle of the damaged courtyard could destroy everyone and everything simply by breathing fire on it all. But what he was looking at was a battle squad of armored and well-armed dragons. He didn't know a lot about dragons. There were none on Amichai lands. The agreement made with Laila's ancestors all those millennia ago had kept the dragons on the north side of the Amichai Mountains. Gruff knew a few weak spots to open up on the beasts' bodies should he be forced to fight one, but he was unclear whether standing around in armor and *not* killing anyone was normal for dragons.

An even bigger question for Gruff, though, was whether bickering was common among dragonkind. Because that seemed to be happening along with the not killing.

"You are a useless human that I should have stomped out of existence years ago!" a dragon with silver scales bellowed down to a well-built warrior woman Gruff had never seen before.

"Every time you speak," the warrior woman boldly shouted back, "all I hear is the long whine of a miserable baby intent on making everyone around it miserable!"

"This coming from a madwoman determined to destroy the entire world!"

The warrior woman leaned in and, in a pretend-whisper they could all hear, replied, "Only when angry voices tell me to!"

A black-scaled dragon snorted a laugh but quickly turned its head away while the silver threw its forearms out to the side, his gaze focused on the other dragons. A clear, universal expression of exasperation and the oft-repeated phrase, "I told you so!"

That's when Queen Keeley foolishly attempted to intervene with, "Please . . . everyone . . . let's calm down and discuss this."

The silver dragon snarled in annoyance and tiredly snapped, "Shut up, woman."

The centaurs immediately readied for another attack in the face of that insult, but they had no time to move because the warrior woman pointed her sword at the silver and screamed, "Oy! You don't talk to her like that! She's a queen and you are *nothing*, Prince Useless!"

"She's not *my* queen!"

"She's still better than you!"

"*That is it!*" the white She-dragon finally bellowed, silencing the other two. "I can't take this anymore! The two of you fighting constantly! This entire trip! I just . . . I can't . . ."

Suddenly the She-dragon put her talons against the sides of her head and swayed a bit.

A gold dragon jumped forward, pushing past the silver and nearly stepping on the warrior woman.

"Sister!" he cried, catching the She-dragon in his forearms.

Behind his helm the silver dragon rolled his eyes and sighed out, "Oh, please!"

"Look what you have done to our poor sister, you *bastard!*"

"It's all right," the She-dragon loudly whispered. "It's just one of my headaches. I need calm and quiet."

"Calm and quiet, Briec," the gold repeated to the silver.

"This is a load of horse shit, you know." He glanced down at the centaurs. "No offense."

Princess Leila now threw her arms up in the air in exasperation, and the She-dragon snarled, "Be nice, Briec!"

The silver let out a growl before finally replying, "Fine," through gritted teeth.

"And, Annwyl . . . ?" the gold gently pushed, still holding his sister.

"But he started it!"

The She-dragon got to her back claws and roared, "*ANNWYL!*"

"Fine!" the warrior woman replied. "I'll let it go."

The She-dragon nodded, smiled. "Thank you. Now why don't we all take a moment to breathe and calm down, eh?"

To Gruff's ears that sounded like a wise plan. One everyone seemed ready to accept until he heard someone good-naturedly calling out from behind one of the buildings, "What's all this yelling, my beautiful girls?"

Queen Keeley's eyes widened in swift panic, and her two younger sisters—the monk and the one who lived in trees—wore the same expression. The tree lover released the monk from the headlock she'd had her in and began running toward the voice. Why one sister had another sister in a headlock, Gruff didn't know, but he'd learned not to ask a long time ago.

"Keep that up," the voice continued, "and you'll awaken an angry She-demon. A She-demon also called your mum."

The younger sister was moving swiftly toward the buildings where harvested grain and vegetables were kept, but she soon realized her mistake when the human queen's father appeared from behind the buildings that were opposite. Those buildings held animals ready for slaughter to feed the tower inhabitants. The acoustics of the surrounding buildings had distorted his voice, and the queen's younger sister realized too late that he wasn't where she'd thought.

He came walking out with a blood-covered axe resting on his shoulder, held there with one hand while the other gripped a blood-soaked sack and a freshly slaughtered pig's head by its ear.

The human queen's father was humming as he came into view, his gaze on the ground.

The younger sister quickly changed direction, but he must have heard her footsteps and lifted his head. He smiled in warm fatherly greeting at the sight of her, but then his gaze moved past her, and Gruff cringed.

"Dragons," Angus Farmerson whispered, stumbling to a stop, his eyes wide as he took in everything before him. "Dragons," he said again.

As Ainsley ran toward their father, Gemma yelled out, "Da! No!"

"DRAGONNNNNNNNNNS!" their father shouted into the morning air.

Ainsley cringed, now running with all her speed toward her father. But she feared she'd never make it in time to save him. Especially not after what he said next.

"*Emma!*" he bellowed at the top of his lungs to their sleeping mother inside the tower, "There are dragons! *Dragonnnnnnns*! There are so many! And they're all beautiful! Bring the children! Maybe if we ask nice, they'll let our little bastards take rides on their backs!"

"*Da!*" Ainsley and her sisters screamed, equally torn between horror, fear, and outright embarrassment.

Gruff had to admit it. He was impressed by the true insanity of the queen's father. With a boldness one only saw in men walking naked through a town square and talking to their "friends . . . the gods," Angus Farmerson happily jogged right into the center of the armed and armored dragons, dragging his fourth oldest behind him. She now had her arms around his waist, attempting to hold him back, but it wasn't working the slightest bit. The man simply kept trotting along. Impressive, since Gruff had once seen the tree-loving female pull an angry bull out of the mud without any help.

"See, girls?" Angus Farmerson demanded of his eldest daughters. "Your mother said I was insane. But I knew I wasn't insane. I saw a dragon that day when I was a child! And now I have proof they exist!"

"Da, please," Queen Keeley begged, quickly using her body— and those massive blacksmith shoulders—to block the warrior woman's view of her father. Who was this woman? Gruff had no idea. But the dragons had called her Annwyl, and that did sound familiar.

"Just come here," the human queen continued to implore her father, desperately adding between gritted teeth, "Right this *second!*"

But if her father heard Queen Keeley, he made no sign, standing amongst all those dragons and gazing up at them. The poor younger sister continued to hold on to her father's waist, trying to drag him away, but he wouldn't be moved.

"Imagine that *I*," the human man rhapsodized, "Angus Farmerson, have met actual dragons. Right here in my own daughter's courtyard." His grin was wide and completely oblivious. "I can't believe my luck!"

"*Daddy!*" the monk daughter barked at her father. "Get over here!"

Again, Gruff was unable to tell if Farmerson had heard his daughter and had chosen to simply ignore her or if he was unaware of anything but the presence of the massive beasts.

"Now," Farmerson tossed over his shoulder, "I don't know if they can understand me, but I'm going to try."

"Please don't!" Queen Keeley begged.

"Hell-ooo, hell-oooo," the human male loudly called up to the dragons, who were now watching him with silent curiosity. He waved, too, which even Gruff found horrifying. "I. Am. Angus. Farmerson," he said, pressing the hand holding a pig's head and blood-soaked bag against his big chest.

Gruff frowned and briefly glanced at his sister. He didn't understand why Farmerson was speaking so . . . very . . . *slowlyyyy*.

"I. Am. The. *Father.* Of. Queen. Keeley." He gave a short gesture toward his mortified eldest daughter. "And. I want *you*"—he pointed at the dragons, pig's blood flying all over—"to know. That *you*. Are safe. *Here.*"

Briallen's eyes grew wide as she locked her gaze with Gruff's. And Gruff knew exactly what his sister was thinking. Of *course* the dragons were safe! Because they were dragons and the rest of them . . . well . . . were *not*. But for some reason, Angus Farmerson felt the need to make the dragons feel safe and welcome. The dragons. The beings dressed in armor, including full helms, with giant swords strapped to their backs.

Farmerson wanted the *dragons* to feel safe. All right, then.

"Now, you all may use our south field to set up camp," Farmerson went on. Sublimely oblivious to . . . well . . . to anything! It was amazing! "And there should be enough bear and deer for you to eat. But please . . . no eating the sheep," he said, pointing a warning finger. "It's not fair to the sheep herders in our valley. Unless, of course, you *pay*. With gold, please," he quickly added. "Not human body parts."

"Da!" Queen Keeley gasped out.

"What? I heard that's how dragons barter with each other. But that won't work here in your little kingdom, now, will it?"

The dragons continued to gaze down at Farmerson with obvious confusion until the lip of the cranky silver dragon curled contemptuously and he opened his big, fang-filled maw.

Briallen grabbed her shield from her back, ready to put herself and centaur armor to the test by getting between the oncoming dragon's flame and the queen's father. Gruff, however, was not about to lose his sister to one human man's delusion. He grabbed her arm before she could gallop across the courtyard and held her in place. At the same moment, a gold dragon slammed his front elbow into the silver's jaw, shutting his snout and forcing the silver dragon back as the gold took a small step forward.

"And I am Gwenvael the Handsome," the gold announced. That's when it occurred to Gruff that the dragons had been speaking in the common tongue all this time. With an ease belied by the shape of a dragon's head and jaw. Gruff had expected a talking dragon to look like a dog chewing bark, but no. The words came out smooth and easy without any strange twisting when the dragon added, "Third-born son and fourth-born offspring of the Dragon Queen, Brigadier General of the Dragon Queen's Southern Armies, Father to the Gwenvael Five and Arlais the Stunning . . . as well as the boy I've been forced to claim as my own."

"Thank you so much, Father!" a male voice yelled from somewhere outside the gates. "My mother is really going to enjoy that one when I send her my next missives."

The gold waved the complaint away. "Oh, ignore him. He's a giant-headed mummy's boy. Anyway, I am delighted to meet you, Lord . . . Angus? Was it?"

"Just call me Angus. No fancy titles for me. Now, this"—he grabbed the arm wrapped around his waist and pulled his daughter around—"is my fourth girl, Ainsley." He put one arm around the petrified girl's shoulders—seemingly unaware when the pig's head smacked her in the face—and used his bloody axe to point behind him. "And the little one there is my girl Gemma. She's a monk now, and we are very proud of her. And next to her, looking just like her beautiful mum, is my eldest, Keeley. She's the queen of these lands, and a better or fairer queen you have never met. Isn't that right, Ainsley?"

"Uhhh . . ."

"The rest of my clan is in the tower with my wife, Emma. Lazy sleepyheads. A few years of being royals and they forget the ways of farmers." He chuckled and asked, "Now who are all your fine-looking friends?"

The gold dragon's grin was wide, showing nothing but row after row of huge, frightening fangs. But it was with apparent joy that he began to introduce those who traveled with him.

"This black dragon here is my brother, Fearghus the Destroyer. This complaining, easily irritated silver bastard is my brother, Briec the Mighty. That glorious, white-haired beauty is my sister, Morfyd the White. And the human, most importantly, is Fearghus's mate and queen of Dark Plains, Annwyl the—"

Still gripping his daughter, Angus spun around to face the warrior woman and exclaim, "Annwyl the Magnificent!"

The human female's shoulders slumped and her expression turned dower. "Well, there's no need to be *sarcastic*."

Ainsley didn't know if she was simply humiliated or terrified.

She thought about it a moment and admitted . . . it was both. She was both humiliated and terrified. And it was all her father's fault! She loved him, more than she loved anyone, but did he always have to be so very . . . Angus?

And did he have to keep hitting her with that damn pig's head?

"You are, aren't you?" her father asked the Mad Queen, finally pulling away from Ainsley and taking that damn pig's head with him. "You're Annwyl the Magnificent. Queen of Dark Plains and Garbhán Isle."

Her father walked over to the Mad Queen, but Gemma and Keeley stood in front of her, not allowing their father to get any closer. Probably a good thing. Who knew what he would do at this point?

Ainsley rushed after her father. To protect him, she told herself. But really it was to get farther away from the dragons.

"Your Majesty," her father said loudly and then, to Ainsley's shock and horror, he bowed. Both arms out so that he had a bloody pig's head hanging from one hand and a bloody axe from the other.

"Da," Gemma growled between clenched teeth.

"He never bowed to me," Keeley complained, which earned her a vicious glare from Gemma. "What? He hasn't! I'm a queen too."

Angus Farmerson rose from his ridiculous bow and smiled at the Mad Queen. "I never thought I'd be so lucky as to meet you, Queen Annwyl."

With narrowed eyes, the Mad Queen studied their father but said nothing.

"I read all about your war against Vateria Flominian, the Unhallowed Empress."

"You did?"

"Joining two armies together, human and dragon, to attack Vateria's palace and then bringing an army of hell's beasts to crush her armies completely..." He nodded. "This old soldier was extremely impressed, Your Majesty."

Gemma frowned and, apparently unable to help herself, turned and asked the Mad Queen, "Hell's beasts?"

"I was dragged to one of the hells once and I became friendly with some of the animals. So they helped me out."

Eyes wide, Gemma demanded, *Why were you dragged to hell?*"

"What does that have to do with anything?"

"It has everything to do with *everything*! Are you one of the undead? Do you even have a soul?"

Crossing her eyes, the Mad Queen resheathed her swords at her back and said on a long sigh, "By the gods . . . monks. All of you are *so* dramatic."

"What's *that* supposed to mean?" Gemma snarled, always defensive when it came to her monkish ways.

"You really don't know? Should I *pray* that you figure it out?"

"All right, that's enough!" the white She-dragon snapped. "I can't hear any more of this bickering. Let's just meet. And talk like normal royals."

"Who planned to kill us?" Gemma demanded. "You did invade *our* lands."

"Because we were going to raze this queendom to the ground," the Mad Queen explained, "and execute all of you if you had slaves. But you don't, so . . ."

"Is that supposed to make us feel better about all of you *being here?*" Gemma exploded.

Gazing at her, the Mad Queen calmly replied, "Yes."

"Wait," Ainsley's father cut in. "I don't understand, Your Majesty. Why did you think my daughter had slaves?"

"Well . . . Queen Beatrix does. A large group of children that had been enslaved by Beatrix escaped from their captors and turned up in . . . uh . . . Lord Angus? Are you all right?"

"By all the unholy gods," the silver dragon growled, "is that man *crying?*"

Ainsley was about to wrap her arms around her father when she heard the same dragon demand, "Wait . . . are *you* crying?"

Ainsley looked up to see tears pouring from the gold dragon's eyes before he sobbed out, "It's all just so sad!"

# CHAPTER 4

Emma Smythe came down to the dining hall to find her husband sobbing; an extremely large golden-blond warrior sobbing along with him; two tall, scarred women trying to calm down Emma's husband; two other large warrior men watching the sobbing spectacle with matching expressions of obvious disgust; and her daughter Keeley standing against a far wall, silently gazing out at nothing.

It had been a weird morning so far. Strange people in her home. Keeley's demon wolves hiding in the children's rooms. And her eight-year-old son announcing that he aspired to "scholarly pursuits" instead of being a farmer or a blacksmith.

She hadn't handled that one well. Shoving the little bastard into the room with all the demon wolves and locking him in. She'd told him he could come out when he changed his attitude.

She really should let him out, but this seemed more important at the moment. Because Keeley not helping her father—as she normally would when he was crying . . . again—but just standing around, staring . . . that was not good. Like that time when Keeley was a child and had managed to hit herself in the head with a shovel she'd just forged. Emma still couldn't explain how Keeley had hit *herself* in the head, but she knew from the dazed look in the child's eyes that she'd hurt her head and they couldn't let her fall asleep for at least twenty-four hours. Just to be on the safe side. Well, adult Keeley had that same dazed expression on her face, and

Emma knew before she delved into anything else, she had to find out what exactly was going on.

Emma walked across the hall to her eldest child and relaxed back against the wall facing outward. Leaning over, she pressed her shoulder against Keeley's.

"What's happening?" Emma asked softly.

"We have visitors."

"I see that. Very large and well-armed visitors." She paused a moment before adding, "Their armor is fabulous, though."

"Fabulous," her daughter quickly agreed. "And magickal."

"What?"

"See how large the males are?"

"Yes."

"They can be larger. Much, much larger. And their armor changes with them. It's wondrous to behold."

"What are you talking about?"

Keeley reached down and scratched her knee. "They're dragons."

Emma chuckled. "You have *got* to stop spending so much time with your father. You're queen now." When her daughter simply stared at her, Emma frowned and glanced at the visitors again. "Really?"

"Did you not look outside?"

No. She hadn't. She'd had too much to do, like most mornings that involved her children.

Squaring her shoulders, Emma walked to the big front portal of the tower and placed her hands on the levers that had been designed so that the children could easily open the heavy doors, or secure them so no one could get in from the outside without battering rams. She brought the levers down and lightly tugged.

As soon as the doors began to ease open, Emma heard the screaming. Panicked, hysterical screaming.

She stepped out but didn't get farther than a few feet because of all the screaming, running people. Crowds of people, many with bags or their children or both.

Emma watched for a few seconds, her mouth slightly open. She had no idea why everyone was running. She didn't see anything that would cause such—

A man abruptly stopped in front of Emma, looked up at the sky, and screamed. A high-pitched scream that had her jerking a bit at the intensity of it. She watched as urine poured from under his leggings, puddling on the ground; the man didn't move until he was shoved forward by several panicked people running by.

Dreading what she might see, Emma lifted her gaze to the sky just the same. And yes . . . flying overhead . . . dragons.

Actual dragons. In the sky above her daughter's territory.

Like the man who'd alerted her to the dragons' presence, she wanted to scream too. But thankfully, she didn't, nor did she piss herself. A good thing, since her fifth-eldest daughter was walking, calmly, through the panicked crowd of people with Emma's sweet Endolyn in her arms.

The six-year-old was pointing at the sky and squealing. Not in fear, though. In complete happiness. Gods, she was so like her father. There wasn't an animal or beast that didn't fascinate the child. Emma's question, though, was why Isadora would think it was a good idea to expose the future blacksmith of the family to bloody *dragons*.

"*Isadora!*" she barked at her daughter, motioning her over with one hand.

When Isadora stood in front of her, Emma began, "I can't believe—"

The sound of crumbling rock and the intensifying screams of the residents had mother and daughters turning toward a building made of brick. Squatting on the roof was a dragon.

Emma took in a quick breath, gawking at the sight. It was a brown dragon, its scales glinting in the two suns, its long brown hair in multiple braids. The talons on each of its claws were the size of a tall human male. Giant wings extended from its back despite the armor that encased the dragon. Armor that matched the armor of the men inside the tower.

"Oh, shit," Emma swore. "Keeley was right. They can shift to human."

It suddenly occurred to Emma that there were dragons *inside* the tower with her youngest children *and* her eldest. The queen!

She turned to bolt inside, but froze when Isadora yelled out, "*Oy! You!*"

Emma spun back around to see Isadora—still holding Endelyon!—yelling at the dragon that had perched on the brick building.

"*Oy!*" she yelled out again, finally catching the animal's attention.

"What the fuck are you doing?" Emma demanded, but her daughter simply waved her off.

"Yeah! You!" Isadora went on. "You gonna pay for that? What you're doing to that roof?"

The dragon looked down at its claws, then back at Emma's daughter. "Ummm . . ."

"Yeah! Exactly! So, unless you want to deal with the mason dwarves and their extremely high prices—get your fat ass off our roof!"

"*What are you doing?*" Emma hissed.

Isadora stepped close, while Endelyon reached over her sister's shoulder hoping to grab hold of the dragons. Because the child was as insane as her father!

"Do you know who manages the money here?" Isadora asked Emma.

"Well—"

"I do! Because no one else is paying attention. If I left it up to you lot, we'd all be living in trees like Ainsley!"

"Excuse me," said a tall, dark-haired woman as she passed between mother and daughters. She had on that foreign armor and wore her brown hair in braids.

"That's the dragon from the roof," Emma said to no one in particular, stunned.

"Da always said they could change to human," Isadora noted.

"And they're in our house. Around your da."

"So? They haven't killed us yet."

"And that calms you?"

"It doesn't make me panic. Not like everyone else out here." She glanced at the locals. "Look at them all. How is any of this helpful?"

"But yelling at dragons while holding your sister is?"

Isadora, barely eighteen summers, curled her lip and snarled,

"Do you want to pay for crumbled brick? Do you have any concept what that costs, Mum? *Do you?*"

Suddenly, in the face of her daughter's irrational anger, Emma forgot all about dragons and the panicked people of the town. She knew someone else would handle all that. She only had to worry about *her* children.

"All right, then." Emma placed her hands on Isadora's shoulders and pushed her back into the tower. "Go deal with your siblings upstairs. And keep Endelyon away from any more dragons. She's plump . . . they might eat her."

Emma faced her eldest child and frowned a bit when she saw Keeley had closed her eyes and was shaking her head. That's when Emma remembered who else was in the dining hall.

"Um . . . no offense," she said to the dragons glowering at her.

The brown She-dragon let out a sigh before refocusing her attention on a warrior—or, Emma guessed, a dragon—with long black hair.

"It's getting pretty bad out there," she told him.

"See if Uncle Bram can handle it."

"I don't know if he's arrived yet."

"Then Aunt Ghleanna."

The She-dragon lowered her brows. "Really? Ghleanna?"

"Do *you* want to do it?"

"I don't want to talk to people. What about . . . is Gwenvael crying?" Before the black-haired dragon could reply, she held up her hand. "I don't want to know. I'll get Ghleanna."

The She-dragon walked out of the tower, and Emma made her way back to her eldest daughter's side.

"All right," she told Keeley. "I now believe there are dragons."

"Told you."

Emma stared at the outsiders. "All of them are dragons, eh? Even the woman with the sleeveless chainmail—useless, by the way—fondling your sobbing father? *She's* a dragon?"

"No. She's not a dragon. She's Annwyl the Bloody, Queen of Dark Plains."

Emma crossed her arms over her chest and did her best not to start yelling. "Are you telling me that not only have you allowed *dragons* into our family home but you've allowed that Demon Cunt—

her official name, by the way, awarded to her by the Dark Elves of Harvest Cove—to molest your sobbing father?"

"She's not molesting. She's comforting. And be glad, because the woman is violently insane, but she seems to like Da."

"Of course she's violently insane. Dark Elves call her *Demon Cunt.*"

"She came here because the enslaved children Gemma released wound up in her territory and she was . . . shall we say . . . livid."

"Because . . . ?"

"She thought we were enslaving children like"—Keeley dropped her voice to a barely there whisper—"Beatrix."

"By the holy hammer of the gods, did that witch tell your father about—"

"She did, but she didn't do it to be mean."

"Are you sure?"

"Trust me . . . I know when a woman is being mean. Besides, she really likes Da."

"Hmmm. Does she?"

"Before you get too testy about her patting Da's shoulder . . ." Keeley pointed to the black-haired dragon.

"Yes. What about him?"

"That's her mate. And I think you have nothing to fear because . . . he's gorgeous."

"You think the dragon is gorgeous?"

"When he's shifted to human . . . ? Quite."

"What is wrong with my daughters?" Emma asked the air. "I mean, I tolerate the centaurs, but lusting after dragons—"

"I am not *lusting* after anyone but Caid of the Scarred Earth Clan. But I'm not blind either. And I seriously doubt that Queen Annwyl is going to give up *that*"—she gestured toward the dragon again—"for our wonderful Da."

"At least your da is human."

*"Mum."*

Once the majority of dragons who'd been in the courtyard had flown off, and the royal dragons went inside the tower with Queen Keeley, the other humans who lived in the town acted exactly as Gruff expected them to act . . . they lost their shit. Some literally.

The screaming. The running. The hysterical sobbing. All typical human reactions to finding out there were dragons flying around one's small, royal-run town.

Not that Gruff could blame any of them. They were weak humans, lucky if they could survive a simple infection or bear attack. Gruff didn't really expect them to challenge beasts that could annihilate most of them by simply taking a step forward. But an orderly exit would have made more sense. At the moment, the only thing the humans were doing was trampling each other.

The only ones Gruff worried about were the human children since they were basically defenseless. And the dragonfear had such hold of their parents, they could easily be buried in the crush of panicked bodies trying to get out of the battered gates. Gruff and his clan did what they could to snatch the small ones before they were lost underfoot, tossing up the ones they rescued to three of his cousins standing on the battlements ready to catch them.

While his tribe did that, the rest of the centaurs, including Princess Laila and her brothers, joined Queen Keeley's two eldest sisters in their attempts to calm down the frenzied mass of humans. Thankfully, they had the help of the religious sects, which surprised Gruff. The various sects were not known for working together. Yet, at the moment, war monks, war priests, and covens of battle witches were doing their best to get the terrified humans to think rationally.

Sadly, though, they were failing. The centaurs were about to be crushed under all the humans desperate to get out.

Gruff was seconds from ordering his sister and Sarff to high ground, whether the battlements or the closest mountainside. He wouldn't lose those closest to him because the ruling clan believed protecting humans from themselves was a good way to safeguard the future of the Amichai. Hysterical humans were worse than stampeding oxen, and they screamed more.

But before Gruff could call out to his sister, who was busy tossing a squealing child up to the battlements, an explosion of flame burst past the opening where the gates used to be.

The screaming worsened and, like the panicked herd they were, the humans abruptly turned, about to charge back the way they'd come. But the flames stopped and a black dragon suddenly appeared in the wall opening. Like all the other dragons, this one was armed and armored, a helm on its head and a sword strapped to its back.

"Everyone calm down," it said. "I didn't mean to startle any of you."

This black dragon was female and spoke with the calmest and most soothing voice Gruff had ever heard. The humans immediately stopped running and screaming. They looked over their shoulders at the She-dragon speaking to them. Of course, that could be the dragonfear, but Gruff thought it was the She-dragon's mellifluous voice.

"I'm Ghleanna," she said, pulling off her helm and revealing short black hair streaked with silver strands. This was different from the other dragons Gruff had seen so far, who had long, thick hair that reached at least past their shoulders or, in some cases, down their backs.

"And I just wanted to stop by and suggest to all of you that you would be much *safer* staying in your homes and going on about your lives. Queen Keeley's armies can protect you . . . *here.* But those of you who insist on running away, out there . . . into the unknown . . . Well," she said with a sigh, shrugging massive dragon shoulders, "neither Queen Keeley, nor Queen Annwyl can be held accountable for what's left of your lives."

Gruff and his sister exchanged glances. What exactly *was* that? What was the She-dragon attempting to do? Reassure? Threaten? He had no idea.

But then a tall man with long silver hair walked around the She-dragon's legs. He was dressed in black robes and had a large black bag over his shoulder that he was busy digging through with both hands . . . while walking. He wasn't looking where he was going and yet he managed to maneuver around the She-dragon with ease.

"*Var!*" he suddenly yelled out.

"Var is out with his unit," the She-dragon told the man. "He'll be gone for hours."

"What?" The man stopped walking and gave a frustrated growl. "You do know I need him, yes?"

"You do know that his grandfather wants him trained as a Dragonwarrior, yes? And if you want to argue with my brother about how he trains his grand-offspring, please be my—"

"No!" the man cut in quickly. "Thank you, but I'd rather not hear that particular speech again. Besides, your brother still hates me."

"He does not hate—" the She-dragon cringed a bit before finishing with—"your existence in his . . . universe."

"How is that helpful?" he asked.

"Well . . ."

"Forget I asked." The man—who Gruff was now certain was simply another dragon in human form—faced the tower. That's when he finally caught sight of hundreds of people standing there . . . frozen in place by their dragonfear. He frowned at first, confused. But then his expression cleared and he immediately focused again on the She-dragon. "What did you do?"

"As I was asked. I calmed the masses. Look how calm they are."

"And you calmed them how?"

"By letting them know that running away was not in their best interest and we can't protect them should they leave town."

"Ghleanna," he sighed. "I'm sure you were asked to come here, *as a human*, to inform the good people that they are safe and had nothing to worry about."

"It was too late for any of that, I'm afraid. They were already hysterical and panicking. So I took another route. But we've gotten to the same place. I mean . . . look at them, Bram. Like calm sheep."

A woman standing right by the gates, clutching a small child to her chest, suddenly burst into tears, and Gruff didn't blame her.

Dragons ate sheep.

If the black She-dragon had gone on, Ainsley wasn't sure what would have happened. But the handsome, silver-haired man stepped in, and before she knew it, the population of Forgetown—Keeley's idea, because even the name of the town must involve blacksmithing somehow—began to calmly return to their homes. A few, Ainsley could tell, had no intention of staying and would probably sneak out when it got dark or they thought no one was looking, but there was nothing anyone could do about that. She was just glad it wasn't the entire town running away. She had a feeling that would do nothing but upset Keeley. Now that she was queen, she took everything so personally.

Ainsley helped the centaurs return children they'd saved from being trampled and escorted some people to their homes. Doing her best to reassure them that her sister would make certain all would be well. That Queen Keeley had complete control of the current situation.

A total lie, but what was she supposed to tell everyone when she had no idea what would happen next? Everything had gone crazy in just a few hours and she felt very helpless. She hated that. Hated feeling . . . adrift.

Gods, she'd give anything to climb one of the forest trees and get some sleep in its branches. But as soon as she returned to the site of the dragons' arrival, Gemma was yelling at her.

"Where the fuck have you been?" her sister demanded.

"I was helping an old lady home. Should I have just shoved her down the road by the back of her neck and told her, 'Good luck, you ancient toad'?"

"Why are you arguing with me? Just do as I tell you!"

"You haven't told me to do anything! And why are you so hysterical?"

"I'm not hysterical. I'm trying to—"

"Fix everything because your god told you to?"

Gemma's nostrils flared and Ainsley squared her shoulders, ready for a fight. But Sheva abruptly appeared on her left and Hilda on her right. They'd both gone off to assist the other religious folk who were helping people back to their homes, but now they were back and doing that thing Gemma hated . . . interrupting.

"Hello, Brother Gemma!"

"Why are you speaking to me, Novitiate?"

Her sister's imperious tone made Ainsley roll her eyes and drop her head back, which only pissed Gemma off more.

"Would you prefer I speak to you, Brother Gemma?" Hilda asked.

"I have absolutely no use for nuns."

"Rude!" Ainsley finally told her sister. "You're being rude. Unnecessarily so."

"You know nothing of the ways of religious orders, so—"

"I know when they're being rude!"

"Brother Gemma—"

Ainsley's sister held her hand up, arm fully outstretched to silence the small group of war monk leaders, made up of different sects, that had come to speak to her. And all because she refused to stop glaring directly at Ainsley.

"Laila," Gemma called out, surprising Ainsley. She'd thought for sure her sister was about to rip her apart in front of the monks. But, still, Gemma's gaze never left Ainsley's. It was getting uncomfortable.

The royal centaur came close to Gemma.

"Why are all of you here and not with my sister in the tower?" Gemma asked.

Leaning in a bit so she could keep her voice low, Laila replied, "She asked me to keep Quinn and Caid out here until they appeared a little less . . ." She briefly glanced at her brothers and finished, "Murderous."

"I don't want her in there alone with—"

"Understood. I'll handle it."

Laila motioned to her small army of centaurs and they advanced toward the tower, Caid moving the fastest in order to get back to his mate, Keeley. Ainsley was impressed that Laila had managed to keep him out of the tower at all. His need to protect Keeley was what Ainsley would definitely call intense.

But Quinn didn't follow his brother immediately, as he usually did in these situations. Instead, he stopped in front of the Torn Moon tribe—a tribe she found fascinating because the rest of the centaurs so obviously avoided them—and told their leader, "You stay here."

Ainsley didn't expect Gruffyn to say anything. He never did. Then again, he didn't really have to.

"Why should my brother stay here?" Gruffyn's sister demanded, pushing herself between the two males.

"Not just him. All of you. And the why is because I don't trust any of you."

"For what reason?"

Quinn moved as close to the other male as he could with Gruffyn's sister standing between them, and Ainsley suddenly realized how much bigger the Torn Moon Clan was than the others. Not the number of them but the size of each individual centaur. Quinn was extremely large, but standing nearly hoof-to-hoof with Gruffyn, he looked like a pony.

"Because," Quinn explained, "I think you knew those dragons were coming to these lands."

Although Quinn made that accusation directly to Gruffyn, it was his sister who responded.

"Are you suggesting we conspired with dragons and the Blood Queen from thousands of leagues away while we've been here with *you* this entire time? Is *that* what you're suggesting?"

"As a matter of fact—"

"Because that sounds *insane!* Are you insane?"

"I'm not insane, and your brother didn't seem exactly surprised by all this."

"Just because my brother isn't shitting and pissing himself like some weak human, that does not make him a traitor to his people."

"I'm not so—"

"Do not take it out on my brother because you royals were oblivious to what was going on all around you this morning! Your lack of observation is not his fault. Blame it on your weak bloodline, Cousin."

Quinn smirked. A smirk that had pissed off many since he'd arrived to protect her family. Ainsley was worried it would piss off Gruffyn and his clan and give Gemma something else to scream about.

"Are you always going to let your sister answer for you, Gruffyn of the Torn Moon Clan?" Quinn asked as condescendingly as he could manage.

"He is when he has nothing to say," Gruffyn's sister replied for the silent centaur.

"Interesting." Quinn finally backed away from the siblings, and Ainsley was surprised by how relieved she felt. She usually enjoyed a little drama in her life as long as she wasn't in the center of it, but the last thing they needed right now was any more fighting.

"You know who I think needs some of your strong protection skills, Cousin?" Quinn said rather than walking away as Ainsley had hoped. "Brother Gemma here. You should keep an eye on her while all this is going on."

"*Princess* Gemma?" Gruffyn's sister mocked. "You want us to protect *her*? Didn't she just cut a man in half last week?"

"That was during a battle," Gemma needlessly added. "It's not like I go around doing that sort of thing for the fun of it."

"She doesn't need our protection," Gruffyn's sister argued. "She has a hoard of sexless human males to protect her. Look at them all. Just standing there." She openly sneered at the war monk leaders still waiting to speak with Gemma. "Like well-fed pets."

"Excellent point," Quinn cheered over the sounds of annoyed muttering from the monks. "But I'm sure Princess Ainsley wouldn't mind a little extra security around so many dragons, would you, Ainsley?"

Ainsley didn't know how she'd ended up in the middle of this, but she was so stunned by the question, she simply gawked at Quinn rather than answering him.

"See?" he asked the lady centaur. "Look how terrified she is by all this."

"*The archer?* I saw her take down a charging bear by putting an arrow through its eye."

Ainsley remembered that. It had been a good hunting day and she had been determined. Her mother had promised that if she took down a bear that morning, she'd make her famous roasted bear ribs for dinner. No way Ainsley was going to miss out on ribs.

"Not only that," Gruffyn's sister went on, "she's got a war monk and a battle nun for friends."

"Both novitiates," Quinn said, his smirk turning into a bright grin. "Young, untrained ladies with no hope of protecting anyone."

Ainsley saw Hilda's gaze narrow on Quinn, but Sheva was quick to remind her that, "Humble. Nuns are humble."

"Quiet, Monk," Hilda shot back.

Quinn gestured at Ainsley. "Now . . . whatever Princess Ainsley needs, I'm sure you lot will have no problem providing it. Yes? Great!"

He headed off toward the tower, and Gruffyn's sister started to follow but her brother quickly yanked her back by the shoulder. A good thing, too, because Quinn's tail lifted and an extremely large load of . . . well . . . shit dropped to the ground, landing exactly where the female centaur's front hooves would have been if Gruffyn hadn't caught her.

"Rude!" the insulted female centaur yelled after Quinn. "Unbelievably rude!"

# CHAPTER 5

Gruffyn wasn't sure if the royal's command was supposed to be a punishment or not, but he could definitely think of worse things to do than protect one of Queen Keeley's younger siblings. He found most of them quite entertaining. Especially the very young one that ran around with her own forge hammer. It was supposed to be for blacksmithing, but Gruff could already tell the child was using it to prepare for battle. Just like her queen sister.

Thankfully, Princess Ainsley was just as entertaining. She lived in trees. She was damn brilliant with a bow. She was friends with an angry nun and a grinning war monk. Most entertaining, though, was her brilliant knack for irritating her older sisters.

She was even more skillful at that than she was with a bow and arrow . . . and she was a master archer.

"Stay here," Brother Gemma ordered Princess Ainsley before she turned to face the war monk elders.

"Apologies, Brothers. So much going on. And I know you have questions and concerns. But before we discuss any of that in detail, let's take a moment to thank our gods for their help this dark day."

The war monks nodded in agreement. Each of them drew a sword or spear and dropped to one or both knees, the pointed end of their weapons in the ground. Heads bowed, they began to pray. Some silently, some much louder. Even Princess Ainsley's war monk friend kneeled in prayer, and the nun folded her hands and bowed her head.

Gruff patiently waited for them to finish but was surprised

when he heard the princess ask, "What exactly are you all praying for?"

It was her monk sister who replied through gritted teeth, clearly annoyed at the interruption, "We are thanking our gods for their protection at this time."

Staring down at all the bowed heads, Princess Ainsley noted, "But they didn't do a fucking thing."

Ainsley heard a grunt and glanced over her shoulder at Gruffyn the centaur. A very large male with black hair, bright blue eyes, and a large black tattoo that went from where his neck met his shoulder blade straight down his entire arm. He quickly looked away when the monks kneeling like pathetic beggars glared at her. But he wasn't fast enough for her to miss seeing his smirk. It was the first time that Ainsley had seen anything that even resembled a smile on his face.

"Our gods," her sister growled, forcing Ainsley to focus on Gemma's still kneeling form, "protected us from the evil of those dragons and the insanity of that foreign queen."

"No, they didn't," Ainsley replied. "Actually . . . I think the dragons are the only reason Queen Annwyl didn't decimate you and your monk friends. Your gods had nothing to do with it."

"The power of our gods influenced your precious dragons," another monk said.

"Don't the dragons have their own gods?" Ainsley asked with true confusion. She could never follow the logic of these religious groups with all their rules and sacrifices. "Why would human gods influence them at all?"

Gemma stood up and faced her. "What are you doing?"

"I'm wondering why my powerful sister is on her knees praying when we have dragons and a crazed queen wandering around our family home. Shouldn't you be doing something? Even if it's the wrong thing. *Something?*"

One of the older war monks, a man with battle scars where half his face should have been, got to his feet and pointed a damning finger.

"Heretic!" he shouted.

Ainsley stared at the monk for a moment before asking, "What's a heretic again? You people keep calling me that, but I have *no* idea what a heretic is. So I don't know whether I should punch you in the face or thank you."

"Brothers in Command," Gemma said to the fanatics now bristling with rage instead of fear, "let us retire to our chosen place for further discussion. All troops will return to their duties. I will be with you in a few minutes."

The war monk elders disbanded; the only two remaining were Gemma and Sheva. Hilda also stayed, but she didn't report to the war monks anyway, so this was not surprising. Still, Sheva, as a novitiate, took a risk standing by Ainsley's side.

Then again, Sheva was probably just bored and didn't want to miss the fight that Ainsley was positive would happen at any second.

Once the elders were gone, Gemma turned to Ainsley and, as she'd been doing since Ainsley bit her face during a fight over toys, the evil bitch punched Ainsley in the tit.

"*Owwww!*" Ainsley screeched, covering her chest with her hands. "*What was that for?*"

"Why do you say shit like that?" Gemma demanded, pacing in front of Ainsley. "I am doing my best to control different sects of war monks who don't necessarily get along. And *you* insist on questioning our gods!"

"I'm not questioning your gods," Ainsley corrected. "I'm questioning *you*. You're dropping to your knees like a—"

"*Don't* you dare," Gemma warned, stopping in her tracks. "And stop questioning everyone's beliefs and religious practices. What people do to worship their gods is their own concern as long as no one else is harmed."

"Don't war monks burn witches?"

From the corner of her eye, Ainsley saw Sheva drop her head into her hands, but she ignored it.

"Is that how you worship your gods?" Ainsley questioned. "By burning women you deem undesirable?"

"Ainsley," her sister snarled in warning.

"I may question, Gemma, but your people burn."

"Do not discuss things you don't understand, little sister. The religious sects that have come here are looking for safety, and Keeley has offered it to them. But they shouldn't have to endure your constant questions and rudeness about how they live and why they choose to believe."

"I don't care about anyone's religious beliefs. I just have no use for fanatics. *Owwwww! Stop punching me in the tits!*"

Gruff cringed a bit when the monk punched her sister in the chest again, surprised Princess Ainsley didn't punch her sister back.

"Now that we understand each other—" the monk said.

"We do?" the princess asked.

"I want you to—"

"I don't report to you, Gemma. I'm not one of your cult members."

Gruff cringed again when the monk grabbed her younger sister by the hair and twisted the dark mane around her fist, pulling the archer down until her head was by her sister's waist.

"For as long as I *breathe*, Ainsley Smythe, you report to me," the monk informed her sister with absolutely no mercy. "Now, while I deal with my monk brothers, and our queen sister deals with that crazed cunt, *you* will clean up the courtyard and grounds so the guards can take their places and the vendors can start setting up their stalls. Understand?"

"You want me to clean up shit?"

"You've mucked out stalls and pens, what's the difference?"

The monk shoved her sister away, her hand still gripping some strands from the royal's head, Gruff noticed.

"The difference," the younger sister replied, rubbing the back of her wounded scalp, "is where the shit came from. Horses and pigs are one thing, but humans—"

"Do it or I'll tell our mother that you shook in fear at the sight of the dragons and that there is no way you'll ever be ready to pick up a sword."

"You don't think I'll ever be ready to pick up a sword anyway, so what does that matter?"

"Because Mum is actually the one who can stop you from doing a gods-damn thing in this life. Would you really enjoy being sent to Aunt Rachel's for training?"

Gruff had no idea who Aunt Rachel was, but the closemouthed smile the monk flashed seemed more like a threat than anything else.

"Make sure she takes care of all this," the monk ordered Gruff and his tribe while pointing to a particularly large pile of human remains as she walked away.

"Picking up human shit and brains," the novitiate monk snickered. "Look at you, moving up in the world."

"Oh, fuck off."

"Why, why, *why*, do you insist on upsetting your sister so?" the future nun asked in confusion. "It's like you want the war monk to cut off your head. They do that, you know? Cut off the heads of family and former friends they deem . . ." She gave a small shrug.

"Heretical," the monk filled in. "And all those elder monks called you a heretic. It's usually the first thing they say before they start the burning."

"They?" the nun asked. "Aren't you one of them?"

"Right." The monk blinked several times. "Yes. *We*. It's usually the first thing *we* say before *we* start the burning."

"I don't understand," the nun continued. "How in the world did *you* find yourself joining a monastery? Had all the other monks been killed off or something and they were desperate to fill their ranks?"

The monk smirked. "We're not having this discussion again."

"But you never give me a straight answer."

"Isn't it enough that I . . . you know . . . pray?"

"So you had no calling?" the nun bluntly asked. "No god whispered your name in the night or showed you a path?"

"The god that calls to *me*, Sister, is steel. And my path is death." The monk smiled. "To be quite honest, I've never been happier."

The princess looked back and forth between the two women before she announced, "And my sister yells at me every time I use the term 'fanatic.'"

Ainsley looked around at the courtyard. "I don't want to do this," she whined. She knew she was whining, but she couldn't help herself. She couldn't ignore the mess in front of her, even if she'd wanted. How could they ask the townspeople to go on with their daily lives as if nothing had happened when the courtyard and streets were filled with human excrement and other . . . remains.

"Your sister does love a good life lesson," Sheva noted, also examining the courtyard.

"I am aware." Before Ainsley's monk sister took her sense of self and chopped it to bits, she'd always loved teaching her siblings how to do things correctly. Once she tried to show Lonnie how to breathe properly. Not while swimming so he wouldn't drown in the nearby lake, just . . . in general. She thought he breathed too fast. For months she attempted to "teach him the *right* way," which did nothing but irritate the family's future farmer.

So forcing Ainsley to clean up shit to keep her "humble" was typical of Gemma.

Ainsley sighed. "Let me get started."

"We can help," Sheva offered. And Ainsley wanted to kiss her.

Hilda, however . . . "What is this *we*, monk?"

"Nuns help others," Sheva pushed back. "I know that for a fact. So let's get you a shovel, Sister Cares-A-Lot."

Hilda turned to Ainsley. "Princess?"

Ainsley glanced around as if searching for something. "Oh, were you expecting me to turn down that offer?"

"Well—"

"Because that won't happen."

Ainsley led the way to a nearby stable that housed the royal guards' horses. Once inside, she grabbed three of the shovels. She was handing out two of them to Sheva and Hilda when Gruffyn walked around her, his soft hide brushing against her arm and side, and began pulling out long-handled shovels and pitchforks and handing them out to his tribe.

"Oh, you don't—"

"But we appreciate it," Hilda quickly cut in before shoving Ainsley toward the open doors.

"Ow!"

"Don't be a baby, Princess."

Ainsley rubbed her shoulder and sneered at Hilda. "I'm not being a—"

Ainsley slammed into something and looked up into the warm brown eyes of one of the royal guards' lieutenants.

"Princess Ainsley." Those warm brown eyes that had so easily fooled her three months ago flashed and instantly went cold. The lieutenant smirked. "How good to see you."

She nodded and silently attempted to move around the man and his small unit, doing her best to keep control of her emotions.

The urge to punch the fucker in the face.

Which was really hard when even his unit snickered as she attempted to pass. Because, apparently, they knew everything.

Just when she thought she was free, though, the lieutenant blocked her escape with that perfect body covered in chainmail and the surcoat with Keeley's crest of two big hammers crossed behind a flaming forge.

"You're not leaving us so soon are you, Princess? I was hoping we could spend some time together . . . again."

Ainsley gripped the shovel tight in both hands, wondering how much trouble she'd catch from Gemma when the righteous monk discovered her younger sister had beaten a man to death with a shit shovel.

No. No. Bashing the man until he screamed for mercy would not be worth it.

"Oh, I see," the lieutenant said, his hand reaching out to caress the handle of her shovel. Near her hands, but not quite touching. "You have such important work to do."

That particular arrow hit its mark, and Ainsley had just lifted her shovel when Hilda yanked her back and stepped up to the lieutenant.

"How dare you, worthless male!"

"Sister, I—"

"Shut up! I should have you crucified!"

The lieutenant blinked his big eyes, the image of innocence. "For what, Sister? What have I done?"

"You know what you've done. And don't pretend you don't!"

Mortified and wanting to be far away, Ainsley turned to walk out the open doors. But her exit was blocked by an extremely large centaur glaring down at her.

She thought the look on his face was one of disgust for her. She didn't blame him. She'd been *so* stupid! All Ainsley wanted to do was climb a tree and stay there until she died of old age. Sadly, she couldn't get past the centaur. There was just so much of him in his natural form.

He reached out to her with one big hand; she had no idea what he wanted until he took the shovel from her.

Gently pushing Ainsley aside, he stepped close to Hilda and, while she was busy dressing down the royal guard, Gruffyn suddenly forced the shovel into the lieutenant's hands.

Shocked, the man looked down at the shovel and then back up at the centaur.

"What's this, then?"

Gruffyn didn't reply, but his sister did.

"Princess Ainsley has orders for you and your lads," she said with a smile. "Clean up the courtyard and streets so everyone can get back to a normal day."

The lieutenant chuckled. "Sorry, centaur. But that's not *our* job. Perhaps—"

"Are you disobeying orders?"

"Orders? From a centaur?"

"From a *princess* of the realm," the female explained. "Sister to Queen Keeley and third in line to the throne."

It always startled Ainsley when anyone said that. It startled her even more that it was true.

"Perhaps your captain didn't explain how these things work," Gruffyn's sister went on, "but when a royal gives you an order, you follow it. To disobey would make you all traitors. Are you and your lads traitors, Lieutenant?"

As one, the centaurs all moved closer. Not just toward the lieutenant but surrounding his men. They moved close, their tails flicking quickly against their hides. Their hooves stomping the ground in a random, unnerving pattern. Their hands on the hilts of their weapons.

"You're not a traitor, are you, Lieutenant?" Gruffyn's sister asked, looking into those eyes Ainsley had been so drawn to. She'd always been a sucker for dreamy eyes. Probably explained her love of deer and why she had to take them down from behind. If she looked into their sweet faces, she would just crumple, and no one would eat meat that night.

The lieutenant's jaw clenched twice before he finally replied, "Of course not."

"Good!"

The centaurs all pushed their shovels and pitchforks into the hands of the royal guard. Sheva and Hilda transferred their shovels last, neither bothering to hide their grins.

"There we are!" Gruffyn's sister cheered before she gestured at Ainsley to go.

A little startled by this outcome, Ainsley hesitated several seconds before she could get her feet to move. She didn't bother to return the lieutenant's gaze. Because she didn't have to see it to know exactly how angry he was at the moment.

When Ainsley was several feet away from the stables, trying to decide where she should go next, she heard the Lieutenant cry out in pain. But when she looked over her shoulder, he was no longer standing in the open stable doorway. Instead, it was just Gruffyn who stood there, casually lowering his back leg when she faced him.

"Sorry!" Gruffyn's sister joyfully called out to the royal guard as the rest of the men rushed to their groaning leader inside the stable. "That was our fault!"

"Queen Keeley," began the white-haired female, a small smile on her face. In her human form, the dragoness was . . . stunning. No other word to use. Even the white hair that should make her look old, did nothing but bring out her bright blue eyes. Eyes that could appear cold and penetrating but, in this instance, appeared warm and caring. As if the last thing she wanted to be doing at this moment was bothering Keeley.

She couldn't explain it, but Keeley felt safer with this She-dragon around. She didn't know why. Maybe it was the effect she seemed to have on Keeley's counterpart. Like Keeley, the Mad Queen seemed calmer with the white dragon nearby.

"Lady Mor—"

"Morfyd is fine. Unless, of course, you prefer that proper titles be used."

Keeley immediately shook her head. "No. Not here. My sister

made me read about the royal protocols, but all those rules . . ." She gave an awkward shrug.

"Yes. It makes one uncomfortable," the dragoness said with a bigger smile. "The fewer uncomfortable protocols there are, the more relaxed Annwyl will be. And we like her *relaxed*," she emphasized. "As much as possible."

"Understood."

"Perhaps," she went on, "you have someone we can work with who could help us arrange for lodgings, food, all that. So you don't have to worry about any of that yourself."

Keeley briefly thought of giving Agathon the job. He'd been Follower of Her Word to her sister Beatrix, but that had been a job he did not want, because he'd lived in constant fear of displeasing either Beatrix or Marius, the Wielder of Hate, Beatrix's husband and the so-called ruling king of Beatrix's territories. Agathon had allowed Gemma to bring him to Keeley's realm and, since arriving, had turned out to be quite helpful.

The problem at the moment, however, was that Agathon was hiding in his room, possibly sobbing. His fear of dragons had sent the poor, sensitive man fleeing as soon as they'd entered the tower.

And Keeley didn't want to add to his stress.

The dragoness stepped closer and lowered her voice. "And maybe someone else to handle your mother."

"My mother?" Keeley asked.

Her mother stood behind the chair Keeley's father was sitting in. He'd—finally—stopped sobbing. Now he just sniffled a little and wiped his eyes. Her mother had her hands on his shoulders, rubbing them, stopping briefly to kiss the top of his graying head. It didn't seem strange to Keeley. It was a typical position for her parents. They loved each other. Had since they'd met. So Keeley was unclear what the dragoness was talking about.

However, Keeley also knew her mother, knew her almost better than herself. So she knew without a doubt that at some point the woman who'd given birth to her was going to say something annoying, rude, or simply despicable. It was in the Smythe bloodline. Her kin literally could not help themselves. How the dragoness would know that, though, Keeley couldn't imagine.

"I'll handle my mother," she promised the dragoness.

"My Keeley has a crown, you know," Keeley heard her mother brag. "A very nice one. I made it for her myself. Do you, Mad Queen, have a crown as well?"

Keeley cringed at the dragoness and mouthed, *Sorry.*

"No," the Mad Queen replied to Keeley's mother. "I don't have a crown. But I do have an empire."

Before Keeley and the dragoness could intervene—because Keeley knew *both* were about to launch themselves at the two women to stop the nasty fight about to take place—the silver dragon pulled the Mad Queen away by dragging her chair across the floor. The harsh noise of the chair legs scraping the stone floor stopped all conversation and potential fights. At the same time, the oh-so-handsome Gwenvael stretched himself across the dining table and greeted Keeley's mother with, "By the gods, you are devastatingly gorgeous, my lady."

But, as a blacksmith, her mother had been dealing with hand-some warriors for decades, and she responded as she would have in her forge years ago . . .

"Oh, fuck off."

"*Mum!*" Keeley barked out, her voice hitting an uncomfortable pitch. "I'm sorry, Lord Gwenvael."

"Don't apologize for me, Keeley."

"I have to. You won't!"

Her mother shrugged. "True."

"It's fine, Queen Keeley. I'm used to—"

"Being told to fuck off?" the black dragon questioned his gold brother with a smirk.

Keeley might have been worried about the Mad Queen's reaction to her mother's rudeness, but the woman was too busy getting into a slap-fight with the silver dragon. Something Keeley had once been informed by one of the war monks was not very "queenly."

When the Mad Queen grabbed the dragon by his long silver hair and began pulling—causing him to spew a torrent of vile words while his brothers did nothing to help but laugh hysterically—Keeley turned back to the dragoness and announced, "I have the perfect person to help you with all you need, Lady Morfyd."

*   *   *

Ainsley had planned to climb a nice tree and maybe get a little sleep, but good manners dictated she should offer the centaurs something to eat. It was the least she could do after Gruffyn and his sister, Briallen, had gotten her out of having to clean up the courtyard and streets. Thankfully, one of the town's pubs was far enough away from the early-morning action that the cook had baked bread and fried meat undisturbed, allowing the small group to eat first meal. In silence. It was the way of the centaurs, because they were centaurs; and Hilda because she was a nun. Ainsley, who usually ate alone these days, also liked to eat in silence simply so she could listen to what was going on all around her. Especially when she found a tall tree where she could eat in peace away from her very not-silent kin. It allowed her to observe the world around her, and what she couldn't see . . . she could hear. Some of what she discovered was local news. Some of it drama between people. She knew of at least six war priests having "forbidden" relationships with either other priests or some randy nuns who also didn't take their vows of abstinence from sex too seriously.

Not that Ainsley blamed them for their transgressions. What god would ask its followers to give up sex anyway? She might regret having fucked the lieutenant because he'd turned out to be such an asshole after the fact, but she didn't regret the actual fucking. That, in the moment, had been quite entertaining. And much needed. She wouldn't give up sex just because of the aftermath. Nor would she give up sex because some higher being demanded it.

If her parents hadn't had sex, Ainsley wouldn't even exist!

A tragic thought, since she did enjoy most of life so immensely.

Sheva leaned back in her chair and let out a healthy belch. "Good food," she added with a grin.

"We can tell you enjoyed it," Hilda drily noted between the slow chewing of each bite she took. She always finished her food after Ainsley and Sheva. Something that would normally annoy Ainsley, but watching the nun slowly and painstakingly chew each and every bit of food was an entertainment all on its own. They'd seen other nuns do the same thing. Something about their "mindfulness practice," which kept them in the present so their thoughts didn't wander to wants and needs that would distract them from their lifelong worship of their chosen gods.

Whatever. Ainsley just knew she couldn't eat that slowly. After years of dining with her family, that wasn't surprising. The Farmerson-Smythe family worked hard, played hard, and ate like starving animals that hadn't seen food for days. The best one could do was protect one's fingers and arms from the onslaught and hope for the best.

"Are you heading back to the tower soon?" the owner of the pub asked Ainsley from behind the bar.

She'd rather not, but she knew she should check on her family. Make sure they hadn't been eaten.

"I am."

"Then can you take your cousin with you, my lady?"

Ainsley didn't know what the man meant until she stood up enough to see her cousin Keran asleep under one of the tables against the wall.

"Oh, for the love of—"

"I'll get her," one of the centaurs grumbled.

"Watch your neck, luv," Sheva warned the centaur. "She's a nasty fighter when she's just waking up."

Ainsley sat again and muttered, "Keran is a nasty fighter all the time."

And she was. A hero of her fighting guild, Keran was one of the few champion fighters still alive to tell tales of her times in the pits. Those tales inevitably bought her a few drinks each night at any pub she went to.

Ainsley wasn't surprised her cousin drank so much. How could she not? Her body was a brutal map of every fight she'd endured. Drinking probably helped with the pain those bouts had left behind.

By the time the centaur brought Keran to the table, she was mostly awake.

"Morning all!" she said cheerily before cringing at the sound of her own voice. Still, it must have been a light night because Keran didn't vomit. That was generally one of the first things she did each day.

Keran glanced around. "Where is everyone? Usually this place is bustling with the morning rush."

Ahhh. To live in Keran's world. Her cousin was completely oblivious to everything around her until someone shoved a sword in her hand and she was ordered to kill. She wasn't part of Keeley's army, but she didn't have to be. She was good wherever they put her. As long as Keran had a sharp weapon at the ready and an enemy to fight, nothing stood in the champion's way.

But when the fighting was over and the children where all safe in their beds, ale had better be waiting for Ainsley's cousin or they'd all regret it.

"So you didn't hear anything this morning?" Briallen asked.

"No. Why?"

The centaur shook her head. "No reason."

"Come on," Ainsley said, standing again. "Let's get you back to the tower and show you . . . everything."

"Are you done?" Sheva asked Hilda.

The nun didn't reply but simply ate the last three pieces of meat on her plate while they all watched her, until Sheva asked with a laugh, "What is wrong with you?"

With a last sip of water from her chalice and not bothering to answer Sheva's question, Hilda stood and led the way outside. There was just something about her that screamed, "I lead and you follow," which they all did. Without question!

They'd been walking back to the tower when a door opened and Ainsley saw her Uncle Archie walk out into the bright morning.

"That's a brothel, you know," Hilda noted.

"No, it's not," Ainsley quickly replied. Before following up with, "How do you know?"

"Mother Superior makes us sing outside to teach the whores they are dirty and disgusting, but our gods love them anyway."

Sheva stopped walking and gawked at the nun. "Tell me you're making that up?"

"When do I ever make anything up? When? Is there anything about me that says I'm creative or interesting enough to make up stories about nuns and whores?"

"Stop calling them whores," Ainsley told Hilda.

"What should I call them?"

She thought a moment. "Businesswomen."

"I prefer whore."

Not in the mood to discuss any further, Ainsley focused on her uncle. But she quickly realized that was a mistake too, as she watched him kiss the woman he'd spent the night with.

"She looks like your mother," Sheva noted.

"I can't discuss that." Ainsley *wouldn't* discuss that. Not now. Not ever. All . . . *that* was between her parents and her uncle.

Wanting to put the brothel behind her, Ainsley set off again. The centaurs continued to follow her. But she'd barely gotten a few feet before Archie called out, "Ho, Niece!"

Ainsley cringed before facing her uncle.

"Little early for you, isn't it?" he asked, laughing at her expense. "This one likes to stay in and sleep, you know," he told the others.

He smiled down at her and teasingly punched her arm. So she punched him back. Hard. In the chest.

"Ow! What was that for?"

"While you're whoring it up, Uncle, our family could have used your help. We have visitors. Dangerous ones."

"What visitors?"

Ainsley waited a beat before announcing, "Dragons."

Archie snorted, then laughed outright. "You *must* stop listening to your father, girl. I know he's my brother, but he was always a—"

"It's true," she said before her uncle could start insulting her father for the next ten minutes, as he'd done many times before. "Ask the centaurs, if you don't believe me."

Archie transferred his mocking gaze to the centaurs, and Gruffyn simply raised his forefinger and pointed at the sky.

Dropping his head back, her uncle stared into the sky for a good two minutes before he finally nodded and said, "Sorry I didn't believe you, sweet Ainsley." He put his hand on her shoulder and stared right at her. "And don't you worry, my love. Your uncle Archie will handle all this."

Gruff watched Ainsley's uncle walk away after his promise. Like his brother, he was a big man. A one-time soldier and now a mason, the one who'd designed the tower and most of the surrounding town, utilizing the help of the mason dwarves to get it done fast and efficiently.

Once he had disappeared around a corner, the monk mused, "He took that surprisingly well."

"He did," the nun agreed. "I mean . . . for your uncle Archie."

Ainsley didn't reply. She was too busy staring off past Briallen. After a few seconds, she looked down; then she lifted her gaze to Gruff, and he saw her expression go from slight confusion to full-on panic.

"Oh, gods," she said to him, eyes wide. "Archie didn't handle that well."

Sheva frowned. "He didn't?"

The royal didn't answer Sheva because she had already started running.

"Ainsley!" Sheva yelled after her. "What's wrong?"

"Archie's gone to slaughter the children!" she yelled over her shoulder.

"*What?* Why?"

"Why do you think?" the princess screamed back. "*Because he's an insane bastard!*"

# CHAPTER 6

Morfyd quickly understood why this human had been chosen to help them—because neither dragon nor human intimidated her.

"Here." The young royal pushed open a door and gestured inside. "This will be your room."

Annwyl stepped inside with Fearghus right behind her.

"Oh, well this is nice—"

"Great" was the reply before the door was pulled closed, rudely trapping the most feared queen in all the lands inside the relatively small room, with a fierce dragon in human form.

"This way," the royal said before moving off.

"What's your name again?" Morfyd asked, following the human female.

"Isadora."

"Oh! Are you called Iz—"

"No." The female turned and stared right at Morfyd. "It's Isadora. It's not Iz. It's not Izzy. And it's definitely *not* Dora. It's Isadora. That's my name. Please call me that."

"Sure, I was just—"

"Thank you."

Isadora continued around the circular hallway. Morfyd glanced back at Gwenvael, but they both quickly looked away from each other before they started to laugh. Because she knew they were about to start laughing.

Isadora pushed open another door and gestured with a sweep of her arm. "This is your room, uh . . . Brack."

"It's Briec."

"I honestly don't care."

Briec glanced inside before stepping into the room. "It's tiny," he noted.

"Grow smaller."

Morfyd covered up her laugh by pretending to cough, but Gwenvael had to spin completely away.

"Do you know who I am?" Briec demanded of the human. "I'm Briec the Mighty, second oldest in the House of Gwalchmai fab Gwyar, fourth in line to the throne of the White Dragon Queen, Shield Hero of the Dragon Wars, and Lord Defender of the Dragon Queen's Throne."

"And I'm Isadora. Too young to leave my parents, but old enough to babysit their efforts to repopulate the entire world with their offspring. And to be quite honest, I have more important things to do than worry about a pompous royal complaining about where he'll sleep after attempting to invade my sister's territories. So, if this room isn't to your liking, m'lord, feel free to find the closest door and exit through it to the vast fields available to you. Or, I don't know," she added with a shrug, "fuck off. Those are your options. Choose wisely."

Isadora stalked off and Briec took in a deep breath, about to blast the child with his flame, but Morfyd stopped him with a quick spell while Gwenvael shoved their brother into his temporary room and shut the door.

"He is *such* a baby!" Gwenvael whispered.

"He could be worse."

"No, he couldn't."

Morfyd nodded. "No. He couldn't."

They continued to follow the girl to another room. She opened the door and, again, gestured with her arm. But before she could say who the room was for, they heard yelling and screaming from down below, followed by rapid stomping coming from the nearby stairs. A few seconds later, a large man with one long braid hanging down his back dashed by.

Frowning, Isadora watched him.

Moments later, another sibling of the human queen charged by as if chased by demons. Three human women followed.

"What's wrong?" Isadora yelled at her sister's back.

"Uncle Archie is going to slaughter the children!"

Instead of joining the chase, Isadora merely rolled her eyes and sighed out, "Honestly! *Again?*"

Gwenvael leaned in close as if he was about to kiss the side of Morfyd's head and whispered against her ear, "We should invade more countries for no reason. Because whatever is going on here is *fabulous!*"

Annwyl sat down and immediately announced, "I like our beds better."

Fearghus the Destroyer gazed at her from across the room. "Really?"

"I'm a queen. I should get a soft bed."

"Annwyl . . . why are we here?"

"Because—"

"No. Don't lie to me. My brothers may take you at your word, but I know better. And I know you were spending a lot of time with The Beast behind closed doors. Because no matter what you and Dagmar may have told all of us, these people are not . . ." He struggled for the right words before finally settling on ". . . masterminds. They're barely minds. We should have just sent an ambassador."

"I was not about to send your uncle Bram alone to unknown lands where child slavery is common."

"Common? Did you not see that poor man's reaction to the news about his daughter? Do you truly believe that was all made up?"

"No. *No.* Not at all," Annwyl insisted. "I truly believe Angus Farmerson is a good man. And he's raised good children . . . mostly. Except for the one."

"But?"

Annwyl lifted her hands and gestured around the room, but she was really talking about Queen Keeley's territories. "But . . . they're not ready for this. Any of it."

"Then we should help them."

"Help them? Help them with what? Surviving? This queen has to fight this battle on her own. But I don't—"

A knock on the door cut Annwyl off and she walked over to answer it. Outside, she found two women, a monk, and a nun pinning a man to the stone floor as he yelled, "I slaughter because I love! I slaughter because I love!"

Annwyl closed the door and turned to her mate. "Yeah. All these people are going to die."

Unwilling to listen to any more shouting, Gruff reached down, grabbing the crazy bastard by his cotton shirt and yanking him up. The nun, the monk, the guild fighter, and Princess Ainsley rolled off the man and hit the floor.

"You don't understand!" the princess's uncle argued, his feet dangling because Gruff refused to put him down.

"Understand that you want to kill your own family?" Briallen demanded. "That seems sane to you?"

"It's better than letting my sweet nieces and nephews become some delicacy on the table of flying lizards!"

"Actually," the gold dragon easily slipped in, "human flesh is quite gamey. Especially when overcooked. So you're not really a delicacy to us. Not only that but humans are so easy to kill. Whereas a good stag with a large pointy rack can put up quite a fight, making one feel as if one has earned the meal. And the meat can be so tender when cooked just . . ."

He glanced around, noticing them all silently gawking at him until his gaze settled on his sister and he asked, "Not helping?"

"Not even a little," the white-haired dragoness replied.

"Sorry."

"See?" the hysterical uncle began screaming again. "*See? All the children must be killed to save them!*"

Gruff, now truly fed up, lifted Princess Ainsley's uncle over the banister. All he had to do was open his hand and their problems would be over. At the very least, the screaming would stop.

"No, no!" the princess yelped. "Don't drop him!"

"Are you sure?" Briallen asked. "The children will be safe."

The royal glanced at Gruff, and he gestured toward her kin with a small tilt of his head. She didn't say anything, but he saw her eyes warm before she gave a shrug and replied, "You do have a point."

Archie Farmerson instantly snapped out of his ongoing hysterics and gasped at his niece.

"*You'd let him kill me?*" he demanded, now grabbing Gruff's forearm and holding on tight. "I'm your dearest uncle!"

"You're my *only* uncle on my father's side. And the Smythes have a bunch. Meaning, you are easily replaced, dearest Uncle Archie."

"You wouldn't!"

The princess raised a brow at Gruff and he let his arm drop for a brief moment, before lifting the man up again.

"Oh, no!" Briallen mockingly exclaimed. "My brother's arm is weakening. However will he hold on?"

"Fine! Fine!" the human said. "What do you want?"

"For you *not* to slaughter the children," the princess immediately replied. "At any time. In the existence of the universe. You swear not to slaughter the children, and I'll ask dear Gruff nicely not to allow you to fall to your death."

"But—"

"You have three seconds, Uncle!"

"Fine! I won't slaughter the children."

Once the princess gave a short nod, Gruff easily hauled the human back over the banister and lowered him to the ground.

When Gruff released him, Archie Farmerson bent over at the waist and put his hands on his knees, taking in and letting out big gulps of air.

Shaking her head, the princess turned to walk away, but her uncle's words stopped her.

"And when your siblings are dying on a spit, about to be devoured by these awful beasts, don't come crying to me, Niece!"

She faced him and pointed her finger. "If you come near my siblings again with anything but friendly uncle banter, I will tell my father *everything*. And that will be all the excuse he'll need to flay your skin from your bones with my mum's blessing. Do we understand each other?"

"As a matter of—"

"*DO YOU UNDERSTAND WHAT MY SISTER IS TELLING*

YOU?" Princess Ainsley's younger sister Isadora abruptly bellowed into her uncle's ear. Every centaur backed away from her because none of them enjoyed loud noises.

Her uncle slowly turned his head to glare at his young niece, his
mouth open in shock.

"Because," she added, now calm, "she sounds perfectly clear
to me."

After an annoyed growl, her uncle said, "I understand."

"Good!" She walked to one of the rooms and threw the door
open. "You. Pretty boy. Inside."

Grinning, the gold dragon slid into the room. "I'm the pretty
one," he told his sister before Princess Isadora leaned in and slammed
the door shut, ignoring the laughter that followed.

She motioned to the white-haired dragoness, but her sister
asked, "What are you doing?"

"Keeley put me in charge of handling our visitors. Right now,
I'm getting the royals their rooms. Although there has been much
complaining."

"There was much complaining," the dragoness confessed. "But
it all came from Briec. He likes to complain. He's really good at it."

"They have *you* doing this?" the princess pushed. "You?"

"Yes. Me. Because, apparently, I don't have enough to do. But,
unlike you, I can't climb trees to get away."

Without another word, the younger royal stormed off, and the
dragoness followed.

There was a long silence after that. Even the royal's uncle managed to keep his mouth shut. It wasn't until the monk finally said,
"Soooo . . . you get to clean up shit while your eighteen-year-old sister handles the royal visitors?" She gave one snort, followed by an
"Ouch."

With a growl of her own, Princess Ainsley spun on her heel and
headed back down the stairs.

Once the royal was gone, the nun faced the monk and asked,
"Have you ever thought of taking a vow of silence?"

"I have. But we both know I'd never keep it."

Gemma gawked at her sister over the big table spread with maps
and scrolls filled with information and asked, "What now?"

Keeley repeated her suggestion, "I think we should talk to Queen Annwyl about an alliance. Working together."

"With *dragons?*"

"Yes. With dragons."

"What is your obsession with strange beings? Speaking of which . . . your demon dogs deserted you."

"Demon *wolves*, and they were frightened like everyone else."

"Not by the dragons but by that *woman!* You can't seriously be suggesting we work with the Mad Queen of Dark Plains."

"She just doesn't seem that bad."

*"You said the same thing about Beatrix!"*

The door opened and Ainsley walked in, giving Gemma a moment to get her anger under control so she could hopefully convince Keeley what a stupid, ridiculous idea joining forces with dragons and a nutter queen would be. Or to beat her in the head until she realized that Gemma was right.

But then Ainsley slammed the door and demanded to know, "Why is my eighteen-year-old sister managing royals while I'm made to clean up shit?"

"You needed to focus on something other than yourself," Gemma responded.

"What does that mean?"

"You made her clean up all that shit and piss in the courtyard?" Keeley asked.

"Someone had to do it."

"Not a princess of the realm."

"It's good for the common folk to see one of us doing manual labor."

"Then you do it!" Ainsley snapped.

"I'm a war monk leader. I'm not touching human shit. Not when I'm one of our war gods' representatives on earth."

Ainsley threw up her hands, but Keeley quickly stepped in to calm her down.

"All right. All right. We have a lot going on right now. We don't have time to turn on each other."

"I can help Isadora," Ainsley suggested.

*"No,"* both Gemma and Keeley said at the same time.

"Why not?"

Gemma started to answer but Keeley cut her off.

"Shut up," she told Gemma before focusing again on Ainsley. "I appreciate the offer, but I put Isadora in charge of the dragon royals for a reason."

"You're saying I can't do it? That I'm incapable?"

"Not incap—"

"Yes," Gemma said. "That's what we're saying."

"That's horse shit."

"Isadora can handle them. They don't frighten her. They don't intimidate her. And she knows how to manage unruly toddlers, which is how most of those dragons act."

"But *I'll* be intimidated?"

"You were definitely frightened."

"So were you. So was Keeley!"

"And we're not handling them either," Keeley interjected.

"But we could if we had to."

Keeley glared at her. "Why?"

Gemma shrugged. "Why what?"

"Why can't you be nice?"

"I don't need nice," Ainsley explained. "I need to understand what I'm doing wrong."

"You're not doing anything wrong," Keeley replied.

"Well . . ."

Keeley stomped her foot. "Gemma!"

"She wants honest! And I'll honestly tell you, Ainsley, that sometimes you're weak."

"*I'm* weak?"

"Not physically. And not with a bow in your hand. But you can't handle this particular situation by shooting one of the dragons in the eye. You need to be strong without weapons. You need to stop hiding in trees."

"I don't *hide* in trees."

"You've been doing it since you were four!"

"Because Beatrix kept trying to kill me!"

"And I always had to save you! You never fought back!"

Gemma stopped and blew out a breath. This was not how she'd

wanted this unavoidable conversation to go. Bringing up old history.

"Look, I'm sorry." Gemma placed her hands on her hips. "I'm sure we can find you *something* to do. You know, to help."

Ainsley walked to the door. "Forget it."

Gemma and Keeley both jumped when the door slammed so hard it nearly came off its hinges.

"See?" Gemma pointed out to a now-glaring Keeley. "Physically she's very strong."

# CHAPTER 7

Gruff watched Princess Ainsley storm down the stairs, out of the main hall, and into the courtyard. He followed by himself, leaving his tribe to see if the centaurs' royal, Princess Laila, needed any assistance managing the dragons and their mad human leader.

He followed the princess through town and, eventually, out of it. She cut through one of the south fields until she reached one of the biggest forests close to Forgetown. Once inside, she found a big, tall tree and proceeded to climb.

Gruff had to admit . . . he loved watching Princess Ainsley climb trees. Her ascent was almost elegant. She wore no special boots. Needed no ropes or gloves. Using nothing but her hands and legs, she scrambled up that tree without disturbing the birds nesting on some of the limbs. Once she'd settled in, he heard her let out a very long sigh, and he knew she wouldn't be moving for a while.

He found his own nearby tree and leaned against the trunk, but the royal's voice caught his attention.

"You don't have to stay," she said, rightly guessing she wasn't alone. "I'm not going anywhere for a while. I need to think. And be depressed. I don't like to move when I'm depressed. So if you have something else to do, feel free to do it."

Gruff shook his head, grunted, and replied, "No. I'll stay."

Not a second later, he heard the leaves rustle, the royal gave a surprised grunt, and before he could even react, she'd hit the ground not ten feet from him.

"By the cock of Ofydd Naw!" he gasped, charging over to her.

"Are you all right?" he demanded as he quickly shifted into human form so he could kneel beside her.

With great care, he slowly turned the royal over, but her eyes were open and she was gawking directly at him when she said, "Did you just speak to me? With *words*?"

Ainsley had been moving to another branch in her favorite tree because the one she'd chosen was a little less comfortable than she'd expected. It was a general tree-climbing move she'd been making since she was four years old, when she couldn't climb into anything bigger than a five-year-old cedar. But when she'd heard the centaur speaking—*to her!*—Ainsley simply lost her footing and fell... forty feet or so.

Thankfully, it wasn't the first time she'd fallen from a tree. After breaking her shoulder when she was ten after a one-hundred-foot drop, Ainsley had taught herself how to fall properly to lessen the damage. How did she do this? By throwing herself from trees over and over until Keeley caught sight of her and put a stop to it with a hysterical harangue about risking her "stupid neck!"

Her specialized training had been invaluable, though, because she'd managed to keep her head, neck, and spine intact in this latest drop.

"Don't move," Gruffyn of the Torn Moon Clan told her. "I'll get help."

Ainsley dismissed his offer with a wave of her hand. "No, no. I'm fine."

"Don't get up!"

But Ainsley was already on her feet and staring down at the centaur still kneeling in front of her. "I've never heard your voice before." And it was *fantastic*. So low, she felt it in the heels of her feet.

She—thankfully—didn't say that, though.

"I actually thought you couldn't speak. Quinn said you could only whinny."

The centaur rolled his eyes and growled, "Bastard," before standing. She watched him rise above her like one of the suns, and it took everything she had not to stare like some pathetic, lovesick girl. Ainsley refused to be lovesick about anything after her experience with the lieutenant.

"You two aren't friends, eh?"

"He's an asshole. And I speak when I feel like it."

"Which makes sense, since your sister seems to enjoy speaking for both of you."

Half his mouth lifted in a smile, and it was fucking adorable!

Gods! What was wrong with her?

Ainsley blew out a breath and turned away from Gruffyn while brushing dirt from her clothes.

"Are you in pain?" he asked.

"Pain?" She realized he was referring to her fall. "Oh! No. No. I'm really fine. My head didn't hit the ground, and—" She lifted her hands, flexed her fingers; lifted each leg and made circles with her ankles. "All my arms and legs work just fine."

When he only gazed at her with doubt, she added, "I used to throw myself from trees so I could learn to fall properly. I know when I'm really hurt."

Ainsley moved away to make sure she truly could walk and wasn't lying to the centaur. Thankfully, she wasn't.

"You *threw* yourself from trees?" he questioned. "Honestly?"

"I never got combat training like Gemma and Keeley. Keeley, being the first child, learned from Dad. He did it to keep her entertained. Gemma learned to fight from the religious fanatics. I had to teach myself."

"By throwing yourself out of trees?"

"I can do forward rolls, too."

This time Gruffyn's entire mouth lifted into a smile that slid into a grin before he told her with a laugh, "That is the most *bizarre* thing I've ever heard anyone say."

Gruff had heard some strange tales in his life, but that was . . . a new one. Maybe not the dumbest or most ridiculous, but definitely the most bizarre. Because who willingly throws themselves out of trees? And then has the nerve to call it "combat training"?

A Farmerson-Smythe child. That's who.

Still . . . Gruff was relieved he didn't have to rush the royal to a local healer. Or, even worse, Sarff. A wonderful healer, but one who didn't really concern herself with her subject's pain tolerance. Though she didn't think suffering was necessarily good for the soul—as some war priests and nuns suggested—she did believe it would remind the sufferer not to do anything "that stupid again during battle."

Which, he had to admit, was an effective policy.

"So did you *fling* yourself off mountains and rocks, too? Or simply forward roll off them?"

"My, you have certainly gotten chatty."

"Sorry. I've just never heard anything so—"

"Bizarre. Yes. Got that."

"If you want me to stop talking—"

"*No.*" She was so emphatic, he did stop talking. After clearing her throat, Princess Ainsley added, "I don't mind you talking at all. It's just . . . I didn't know you could."

"Yes. Because you thought centaurs whinny."

"Blame Quinn for that!"

"I blame Quinn of the Scarred Earth Clan and his kin for many things. What's one more?"

The royal dropped to the ground, her back against the tree's trunk. "I have noticed that your two clans don't seem very . . . close."

"Actually, our two clans are cousins by bloodline."

"Really?"

"Really."

Gruff sat on the ground across from the royal, giving himself a few extra seconds to get adjusted to the way his human body was supposed to move. He didn't use it very much, so he wasn't as familiar with exactly what he could do with only two legs.

"Cousins by blood," the royal repeated. "Huh."

"Yes. But despite that connection, we hate them."

The royal grinned. "I have to say, centaur, I am enjoying our first conversation."

The Commander General of the Old King's armies looked around the room at the dukes and barons. A gruff, hard man who had spent almost his entire life in the army, he acknowledged nearly everyone in the room . . . but Beatrix.

She knew why. She was a woman. Not even a pretty one. Why would he show her any respect? Even as a queen.

The Commander General had no use for women he wasn't about to fuck or murder or hold hostage to get something he wanted from an enemy. The Old King had ruled alone for decades with no queen by his side. Just consorts who had no say in much of anything. Women easily tossed away should they irritate the Old King's thin nerves. That's what the Commander General was used to and what he expected from all women.

That's not what he got from Beatrix, though, and he hated her for it.

Quite used to being hated, Beatrix didn't let it bother her. The only reason she hadn't had his throat cut yet was because the Commander General had the full loyalty of the Old King's army. To dismiss him as just another useless human would be a mistake on her part, and she knew it. So, she bided her time. It was one of her best skills . . . biding time.

As a woman in the Old Kingdom, Beatrix had to have uncommon skills to get anything done. Because she had no beauty. She had no charm. She had no warmth. She had none of those things other women possessed in abundance, the qualities that helped them manage through life. But Beatrix didn't plan to "manage" her way through life. She would rule.

Her time was coming; she just needed to deal with a few of the old war horses that had remained part of the fabric of the Old Kingdom. The ones who still expected her husband to be giving the orders, making the rules, building the empire. But Marius, the Wielder of Hate, had no vision. He had no power beyond what he'd inherited from his dead father and the sword he'd used against his many half brothers and male cousins. And he had no intelligence beyond that of the basest animal. She could distract the man with a pretty girl and a pint of ale the way one could distract a barn cat with a mouse.

Sadly, the Commander General was not as easily fooled, which meant every time his gaze passed over her, she made sure she was smiling.

Not to make him feel comfortable, though. Her smiles never

made anyone feel comfortable. She'd learned that from her own family. When Beatrix smiled, she made others feel anything but comfortable and she was fine with that.

"Perhaps I should discuss this with His Majesty," the Commander General remarked, his gaze on a duke across the room.

"Unfortunately, His Majesty is not available at this time," Ivan the Mystic explained, and it was clear from the way the Commander General clenched his jaw that his hatred of Ivan was much more profound than it was of Beatrix.

She'd met Ivan a year into her time in the Old Kingdom. She'd found that he'd originally trained to be a monk but had finally left the harsh life of self-denial and hard work, delving instead into a life of witchcraft and indulgence. For many royals, this would be a reason to keep Ivan the Mystic away from the throne, but Ivan had turned out to have a wealth of knowledge and useful gossip. He'd fucked many of the wives and older daughters of the men currently in the room, and these women had told him *everything*.

Ivan had a way with women. It didn't work on Beatrix, but he seemed to enjoy that. He seemed to enjoy the fact that physically, neither of them enticed the other. That knowledge made their relationship the most real either had ever had. Beatrix did not question Ivan's loyalty because they both wanted the same thing. Power. Just different kinds. He wanted the power of the gods, and she wanted the power of an empress.

She'd make sure they both got what they wanted.

"Where is the king?" the Commander General demanded.

"Not here. But Her Majesty, Queen Beatrix, is available. Tell her what you must, and she will—"

"I don't have time to waste—"

"Now, now. Before you say anything you cannot take back, Commander General, perhaps you'd like to—"

Ivan stopped speaking when the Commander General stomped his way across the room, plate armor rattling as he moved.

When he snatched the door open, Beatrix asked, "Is this about the Blood Queen of Dark Plains?"

The Commander General froze in the doorway.

"She's crossed the Amichai Mountains . . . yes?"

"Did your male *witch* tell you that?"

"No. My spies did. I have spies everywhere, Commander General. You really should keep that in mind."

He faced her, and she found it interesting how his big body nearly filled the doorway. There was so much of him, especially covered in his plate armor. Must be terrifying for his enemies on the field of battle. To see something like that tearing toward them, big battle-axe in hand, maybe screaming a war cry. An interesting thought but, unlike her sisters, Beatrix didn't need to go to a battlefield to witness such encounters up close. She had others provide that information to her while she remained in safety. After the loss of Agathon, she'd brought on several new Keepers of the Word. There was only supposed to be one who worked directly with the king, but she'd changed that tradition and made the new Keepers part of her spy network. A network Ivan managed for her.

"Yes," the Commander General said. "The Blood Queen is here. In our lands. And she's not alone. She brings—"

"Dragons. Yes. I know."

"You don't seem too worried," he said, and she could hear the accusation in the man's voice.

"Because I'm not. I don't fear a madwoman. Nor should you."

"A madwoman that, I've been told, has come here with an army of *dragons*. We can't fight dragons."

"Dear Duke Hitchbrook"—she gestured to the duke—"already has his men building siege weapons designed to handle dragons coming at us from the air, while Baron Hoffenmyer has been in charge of weapons that can destroy them should they attack from land."

His eyes narrowed on her. "You *want* to fight dragons . . . ?"

"Of course I don't. What sane person wants to fight dragons? But that land beyond the Amichai Mountains should not be ruled by an insane woman who fucks dragons." She glanced at Ivan. "I don't even *want* to know how she manages that."

"We'll have to ask before we take her head," Ivan joked.

"It's insane, what you're planning," the Commander General said plainly, stepping back into the room. "For centuries we have never ventured over the Amichai Mountains, and they have never come here. And for good reason. The Mad Queen is not the only ruler in those lands. There are many others, and not all of them are insane. Now you've opened the doorway to their breaking that un-spoken but iron pact we've upheld for so long."

"Nothing lasts forever, Commander General. And, eventually, one of them would have come here to take what they think is theirs. We're just striking first."

"We're not ready for an onslaught from dragons."

"They're not going to attack us. I doubt they've even attacked my sister."

"And you know this . . . how?"

"While the Mad Queen may wear the crown, she is not the one who runs those territories."

"You speak of the fabled Dragon Queen?"

"No. I mean The Beast."

"Who's The Beast?"

"Someone actually worthy of my concern. And trust me, that one has not traveled into our lands. Not yet. You need only think of the Mad Queen and her army coming here as a scouting party rather than a battle-ready army."

"You think a queen has come here merely to scout these territo-ries?"

"If she were here to fight, she'd have laid my sister's pathetic lit-tle town to waste and been on her way here. She's not."

"Maybe because she's too busy picking the remains of the townspeople from her teeth?"

"Anything is a possibility, but no. I've studied the Blood Queen closely. I know her better than she knows herself."

"You *know* a madwoman?"

"Even the insane have patterns, Commander General. Don't worry. When they come—and they will come—I will make sure we are more than ready for them. Dragons and all."

"And if your sister aligns herself with the Blood Queen? Com-bines her army with theirs?"

Beatrix chuckled at the thought.

"If that were to happen, the alliance wouldn't last long. Not with my sister on her very high, moral horse. As soon as that mad-woman does something reprehensible—they will tear each other apart."

The Commander General stepped closer and, for the first time, he looked at Beatrix with something akin to . . . respect?

Perhaps. But she wouldn't count on that just yet.

"And if that happens, we will be in an even better position," she added. "Just make sure my armies are ready when I need them."

"*Your* armies?"

"Do you know where your king is right now?" she asked. "He's burning down a little town about one hundred leagues away from here because the baron did not take him seriously. He could have had one of your military units handle that, but he wanted to do it himself. Felt it was necessary to make his point. I, in comparison, don't have time for nonsense. I have an empire to build. So I need to know."

"Know what?"

"Do you want to lead the army of a kingdom? Or the army of an empire?"


"Seven thousand years?" Ainsley asked. "You and your tribe have been nursing a grudge for seven thousand years? Really?"

"Yes. Really. It's my job. I am—"

"The Grudge Holder. Yes. I . . . heard that part." She shrugged, suddenly depressed. "At least you have a job. Apparently, I don't deserve a job because I'm weak and pathetic. I don't deserve to live because I didn't fight back against Beatrix when I was still in my crib."

"Is that what your sisters *actually* said?"

"It was close."

He scoffed and flashed that damn smile again. Ainsley had only ever seen him glare or roll his eyes. No one who looked that angry should have a smile so powerful. The smile didn't make him appear any less angry, but it did make him damn gorgeous.

"You know," he said, "you don't have to wait until someone gives you a job. I was holding grudges long before I was given the title."

"That sounds great, but Gemma never lets me do anything. She barely lets me out of her sight." She paused a moment before adding, "Except when they're completely ignoring my existence on the planet and could not care less what I'm up to."

Ainsley relaxed her shoulders and elaborated, "You know, I followed Gemma to her monastery, fought in a battle that decimated three-quarters of her brotherhood, and came home alive . . . and no one in my family even noticed I'd been gone. Gemma barely noticed I was there when it was happening. It was *Quinn* who watched my back. Keeley didn't even realize I wasn't around for all that time, and she watches my other siblings like a hawk. My sisters hate me, don't they?" she finally asked out loud.

"They don't hate you," he argued. "I know hate. Revel in it like good-fitting armor. There's no hate there. Although I do sense irritation."

"I don't know why. I'm delightful."

"Except maybe when you tell your monk sister she's just a puppet for the gods. I could see how that would get on her nerves."

"All I do is ask questions."

"Leading questions. When you aren't outright saying that she's stupid."

Ainsley cringed. "Am I really that bad?"

"Yes."

"Couldn't even lie to me, eh?"

"I'm known for many things, but lying isn't one of them. Which is why I can tell you that sitting around, waiting for your sisters to *give* you a job, is not what I'd call a wise course of action."

"I followed Gemma into battle without asking first. And then returned to fight in the battle against Cyrus the Honored—"

"I remember. You were good."

"I was. But still, they treat me like I'm . . ." She searched for the right word.

"Their younger sister?"

She nodded. "Exactly. One moment, they're ordering me to shoot arrows into someone's chest. The next, they're acting like I still can't put on my own boots without their help. It's infuriating."

"Then take your own path. Find your own way. Stop asking for permission. Definitely stop hiding in trees when they hurt your feelings."

"I wasn't hiding."

"What would you call it, then?"

"Getting a few moments to myself."

"Hiding."

She glared at him across the small space between them.

"Let me guess," he teased, "you liked it better when I just grunted?"

Gruff didn't know why he'd felt the need to have a discussion with Princess Ainsley, but he was glad he had. Despite his throat being sore from so much conversation, he enjoyed seeing her smile again. To see her happy. It was a nice change of pace.

She started to ask him something but stopped when they both heard a strange, mournful noise coming from deeper in the woods.

"Oh, no," she gasped after listening to the sound for a few more seconds. "That's Gemma's horse."

Gruff raised a brow. "Horses don't sound like that."

"Ones that were dead and brought back to life by necromancers do."

He scowled at the mention of that poor animal. It was some undead thing that the queen and her monk sister refused to put down. He didn't know why. It was barely alive. In fact, at least half of it wasn't alive at all. Then he'd heard that Brother Gemma had been trained in necromancy before he'd actually seen her in action. He'd watched her raise gutted soldiers from the dead so they could briefly fight for their side. "Briefly" being the key word. Not long after running into a group of their enemies and proceeding to tear them apart with bare hands, those things would crumble into a small pile of bones and goopy remains that would be finished off by crows and vultures. But apparently something had "gone wrong" with that horse. It had not died. Instead, half of it looked alive and healthy and the other half . . . did not.

His tribe avoided the thing at Sarff's suggestion. Not that any of them wanted to be around something half-dead. But Gruff believed it should be put down. Humans did it when a horse broke its leg. Why wouldn't they do the same thing for that poor half-dead animal?

Princess Ainsley got to her feet and made her way deeper into the woods, following the sound. Gruff, of course, followed her.

Not because he'd been commanded to keep an eye on her but because he didn't want to find her half-eaten remains a few hours from now. He liked the moody royal. In a completely platonic way . . . in case anyone asked.

As they came around an extremely wide tree that had probably grown in the forest since the beginning of time, they both came to an abrupt stop. Silently, they watched the half-dead horse walking through the woods. Next to it was the Mad Queen of Garbhán Isle.

It seemed the foreigner needed to get away from the princess's family too. But to spend that time with a half-dead animal . . . ?

Gruff shuddered a little, and it must have been more noticeable than he thought because both the half-dead horse and the Mad Queen stopped walking and looked over at them.

"Should I run?" Princess Ainsley asked quietly through gritted teeth. "I feel like I should run."

He understood that feeling. Reason told him to grab the royal and bolt as if an army of demons were right behind them. But the prey animal inside him, the one Gruff trusted above all else, told him he was safe.

He didn't understand that. How could it think either of them was safe from those two . . . things?

When the half-dead and the mostly crazed simply stared at them, Princess Ainsley cleared her throat and said, "Everything all right, Your Majest—"

The Mad Queen's glower was so brutal that Gruff understood why the princess's words stumbled to a stop before she tried again. "Everything all right . . ." She swallowed, before finishing with a high-pitched, "Annwyl?"

The Mad Queen's face relaxed and she tossed her head to get the hair out of her eyes.

"Everything is fine," she replied, moving around the horse and stroking the side of the face that hadn't decayed so badly one could see the horse's teeth. "I found her going somewhere and I wanted to make sure she was all right."

The half-dead horse gently pushed past the queen and continued on.

"I think she's looking for something," she said, again following.

"We should go with them," Princess Ainsley told Gruff.

"I can go. You should go back and tell your sisters—"

But she was already following behind the half-dead horse and the Mad Queen. Completely ignoring her own safety, and irritating him beyond reason.

Yes. She was very good at being irritating.

"Which sister are you again?"

"I'm Ainsley. Fourth oldest."

Annwyl the Bloody glanced back at her. "The archer, yes?"

"Um . . . yes. How did you hear about that?"

"I hear about lots of things. When you're insane, no one thinks you're listening."

That was such a strange comment, Ainsley didn't know how to respond. So she didn't.

"What's this horse's name?" the royal asked.

"Kriegszorn. She's my sister Gemma's horse."

"So the monk is a necromancer."

Ainsley blinked. She didn't know how the queen had made such a leap.

"Don't worry," the Mad Queen went on. "I don't judge. My son is a necromancer. And we've had more than one of his failures running around our home. The worst, though, was the headless dog. I don't know what happened there. And it just wouldn't die. But it had no head, so the hole—" She moved her hands around her neck. "I guess, where the food goes down . . . it developed teeth and some fangs. And it would just eat scraps off the floor . . . without its head."

Her entire body shuddered, and she waved her hands as if trying to dispel the memory. "I finally told my son, 'I don't care what you do with it, my lad, but you get it the battle fuck out of my house.' The next day it was gone, and I was never so grateful." She shuddered again.

The queen looked back at Ainsley and added, "I must say, I'm very glad this one has her head."

Unable to hide the disgust in her voice and, probably, on her face, Ainsley replied, "Me too."

* * *

Gruff was glad when the horse finally stopped walking because that meant the horrifying discussion the Mad Queen was having with Princess Ainsley also ended. He really needed that story to end.

They'd arrived next to one of the larger swamps located deep within these woods. For food and fresh water, everyone stuck to the rivers. Both human and centaur. Because the swamps could be dangerous. One never knew what was hiding in those murky waters. Or in the trees, for that matter. Lots of snakes lurked around and in these swamps. Small ones that had enough poison to take down an entire herd of his brethren; and long, wide ones that could coil around their victims to crush them before slowly swallowing them whole.

Like all horses and centaurs, Gruff did not like snakes.

Which meant he was more than ready to exit this part of the woods as quickly as possible. And was about to say as much when he heard a strange sound, different from the strange sounds the half-dead horse had been making.

It was small and if he didn't have the superior hearing of a prey animal, he never would have heard it.

Shifting to his natural form, he slowly made his way to the edge of the swamp. Carefully, he leaned over, trying to get a fix on where that sound was coming from, when something sprang out of the dark water toward his face.

He didn't bother to go for one of his weapons but simply caught the thing in his fist, squeezing tight, and forcing the snake's mouth to remain open so it couldn't sink its fangs into his arm. While the thing he held twisted and turned, trying to get away or, at the very least, poison him, another snake leaped from the water at Princess Ainsley. Before he could even call out a warning, she had her bow off her shoulder and an arrow nocked. He saw the snake flop back into the swamp, the royal's signature shaft extending from the reptile's throat.

One of the giant swamp snakes slithered out of the water and managed to wrap its upper body around the Mad Queen's leg. She grabbed its head with both hands and forcefully pried its mouth open until she'd torn the jaw off. She let the rest of the snake's body slip back to the ground, but she held on to that jaw with all its fangs. Gruff had a feeling part or all of those remains were going to end up in her armor or on the hilt of one of her swords.

Another small snake launched itself from the swamp right onto Brother Gemma's half-dead horse. It dug its fangs into the thing, but after a few seconds, the snake fell off. Dead. Its body decaying right in front of them.

The half-dead horse, however . . . ? She was fine. She didn't even appear annoyed.

"I see something!" the princess called out before splashing into the swamp and wading over to some high grass.

"*Princess Ainsley!*" Gruff shouted. He charged in after her, catching her around the waist and lifting her out of the water, then quickly rushing out again. As Gruff moved, he sensed something leaping out at him, but before he could turn to deal with it, he felt a searing pain shoot across his backside. Just as quickly that pain was gone. When he was once again on land, he looked over his shoulder, expecting to see some poisonous snake attached to his ass, but instead there were whiffs of smoke drifting up from his hide. He could see that some hairs had been singed. Confused, his gaze moved to the Mad Queen. She was standing on the other side of the half-dead Kriegszorn and, with a shake of her head, she said, "Trust me, centaur. You do *not* want to know what just happened." She stroked Kriegszorn's head. "But you do owe this one your life."

Deciding it was in his best interest to follow the Mad Queen's suggestion, Gruff lowered the royal to the ground. Before he could yell at her never to do that again, she faced him, her hands cupped together. Smiling, she slowly opened them to reveal what she held.

"What the fuck is that?" he demanded.

"It's a baby bird."

The Mad Queen leaned in and, after taking a look, grimaced and asked, "Is it?"

# CHAPTER 8

Gemma was standing by the open front doors, talking with a messenger. She needed him to track down her cohorts— fellow monks she'd trained with and now had lifelong bonds with—and order them back to the tower. She'd sent them off to check on various religious sects located at the boundaries of Keeley's and Beatrix's territories. It was an important task, but she'd feel better if they were back here. At least while there were dragons sleeping near her siblings.

As she gave the last of her orders and scrolls to the messenger, Gemma glanced up in time to see Ainsley walking toward her with the centaur ordered to protect her. And right beside them was the Mad Queen of Garbhán Isle! A woman who, last Gemma had heard, was upstairs in the room she'd been given. But no. She wasn't there. She was walking along with her ridiculous sister! Who should know better!

She motioned Keeley over.

"See what I mean?" Gemma demanded, gesturing at Ainsley and Queen Annwyl.

Keeley shrugged. "What?"

"What do you mean, 'what'? Aren't you the slightest bit concerned about this?"

"Would you prefer to see Ainsley dragging that woman like she drags the elks she brings home for dinner? Two arrows in her body?"

"I'm concerned about who Ainsley's making friends with. We both know she has horrible taste in friends. And men."

"We both promised each other we wouldn't bring that idiot guard up in front of Ainsley because *I* will not be responsible for pulling an arrow out of your ass when she shoves it there." Keeley glanced out the doors, gauging how far away Ainsley still was before stepping close to Gemma and whispering, "Stop being such a bitch to her."

"I'm—"

"Don't deny it. We both know when you panic, you take it out on Ainsley. And she didn't do anything wrong." Keeley rammed her finger against Gemma's chest. "So, when she gets over here"— she jabbed her finger to emphasize each word—"you. Be. *Nice.*"

Ainsley walked in between Gemma and Keeley. She had her hands cupped together and, with a smile, slowly lifted her top hand so they could see what she currently held.

Keeley, gasping, took a step back and ordered, "*Get that fucking thing out of here!*"

Ainsley immediately closed her hands again and gawked at her sister. "Are you serious right now?"

"You can't keep that thing here, Ainsley."

"It's a baby!"

"It is a dangerous beast that I won't have around my family!"

Gemma and Ainsley glanced at each other before Ainsley reminded Keeley, "You have demon dogs with blood for drool and fire where their eyes should be. And you're worried about *this* little bird? It fits into my hand!"

"Those particular swamp birds are *not* meant to be around human beings."

"Half of Gemma's horse is dead, and pieces fall out of it constantly, and you don't mind when it wanders into the main hall while we're eating."

"Don't bring Kriegszorn into this," Gemma chastised. "She adores you!"

"And I adore her! But I'm not blind to the fact that half of her is dead and that she can breathe fire! You were both concerned when the dragons did that!"

Smirking, Gemma said to Keeley, "She does have a point."

Her elder sister glared at her. "What are you doing?"

Shrugging and lifting her hands, Gemma pouted and said, "I'm just being nice."

"I hate you," Keeley snarled.

"I'm keeping it," Ainsley announced. "And that's the end of this discussion."

What fascinated Gemma was that, as queen, Keeley could order their sister to get rid of the thing. She could order her royal guards to take it from Ainsley and kill it right in front of her. But it didn't even occur to Keeley to demand anything. Instead, she just said, "Fine. But if that thing starts to burrow its way through your stomach, don't come complaining to me."

"I'll keep that in mind."

"And just so you know, those things are mean—"

"So's Gemma."

"Hey!"

"They grow incredibly fast—"

"So do our brothers. As it is, the baby"—she gestured to their three-year-old brother, who was trying to reach a basket of warm bread with one pudgy arm—"looks ready to pick up the dining table and tilt all the food into his mouth."

"And they smell."

"Then I'll bathe it."

"Well, if you already have it in water," Keeley muttered, but still loudly enough for everyone to hear, "then you might as well drown it while you still can."

The Mad Queen was easing past the bickering sisters when Keeley said that, and the foreign royal cringed in horror at the statement.

"Eeesh," she said before moving past.

"Really?" Keeley glared at the Mad Queen's back. "They call *you* the Blood Queen!"

"Not because I ever told anyone to drown a baby bird!" the royal shot back.

Gemma nodded. "She has a point."

"Shut. *Up*."

Hilda found Ainsley in her room, fussing over what she said was a bird—Hilda had her doubts—and complaining about her sisters. As usual.

What was unusual was the centaur standing by Ainsley's bookshelf, flipping through books. She knew the centaurs took their commitments seriously, and this one had committed to protecting the princess, but standing around a royal's room while she put some odd-looking creature into a small metal box seemed above and beyond.

"Will it survive in there?" Hilda asked, now looking at the creature over Ainsley's shoulder.

"It will once I fix the box up for her."

"How do you know it's female?"

"It's a guess based on her will to survive."

When Ainsley grinned at her, Hilda knew that bird wasn't going anywhere. Few things brought the royal actual joy, so the nun would make sure nothing happened to the poor little thing. Despite its smell.

"So what did you find out from your sisters about Isadora's new role and your lack of one?" she asked, sitting on the end of the bed.

"I found out they hate me."

"They do *not* hate you," the centaur contradicted from his corner of the room. And it took all of Hilda's strength and training not to jump off the bed in shock.

Hilda and her fellow sisters had been living in Forgetown for more than a year, and not once in all that time had she ever heard this particular centaur say . . . anything. Ever. She and Sheva had speculated that maybe he'd lost his ability to speak during battle, though he had no scars on his throat.

"Fine," Ainsley said, carefully tucking soft fabric into the steel box, so her stinky bird had something comfortable to lie upon. "They barely tolerate me and find me annoying."

The centaur rolled his eyes and looked back at the book he held in his hands.

"What do you think . . . um . . . Gruffyn?" Hilda was pretty sure that was his name, but who knew? There were so many centaurs, and she had no interest in learning any more names than necessary.

The centaur grunted, and Hilda quickly realized she wouldn't be getting full sentences from him as Ainsley did.

"Well, as long as you two have worked things out."

"Nothing to work out," Ainsley replied. "I just need to ignore my sisters and find my own way."

"And you plan to do that . . . how?"

"I have no idea."

"As always, you have *such* a vision."

"Look—" Ainsley began, pointing her forefinger at Hilda. But they both paused to stare at the bird gripping the entire tip with its beak.

"What's your bird doing?" Hilda asked. "And is that blood?"

"It is." She shook her hand, but the bird held on. The blood, however, flew. "And it is on there firmly."

The centaur grunted and Ainsley growled, "I know Keeley was right, but we're not telling her that."

The grunt he'd made sounded the same as the one the centaur had given Hilda earlier, so she wondered how Ainsley could possibly understand him. But he didn't correct the royal, so . . .

"If I can train a hawk, I can train this . . . swamp bird. You'll all see."

What Hilda enjoyed seeing was Ainsley's desperate attempts to get that smelly thing off her finger. Especially when the biting got more intense and it actually began to hurt.

At first it was funny, but when the blood began to flow heavily and drip onto her bed, Hilda jumped in to help Ainsley remove the thing. It wasn't just that the bird was holding on but that it had its *fangs* dug in. Why a being so young had fangs already—it didn't even have feathers yet—she didn't know. More important, why did a *bird* have fangs at all?

When they finally pried the creature off and Hilda put it back in its box, the centaur wrapped a cloth around Ainsley's finger to stanch the flow. But it kept coming.

"I think we need a healer," Hilda said.

"Preferably before I die of blood loss."

"So it bit you?" Ainsley's queen sister asked while Sarff took care of Ainsley's finger.

Annoyingly, Keeley had her chin resting on her open palm and her elbow on the big dining table, and she was smirking. It was the smirk that aggravated Ainsley the most.

"No," she lied. "It didn't bite me."

"Then what happened?" Keeley blinked her big eyes, trying to look as if these were innocent questions. But she was *not* innocent in the least! "Because those look like bite marks."

Ainsley thought a moment before replying, "Gruff bit me."

"Gruff?"

Using her other hand, she pointed at the centaur standing across the hall reading one of the books he'd taken from her room. She didn't even know which book. Keeley had put those books in her room and Ainsley hadn't ever looked at them.

Keeley gazed at the centaur. "Gruff . . . of the Torn Moon Clan? One of the warrior tribes of the Amichai. *He* bit you?"

"It was an accident, but . . . yes."

"Gruff?" she called out.

"Gruffyn is his full name," Ainsley corrected.

"Gruffyn? Did you bite my sister?"

Gruff slowly looked up from his book at the roomful of people, centaurs, and a couple of dragons staring at him expectantly before he replied with a grunt.

"See?" Ainsley said, smiling.

"I think," Sarff said, leaning in closer to Ainsley's finger, "you've got poison in this wound."

"You can draw that out, though, can't—*by the unholy powers of the gods!*" Ainsley exploded before looking down at her wounded hand.

With her mouth hanging open and tears streaming down her face, she gawked at Sarff of the Torn Moon Clan. "What the fuck did you just do?"

Holding a sharp and bloody knife in her left hand, the female centaur replied, "I cut the tip of your finger off."

Shocked, Ainsley looked up at Gruff, but he was busy grimacing. Not in disgust but something else. Had he known this was going to happen? She wasn't sure and, at the moment, wasn't going to ask, because a crazy centaur had just cut off her finger!

"Why . . . why . . . why . . ." Ainsley blew out a breath, tried again. "Why would you do that?"

"Because it was either cut off the tip of your finger now or watch you slowly die while your skin peeled off ten minutes from now. I went with the finger."

"But . . . you do know that it won't grow back, yes?"

"Fingertip. Death. These were your two options."

Keeley had her hand over her mouth, eyes wide in shock. But as soon as she saw Ainsley looking at her, she dropped her hand and asked, "So did Gruffyn also poison you?"

Realizing Keeley was not willing to let this go even after her own sibling had been maimed, Ainsley growled out between gritted teeth, "It was an accident. Gruffyn didn't mean to." Because when Ainsley made a commitment, she stuck with it! Even if that commitment was to a lie.

At a stalemate, the siblings stared at each other until Ainsley heard the gold dragon say to Gemma, "I can't express to you how entertaining this queendom is. If I could, I'd move here!"

"You let them believe that poor centaur poisoned you?" Sheva demanded before rolling off the desk she'd been splayed across and landing on the floor. The fall didn't stop her from laughing, though. Because how could it? She'd never heard anything more ridiculous in her entire life!

"I had no choice!"

"You could have told them the truth," Hilda unnecessarily pointed out, knowing Sheva was vastly entertained by the bickering between Ainsley and her older sisters.

"And let Keeley think she won? No."

"You'd rather Gruffyn suffer?"

"Oh, he's not suffering!"

Hilda shook her head and adjusted her religious habit. "At least when your finger heals, it won't look too bad. From the little I know, it appears Sarff did a very good job."

"Did she give you any warning at all?" Sheva asked, pretty sure what the answer would be. When Ainsley snarled and looked away, Sheva started laughing again. A reaction that pissed off her friend.

"This isn't funny!" Ainsley whined. She did have a tendency to whine. "I lost part of my finger!"

"Do not exaggerate," Hilda chastised. "You lost the tip of your finger."

"Just the tip!" Sheva gasped out before she choked a little on her own laughter.

The door opened and Gemma walked into the private offices of their order's elders. When she saw the three women, she stopped and asked, "What's going on?"

Holding her injured hand with the other, Ainsley said, "Nothing."

"Why are you in here?"

"No reason."

Sheva's leader smirked and asked, "And how's the finger?"

Hilda shoved Ainsley against the closest wall and yanked from her hands the bow and arrow she'd been about to shoot her sister with.

"That good?" Gemma joked.

Hilda pinned Ainsley to the wall and held her there while their friend snarled and cursed as she tried to get her hands on her sister.

Gemma turned to Sheva. "Don't you have things to do, Novitiate?"

Clearing her throat, she said, "I'm assisting Princess Ainsley."

"With what, exactly?"

"Her duties."

"Which are?"

"Important."

Gemma closed her eyes and let out a sigh. "Whatever you do, Brother Sheva, whenever Master General Ragna returns, please don't let her know that you have nothing to do. Because then she'll give you something to do and none of us will ever see you again."

"Yes, Brother."

"Make sure to change that bandage regularly, Ainsley," she told her sister on the way out the door. "I'd hate for an infection to develop."

Hilda almost lost her grip on the royal but managed to keep her from catching Brother Gemma by the hair.

"Bitch!" Ainsley barked after the door slammed closed.

"I am so glad I never had siblings," Hilda announced.

Yanking her bow back from the nun, Ainsley warned, "As far as my family is concerned, Gruff of the Torn Moon Clan bit me and accidentally poisoned me. Understand?"

"You can't keep using him for your lies, Ainsley."

"I won't!"

"Unless you're poisoned by a disgusting bird." Sheva sat up, her laughter finally under control.

"Where is that bird anyway?" Hilda asked.

When Ainsley didn't answer, they both focused on her and waited. Finally, she admitted, "It's in the walls somewhere. I can hear it moving around but I can't find it."

Sheva fell back against the floor, laughter spilling out of her once again as she barely dodged the boot flung at her head by a princess.

"How do you feel?"

The royal looked up at him through her lashes and replied, "Like I'm missing a finger."

"Not all of it."

Gruff had to work hard not to laugh at her angry sneer.

"I don't know why you're growling at me," he continued. "You're the one accusing me of being a poisoner."

"By accident! I said you *accidentally* poisoned me. I didn't, at any time, say you were an intentional poisoner."

"Yes. That makes a huge difference to centaurs who already hate me."

"You hate them more," she reminded him.

"That's very true."

The princess, arms folded over her chest, had found the quietest corner in the main hall so she could glare at everyone standing around enjoying some wine. As Gruff's orders to protect her had not been changed, he stood beside Ainsley.

"I do not want to be here," she said.

"You're a royal now, and this activity is an important part of royal politics. The performance of royals pretending they like each other in the hopes that one day the royal with the bigger army won't destroy them and may even help them win a different war."

"You really think my sister is going to ask for an alliance with Annwyl the Bloody?"

"She'd be a fool not to."

Princess Ainsley leaned in close and whispered, "My sister

thinks the woman eats babies. I can't imagine she'd want an alliance with her."

"Maybe she's figured out I don't eat babies," Annwyl the Bloody whispered beside them.

Gruff had no idea when the woman had sidled up next to them; there were few who could get that close to him without his knowing. And yet she had. All while in a dress she clearly hated, since she kept tugging at the bodice and moving her shoulders around. She was, however, dressed appropriately for this feast in honor of the Mad Queen. It was amusing, though, that the Mad Queen didn't seem to want to attend any more than the princess did.

"Does this look all right on me?" she asked, again tugging at the material.

"It does," the princess promised. "You look very . . . proper."

The Mad Queen stuck her tongue out, made a sound of disgust, and rolled her eyes. All at the same time.

"Morfyd knows I hate this sort of horse shit, but she insisted I come. I'd rather eat in my room and read a book. Your father has a lovely library, by the way."

"You could have said no," Princess Ainsley reminded her.

"Yes. But then I'd have to hear about it. When Morfyd chastises someone . . . even if you're just in the room—"

"Yeah!" the princess heartily agreed; the two women stared at each other and nodded. "You feel such guilt when you didn't do anything wrong. I thought that was just me!"

"No. She makes all of us feel that way. She could be yelling at one of Dagmar's dogs and you just feel like you should be the one slinking off into the corner and whining."

"Who's Dagmar?"

"Dagmar Reinholdt. My battle lord. Our enemies call her The Beast."

"A mighty warrior, then."

"No." The Mad Queen shook her head. "She's never been in a battle except by accident. She can't even swing a sword. One time she tried to yank a small chopping axe away from one of her daughters and somehow ended up hitting herself in the head and breaking her spectacles."

"Spectacles? You mean to help her see?"

"Without them, she's blind as a bat."

"And . . . and . . . *this* woman is your battle lord?"

"If you ever meet her, you'll understand. I didn't even name her The Beast." She dropped her voice again to a whisper. "Her family did."

She tugged at her dress again, but this time she tugged too hard, and the garment ripped. Luckily, the Mad Queen had her breasts bound, so Gruff didn't have to see what was going on there. Because above and below the binding were many, many scars.

"Oh, for fuck's sake!" she snapped before turning and walking out the back door.

After they watched her disappear, Princess Ainsley turned to Gruff and said, "I like her."

"That does not surprise me in the least."

"There's a bird on your head."

Ainsley looked at the black dragon sitting across from her at the long dining table. "Pardon?"

"There's a tiny, baby bird on your head. The poisonous one, I think."

"Oh . . . uh . . ." It wasn't so much that the fucking thing was creeping around the tower or even that it seemed to have nested in her damn hair. It was that it had found *her*! Out of all these people, this little bird had tracked her down and had made itself at home. In her hair.

Ainsley's father came over and stared at the top of her head in a manner that could only be described as goofy. His head tilted back and forth as he studied the thing that had nearly killed his daughter.

"Look at what my girl found!" he exclaimed to the table of visiting royals dining with the adults of her family. Even Keran had made an appearance. Not in a dress. But she'd washed her hair . . . so that was impressive. Uncle Archie had attempted to attend but was immediately ordered away by Angus. Ainsley hadn't told her father what Archie had done, but word had made its way to him—and he had not been happy. So Archie had been banished.

Ainsley wished she could say her uncle had gone quietly, but there had been much stomping and cursing and complaining that her father "didn't understand! It was for their own good! Do you *want* your children eaten by dragons? Well . . . *do you?*"

"Is that the thing that poisoned her?" Gemma asked. "Kill it, Da!"

"No, no, no! We won't be thinking of doing that to such a wee thing." Her father leaned in closer. "The poisoning was an accident. These swamp birds are born with poison in their baby fangs to protect them from predators."

"Why does it have baby fangs?" Ainsley's mother wanted to know.

"What's really interesting, though," her father went on, ignoring his wife, "is that most of the mother birds have three eggs. If all three hatch, she'll only raise one."

"She lets the others die?" Keeley asked.

"No. She drowns them. Just stomps them down with her webbed feet until they're covered by water, holding them there until they're *dead*."

Keeley's mouth briefly opened, and Laila suggested, "Perhaps this is not appropriate dinner discussion. About bird mothers killing their babies."

"But that's what's amazing!" her father cheered.

"That they're murderous birds, and you should have killed the thing sitting on your daughter's head by now so it doesn't peck the rest of your human offspring to death?" the silver dragon asked before practically inhaling the meat off a massive rib bone, which was disturbing enough. But Ainsley couldn't help but stare when he began to eat the remaining bone as well. The crunching sound . . .

"Oh, Ainsley will be fine," her father said dismissively. Not remotely concerned that the damn bird was snuggling down into her hair as if her head was its literal bed. "No. What's fascinating is that the extra little ones don't usually survive the drowning. The fact this one did says it's determined to live. And because Ainsley saved it, this little one already sees her as its mother! This wee thing will be loyal to you, my darling girl, until the end, which will be a long time. There are some who believe these birds are immortal."

Her father suddenly hugged Ainsley's shoulders. "You're going to have that bird as your pet forever! Isn't that lovely?"

Closing her eyes, Ainsley put her elbows on the table and pressed her fingers against her forehead and cheeks.

"Ainsley," Keeley said innocently, sitting at the head of the table and picking up a piece of meat off her plate, "is this situation also Gruffyn's fault?"

Slowly lowering her hands, Ainsley turned her head and sneered at her sister, mere seconds from telling her to fuck off, too. But the days-old bird that had made itself at home in her hair planted its little wings on her scalp, raised its little body, and let out a bone-chilling screech that even disturbed the dragons.

There was only one who didn't seem concerned about Ainsley's hair-bird.

"See?" her father cheered, sitting back in his chair. "Already so protective of my baby girl! I love this bird!"

Keeley closed her eyes and worked hard not to initiate one of their family arguments in front of a foreign queen. There were lots of reasons that would be a bad idea, but mostly she simply didn't want to be embarrassed. Life was hard enough without adding the humiliation of her father thinking a poisonous bird that had nested in her sister's hair was a good pet.

To calm herself, Keeley reached under the table and handed the rib she'd been holding to the demon wolf who was pressed up against her leg. Her friend was still extremely wary of the Mad Queen, but he wanted to be close to Keeley. She appreciated the risk he was taking just for her and was reassured by his presence. She was also glad he took the rib. He hadn't been eating since the foreign queen had arrived. He always ate. Always. He was never *not* hungry.

She dug her fingers into his fur and focused on the Mad Queen.

"So . . . Queen—"

"Annwyl."

"Yes. Queen Annwyl."

"Just Annwyl." She hadn't even stopped eating to speak or looked at Keeley at all. Lovely.

Keeley glanced over at the dragons. The female dragon with the white hair and her black dragon brother both nodded at Keeley.

"All right. Annwyl. Is the food to your liking, Annwyl?"

"Aye. It's fine. *Ow!*" Annwyl looked up from her food long enough to glower at the female dragon sitting catty-corner from her.

*Be. Nice!* The dragoness mouthed to the Mad Queen.

*I was!*

*Liar! Now be nice!*

Did they think that Keeley couldn't see them? Because . . . she could. *Everyone* could see them.

The foreign queen cleared her throat and said to Keeley, "The meat is quite tender. And well-seasoned."

"Excellent. I'm glad you're enjoying it."

Keeley took a few more bites, then asked, "Not to get too serious over dinner, but"—she shrugged—"what do you think about our defenses? The preparations we have made against possible attacks by our enemies?"

"Do you mean if you are suddenly attacked by Beatrix?"

"I guess that's the best place to start."

The Mad Queen paused thoughtfully before announcing, "If your sister attacked now, her armies would kill all of you and your subjects and raze this entire town to the ground. It would be like none of you ever existed."

Keeley, horrified, gawked at the foreign queen. Actually, they all did, except the silver dragon, who rolled his eyes and went back to eating, and Gwenvael, who snorted, which he quickly attempted to muffle but couldn't. He excused himself and made a hasty exit through the front doors. Once he was outside, they could all hear his raucous laughter.

"Annwyl!" the dragoness squeaked.

"What?" the Mad Queen glared at her. "You want me to lie, too?"

"*Yes!*"

"You never made that clear." She picked up another rib off her plate. "You just said to be nice."

# CHAPTER 9

Ainsley woke up early. She was in her favorite tree near the big lake. She hadn't planned to stay in a tree the night before, but after the disaster that was "Queen Keeley's first royal banquet with foreign interests"—as Keeley's Keeper of the Word had called it—Ainsley knew she couldn't stay in the tower and risk her bird. She hadn't really planned on keeping the ugly thing after it had poisoned her and caused the loss of a finger she needed for her archery, but when it opened its mouth and silently demanded food, she just melted. It seemed so small and defenseless.

Once she had made that decision, she went to her father and asked what to feed it . . . turned out it was a meat eater. Even only a few days old, it wanted raw meat. Fresh or rotting. Shuddering at the thought, she'd grabbed some leftover meat from the banquet and took the chick to her tree. She'd climbed and, once settled among the leaves, fed him. Or her. She wasn't sure yet which one it was. But she'd started to hate calling it . . . it.

After feeding, the bird settled down on her head and went to sleep. She knew it was asleep because it growled. According to her father, growling in their sleep was just something these birds did. The first time it did that, she briefly entertained the idea of tossing it from the tree. The sound was that loud and off-putting. But, in time, she grew used to it.

Now, as she carefully straightened up, trying not to wake the bird, he began screeching. The sound seemed louder than it had

THE HERETIC ROYAL • 113

been the night before. She took the chick down and he automatically opened his mouth; again demanding to be fed.

Thankfully, she still had some meat left, so that's what she gave him. The food quieted him down, which was good because a few minutes later, she saw Keeley, Gemma, Laila, Caid, and Quinn all walking toward the lake. She doubted Gemma would recognize the demanding call of her bird, but she knew Keeley would, which would lead to yet another fight. It was too early for all that, so she did not announce her presence.

Keeley sat on a boulder by the lake and asked her sister, her centaur lover, and her centaur friends, "Is Queen Annwyl right? Are we doomed? Am I killing my own people because I'm not prepared?"

"I don't think we can trust anything that woman says," Gemma replied. "She's clearly insane and her name is Annwyl the *Bloody*. She doesn't even have a last name. In those lands, no one gets more than a first name until they earn it. Meaning that she *earned* Annwyl the Bloody. And the Mad Queen of Garbhán Isle. *And* the Blood Queen. She didn't take those names for herself. They were *given* to her by her own people. So excuse me if I don't feel the need to listen to the opinions of any royal like that."

"My dearest love—" Quinn began.

Gemma sighed. "Please stop that."

"—heart of my hearts—"

"I *will* break your nose again if I must."

"—ruler of my loins—"

Gemma laughed, and Ainsley was glad to see it. She felt that Quinn kept her sister balanced. A little less religious fervor and a little more . . . well . . . sanity.

"—I think we are past the 'She's the mad queen of a faraway land and we need to stay away from her' stage of this situation. Annwyl the Bloody is here. Now. We need to decide what we do from this point on."

"Quinn is right," Laila said.

"Shocking opinion," Caid grumbled after his sister's comment.

"Don't keep going on," Laila told her dark-haired brother. "We know exactly how you feel about all this. We don't need you to repeat it. Instead, we must decide what we will do next. Do we ask the dragons to vacate our lands in the next two days—and be willing to back our request up with force—or ask for their help?"

"Why the next two days? Why not this very second?"

"We all know it's not easy to move an army."

"Oh, please!" Caid barked. "All they have to do is fly away and take their insane queen with them. And, Sister, in answer to your question, I think they should go."

"I agree with Caid," Gemma said.

Quinn shrugged his massive shoulders. "I, too, would like them gone—"

"Good."

"But, dear Brother, I think that would be foolish."

That's when Caid roared, "*You are so weak!* You're just afraid to tell them to go."

"Do you think I truly *want* dragons on these lands?" Quinn snapped back. "But their being here is, in fact, *not* the biggest issue."

"Then enlighten us, Brother. What is the biggest issue?"

"They went over the Amichai Mountains to get here, dumb ass! We both know that means our father has been alerted to their presence and has already assembled a war council of all the clans. He'll be ready for battle whether it's necessary or not, which would put *all* our people at risk! Is that what you want? To have those things taking their flames to our mountains? Risking the foals and yearlings? Like anything that bleeds, the dragons can be defeated. But at what cost?"

Ainsley couldn't help but smile a little. To everyone around them, Quinn might seem nothing more than a spoiled prince who could fight well enough but took nothing seriously. She, however, had always known differently. Just as Gemma had eventually learned. It was probably why her sister was so in love with him. Because he wasn't what he seemed. Not completely. So his rational thoughts and concerns about the current situation had been perfectly expressed. Plain to see, because Caid abruptly calmed down; his shoulders dropping a little at the realization of what could eventually be lost if they didn't manage to keep their wits about them.

"I think," Quinn calmly went on, "making them our enemy is not the way."

"No one said we should make them our enemy," Caid replied, shifting to his natural form and walking into the lake until it nearly reached his tail. "I just don't think we should align ourselves with someone who was named the Blood Queen by her own people."

"A people she's kept safe all these years. We shouldn't under-estimate her simply because she's . . . different."

"Different? Is that what we're calling her now? The Different Queen? What should we call the dragons? Large lizards?"

"Which are you more worried about, Brother? Her or the dragons?"

"Both!" Caid barked, his tail practically slapping back and forth. Ainsley never approached a horse with a tail moving like that. "Those dragons are more than happy to unleash that woman on the world before they come in to dine on the remains of her rage! And I'd prefer we not be one of their meals."

Laila held up her hand, silencing her brothers before Quinn could reply. She turned to Ainsley's eldest sister, who had been silent the entire time, and asked, "What do you think, Keeley?"

Staring out across the lake, Keeley replied, "Before I decide anything . . . I need to talk to her. Alone. Queen to queen."

"No!" Caid said with much force. "Absolutely not. You're not meeting that woman alone."

"I need to, Caid." She gave a little shake of her head and let out a long breath. "Right now, we are preparing for a fight between two city states. And whoever wins gets both. But knowing who my sis-ter really is . . . what she's really about, I'm certain she's not fighting to increase her territory. In fact, the more I think about it, the more I'm sure she doesn't care about me at all. She's using me, *us*, as a distraction while she prepares her armies to create an empire in the most brutal way she can. Because that's who Beatrix is. Despite her dainty dresses and quietly read books, she is a brutal warrior queen who will swallow us whole and leave nothing behind."

Keeley absently rubbed her stomach as she spoke those words, and Ainsley would bet her sister didn't even realize what she was doing in that moment. Yet Keeley made the same motion anytime she spoke seriously of Beatrix. She rubbed her stomach because that's where Beatrix had shoved the knife into Keeley's gut and opened her up. Trying, and damn-near succeeding, to kill the one person who had always protected her. Why had she done that to someone who loved her so? Because, in that moment, Keeley had been in her way. That's who Beatrix was. Who she had always been. A soulless, heartless bitch who would crush anyone who stepped in her path, whether stranger or friend. Guilty or innocent. And someone like that, someone so willfully, even *happily*, cruel could never rule.

Never.

"I already know what my sister is capable of," Keeley continued, "and we're going to need help to stop her. If that means aligning ourselves with the Mad Queen of Garbhán Isle, then so be it. But I'll talk to her first." Keeley got to her feet, pausing briefly to wipe the dirt off her ass. "Alone."

With those words, Keeley headed back to the tower. As the others followed, Caid briefly stopped to shake the water off his hide.

Once they were gone, Ainsley's mind began to turn. She wanted to help. *Needed* to help, but she knew her sisters would never—

"It's wonderful to listen to others' true thoughts without being seen, isn't it?"

That voice sounded as if it was right next to her, but Ainsley didn't see anyone. She turned her head, looking from side to side out of the tree, her eyes open wide in near-panic as she desperately searched for the speaker, but she saw noth—

Ainsley caught sight of something out of the corner of her eye and had her arrow nocked and nearly unleashed when one giant gold talon, more than the length of her, gently pressed against her, stopping her from lifting her bow.

"Nothing to fear, Princess Ainsley. Just doing what you were doing . . . being nosey."

Insulted, she snapped back, "I was not being—"

"Don't lie." The talon pulled away. Ainsley kept her grip on her bow, despite the pain it caused to her wounded hand, but she didn't raise the weapon again. Not yet. "I have two older brothers that treat me like shit, too. I know what we have to do to survive in such a household. Meaning, we both know exactly what you were doing."

He abruptly appeared in front of her in all his gold-dragon glory, his snout so close to her, she could see each and every bright, white fang in his head.

It was . . . discomforting.

Refusing to feel afraid any longer, Ainsley noted, "They're my family. I can listen to them all I want. But why were you listening to Queen Keeley's conversation? Were you spying as part of an evil plot against my kin?"

The dragon took in a breath, and for a brief, horribly frightening moment, Ainsley thought she was going to die a sad, fiery death all because she'd snapped at him. She was just trying to sound unafraid! She shouldn't die for that!

There was no fiery death, however. The dragon simply let out his breath and said, "While I make it my life's mission to torment my brothers on a daily basis—simply for my own amusement—"

"Of course."

"—they are still my family. And I want my family safe. I need to know if you and *your* family are plotting to kill us all while we sleep in your lumpy, tiny beds."

Ainsley gazed at the dragon for a long moment. And what she saw there . . .

Because it had never really occurred to her that dragons could—and would—be as protective of their kin as she was of her own. Her panic and fear drifted away for the first time since the dragons had dropped down into the courtyard and made themselves known. Because what she saw in the eyes of this gold dragon was something she had *never* seen in Beatrix's cold, dead orbs.

A soul.

Without even realizing it, she'd automatically assumed these beasts didn't have the one thing that most humans had. That thing inside that made one caring and loving to something other than oneself. Whether it was a pet, a husband or wife, one's children, or even some feral barn cat that hissed every time someone came near.

Gods, she missed that cat.

Realizing the connection she had with a being so vastly different from her, Ainsley smiled and said, "I promise, Prince Gwenvael, we are *not* plotting to kill you or anyone else in their bed. My sister Keeley would never, *ever* allow it."

"Please. Call me Gwenvael. Dragons aren't fussy about titles unless someone is really making us mad. And Annwyl hates titles altogether. The bowing and scraping irritates her beyond reason. I would ask one favor, though."

"Yes?"

"Could you assist me with the centaur currently pressing his spear against my cock. He is my very close friend, my cock, and I'd hate to lose him . . . or the two friends right next to him."

Ainsley leaned over so she could see through the leaves and branches. Standing directly under Gwenvael was Gruffyn, the tip of his spear shoved straight up and disappearing into the poor dragon's . . . uh . . . well . . . nether regions.

"Do anything to harm her," Gruff growled out, so angry he was forgoing his usual grunts, "and the rest of your long dragon years will be very. Sad. *Indeed.*"

"Gruff! Wait!" he heard Princess Ainsley call out before she scrambled down the tree. When she finally reached the ground, he immediately noticed she had that bird in her hair. Again.

"This isn't necessary," she told him.

"It isn't? Because you seemed to be in danger."

"I wasn't. It was just a conversation. I promise. You can stop—"

"Abusing my cock," the dragon said.

This hadn't been Gruff's plan when he went looking for Princess Ainsley this morning. He'd just gone to check on her. To make sure she was feeling all right after the previous day's . . . Bless the horse gods! What could he call the events of yesterday? "Activities" didn't seem right or remotely strong enough.

Well, whatever the right word, he'd searched for her. Not hard, knowing most of her favorite trees, which was why he'd headed first to the tree beside the big lake. That's where she seemed to spend most of her time. Centaurs liked to communally bathe in this lake and he usually made sure to attend to ease his royals' concerns about the loyalty of his clan. However, he always stood back and watched rather than getting into the water with the rest of them. And one time, he'd leaned against a large old tree, heavy in limbs and leaves. That's where he'd first heard her breathing coming from one of the branches. He didn't say anything or draw attention to her. He knew that the human royal probably just needed some time to herself. Especially coming from such a big family that spent as much time together as they all did. After that, he was able to find her other favorite trees easily. He simply listened for her breathing.

And that had been his plan this morning as the two suns peeked over the horizon and began to fill up the valley with their bright light. What he hadn't expected was to find the big gold dragon poking its giant head into the leaves like he was about to swallow the princess whole. Gruff doubted he could challenge the beast head-on, in a more honorable fashion. So he'd gone for every male's weakest point—no matter the species—which he'd found tucked up inside the dragon's body like a turtle's genitals. Even better... there were no scales covering the dragon's groin, allowing Gruff to use his long spear in a completely inappropriate way. Now, if the dragon decided to move in any direction, Gruff could rip that cock open from tip to balls before being tragically crushed to death.

A solid plan that would allow the princess to run for her life. But she didn't run. Instead, Princess Ainsley begged him to stop.

He hadn't expected that either.

He also didn't like it. Why was she so protective of this dragon?

Was it the long, luxurious gold hair that made her so defensive? Or those shiny gold scales? Or maybe it was that pretty face the dragon had every time he shifted to human form?

No. Gruff didn't like any of that.

His grip tightened on his spear, but then that ugly bird hissed at him because Gruff was upsetting its mistress.

"Really. I'm fine," Princess Ainsley insisted.

She held her hand out, and Gruff took a few long seconds to debate what he should do. Part of him really wanted to shove his spear up and be done with the matter, but he knew the princess had a good sense of when she was in danger and when she wasn't. If she had really felt threatened, she'd have made a run for it by now.

And yet... he really wanted to destroy this dragon's cock!

No. No. He wouldn't do that. Not unprovoked anyway. Although he felt provoked. And why was that? Because instead of threatening the royal, he'd discovered the dragon had been, basically, chatting her up? Didn't this one already have a mate? What was he doing, chatting up young human women alone in trees?

That urge to ram his spear upward almost took over, but he fought it hard. To do such a thing would cause more than a damaged cock. It would cause war. Because this wasn't just any dragon. It was a royal one.

Finally, with one hand still holding his spear up—and pressed against the beast's scaleless groin—Gruff reached out with the other to grasp Princess Ainsley. Her fingers intertwined with his and, keeping a tight grip, she tugged him away. And, to his disgust, like one of her father's pet lap-pigs, he let her.

Once Gruff and his spear had been removed, the gold dragon let out a long, relieved breath, his front claws resting on his knees, his giant head bowed down. He then took several more breaths to calm himself down.

"Thank you, Ainsley," the dragon said. "I am so fond of Darryl."

Ainsley glanced at Gruff before asking, "Darryl?"

"That's his name. Darryl the Stalwart. Actually, he has a longer name, but you don't need to hear all that. You're a little young."

Disgusted, Gruff rolled his eyes, and that's when the dragon finally focused on him. "I see we have a protective knight for our fair damsel."

Gruff grunted and, to his surprise, the dragon laughed and took several big steps away from him and his spear.

Flames surrounded the beast until finally a man with long golden hair stood where the dragon had once been. His chainmail, which had been open at the waist in his natural form so his back legs could move freely as a dragon, now encased his human form like leggings while all of it, including his weapons, had shrunk in size.

"That armor and chainmail are *amazing*," Ainsley noted, apparently unaware she was still holding Gruff's hand. "My sister Keeley is definitely going to want to know how you guys make that!"

"I like your sister."

Ainsley stopped walking, arms crossed over her chest, and looked up at Gwenvael.

"No, no," he said quickly. "Not the monk. She seems a little . . ."

"Self-righteous?"

They began walking around the lake again. They'd left a very unhappy Gruff by Ainsley's favorite tree, allowing her to talk in private with Gwenvael the Handsome. Not because she didn't trust the centaur to keep her secrets—actually, she did trust him to do that—but because he so clearly disliked the gold dragon. Every time Gwenvael spoke, Gruff growled. It got so bad, she could barely hear anything the dragon was saying. In the end, it was just safer to leave him behind while Ainsley and Gwenvael went on a walk around the lake. Not far enough away for Gruff to be concerned about her safety but far enough that she didn't have to hear all that damn growling!

"I was going to say uptight, but self-righteous works as well. No, I speak of your other sister. The queen."

"Keeley."

"Yes. I like Keeley. I like her calm nature. I think she'd be a good counterpart to Annwyl. Who is less calm."

"A counterpart for what?"

"An alliance."

"Why would you need us for an alliance?"

The dragon glanced at her before explaining. "For thousands of years, our two lands have been divided. Dragons, minotaurs, and centaurs on one side of the Mountains of Dark Despair and Indescribable Pain. Dwarves, elves, and centaurs on the other side."

"We actually call them the Amichai Mountains," Ainsley said.

"Why?"

She shrugged. "Because we don't live in constant darkness and misery . . . ?"

"Neither do we, really, but our ancestors did have a pithy way with names," he joked. "But they also strongly believed that this was how our peoples would survive."

"And you think they were right."

"It doesn't matter what I think. Because the lines have been crossed. Children from your side have come to our lands and we've come to yours. Even worse, those children were being used as slave labor and came through tunnels that *your* Beatrix has built. As the minotaurs have taught my people over the years, the only reason to dig tunnels is to stage invasions."

"You were invaded by minotaurs?"

"We were. They killed the queen."

Ainsley frowned. "The Dragon Queen?"

"No. Annwyl. They killed Annwyl. And then a god brought her back. She's been alive ever since."

"Yeahhhhh. You may not want to mention *any* of that to my monk sister."

"Isn't she a necromancer? Bringing things back from the dead is what she does."

"She's also a religious fanatic with an itchy sword hand. Right now, she just thinks Annwyl is insane. But if Gemma starts believing the Queen of Garbhán Isle is actually born of pure evil . . ."

"Understood. Although you may not want to mention your Brother Gemma's fanaticism since she's so close to Queen Keeley's throne. Fanatics unnerve Annwyl. We don't want her unnerved."

"I'm guessing we don't, and I'll keep that in mind."

"But this is what I'm talking about."

"You mean how religious fervor and insanity are basically the same thing?"

Gwenvael grinned and it was as if the two suns were shining right down on Ainsley's head from only a few feet away. As a human, the dragon was stunning. She imagined that his mate must be an astounding beauty. Even more beautiful than Morfyd. Who else would feel confident enough to claim this dragon as her own?

"Actually, I was talking about the give and take of our current negotiation," he explained. "That, of course, does not mean I don't agree with you. That being said, my mother and sister are both witches and expertly deal with many gods, which has taught me not to judge those who choose to worship such power as long as they bring harm to no one."

He frowned. "What's wrong? What did I say?"

"You brought up negotiation, but . . . I can't negotiate anything. My sisters don't take me seriously and they don't involve me in anything that has to do with Keeley's queendom. I can't help you."

"You have more power than you realize, sweet Ainsley. You just need to learn how to wield it." He pressed his hand to his chest and gave a small bow. "So, Your Royal Highness, let me be the first to teach you the many devious ways of the sneaky, nosey sibling."

"Oh, Prince Gwenvael," she said, laughing, "I am *so* eager to learn."

# CHAPTER 10

Quinn took a turn around the courtyard and market. The shops were active again, he was glad to see. And quieter than usual, but he could see that fewer residents had fled than he'd thought. He would guess those working the market made the other residents feel calmer, while the lavish money spent by the dragons in their human form encouraged the tradespeople to risk their lives.

He'd always found that coin could calm the most terrified of humans.

Caid had offered to accompany Quinn on his walk, but that was always a bad idea. All that glaring put the locals on edge; it definitely wouldn't help now.

Nearing the tower with two whole chickens and fresh bread in a bag hanging off his shoulder, Quinn caught sight of Ainsley. He'd felt bad for her the last two days. Gemma was being harder on her than usual. He knew why, too. Fear. She was so worried about her siblings that she could barely see straight. All she could envision was their death among dragon flame or at the tip of a sword held by soldiers in Queen Beatrix's colors. And because Gemma didn't panic like Keeley—who'd thrown up at least three times the day before once she was alone in her rooms—she turned full soldier. Giving orders and expecting them to be obeyed by siblings who'd never obeyed much of anything except their parents and, occasionally, Keeley. Of course, what he called "full soldier," her kin called, "Mean Gemma."

And, sadly, Ainsley got the brunt of Gemma's bossiness because she was the oldest of the younger siblings and because she took it. She took it like a champ but that didn't mean it was fair. Not when she tried so hard.

He decided to go over and offer to share his chicken and bread with her in the hope he could give her some words of encouragement. But as he started walking toward her, he watched something horrifying unfold.

Gruffyn of the Torn Moon Clan coming up behind her in his human form—which was strange because he stayed centaur most of the time, having no desire to make the humans around him feel any ease at all with the presence of centaurs on their lands—and grabbing her arm. Then, standing a few feet away from the front tower steps, they began to . . . bicker. He'd say something; then she'd reply. Testily.

Not only that but Gruffyn was speaking. To Ainsley. With words.

Quinn practically bolted over to them, but they suddenly turned away from the tower and stalked off into a crowd. By the time he reached the place where they'd been standing, he couldn't spot either of them.

Now he was running. Into the tower and over to the dining table where the family was eating their first meal. Dropping his bag of food onto the table, he reached into a chair, wrapped his arms around Laila's waist, and carried her out of the main hall.

"Where the hells are you going?" Caid demanded from behind them.

"Nothing!" he called back. "Just need to talk to my sister about a toe infection!"

"Ewww," he heard Isadora complain before he closed the door to the war room and put his sister on the ground.

"What is wrong with you?" she asked.

"We have a problem."

"Oh, gods. Please don't tell me one of the dragons killed someone."

"No. It's worse. Gruffyn was talking to Ainsley."

His sister gazed at him for what felt like forever before replying, "Uh-huh."

"Gruffyn!" he pushed. "Gruff. *Yn*. Was talking to our little Ainsley."

"Ainsley is hardly little, and Keeley told me the women of their bloodline have growth spurts. Did you know that Keran used to be barely five feet when she was seventeen and then, over one summer . . . boom."

"What are you talking about?"

"What are *you* talking about? You're acting insane."

"Gruffyn!"

"Right."

"Of the Torn Moon Clan."

"I'm with you."

"Was *talking* to Ainsley."

She blinked. Thought a moment, and finally said, "Ohhhh." She blinked again. "I didn't think he could speak. I just assumed Sarff had removed his voice box and was planning to use that to control his soul."

"What?"

"Sorry, sorry. Just my assumptions. Okay." She took in a breath, "So what you're saying is Gruffyn can speak, and he was speaking to Ainsley. Yes. And?"

"What do you mean 'and'?"

"I mean . . . 'and.' I don't understand why that knowledge necessitated my leaving first meal."

"You don't see the problem here?"

"Other than my first meal getting cold . . . ? No."

He stepped close to his sister, bringing his face down so he could look her directly in the eyes. "Gruffyn of the Torn Moon Clan was *talking* to Ainsley."

"Uh-huh."

"You know what that means."

"Dialogue?"

"Laila!"

She laughed. "Are you truly worried about Ainsley and Gruffyn—"

"Fucking? Yes!"

"Should I tell Brother Gemma she should find a more loyal centaur for her monkish bed?"

"What?" He stepped back from his sister, insulted. "How dare you!"

"Then I truly do not understand. What do you care who Ainsley is fucking if you do not desire her?"

"Sister, she didn't just pick a centaur. She picked Gruffyn—"

"You *think* she's picked Gruffyn. There's no evidence."

"—his Clan's Grudge Holder."

She frowned. "Wait. Do you think Gruffyn is getting close to her to—"

"Get close to a throne? Yes. That is exactly what I think! If anything happens to Keeley or Gemma, Ainsley becomes queen and Gruffyn will suddenly be in charge of an entire army that he can order to take back what he considers his family's birthright."

Laila shook her head. "Look, I don't like the Torn Moon Clan any more than you do. The fact that they can't let a seven-*thousand*-year-old grudge go is, quite honestly, annoying. But I can't imagine Gruffyn using anyone that way. I don't think he could be bothered. He hates *everyone*."

"Right," Quinn agreed, again stepping close to his sister. "But he's *talking* to Ainsley."

"So you're just going to take orders from a dragon?"

Ainsley scratched her head. It was itchy now that her bird had moved to a spot on her neck, underneath her hair. Now no one could see him and people had stopped asking stupid questions. "I am not taking orders from anyone. Gwenvael and I are *plotting*!"

Gruff threw up his hands. "*How is that better?*"

"Wait, wait, wait," Briallen interrupted before tearing a whole, cooked chicken in half with her bare hands. "How is plotting *not* treachery?"

"I'd never betray my family."

"Good to know." She offered half the chicken to her brother, but he waved it off, so she gave it to Sarff. "But you are, and I'm using your word, *plotting* with a dragon against your sister."

"No. Not against. I'm trying to help her build an alliance with Annwyl the Bloody."

Sarff took a bite out of her chicken and thoughtfully chewed before replying, "We could use some of that dragon fire power."

"What?"

"Am I wrong?" Briallen asked her brother. "They're massive giants with the ability to breathe fire. It would be better to have them on our side than lose them to Beatrix."

"Which I agree with. But to be led by that smug bastard—"

"You just don't like him," Ainsley accused.

"I hate him. I thought that was clear." Gruff looked at his sister and Sarff. "Was I not clear? About my hatred of the gold dragon?"

"You were clear," Briallen said before taking another bite of chicken.

"Like the suns," Sarff added. "But we can't trust Queen Keeley will get this right."

"Why? She's set up alliances with dwarves and truces between religious factions that used to decimate each other for fun."

"All impressive," Sarff said. "But let's be honest . . . Queen Keeley is not really the problem."

"Exactly!" Ainsley practically cheered. She was so relieved that at least one of them understood what she was trying to do.

"That's the point," Gruff growled. "Queen Annwyl *is* a problem. For everyone! And you want to be the one to deal with her?"

"Just to get things rolling. Just to let her know that my sister would make an excellent comrade in arms."

"Which all may work out as you planned. *Or*, instead, she may just cut off Queen Keeley's head and wear it like a hat."

"No one is faster than me and my bow."

"It's good to hear you can still use your bow," Sarff remarked.

"Why? Because you chopped off my finger without even warning me?"

"Yes."

"Ainsley—"

"It loves me," she said to Gruff. "It'll protect me."

"I find it so disturbing you talk about your bow like that."

"I was talking about my bird."

"Oh. Why?"

"Because," Sarff interjected, "it's why she can't use a bow anymore."

"I can use a bow. You just said I can use a bow."

"Can we stop discussing your bloody bow?" Gruff demanded.

"You're right," Ainsley agreed.

"I just need you to answer one question for me."

"Which is?"

"Are you with me, Gruffyn of the Torn Moon Clan? Or not?"

"Fine," Gruff growled. "But we're not leaving you alone with her. One, or all of us"—he gestured to his sister and Sarff, then at the rest of his clan, who were taking apples off the trees and eating them—"need to be around you when you talk to that woman."

"That actually sounds like a good idea," Ainsley admitted. "But we don't tell my family anything. Ever. Until the end of time."

"Why?" Briallen asked.

"If Gemma even *thinks* I'm trying to intervene in any way, she will send me to a nunnery. And she'll say it's for my own good. Which is just hurtful, but that's beside the point."

"What about your two friends?" Sarff asked. "The nun and the monk."

"What about them?"

"They're smart and good with weapons. I think we can both agree that it would be better to bring them in now than it would be to drag them in later when all hells have broken loose."

Ainsley nodded. "You have an excellent point."

Sarff smiled, a tight scar on her jaw stretching as she did so. "I always do, sweet girl."

Gruff tried sitting on the high wooden stool once more, but he couldn't seem to find the right place to put his human ass.

He didn't know how humans managed their bodies. They seemed so . . . confusing. And yet appeared so simple.

"What are you doing?" Ainsley whispered.

"Trying to sit on this stupid stool."

"I leave you alone for five minutes . . ." she teased before reaching up and grabbing his shoulders. Once he'd stopped moving, she used her hands to guide him back until his ass hit the stool. His human knees automatically bent, and he was suddenly sitting.

He looked down at himself. Nodded.

"Comfortable?"

He grunted in reply and she smiled, walked away.

Gruff watched her move across the room, toward the Mad Queen. She didn't realize it, but she moved like her older sisters. Like she was swaggering into battle.

"Gruffyn?"

Gruff looked away from Princess Ainsley to Princess Laila, who now stood in front of him.

"Come with me."

It was an order, so he followed her through the main hall—after gesturing to Briallen to keep an eye on Ainsley—and out one of the doors that led into a hallway. He thought the princess was leading him to the kitchens, but she stopped a few feet into the hallway and smiled up at him.

"You have been doing an excellent job of protecting Princess Ainsley. It's been greatly appreciated."

He grunted at her and watched as she seemed to wait for something more. What, exactly, was she expecting?

When the silence had stretched on for over a minute, she finally said, "Now that things have settled down, you and your clan can return to your previous duties."

Gruff didn't respond. He didn't even grunt. He was too busy thinking of how he could fix this. Because he was not leaving Princess Ainsley on her own. Although she seemed to have a way with the dragons and was becoming more comfortable around them, he wasn't at all sure she could manage the same thing with the Mad Queen.

But he also wasn't going to break her trust and explain to Princess Laila why he was about to refuse the command she'd just given. Not when he knew that as soon as he told Laila, she'd run and tell her idiot brothers and it all would get back to the monk sister. He wouldn't put anyone through that kind of suffering.

Then he almost smiled. His sister. She could take care of this for him. One conversation with Briallen of the Torn Moon Clan and everything would be as he needed it.

"All right," Princess Laila said when Gruff didn't respond at all. "Well, any questions, please let me—"

"Oh, there you are, Princess Laila!" Angus Farmerson called out as he made his way down the hall.

"Angus. What can I do for you?"

"Well, first I want to say"—he put his hand on Gruffyn's shoulder and lowered his usually loud voice—"what great work Gruffyn and his clan have done for my girl Ainsley. I was worried that she wouldn't let anyone protect her while our new friends were here. I worry about her like I worry about all my children, but she always thinks she's capable of defending herself against anyone. So it's been a comfort to know that dear Gruffyn here is watching out for my Ainsley."

"Well, actually—"

"You see, my girl doesn't get along with many people. Her acceptance of Gruffyn and his clan is practically a miracle, and it keeps my Gemma off her back for once. So, I was wondering if we could keep things as they are? Just for a bit. Until everyone is a little more settled with all these new beings roaming about. Is that all right with you?"

Princess Laila opened her mouth, and Gruff truly thought she was going to deny Angus Farmerson's request.

But who could deny that man anything? It was his face. It was just so weirdly hard and sweet-looking at the same time.

Her Royal Highness briefly closed her eyes before announcing, "Of course, Angus. I'm sure Gruffyn and his clan wouldn't mind. Would you, Gruffyn?"

Gruff grunted, and Angus slapped him on the back. "Thank you, dear boy! I appreciate it." He put a blunt finger against his lips. "But shhh. Not a word to my Ainsley. She gets mad when she thinks we're being overprotective."

"Don't worry, Angus. Your secret is safe with us."

He gave Princess Laila a brief but tight hug before walking away.

Once they were alone again, the royal faced him. "Well . . . you have your orders."

Gruff nodded and returned to the main hall.

He'd just gotten his butt perfectly situated on the stool when Angus Farmerson, a loaf of bread gripped in his hand, motioned several of his younger children up from the table.

"We're going to the east fields!" he called out to his elder daughters.

"Whatever you do, Daddy," Gemma replied, "do not go to the south fields."

A bite of bread half-hanging out of his mouth, the queen's father stopped. "What does that mean?"

"It means stay away from the dragons."

"I said we were going to the east—"

*"Daddy!"*

"Fine!" He urged his children out the doors while loudly muttering, "Guess no flying trip requests today for our new friends, little ones. Because someone *is an ungrateful daughter!*"

That last bellowed bit had Gruff gazing at Angus Farmerson, which was when the man gave him a very large wink.

Before Gruff could ask what the hell that was, Princess Laila's idiot brother, the light-haired one, was suddenly right by his side.

"What was that about?" the idiot demanded.

Gruff stared at him.

"Are you going to answer me?"

"My brother doesn't have to answer you!" Briallen argued, stepping in front of Gruff and pushing her chest against the royal's to force him back. Gruff didn't even know where his sister had come from! It was as if she'd appeared from the air! "My brother doesn't have to say a word to anyone if he doesn't want to! *It's the law!*"

The royal frowned. "What law?"

"The laws of our gods."

Gruff watched the poor centaur. It was clear the royal wanted to argue that point with Briallen, but he had no clue what to say. Who would? The law was insane. Just like Gruff's sister.

With a snarl, the royal eventually stomped off and Briallen turned to grin at Gruff. He grunted and she warmly replied, "I love you too."

Beatrix entered Ivan's private chambers while her personal guards were allowed to wait out in the hallway because everything inside made them so uncomfortable.

"Any word from Commander Beaton?" she asked.

"No, Your Majesty. We know he's reached the main town of Wilforden. But no word whether he's met and talked to the baron."

"All right." She moved toward the big altar where Ivan stood, working on something at the center of it. "But as soon as you hear—"

Out of the corner of her eye, Beatrix saw something, mostly hidden in the dark shadows.

She immediately stopped and pointed. "What is that?"

Ivan smirked. "That is my new assistant, Maisie."

"New assistant? I know we lost the male you worked with, but what about the other female? The fat one?"

"Penelope had an unfortunate accident. We'll miss her."

No, she wouldn't. Beatrix barely remembered the woman except that she was fat and very blond.

This one was much thinner, it seemed. Yet she hid in the shadows. She must be paranoid, Beatrix thought. The thin, pretty ones, Beatrix had always noticed, enjoyed being seen by nearly everyone.

"Come out into the light," Beatrix ordered. "Let me see you." But this Maisie only shook her head and stepped deeper into the darkness.

"Maisie, now don't be shy," Ivan purred. "Come out here and show our queen your lovely face."

After a long, rather painful sigh, the woman moved into the light. And Beatrix quickly motioned her back with both hands.

"Go, go, go. Don't need to see any more of that."

"My Queen, don't be so cruel." Ivan laughed.

"You could have warned me!"

"I *can* hear you," the woman snarled from the dark.

Ivan laughed. "Nothing personal, my sweet girl. And our wonderful queen is known for her directness. But we all know that your face is not your best feature."

"*My* face is not my best feature," Beatrix shot back. "*That* is a horror show!"

"*I'm right here!*"

"Sorry. Sorry," Beatrix apologized, shuddering.

She moved to the altar, opposite Ivan, so she didn't have to look at that woman anymore. "Now that we know it wasn't her beauty that attracted you to your new assistant—"

"By the gods," came hoarsely from the darkness.

"—what qualifies her to be working here and forcing me to possibly see that face every day?"

"She has mighty skills with herbs."

Beatrix couldn't help but smirk. "A poisoner?" She looked over her shoulder into the darkness. "Come near my food or drink, little girl, and I'll make sure you're skinned while still breathing."

"She has no desire to destroy the woman who will be giving her so much, Your Majesty."

"And what am I giving her?"

"Vengeance," came that voice from the darkness.

Beatrix never had time for those seeking revenge. It was a boring motivation. Spending one's entire life trying to kill someone who did whatever. Not when unmitigated power was revenge enough.

"For what? Because someone burned off half your pretty face?" Beatrix asked.

"No. Because your sister's army killed my family."

Beatrix faced the shadows but the woman had stepped into the light.

"*My* sister?" she asked, incredulous. "You expect me to believe that *she* did this to you?"

"It was during the battle against Duke Covanshire. They burned our village to the ground and my family with it."

"*You* survived."

"I was out in the Northwoods harvesting—"

"Poison?"

"Herbs can heal, Your Majesty. Or they can kill. My mother taught me both."

"But *my* sister burning down a village? Anyone's village?"

"I don't know if it was by accident or on purpose. I just know it happened. And now I don't sleep."

Beatrix stared at the woman. It wasn't easy, with that face. But she liked the way Maisie gazed right back. Not flinching even though she was facing a queen. It wasn't the look Beatrix got from men. That direct challenge they gave her.

No. This woman's gaze told Beatrix something different. Her expression was filled with rage and hate and destruction. Something Beatrix could use.

"Welcome to my queendom, dear Maisie."

Without another word, the poisoner skulked back into the shadows and made herself at home.

Ainsley smoothed down her shirt, squared her shoulders and—with complete confidence—walked across the main hall until she stood in front of Queen Annwyl and Keeley.

"Morn—"

"What are you doing?" Gemma asked, stepping directly in front of Ainsley. Because she was the same height as her sister, Ainsley couldn't see around her, which made it impossible to talk to the two queens.

"Just coming over to say—"

"Why don't *you* go help Daddy in the east fields?"

Ainsley didn't understand what was happening. Gemma knew that her sister didn't farm. Nothing bored her more than harvesting fields or dealing with grumpy cows. When she'd turned eleven, she was supposed to spend one whole year with her father, tending the land they lived on. By the fourth month, her father took her to their mother's forge and left her there. Although that apprenticeship only lasted eight months, it helped Ainsley understand she didn't want to be a blacksmith either, even though she took her mother's family name. The only reason she'd stayed so long at the forge was because her mother loved the arrowheads Ainsley forged and they sold well to the soldiers and warriors coming through town. Other than that, though, Ainsley's family knew she was not a farmer or a blacksmith.

So why the fuck would Gemma try to force her to . . .

"You don't want me talking to Queen Annwyl," Ainsley guessed.

"That's not it."

"Liar. You're a lying monk."

"It's just this isn't the time for chatting." She stepped closer and lowered her voice. "We're hoping to have a serious discussion with Queen Annwyl, and I'm worried your presence will be a distraction."

"A distraction? Greeting a guest is, to *you*, a distraction? Or only when *I* am the one greeting the guest?"

"It's not like that, Ainsley. You can just talk to her later."

Ainsley wanted to respond but she knew that every word out of her mouth would be hysterical screaming, which would only prove to her sisters that she was nothing but a useless baby who needed to be kept away from royals and dragons and anyone else they deemed important.

So, when Ainsley was sure she would *not* wrap her hands around her sister's throat and choke the very life from her, she spun away, stalked past a silent Gruffyn, and out the open front doors. Never looking back.

Gemma winced as her younger sister stormed out the door; the centaur gave one last glower before he followed Ainsley as her protection.

"You know," the Mad Queen remarked, standing right beside Gemma now, "the last time I saw my brother alive, I gave him that same look your sister just gave you." She paused, then added, "Then I took his fucking head."

Slowly, Gemma turned to look directly at the woman speaking to her.

"I put it on a pike outside my encampment. Fearghus wanted me to take it down after a few days. Said the crows had pecked out his eyes. But I wanted everyone to see. To understand."

She knew she shouldn't ask, but she couldn't help herself. "Understand what?"

"That his kingdom was now mine. Just like his head."

Gemma didn't know what to say to any of that. Instead, she simply stood there, quietly horrified.

As she gawked at the foreign royal, the Mad Queen's dragon mate came bounding down the stairs and immediately headed for the door.

"I need to stretch my wings," he informed her. "Care to join me?"

Queen Annwyl held up a finger and said to Keeley, "Did you want to speak with me?"

Instead of saying she did want to have a queen-to-queen audience, Keeley shook her head and sort of . . . squeaked?

Not that Gemma blamed her sister at all. The whole brother's-head-on-a-pike thing was, at the very least . . . *off-putting*! Meaning that silence and no private meetings between the pair were probably the best approach. At least for the moment.

"All right, then," the Mad Queen replied before following the dragon outside.

"What was I supposed to do with that story?" Keeley demanded in a panicked whisper.

"I honestly didn't know if that was a warning to me . . . to you . . . or to the screeching voices in her head."

Keeley gestured toward the open doorway. "Do you think they'll be leaving from the courtyard?"

The sisters looked at each other, then bolted to the entrance. When they reached the steps in front of the tower, they came to an abrupt halt.

Queen Annwyl was just swinging her leg over the dragon's neck, her hands clinging to his hair. She said something to Princess Morfyd, who was standing a few feet away in her human form and then they both laughed, neither female bickering for once.

Taking a few seconds, the Mad Queen settled her ass onto the black dragon's back and tied her wild brown hair off her face with a leather strip. It was the first time Gemma had ever seen the foreign royal's face clearly. The scars she bore from past battles were easy to see now. They bore witness to the victories she'd won because she was still breathing. Somehow. Despite the brutal scars. She had one that went straight across her face from her temple, all the way down, missing her eye but slashing her nose, her lips, her jaw until it reached a nasty end in her neck just above the main artery that would have killed her instantly on the battlefield. Another messy scar showed that her cheek had been ripped open and, at some point, hastily and poorly sewn shut. Her other eye had a gash just above the brow that looked like a hatchet had struck it. Smaller, less horrifying marks crisscrossed her throat.

And yet, despite what Gemma would take as obvious evidence that this woman had been through untold horror on the battlefield that must have brought on her madness, her obvious joy at being on the dragon's back was palpable. She looked as if she couldn't imagine being anywhere else in the world.

Gemma could see that this woman was absolutely jubilant to be with the one she loved. Even if that "one" was a dragon.

And yet this same woman had taken her brother's head, put it on a pike, and then bragged about it.

The black dragon unfurled his wings. Not straight out but up to avoid the nearby buildings. When he dragged them down, his claws left the ground, and he was airborne.

Gemma and her sister watched the pair fly off until they were no longer in sight.

"I'll try again tomorrow. In the morning," Keeley eventually said, her voice confident.

"You sure?"

Keeley faced Gemma. "We just watched that woman mount a dragon ten, twenty times her size and fly off. We need *her* as an ally."

"She cut off her own brother's head and put it on a pike as a trophy."

"I know."

"That doesn't worry you?"

"Right now, everything worries me. But I am *not* letting Annwyl the Bloody, friend and mate to royal dragons, align her armies with Beatrix."

"She might *be* Beatrix."

"She's not."

"Keeley—"

"She's *not*."

"After that story about her *own* brother, how do you know that?"

"Because Annwyl clearly loves that dragon. *Trusts* him not to throw her off his back midair. He means something to her. His whole family does. And the way she loves them is the way she loves her queendom. Her people. With all her heart and soul."

Gemma crossed her arms in front of her chest. "So?"

"Gemma . . . Beatrix has never loved or trusted *anything*."

# CHAPTER 11

Princess Ainsley kept stopping, opening her mouth as if she was about to say something, and then storming off again. It went on for a good ten minutes before the nun and the monk caught up with her and the centaur.

Still too angry to speak, the princess stomped away from them, and they both turned to Gruff. He didn't really know what to tell them, though. What had happened hadn't been an explosion of anger. Or a fight to the death between siblings. It had been something else. Something a lot more hurtful, he'd guess.

No one could think of anything to say, so they followed the princess. As she had with him, Ainsley kept stopping, facing them, opening her mouth to say something, and then stomping off again. It happened at least five times before they briefly lost sight of her when she went around a huge boulder.

When Gruff caught up with her, she was standing by the far end of the boulder, peeking around it. She held up her hand and Gruff motioned to the others to stop before he silently moved up behind her. Leaning over the royal, he looked around the boulder as well and saw a tall man dressed in chainmail, speaking to someone draped in a cape that covered the person's entire body, from head to toes. He couldn't even see a face.

The tall man, Gruff guessed, was a dragon in human form based on the size of him. The two spoke in whispers and then the one in the cape disappeared into the nearby woods.

"It's rude to watch people," the dragon said after his comrade disappeared.

"And it's rude to betray my sister!" the princess yelled as she came around the boulder, shaking off Gruff's hand when he tried to stop her.

"Who are you? Who are you working for?" Before Princess Ainsley even reached the man, who still had his back to them, she had her bow out and an arrow nocked. "I will kill you where you stand if you don't tell me what's happening."

Ainsley knew she spoke to a dragon, but she didn't care. She reasoned that if she could release her arrow before he completely shifted, it would go through his eye and into his brain. She doubted even a dragon could withstand that.

His head tipped to the side, and he squinted. "You really would, wouldn't you? Unleash that arrow on me."

"What do you think? Now tell me what's going on before I get testy."

With a sigh, he pulled a small case out of the travel bag slung over his shoulder and opened it. She watched as he put a set of spectacles on his face, adjusting the thin metal arms carefully over his ears.

Once done, he focused on Ainsley again and this time seemed much less annoyed.

"Ahhh. Princess Ainsley. I'm Unnvar Reinholdt. First born son of Dagmar Reinholdt, prince royal of the House of Gwalchmai fab Gwyar, and my mother's absolute favorite."

Ainsley lowered her bow. "Your father is Gwenvael?" she guessed.

"Tragically. But my mother is—"

"Dagmar Reinholdt. Queen Annwyl's battle lord. The battle lord who has never been in a battle."

"That's incorrect. My mother has never *raised a sword* in battle, but she has been in battle and is greatly feared in our lands for many reasons. Pray you never find out what those are."

"Are you betraying my sister?" Ainsley demanded.

He didn't answer right away, his gaze focused over her head. "Are you going to introduce me to your medley of friends?"

"Are you going to answer my question?"

He gave a strained smile. "You first."

Ainsley thought about fighting him over all that but decided against it. There was just something about him . . .

"This is Gruffyn of the Torn Moon Clan. Brother Sheva, novitiate of the Order of Righteous Valor. And Sister Hilda of the—"

"Sister Hilda's fine," Hilda told them.

"Sister Hilda's fine," Ainsley repeated.

Gwenvael's son studied Ainsley for a long time before he asked, "And do you trust them?"

"With my life," she answered honestly.

"Fine." Unnvar seemed to take Ainsley at her word, because he immediately held up a piece of parchment. "From one of my mother's many spies. But it's not about your queen. It's about one of the commanders of Queen Beatrix's armies."

"What about him?"

"He's in neutral territory."

"And?"

"And you don't want him to be there. He is attempting to make it *not* neutral but an ally of Queen Beatrix instead."

He gazed at her through those round pieces of glass, and Ainsley couldn't help but ask, "Do you really need those?"

"Why else would I wear them?"

"But do dragons need spectacles?"

"Some of the very old ones do."

"But you're young and, again, a dragon."

"*Half* dragon. My mother is very human, and although I was born with eyes that worked perfectly, I did eventually inherit her only flaw." He held up the parchment. "Anyway, I have to get this to Uncle Bram so he can take it to your sisters. And, I surmise, prove my loyalty to you."

He tried to step around her, but Ainsley held up a hand. "Give it to my sisters . . . why? Exactly?" When he only stared at her, she added, "What do you expect them to do with that information?"

"If it were up to *me*—and as has been pointed out to me several times today, it's not—I'd send some of my best people to capture Beatrix's emissary and bring him back here for interrogation."

Ainsley burst out laughing, but Unnvar's expression didn't change. He didn't appear hurt or amused, either. Simply curious.

"I don't understand what's so humorous."

"My sisters aren't going to do any of that. Ever."

"But it does make sense, yes?"

"It does. But when you use the word 'interrogation,' I'm sure you mean torture, and there's no way on this earth Keeley is ever going to agree to that."

He paused thoughtfully before announcing, "I can get my aunt Annwyl to do the interrogation. She's done it before."

"She's tortured people?"

"Just enemy males who've attacked first. And only when she desperately needs information. Otherwise, she just cuts off their heads to be done with it."

Deciding to ignore the last part, Ainsley asked, "Torture them how?"

"My aunt is not subtle. She just starts cutting off body parts until she gets what she needs."

"Okay," Ainsley shook her head and waved her arms. "No. No. No. No, no, no, no, no. That's just not going to work. Not for my sister. Not for me. Just no."

"Then what would you sugg—"

Ainsley snatched the parchment from Unnvar's hand. "I'll take care of it."

"How?" Sheva asked, reminding Ainsley she wasn't alone with this dragon. Or human. Or whatever the hells he was.

"I'm going to get this"—she glanced at the parchment—"Beaton person and bring him here myself. We'll decide what to do from there."

"This 'Beaton person,' as you call him," Unnvar explained, "has been a commander in the Old King's armies since long before your sisters claimed their crowns, which means he did not come by that title lightly. I'm assuming he's not a man to be toyed with."

"I'm not going to be *toying* with anyone."

"It's doubtful he's alone. A man of his rank would have at least two hundred soldiers at his disposal. Meaning that you might want to bring someone with you."

She looked over at Hilda and Sheva. "What are you two up to?"

Hilda raised a single brow. "Doing anything but this?"

Gruff couldn't believe the royal was being so stupid. All because her sisters acted like . . . well . . . sisters? She was willing to risk her life to prove some point?

"Come on," Princess Ainsley pushed her wisely reluctant friends. "It'll be fun!"

"It will be anything *but* fun," the nun argued.

"You are going to get us in so much trouble," the monk added.

"You love trouble."

"Other people's trouble. Not my own."

"Believe it or not," the princess replied, "I am not stupid enough to go do something like this by myself. And both of you were looking for something more meaningful to do."

"I was?" the nun asked.

"No, I wasn't!" the monk shot back.

"Plcccccccasc," she whined to her friends. "Please, please, please! I promise to provide everything we need, and after we're done, I'll make sure you're amply rewarded so that you can buy new . . ." She gestured at Sister Hilda. "Buy new habits and body-covering robes." She waved a hand at Brother Sheva. "And something grand for you to sacrifice to your all-important gods! Won't that be nice?"

"What about when your sisters notice you're missing?" the prince asked.

The three women gazed at each other for so long that Gruff thought maybe the royal would back out of her risky scheme. But then they all suddenly howled in laughter, bending over at the waist and occasionally choking. So entertained were they, the laughter went on for some time before the princess said—between wiping her eyes and little hiccups—to Prince Unnvar, "They'll never notice I'm gone. Don't even worry about that."

When the laughter finally ended, Princess Ainsley said to Gruff without turning around, "I know you're not happy about any of this, but you can stop glaring at the back of my head."

He grunted and she faced him. "You don't have to worry about us, you know. I promise, we'll be fine." Gruff didn't reply. "Just don't say anything to anyone." Still nothing. "We both know I can take care of myself." More nothing. "I mean, yes, I'm a royal. And my potential capture by the enemy would be a very bad thing, but you know I won't let that happen." Even more nothing. "You're being completely irrational about all this. I'll be fine." Absolutely nothing. "I don't need a babysitter, Gruffyn!" Not a word.

"*Fine!*" she exploded. "Your lot can come. But do not forget that *I'm* in charge. Not you. Not your sister." She held up her bandaged hand. "Definitely not Sarff. Are we clear?"

Gruff grunted, and she let out an annoyed breath. "Thank you."

Brother Sheva glanced at Sister Hilda and asked, "What did we just watch?"

"I've stopped asking that question."

"We leave tonight," Ainsley told them as she led the way back to the tower. "After dinner, which I won't be attending. They'll be expecting that after the way Gemma pissed me off. When I don't show up the next few nights for dinner, they won't even notice."

"Are you sure about this?" Sheva asked again.

The monk was not worrying about herself but about Ainsley, which Ainsley greatly appreciated.

"I'm sure. I need to get out of here. And to be able to do something useful—"

"And dangerous," Hilda added.

"After dragons, are you really that worried about taking on some lowly commander in Beatrix's army?"

"Is that what you're up to, Your Majesty?"

Ainsley froze at the sound of that voice, her entire *being* cringing. Looking to her left, she saw Master General Ragna of the Order of Righteous Valor—Gemma's order!—and quickly forced a smile.

"Oh. You're back, Ragna!" She hated how high-pitched her voice sounded.

"Yes, I am!" Ragna mockingly squeaked back at her. "I was traveling with your sister's cohorts—Brother Kir, Brother Katla, and Brother Shona—"

"I don't care," Ainsley muttered.

"—and when they got the orders to come back, I came too. I sensed there was drama afoot now that your sister Gemma is in charge of my beloved brotherhood. And by the war gods, I was right. So. Much. Drama." She stepped away from the tree she'd been relaxing against and walked toward Ainsley. "My army is not far behind, which is good since we are now overrun with dragons that your sister seems unable to get rid of." She pointed at the sky, and they all looked up to see several of the giant beasts flying by. "Such fun I've missed. But it seems that you, my lady, have found more fun!"

Ainsley let the façade drop. When it came to Ragna, she didn't know why she had bothered in the first place. The woman was such a force within her order that she had her own army. When she walked by, other Order of Righteous Valor monks stopped talking and desperately waited for her to leave. She was feared and respected by other orders, feared and avoided by the battle priests and the nuns, as well, and feared and loathed by nearly every witch's coven in the known universe.

She was, to put it bluntly, an unpleasant person to be around, who represented everything Ainsley hated about these god worshippers. Because Ragna was more than a disciple; she was a militant follower who would do anything if she felt it was in the best interest of her war gods. And Ainsley meant *anything*. The woman had no loyalty to human beings. Her loyalty was only to her gods.

Despite that, Ragna had always been . . . well . . . Ainsley wouldn't call it kind. Or nice. Perhaps the best way to put it was that Ragna had always been decent to Ainsley. Even helping when she could . . . or if she wanted to.

Things had changed, however, since Gemma took the Grand Master title of the Order of Righteous Valor. While the brotherhood and all the other orders had heaved a sigh of relief at the assignment, Ragna had felt betrayed. With the other elders of their order dead, Ragna had assumed she'd take over the brotherhood. Her experience of the battlefield was legendary. When that didn't happen . . .

Ragna would never turn her army on her own brothers—at least not without orders from the war gods she worshipped—but she wasn't happy about any of the recent changes and wasn't afraid to let anyone know about that unhappiness, including Ainsley.

To get rid of Ragna for a bit, Gemma had sent her cohorts out to check in with all the other religious orders that lived within Keeley's territories; she had ordered Ragna and her army to go with them for protection. A protection it was doubtful Gemma's friends needed. But Ainsley couldn't blame her sister. It had to be hard to be constantly glared at by Master General Ragna.

"So, tell me," Ragna ordered in a lighthearted way that didn't belie the fact it was definitely a command, "what are you up to, Princess?"

Ainsley knew she could lie, but what would be the point? At least where Ragna was concerned. Knowing it would be a waste of time and breath, she simply revealed, "I'm going into neutral territories to track down some commander of Beatrix's army who's trying to arrange an alliance with one of the dukes—"

"Baron," Hilda corrected.

"Whatever. Hilda and Sheva offered to go with me—"

"Well—" Sheva began.

"—and Gruffyn insisted that his clan also come along as our protection."

"And once you have this commander, what do you plan to do with him?" Ragna asked.

"Bring him back here, slap him around a little until he tells us what he knows. Then, maybe, have him put on trial for any war crimes we can prove."

Ragna's gaze slowly moved over Ainsley and her entire group before she said, "Good luck."

She walked away and, stunned, Ainsley turned to Sheva and Hilda. Both could only shrug, being as confused as she was.

"That's it?" Ainsley finally asked Ragna's retreating form.

"If anyone asks, Brother Batsheva," the Master General addressed Sheva, "tell them your novitiate training is under my command now and you're following my orders. Understand?"

"Uh . . . yes, Brother."

"And Sister Hilda . . ." Ragna flicked her hands out even as she kept walking away. "Well, quite honestly, I'm sure your fellow sisters will be glad to see you go. I can say with pure honesty they dislike you even more than they dislike me. But your Mother Superior is too afraid to do anything about it."

None of them could argue with that, so they didn't bother.

Once Ragna disappeared, Sheva asked with unusual dourness, "Do you really think I'm reporting to her now?"

"Would that be so bad?" Hilda wanted to know.

"Yes."

"Because when we get back, she'll actually make you work and won't be easily fooled by your lies?"

Sheva nodded. "Exactly."

# CHAPTER 12

"The four of you stay here in case the idiot twins start looking for us for some reason."

"But what do I *say*?" Drych asked, referring to Princess Laila's brothers. "If they ask questions. They do like to ask questions." Like Gruff, Drych didn't feel the need to speak unless necessary.

"You don't say anything," Briallen told him while she haphazardly shoved things into her travel bag. A bag that Gruff would repack for her with things she actually needed. "You just do what Gruff does. Grunt. If they ask you more questions, grunt again."

"But you won't be here to get between those two and me. I don't want to talk to them. They annoy me."

"Everyone annoys you," Gruff noted.

"Yes! That's true. And yet you're leaving me behind!"

"I can do it," Eirlys said. Eirlys was the daughter of his mother's second-in-command. She'd been ordered to go with Gruff and the others to help fight against Queen Beatrix because her entire family found Eirlys annoying. So did Gruff but he avoided speaking to her and, eventually, she'd wander away.

"You know not to approach them first?" Briallen asked. "Let the royals come to you."

"I avoid the royals most days," Eirlys replied in that very high-pitched voice. "Because according to Prince Caid, he finds me irritating and a pest."

Gruff and Briallen exchanged a glance before Gruff admitted, "She's absolutely perfect."

* * *

"Please don't tell anyone."

"I don't like you doing this."

"I'm not going alone." Ainsley took her father's hand and tugged until he sat on her bed, her travel bag between them. "I've got Sheva and Hilda. Plus Gruff and his clan."

"But none of your sisters."

"Well one *is* queen, so she's busy. The others are too young. And one is a raging psychotic."

"Gemma doesn't mean—"

"To be a bitch?"

"To be so scared. All this is very overwhelming for her. And she just got command of her order . . ."

"Da, I know. Which is why I'm no longer waiting for either of them to *give* me anything. They both have bigger things to worry about, and I need to start doing things on my own. But I want *you* to know where I am so you don't worry."

"Your mother will worry too."

"Uh-huh."

"Anyway," he continued, "what do you want me to tell them if they notice you're gone?"

"They won't."

"Ainsley—"

"They won't. Trust me. But I do need a favor."

"Get between Gruffyn and Laila again? Because you were spot-on about that."

"I don't need a protection detail, but Laila hates it when her people have nothing to do. Now that she's given her orders, I don't think she'll bother us again. But I do need you for this."

Ainsley reached under her hair and lifted the bird off her neck. She held the creature out to her father.

"Can you?" He was already beginning to screech a little because he was hungry.

"Of course!" Her father took the chick in his hands, smiling. "I'll make a space for him in your room. Not a cage but someplace where he won't be at risk from your sister's wolves. Or those two cats that keep sneaking in here."

"I think Endelyon keeps feeding those nasty things."

"Or Isadora." Angus shrugged at Ainsley's questioning look. "She likes cats."

That was actually a good thing. Beatrix had never liked any animals. Even the birds singing early in the morning had upset her and they were high in the trees, not inside their house! So Ainsley thought it important that the rest of her siblings had a warm spot for some sort of animal.

"Tell me, Daughter," her father said, sounding far too sad, "have I let you down? Let the family down?"

"What?"

He petted the chick's head with his pinky, soothing the cranky bird. "Maybe if I'd been a better father—"

"No, no, *no!* Don't you dare even think that!" she ordered. "Beatrix was born as she is. Cold and heartless. Not because of you and Mum but *in spite* of the love and care you and Mum and Keeley gave her. You can't take any of what she's done on yourselves. Especially when you and Mum have more than a thousand well-adapted children who prove what loving parents you are."

"You do not have over a thousand siblings."

"You and Mum are like dogs that keep breeding. Every season a new litter."

"Do not compare your parents to dogs, spoiled child!"

Chuckling, Ainsley leaned over her bag and kissed her father's cheek. "You are an amazing father, and whatever is happening with Beatrix is her own fault and her loss."

"Thanks, luv." He stood, cuddling the bird close to his big chest. "Before you pick a horse to ride on this—"

"Expedition."

"Ooooo-kay. Before you pick a horse for your expedition, go see Gemma's horse."

"Da, if I take Kriegszorn, Gemma is definitely going to know—"

"Just do as I ask!" He stomped to the door. "Can't any of my children simply do as I ask?"

"I'm sure that a few of the *thousands* out there—"

*"Ainsley Smythe, you know damn well and good that you do* not *have thousands of siblings!"*

"Well, if you want to keep it that way, maybe you and Mum

should take a night off. And it was unnecessary to slam the door like that!"

After sending his fellow centaurs to wait for him and the royal outside the town gates, Gruff went looking for Princess Ainsley. He'd thought she would have met him earlier, but after waiting nearly half the hour he decided to search her out.

Perhaps she'd changed her mind and had decided she didn't want to do anything this senseless. But Gruff knew better. The royal was too stubborn to change her mind if the decision would in any way please her elder sisters. It was more likely she'd already been found out and her sisters had her chained up in her bedroom with that strange bird of hers keeping watch.

Gruff was almost back to the tower when he heard someone whistling. He stopped and looked around until he saw Angus Farmerson gesturing him over.

When Gruff reached him, the man whispered, "You can find my girl at the stable where Gemma's horse is kept."

"Why are you whispering?" Gruff asked.

Farmerson leaned back. "Never heard you speak before, boy. Didn't know you could. And I don't know why I'm whispering."

"Which horse?" Gruff asked, because the monk had two horses. And one of them was half-dead.

"The almost dead one," Farmerson replied, ruining Gruff's night.

"Of course."

The human started to walk off, but he abruptly stopped and faced Gruff again. "You will take good care of my girl, yeah?"

"With my life, sir."

Farmerson nodded and patted Gruff's shoulder before heading back to the tower.

So many children, and Angus Farmerson loved each and every one of them. Even Queen Beatrix. That's why her betrayal hurt him so much. If he didn't care about her, why would he be so devastated every time she was mentioned? Why would his children do their best to hide the truth of what she was up to from him? But Farmerson never let his disappointment in one child affect how he treated the remainder of his offspring.

Gruff appreciated that. Appreciated the kindness that had clearly rubbed off Angus Farmerson onto his fourth eldest.

The half-dead thing that Brother Gemma insisted on keeping around had its own stable far from the tower, the market, or any other main building. But it was still close enough so that the thing could be checked up on when necessary. A good idea considering this was not an animal one wanted wandering around the countryside.

Gruff had accidentally passed the dead thing in its stable a few times. When he had, it was always disturbing. Not because it was doing anything supernatural or evil. It had, in fact, been doing something normal horses do all the time: grazing. And, depending on the way he walked up to it and the direction it was standing, he might see just that. A horse grazing. But other times he would come up to it from the "wrong side" as he called it and witness the dead thing chewing grass or eating animals from the side that was decayed. That side had no skin and most of the flesh was dropping off. He'd see that one eye staring at him and the skeletal head chewing, chewing, chewing away in a grotesque display of unholiness.

The first time he'd witnessed that, his prey animal had screamed inside him, begging him to run. As far and as fast as he could. It took absolutely everything he had not to reveal the disgust and panic that was building inside him; not to bolt off into the surrounding forests and never return. The few times he'd seen the horse after that, he'd been less reactive. Calmer. But still filled with disgust and horror. It was to be expected, though. He was only a centaur. Not a demon used to witnessing such disgusting and unholy things chewing, chewing, chewing on an apple. That one eye staring at him.

Gruff shuddered and did his best to put the image out of his head. He was just here to find out if Ainsley still wanted to make this insane journey and, if she did, get moving.

Yet Gruff halted abruptly when a bright ball of multicolor lights exploded out from the trees. He knew it came from the stable and he shifted to his natural form and ran toward it, battle-axe and spear at the ready.

When he reached the path that crossed in front of the horse's stable, he found Sister Hilda on her knees, hands clasped in front of her, eyes closed tight as she prayed hard to her gods. Prayed for their protection and guidance, he assumed.

Standing a few feet farther down was Brother Sheva. She did not pray. She was not on her knees in the dirt. But she had her back to the nearby stable and her hand gripping the hilt of her sword. If the monk saw him, she said nothing as Gruff trotted by.

Gruff continued until he reached the stable. Right next to it was the enclosed pasture that the dead thing spent most of its time in. The stable doors were left open so it could come and go into the pasture as it liked.

Unlike the previous day, Gruff didn't think the thing had gotten out again. The light was too great. He could actually feel that light because it was filled with magicks, and it pounded against him in waves as he moved closer. His trot slowed to a cautious walk until he saw Ainsley standing by the fence. She didn't even turn to him when he stopped next to her. She only gazed straight ahead. He wasn't even sure she was aware he'd arrived.

Dreading what he might see, Gruff turned his head toward the middle of the pasture in time to watch in horror as something slid out of the dead thing's birth canal and dropped onto the ground.

It wasn't the only one. There was already another, a white one, and it had torn its way out of the membrane that had surrounded it and now stood on shaky legs.

The dead thing moved forward, away from its offspring and seemed to start the process all over again. Normally a mare lay on its side to deliver a foal; this thing just stood strong until whatever was in it slid out. There was no struggle. No waiting. No distress. And there was more than one. With horses, there was rarely more than one foal. If, by some miracle, a mare had twins, it was rare the second one survived.

And there were never triplets. Not live ones.

Yet the black-colored second foal was already kicking its way to its feet while the first already appeared bigger than when Gruff had first seen it.

The third, a gray with white hooves, came sliding out of its mother and crashed to the ground, pure light exploding all around it. The half-dead thing trotted away, the placenta already expelled as she moved. A few seconds later, the first foal was trotting on its own and was now tripled in size. The second was a minute or two behind the first. But the third was on its hooves and running around the pasture within seconds. That's the one the half-dead thing went to and nuzzled first. Then she led it over to stand in front of Princess Ainsley.

The royal gazed at the gray foal for a very long, silent moment before she asked, "Do . . . do you . . . um . . . want me to ride . . ." The royal leaned over as far as her body would allow so she could look under the foal. "Him," she said when she was upright again. "Do you want me to ride him?"

The foal put its now huge head over the fence and Gruff took several steps back, but other than leaning away a bit, the princess kept her feet planted.

Letting out a breath, she slowly reached her hand out to touch the foal's head.

Worried about what she was going to do, about the risk she was taking, Gruff softly began, "Princess Ains—"

The undead thing was suddenly there, at the fence, her half-decayed head coming at him, fangs flashing, a warning hiss exploding from the back of her throat.

Gruff backed up a few feet more, and that seemed to calm the mother down.

"It's all right, Gruff," the princess told him as she gently and carefully placed her hand on the foal's head.

She had to raise her arm now so she could reach its head and muzzle. The foal towered over her, appearing full grown and, even stranger, completely normal.

All the skin was on it. There was no decay, no fangs. Its eyes didn't change color. It looked like a beautifully bred gray horse that one would pay a small fortune to have. Yet it had been born only in the last few minutes and was now fully grown. As were its two siblings.

Once she began petting its head, the foal nuzzled her arm and licked it. Again, nothing strange about that. No destroyed flesh where its tongue had been. No cries of pain from the princess.

Everything seemed normal.

Except this wasn't normal! Not in any way!

Gruff heard footsteps and looked behind him to see Sister Hilda walking up to the fence, her hands still clasped in front of her.

Brother Sheva followed behind her, desperately whispering, *"What the fuck are you doing, crazy nun?"*

"My god told me to come here," Sister Hilda replied, harshly panting after each sentence. "That I would be rewarded. So I put myself in the hands of my god."

She reached the fence and waited. The black foal, also now fully grown, trotted over to her. She didn't move. Didn't try to touch it. Without prompting, it put its head over the fence and nuzzled the nun.

Despite whimpering softly in fear, Sister Hilda carefully stroked the side of the horse's face. And stayed still as it sniffed her.

Gruff expected to see the last foal—the white one that had been born first—trotting to the fence, too, but it didn't. Looking around the pasture, he quickly realized that foal was gone.

Cringing, Gruff slowly turned and Brother Sheva, busy watching the nun with a distinct look of disgust on her face, moved her gaze to his. They stared at each other a long moment before the monk said, "It's behind me . . . isn't it?"

Gruff nodded, unable to speak. It wasn't that the horse had gotten out of the pasture. The half-dead thing did that all the time. It was that Gruff hadn't seen it jump out. It was simply there one second and gone the next. Only to arrive behind the poor monk, who was about to soil her leggings if her expression was anything to go by.

"It's going to kill me, isn't it?" she asked.

"I don't think so," he managed to get out. "But I'm not really positive."

"It's all right," Princess Ainsley said to her friends. "Kriegszorn is rewarding us with her offspring. We'll be perfectly safe with them."

"She told you that?" the monk demanded. She still hadn't turned around to look at the white stallion with a diamond-shaped brown spot on its forehead.

"No. It's a guess. But I'm going with it." Ainsley lowered her hand and stepped back from the fence. "I'm going into the stable now to get his tack. I suggest you ladies do the same."

"We're bringing them with us?" Sheva asked.

"We do not turn down a gift—"

"From a monster?"

The half-dead thing was suddenly on the monk's right—Gruff didn't see it leave the pasture either—and leaned in close to hiss right in her ear. To Brother Sheva's credit, although startled, she didn't run. She simply leaned her head away from the fanged maw hissing at her.

"A gift from a good friend," the princess amended. When she walked by Sheva, she grabbed the monk's hand and dragged her toward the stable. The nun followed silently.

Leaving Gruff outside with the half-dead thing and her unholy spawn.

Silently and without moving, they all stared at him. He grunted. And, as one, they grunted back.

Deciding this was too much, even for him, Gruff called out toward the stable, "I'll be waiting at the meeting spot, Your Royal Highness." Then he walked away.

No. He didn't run. Because he knew running would just turn him into prey. And whatever these things were, the one thing they were *not* . . . was prey.

# CHAPTER 13

Keeley came down the stairs. She was looking for Gemma but, other than her youngest siblings, she only saw the royal dragons, Queen Annwyl, and Isadora.

Her fifth eldest sister stood by the open double doors, working diligently on a parchment tacked to a thin piece of wood that had been sanded and oiled so that it was smooth. It included a little well that held some black ink, and she dipped a quill into it every few words. A very nice writing surface that her sister could carry anywhere.

Isadora had probably made it herself. She did love working with wood.

"Have you seen Gemma?" she asked her sister.

"No."

Keeley briefly watched Queen Annwyl play with little Endelyon. Her sister had her small silver hammer, and the foreign royal had a wooden training short sword. They mock-battled across one of the dining tables. The queen was moving much slower and hitting much lighter than she had when Keeley had challenged her.

"Gemma isn't harassing Ainsley again, is she?"

"I haven't seen Ainsley this morning," Isadora replied. "She's probably up a tree."

"Which tree?"

"I don't know. Any tree. If there's a tree taller than six feet, she's probably climbed it, which means they are all available to her. Why do you care anyway?"

"I feel bad. Gemma's been—"

"Awful?"

"She's always been protective of all of you."

"Yeah. Like one of those dogs that picks up her annoying pups by the neck and shakes them until they whimper and cower."

"She's not that bad."

"You cuddle, Keeley," Isadora explained. "Gemma shakes. It's just how you two deal with us."

"Should I talk to Gemma about it?"

Her sister looked up from whatever she was working on. "Why?"

"To calm her down a bit?"

"You expect Gemma to calm down with dragons *literally* sitting on top of our tower?" she scoffed. "We're lucky she hasn't screamed hysterically and started killing everybody with one of her axes." She glanced off. "That woman has so many axes."

Isadora went back to writing. "I promise you, you're better off not getting involved. We all know how to handle Gemma."

"You do?"

"Yes. I just walk away. She yells, but she never chases me down. Endelyon over there, throws her little hammer at her head. That usually puts a stop to her hysterical rants about anyone's safety. Rexie"—Rex was a year younger than Endelyon—"tells her he's going to study magicks so he can be a witch one day. She gets so upset that she cuddles him for hours and tells him all witches are evil."

"He wants to be a witch?"

"Of course not. He wants to be a farmer, but it's a quick way to get her to back off. And Duncan"—born a couple of years after Isadora—"panics with her."

"He panics?" She'd never seen her younger brother panic.

"No. He just emulates her until she becomes concerned that he's panicking too much and then she spends the rest of her time trying to calm him down. Not surprisingly, he gets extra food out of it."

"He eats so much."

"He's going to be a giant. Oh, by the way, he needs a new bed. His legs are now hanging so far over the end that he can comfortably place them on the floor when he's lying down with his head against the wall."

"Can you just take care of that?"

"Of course."

When Keeley continued to stand there—watching Annwyl the Bloody take a "brutal" hammer hit to the head and cough up nonexistent blood before dropping dramatically on the dining table so that Endelyon could put her foot onto the woman's chest, hold up her weapon, and roar out, "*Victory!*" to the entertainment of the dragons watching—Isadora asked, "Is there something else?"

"Just trying to figure out how to ask Queen Annwyl for a private meeting. Just the two of us."

"You want a meeting?"

"Private meeting. Yes."

Isadora looked up from her parchment and barked across the room, "Oy! Annwyl?"

"By the gods!" Keeley desperately whispered. "What are you doing?"

"You got some time to meet with my sister? She'd like to talk to you in private."

"I think I'm dead," the royal replied, her eyes still closed, her arms spread wide on the table.

"She's dead!" Endelyon let them all know.

"You can kill her again later, Endelyon."

Endelyon rolled her eyes. "Fine." She took her foot off the royal's chest and added, "I give you your life, Your Majesty! But doom will come!"

"Excellent," Queen Annwyl said, sitting up. "Now remember what I taught you."

"All boys are icky, and *by this hammer, I rule!*"

Grinning, she wrapped her hands around Endelyon's waist and lifted her off the table. "Excellent! You're a brilliant student. And much nicer than my daughter."

"Can I hit her with my hammer when I meet her?"

"Of course you can!"

"Do not hit my daughter with your hammer, tiny child," Prince Fearghus admonished Keeley's sister.

"Yay!" Endelyon cheered, waving her hammer and running toward the open door at the back of the hall. "I get to hit Prince Fearghus's daughter with a hammer!"

The royal dragon looked at his mate, his hands held out at his sides, and asked her, "Why?"

Giving a little chuckle, Queen Annwyl turned toward Keeley. "I hear you have some beautiful lakes around here. I'd love to see one."

Keeley took in a breath and smiled. "Absolutely."

"Did you call me 'Your Royal Highness'?"

Gruff frowned at Princess Ainsley's question, probably because he hadn't said much of anything to her in the last few hours. They'd ridden through the night, the animals—he guessed he could call them that—which the three human women rode seemed to have an endless supply of energy. It was the centaurs that had to take a break. They were walking toward a river not too far from the road to eat something and cool off a bit. In fact, when Gruff thought about it, he realized the entire group had not said much at all. And when they did speak, it was strictly for informational purposes. No chitchat. Gruff loathed chitchat, so he was fine with that. He hoped there would be no idle conversation for the next few days.

"I haven't called you anything," he replied.

"Not today. When we were at the stable last night—"

"With the devil horses?"

"Stop calling them that."

"What would you call anything that was fully grown within minutes of birth?"

"Our transportation. And can we move on from that, please?"

"Fine."

"So did you?"

"Did I what?"

"Call me 'Your Royal Highness'?"

He shrugged. "Probably. That's your title, isn't it?"

"That's my title, but you don't really think of me that way, do you? I'm Ainsley . . . right?"

"Right. Princess Ainsley."

"You think of me as *Princess* Ainsley? Seriously?"

"How am I supposed to think of you?"

"As Ainsley! Your friend, Ainsley!"

"We're friends?"

The royal sneered at him and tapped her heels against her . . . oh, fine! Her horse! He felt stupid calling them just "animals." So he'd call them horses and pretend they weren't weird, unholy beasts spit up from the very pits of all the hells.

"Smooooth," his sister mocked, now walking next to him and watching Princess Ains—

Fuck! Fine! And watching *Ainsley* catch up with the nun and monk.

"What was I supposed to say to her?" he asked.

"Anything but what you did say." She shook her head and laughed. "Daddy's right. You're a mess."

"She's a royal. Not my friend."

"A mess," she repeated, still laughing. Which he did not appreciate.

They didn't go to the lake first. They went to the queen mother's forge. And it was, to Annwyl's surprise, a true, functioning forge; with several master blacksmiths and their multiple apprentices. She was not surprised to see them all working on weapons and armor for the queen's army, turning out quality that was quite impressive.

What did surprise Annwyl was that the queen mother was actually working at the forge herself. She had her own area where she created swords and spears. They walked in on her hammering blade steel at her station while wearing a sleeveless black leather tunic and black leather leggings. She had her hair piled on top of her head in a messy knot to keep it out of her face, and strapped to her back was her youngest child. How the child slept through so much noise and heat, Annwyl didn't know. When Annwyl's daughter was that young and napping, she would wake up long enough to fling things at her mother's head if Annwyl made the mistake of turning the page of a book. Then she'd screech, *"Noise!"*

Of course, now that Talwyn was an adult, Annwyl simply chucked the flung object back and then they screamed at each other until Fearghus or Talan—her son and Talwyn's twin—stepped in and calmed them down.

She missed her children. They were in the Northlands studying battle techniques and magicks under their uncle-by-mating Ragnar the Cunning. Her son wrote her regularly, and Talwyn kept in touch with her father. Although that wasn't the same as having them close by, she knew it was all for the best. She wanted her children prepared for anything that came their way because *everything* was out to get them. Already at risk because they were the offspring of the Mad Queen, her twins were the product of a human mother and dragon father, which made them a target for every religious zealot and bloodline-purist bigot the world over. Meaning that Talan and Talwyn were not only preparing for their future as rulers of Annwyl's territories—and, possibly, rulers of dragons—but also as rulers of all the other dragon-human offspring that roamed her lands. A breed of beings that produced no two alike. Some resembled their dragon kin, with wings and scales like every other dragon, though sometimes much smaller. Although she had noticed the smaller dragons also tended to be much meaner than the big ones. Like one of those tiny dogs for fancy royals that had been bred over generations from what was once a giant dog. Which meant that what they might lack in size, they more than made up for in homicidal rage.

Then there were others that took after their human parent, appearing like any other person around them, walking on two legs, waving "hello" with two hands, glaring with two eyes, and yelling "fuck off" with one mouth. All very common among human beings . . . until those same beings were threatened and suddenly discovered they could destroy an entire village with a flame mightier than even their dragon parent possessed.

Some were also rich in magicks, creating a new breed of witches. While others were so unbelievably strong and battle-ready at birth that, Annwyl was sure they would one day lead her legions.

Then there were others who were simply . . . average. With nothing special about them other than who their parents were. Those were the ones Annwyl worried about the most. The ones who simply wanted to live their lives as average citizens of her lands without being dragged from their house and burned alive or attacked in their caves by angry mobs with spears.

Talan and Talwyn, as future rulers, had an amazing destiny in front of them, but only if they survived those determined to destroy them and all their kind first.

That was why Annwyl couldn't simply continue to ignore what was happening on the other side of the Mountains of Dark Despair and Indescribable Pain. Whatever wars they might have, whatever battles, plagues or droughts or other natural or unnatural disasters, the people of the Old King had not been the worry of Annwyl or any ruler of Dark Plains. That very high and very ominous mountain ridge, spanning the Old King's lands from one sea to the other had been a very hard and permanent line that was never crossed. The few who did—travelers looking for adventure and merchants looking for more interesting wares—rarely moved past the villages closest to the base of the mountain. Why? Because those who traveled farther into the territories rarely returned. Just as those traveling from Keeley's territories into Annwyl's came to nasty ends too. Troops stationed close to the mountains often found the remains of foreign travelers half buried in swamps or lakes. Usually they were the victims of thieves or, if they'd brought children with them, slavers that Annwyl still spent her time hunting down and destroying.

She had to hunt slavers. It was the one thing she couldn't stand. The subjugation of human beings.

Her father hadn't had slaves in the common sense but indentured servants. And his cruelty to them was enough to impress upon her that someone who thought they literally *owned* another human being wouldn't be any kinder. When her brother took the throne, he started allowing slavers to sell their human wares in nearby town squares. Not only that but he definitely liked the idea of owning females and children for his amusement. Annwyl had argued with her brother about what he was doing. In fact, she had become so much of an annoyance to him that he'd eventually attempted to marry her off to the first duke that was willing to take on an "untamed royal." Her brother had Annwyl forced into a white gown with garlands in her hair, then chained her up inside a carriage and sent her out of his life. Too bad for him that the rebels—also fighting the many poor decisions her brother was making as ruler—ambushed the entourage accompanying her. Because he knew "how difficult" his younger sister could be, her brother had sent an entire company of soldiers as escorts. Meaning that what should have been a quick assault on some royals and a few guards turned into a fierce battle with much bloodshed.

One of the rebels had actually released Annwyl from her bindings and ordered her to run.

But she didn't run. Annwyl instead picked up a sword from a dead rebel's hand and proceeded to slaughter as many of her brother's soldiers as she could. Despite her lack of sword training, it hadn't been hard for her to kill the first time, or the many times after that. Annwyl simply let her rage do all the work. All she had to do was remind herself of what those soldiers had done when they'd invaded helpless villages. What her brother had *allowed* them to do. She'd hear them joking about it all as if tormenting defenseless human beings was some kind of fun hobby. And they were already planning to do the same to the rebel fighters. Planning to torment their families to destroy the rebels' commitment to their cause. Annwyl, however, wasn't going to let that happen. Not because she had some great loyalty to the men who fought her brother—at least not then—but because she knew the only ones that would truly suffer were the women and girls. The ones who didn't fight, who waited at home for their men to return. They would one day have their doors kicked in and their lives destroyed, all to make a point to anyone who might even be considering rebellion against the king.

Merely thinking of those poor women allowed Annwyl to unleash her barely contained rage on those loyal to her brother. When she could finally see again without a haze of red in front of her, Annwyl stood among the hacked and brutalized bodies of her brother's soldiers, her white gown now dark red because it had been saturated with her enemies' blood.

A few of the rebels had gawked at her before one called out the name that would characterize her ever after: "Annwyl the Bloody!" They had all cheered and laughed, and it had never occurred to Annwyl that the moniker would stick and become her name forever. Even as queen. Now she realized she was even known as

Annwyl the Bloody in lands she knew nothing about. A name that brought fear to beings thousands of leagues away from Garbhán Isle.

Her brother would have loved to possess that kind of reputation. He would have rolled around in it like a dog rolling around in another dog's piss. But Annwyl didn't enjoy peasants quaking in fear at the mention of her name. She wanted corrupt rulers doing that. Sadly, she hadn't figured out how to achieve one without the other, which meant she had to let those who didn't know better live in constant fear of her and her soldiers until she could prove them wrong.

Unfortunate but necessary in days like these.

Annwyl gasped and moved straight across the forge to a row of finished weapons hanging from a far wall. She had her hand out and her fingers almost on the steel when she stopped and glanced at Queen Keeley and her mother.

"May I?" she asked.

Mother and daughter appeared slightly surprised that she had bothered asking; the pair exchanged brief glances before the queen mother gave a small nod.

Grinning, Annwyl picked up a long-handled battle-axe. It was almost as tall as she, all steel, and had a glorious double axe-head with a lovely detailed design on both sides. It wasn't quite a halberd since it had no spear at the very top, and the long steel handle was solid, yet not so heavy that she struggled. She swung the weapon to the right, then left, before slamming it down in front of her.

Annwyl couldn't believe the quality of the weapon, and she fell in love with it almost immediately. True, the two swords strapped to her back were her absolute favorites. Given to her by Fearghus, they were everything she needed in a weapon. But, like jewelry, who said she could only have one or two pieces? Especially when a weapon was so beautifully crafted.

"How much?" she asked the queen mother.

"Oh, well . . . that is one of my best-made weapons. Can cut through an entire man if you have the strength for it."

"I do. So what's your price?"

"Um . . ." The queen mother looked at her daughter before replying, "Ten thousand—"

"Mum," Queen Keeley snapped, unwilling to let her mother finish.

"Of course. You're right, Keeley." She returned her gaze to Annwyl's. "Five thousand—"

"Mum!"

Cracking her very large shoulders, the queen mother finally announced, "It's yours. No cost. As a gift, Queen Annwyl."

"Please," Queen Keeley insisted when Annwyl hesitated. "It's some of my mother's best work, and I think you'll enjoy—"

"Mercilessly killing all your victims with it, crazed wench."

"*Mum!*"

# CHAPTER 14

Ainsley crouched down by the river and filled her flask. The gray horse moved in next to her, lowering its head to drink. Then Sheva's white mare stood on her left side to drink.

And, for the first time, Ainsley felt trapped. Having these particular animals next to her was unnerving. Not that she didn't appreciate having such a fine, tireless animal to ride. But she couldn't forget how they'd come into this world. They *seemed* normal, but she wondered what their normal-looking hides might conceal.

Which was why she wished she had one of her father's horses. The travel party would have had to stop for more breaks, but at least those horses wouldn't make Ainsley feel ... well ... trapped!

Staying crouched, Ainsley eased back. Step by crouching step until she'd crouch-stepped away from the two horses on either side of her and right into the long front legs of Hilda's black stallion. The beast glared down at her and, without meaning to, Ainsley let out a startled squeak that she was glad her sisters weren't around to hear. She was embarrassed by that weak sound, and it did nothing but annoy Hilda's horse; his large head came down and snapped at her.

She ducked but didn't really need to, because the gray stallion rammed his equally large head into his brother's. The two began battering each other with their bodies and Ainsley had to scramble across the ground to get away from them. Sheva's mare charged in but didn't stop the fight as Ainsley had hoped she'd do, but instead joined in, leaning over Ainsley to bite one brother; rearing up over Ainsley to attack her other brother with her front hooves.

Ainsley rolled and ducked, but every time she thought she'd found a way out of the melee, she quickly discovered her exit was blocked by stomping hooves or snapping jaws.

"I should have said no!" she kept repeating out loud. "I should have said no!" And she should have! She wanted her old horse back. The horse she'd ridden to Gemma's old monastery hadn't been the best horse she'd ever been on, but at least he'd never crush her skull in while busy fighting one of his siblings.

A hoof kicked her in the side and she rolled over two times, landing on her back as front hooves hovered over her, about to slam down on her chest. She didn't have time to scream as she attempted to roll away again, but many hands suddenly gripped her, and she was quickly yanked out of the way.

"You all right?" Gruff demanded. When she nodded, he released her and charged into the middle of the fight, his sister by his side.

Ainsley was helped up by Hilda, Sheva, Sarff, and a few of the other centaurs. She nodded her thanks and pressed her hand against her side, wincing a bit.

"You hurt?" Sarff asked.

"One of them back-kicked me, but I don't think it's broken—owwww! Beastly female!"

"Stop yer whining, girl! No wonder your sisters don't think you can handle anything. A little pain and—"

"Owwww! Why are you making it worse?"

"I'm not. Just making sure you're right about no break."

"I've had broken ribs before. I know what they feel like."

Hands still pressing against her side, Sarff looked at Ainsley and guessed, "Fallen out of a few trees, have you?"

"When I was younger, yes. But I've also been trampled by stampeding pigs and was once kicked by a cow. So, yes, I know what broken ribs feel like."

"You do because, as you said, these ribs are not broken." Sarff reached into her travel bag, allowing Ainsley to let out a breath now that the increased pain had dissipated. But the centaur was soon back, her fingers under Ainsley's tunic, smearing something directly onto her bare skin.

"What is that?" Ainsley wanted to know . . . immediately!

"Such squawking from you, child. I don't know how the queen mother puts up with any of you."

"By having her older children take care of the younger ones while she went off to her forge. Now what are you putting on me?"

"It will curb the pain until the area heals." She closed the jar, dropped it back into her bag, and wiped her hands on a cloth. "Remind me tonight to put more on when we stop. You won't sleep if I don't, because the pain will be too great and you won't feel like riding anywhere come morning. Understand?"

Ainsley nodded, noting that Kriegszorn's offspring were back drinking water from the river. They were calm and relaxed as Briallen talked to each one, patting a neck or stroking a hip. Gruff returned to her side.

"Sure you're all right?" he asked.

"The girl's fine," Sarff informed him. "Sturdy farm stock, like her father."

Ainsley cringed at that. She never wanted to be thought of as "sturdy farm stock." She wasn't one of her father's sheep!

"Thank you," she said to Sarff with as much sarcasm as she could muster.

"Welcome!"

Sarff walked off, oblivious, and Gruff stared at Ainsley. Just stared.

"Why are you looking at me like that?"

He jerked his head toward the horses. "You can't keep setting them off."

"I did no such thing!"

"Are you sure? You know sometimes you can be a little skittish."

"I am not skittish! And the gray horse—"

"You should give him a name."

Ainsley glanced around, wondering if the centaur was teasing her and everyone else was in on it, but no. "What?" she finally asked.

"You should name him. It's a sign of respect."

"For a horse?" She held her hands up when he got that irritated look on his face. He was worse than Keeley about this sort of thing. "Fine. I'll call him—"

"Do not call him Demon Fire."

Ainsley tensed. That's exactly what she'd been about to call the gray horse. Mostly to piss off Keeley, but still.

"How did you know...?" She shook her head. "Forget it. I don't want to know how you know. Instead, I'll name him... Lord Paladin."

Gruff grunted. It was a long one too.

"What now?"

"Did you name him that just to piss off Princess Gemma?"

Ainsley grinned. "Yes."

"It's just us," Keeley said. "You and me. No court surrounding us. No armies or subjects."

"Or your mother."

"Yes. So let's just be honest with each other."

The Mad Queen, standing on a boulder a few steps into the lake, nodded. "All right."

"Excellent." Keeley took in a breath, then asked, "Why do you think I'm going to get all my people killed?"

Keeley watched the foreign queen's face contort into all sorts of expressions as she struggled for a reply. It got so bad, Keeley couldn't stand it anymore.

"You can just be straightforward since Princess Laila and Princess Morfyd aren't here to yell at us about how we're mishandling the etiquette of our current situation."

"I'm not sure you really want to hear what I—"

"Just tell me."

"Fine," Annwyl said, briefly tossing her hands into the air. "You're weak."

Keeley couldn't help but snort at that.

"I've been called many things over the years, Queen Annwyl. Especially as a female blacksmith with an almost all-male clientele. And yet no one has ever called *me* weak."

"I don't mean your physical strength, Keeley. I mean *you*. The person. You are a weak person."

Unable to hide her hurt at the foreign queen's words, Keeley asked, "Why would you say that?"

"You don't see it . . . do you?"

"See what?"

Annwyl leaped from the boulder to the lakeside and didn't even get her feet wet.

"You're a good person, Keeley," she said, surprising her fellow royal. "A truly good person who is honest in word and deed. A person who became queen not because she was born to it or because she wanted unlimited power but because she knew she had to rule in order to protect all those around her."

Keeley didn't really see what was wrong with any of that. How did that make her weak? Wasn't a good, kind ruler what everyone at least *said* they wanted? So why did the foreign queen seem to be holding kindness against her?

"Beatrix will use that kindness," Annwyl continued, "that goodness, to destroy you and your people with you. And the worst part . . . ? You'll let her."

Gemma unrolled an ancient scroll across a plain wooden table in the middle of the repurposed soldiers' barracks now used for meetings with the elder brothers of the monk orders. She wanted them to feel they could speak their minds without worrying about centaurs or nervous soldiers fearing a sudden religious rebellion.

Allowing honesty here and now prevented whispered plots later. And Gemma knew her queen sister didn't care about the private meetings; Keeley was more than happy to hear the concerns and complaints of the orders and was always willing to assist them as long as it didn't infringe on the freedoms of other religious or nonreligious residents.

Although Gemma had to admit, it wasn't easy managing so many religious leaders. All those voices bitching about this or that. But she knew the war monk orders could not survive if they didn't learn to not only work together but also allow the freedoms of others. Including those they'd once burned at the stake. A hard change for many of the elder monks, but one that was necessary. Because it was the one thing Keeley would not allow. Persecution for a person's beliefs or lack of them.

"I'm gone for a few days and you invite dragons into your sister's territory," a voice said from the doorway.

Gemma let out a long sigh before she lifted her gaze to Ragna's.

She'd really been hoping that Ragna would be gone for a lot longer than a few days, but Gemma had made the mistake of sending her off with Shona, Katla, and Kir. Her longtime cohorts and closest friends. She knew she might have to call them back a little early if something came up, but never thought it would be within days of sending them out! And when they'd returned, Ragna had come with them. Even leaving her army to follow. She didn't go anywhere without her bloody army.

"I didn't *invite* them in, Ragna. They came of their own volition."

"And you let them stay," she said with a telling smile. Telling because Ragna rarely smiled unless she was disrupting someone's life. The woman loved disruption.

"What was I supposed to do? Challenge the biggest dragon to a fistfight? Winner take all? Does that *seem* like a good idea to you?"

"This town is filled with monks, priests, even witches. All of them trained to fight all manner of things, but instead, you invited dragons to dinner with your sister the queen. Brilliant plan. Next, you'll invite demons into your home . . . oh wait. Your sister is already feeding demons under her table."

"No," Gemma disagreed. "My sister doesn't feed her wolves under the table. She feeds them right out in the open. Without a worry in the world about who thinks that might be strange."

"And to top it all off," Ragna continued, "you bring in that monstrosity—Annwyl the Bloody. She rips babies from still-breathing mothers and, if they survive, she forces them into her armies when they are barely ten summers old."

Gemma frowned. "You really believe that?"

"It's what everyone says, Brother Gemma."

"Really? Because they also say that before you burn witches, you cut off their breasts and fry them up in a pan along with onions and a thick pink sauce. Should we all believe that, too?"

Ragna reared back a bit, as if she'd been hit. "They actually say that about me?"

Gemma blinked in surprise. "For . . . decades. You really didn't know that?"

"No! Ewwww! That's vile! I burn witches, but only because they deserve it. But I've never cut off or eaten anything from them or anyone else! That's disgusting! Tell me, right now, who is spreading these horrific lies? Tell me! I want to know who says such things!"

Gemma shrugged. "Um . . . *everyone?*"

"What do you mean, 'everyone'?"

"Quite honestly, Brother . . . it was *literally* the first thing I ever heard about you. The *first* thing."

"And you believed it?"

"Welllll . . ."

"Brother Gemma! How could you believe something so ridiculous?"

"How could you believe that Annwyl the Bloody cuts babies out of the wombs of their mothers?"

"Because that one is probably true."

"Ohhhhh," Gemma sighed out, "Brother Ragna . . ."

"What do you mean I'll 'let her'?" Keeley exclaimed. "Why would I ever do that? *Ever?*"

Annwyl lifted her arms away from her hips, then let them drop. "Because you still want to believe in her?"

Keeley snorted. "Really?" She lifted her plain cotton shirt to just below her breasts, exposing the wicked scar across her lower stomach. "I know exactly how far my sister will go to get what she wants. I have no doubts."

The foreign queen gave a small smirk and crossed her arms. Her muscles strained the links of her sleeveless chainmail tunic, which seemed to be the only thing she was comfortable wearing.

"Beatrix did that to you?" Annwyl asked.

"Yes."

"And you think that changes anything?"

"It proves I know who my sister is and how far she'll go to obtain power. I see very clearly when it comes to Beatrix."

"Really?"

"Really."

Annwyl nodded. "Let me tell you what I see. At some point, when your sister decides she's ready to advance into these lands, she'll have one of your young siblings taken from you. Or maybe she'll take all the young ones. It won't be the older sisters or your parents because they will likely fight to the death, preferring to sacrifice themselves rather than become a tool for Beatrix to wield against you. It will also be the young ones because at that age, all they want to do is survive. After a few months—perhaps even a year—she will contact you. Let you know the child or children are fine. That all she wants is an alliance. Because of the strong connection you have with your siblings and your desperation to have them returned to you alive, you will agree because you'll agree to anything at that point. So an alliance will be struck. Your siblings will be returned, and everything will seem safe and sane to you. Then in a few months or maybe another year, Beatrix will have her armies ride into your territories and lay waste to everything you love while she focuses *her* attention on a new target, which will likely be my territory and my people. When she does finally make that move, all of you will be long gone. Not even a memory, because she will ban the mention of your names. Not because she feels bad about what she did—and, side note, she *won't* feel bad—but because she wants to forever remove the stain of her peasant upbringing. In the end, all you've sacrificed will be for nothing. Because she'll have killed your siblings anyway."

She took several steps closer. "It's been two years, Keeley, and she hasn't attacked your territories even once. Instead, she lets her brothers-in-law attack you. Or she lets her king husband send in small groups for blitz assaults that can be wiped out with a single blast of dragon fire. What do you think she's doing when she allows this? Do you think she's just waiting for you to get strong enough and amass a big enough army so it can be a fair fight? No. She's letting you battle all the other challengers to her throne first. Whoever is left standing after all that will be the ones she unleashes her much stronger army on. And to your sister, it won't matter if the army her soldiers take on is yours or one of the Old King's sons. To Beatrix, it simply doesn't matter, because you mean *nothing* to her.

You never have. That's the difference between the two of you. You once loved her. She was your sister. Your blood. But to her, you might as well be a favored pet she once had when she was growing up. A dog or a cat. So . . . understand what I'm telling you. She will use your family to get exactly what she wants."

Her entire body numb now, Keeley softly asked, "Is that what you would do?"

"What? No!" Annwyl jerked a bit, eyes blinking wide. "Of course not! I would never steal someone's child! Why would you even ask that?"

"You seem quite clear on what you think Beatrix's plan will be. How could you know any of that if it wasn't something you would consider doing?"

Annwyl pulled off the weapons strapped to her back and tossed them to the ground, then grabbed the bottom of her chainmail shirt and lifted it up and over her head. She wore cloth bindings tied tight around her breasts, probably to keep them out of her way in a fight.

With the shirt hanging loosely from her hand, the foreign queen turned away from Keeley, exposing her back. The woman was riddled with scars, but these particular ones were different from the others. Somehow more brutal and much older.

"Once," Annwyl began, "my brother released our father's war dogs on me. He said it was a joke, but we all knew that was a lie."

Keeley frowned. Those scars weren't from bites. Was she lying?

"I got away from the dogs by climbing one of the army's siege weapons and waiting until their trainer got them all back in their cages. But by then, my rage had taken over and I tracked my brother down inside the main hall and attacked him with one of the meat knives on the dining table." The Mad Queen began to pace in front of Keeley. "We fought like wild animals on the floor, the guards unwilling to step in to stop us because they didn't want to get hurt. Our father eventually arrived and pulled us apart. I told him what had happened, and he believed me because my brother was a chronic liar. But despite that he proceeded to beat us both within an inch of our lives. It took us *weeks* to recover, and the matter was never discussed again."

"If your father believed your brother attacked you, then why . . . ?"

She stopped pacing but didn't look at Keeley. "My father wanted us to know that our lives and deaths were at *his* pleasure. Not ours. The only one allowed to kill either me or my brother was him."

Annwyl finally faced Keeley. "When he beat me and my brother, I saw the look in his eyes. There was nothing there. We only existed for what we could do for him. My brother would carry on the bloodline and continue the rule my father had been battering his people with for decades. And, when old enough, I would be handed off to the most important duke or baron he needed to keep under his control." She scratched a small spot on her forehead with her thumbnail. "So when you ask how I know what Beatrix would do . . . that's how I know. Because it's exactly what my father would have done. He was a cruel, heartless leader, but he wasn't dumb. Neither is your sister." Annwyl moved closer to Keeley. "And she will use the love you have for your family against you. Because she knows you'll do anything to protect them. That's what makes you weak. That's why Beatrix will win."

"You know, Queen Annwyl, you care about your family as much as I do. Why doesn't that make you weak?"

"Because they know . . . *everyone* knows what I bring should any of them come for my family." The Mad Queen moved in so close, Keeley could feel her breath on her face. Clearly see each time the woman's face twitched as she struggled to control her rage. "Because when it comes to protecting my kin, whether human or dragon, I am the maddest cunt any of my enemies will ever have the displeasure of meeting. They know that there would be no alliance. There would be no peace. There would only be blood and death and my enemies screaming as I send them *in pieces back to their gods.*"

Their gazes locked, and Annwyl asked, "Can you, Queen Keeley, say the same?"

As soon as Shona shoved open the door of the barracks door and rushed into the room, Gemma knew something was wrong. But whatever Shona was about to say was silenced when she caught sight of Ragna.

"Oh . . . Master General Ragna. You're here."

"I am, Brother Shona," Ragna said with a grin. "And *you're* here. What a delight for us all!"

Gemma rolled her eyes. Gods, this woman!

"Can you give us a moment, Brother?" Gemma asked.

"Of course." She looked back and forth between the two friends before finally leaving.

"She is going to make your life very miserable," Shona warned.

"She's going to try. Now what's up?"

"Did you know your sister is going to have a private meeting with that foreign queen?"

Gemma did know. She'd been working with one of the dragons, Lord Bram, to set up a good time and place for this all-important private meeting of queens. A private meeting that Gemma and a few of her most trusted soldiers would observe in case the Mad Queen decided to prove she'd been aptly named.

"Yes. I know about it. It'll be happening tonight."

"Tonight?" Shona repeated. "Gemma, Keeley's talking to her now. Alone. Just the two of them."

It took Gemma a moment to understand what her friend was saying before she growled out, "By the war gods of all nations . . . *my idiot sister will be the death of me!*"

"You're right, you know," Keeley finally admitted. "I do still want to believe Beatrix would never hurt our brothers and sisters if I just gave her what she wanted."

"You want to believe it," Annwyl said, sitting next to Keeley on the tree stump, "because a normal person would never harm their own kin. But it's less about you believing her and more about you having no other choice."

"But if they took *your* children—"

"My children are . . . different. Taking one of them brings the wrath of the other. They're twins, you know. But even then, if someone managed to take both, that would unleash their cousin Rhian, and no one wants that. The combined strength of the three is . . . formidable. And to outright kill them would bring . . ." She looked at Keeley. "Well, that would bring me and my rage, and that's a risk only the foolish and truly insane would take."

Keeley turned a bit so she could look right at the foreign royal. "Annwyl, we need to find a way to trust each other. You need me and my family line to hold this queendom and to expand our territorial line so that Beatrix and her army become meaningless. I need you and your soldiers to help us do that."

"And I need to know that when the time comes, you'll kill your sister."

Shocked, Keeley asked, "What?"

"Was I unclear?"

"I . . . uh . . ."

"As long as she lives, your throne will be under threat. And from what I can tell, a great threat, because she's only been queen for two years and yet she's managed to take complete control of a male-only dynasty. Is she even twenty yet?"

"Twenty-five."

Annwyl tossed up her hands. "Your sister will need to *go*. But I honestly don't think you have it in you to do it."

"Not everyone's comfortable cutting off their sibling's head," Keeley sneered.

"Royals are. That's how they become royals. That's how they keep their thrones. Either you get ready to be that kind of royal or you give up your queendom now. And I took my brother's head because he was an utter monster."

Keeley wasn't going to give up her throne. Not because she wanted it so badly but because Annwyl was right. She wanted to keep everyone safe. It was amazing how corrupting being king or queen could be. Beatrix may have been born that way, but that didn't mean their siblings weren't also at risk of becoming murderous vipers, ready to destroy each other for a chance to rule these territories. No, she wouldn't put her brothers and sisters at risk of becoming like the Old King's murderous sons.

"I need to think. Can we talk again later?" Keeley asked Annwyl.

"Of course."

Keeley stood, but the Mad Queen didn't follow. "Would you like to walk back to the tower together?"

"No, thank you." Annwyl stretched her long legs out and focused on the placid water. "I think I'll stay here for a bit."

Without anything left to say, Keeley headed back to the tower.

She was so lost in her thoughts that she didn't know she wasn't alone until she crashed into Gemma and her three monk cohorts, Kir, Katla, and Shona.

"Oh. Hello," she said when she saw her younger sister glaring up at her.

"Are you all right?"

"Fine, fine," Keeley said, her gaze moving around the woods she stood in. "Let me ask you, Gemma . . . could you take Beatrix's head if you were ordered to?"

"Yes."

There hadn't even been a pause. No delay. No thoughtful chin tapping. Nothing!

"What do you mean yes?" Keeley demanded.

"I mean yes. Ordered or not, I could take Beatrix's head. It's not like she doesn't deserve it."

"She already tried when we were in the Old King's palace," Brother Katla volunteered.

"But Beatrix's soldiers protected her," Brother Kir finished.

"She's your sister," Keeley felt the need to remind Gemma.

"Not by my choice. Besides, she's a murderous slaver who gutted you. It wouldn't exactly be a hard chore for me if you ever gave the order."

"You really mean that, don't you?"

"Keeley, if it hadn't been for you, I would have killed Beatrix before I left to join the monastery."

Ragna had seen Brother Gemma and her cohorts meet outside the barracks and she'd had every intention of following them so she could find out what they were hiding. But before she could set off after them, she saw another order of war monks heading around from the other side of the barracks she was hiding behind. They had their shields with them, which was strange. All war monks kept their swords and knives strapped to them at all times, but their shields usually rested beside their bunks until needed for battle.

More curious about what this particular order was up to than Gemma and her useless friends, Ragna changed direction and followed them.

They moved silently and quickly, as any decent war monk was trained to do, but one of them was clearly reacting to something.

Ragna paused for a moment, taking several quiet but deep breaths to ease her racing heart. A god. This monk was hearing from a god. It had happened to Ragna more than once since she'd been called. It wasn't so much a voice that she heard. War gods were never so obvious as to show up in a form humans could accept; nor did they simply chat with their disciples or bother becoming a booming voice in one's head. The gods called to their most loyal and dedicated in ways not easily described to those who had not been so wonderfully blessed. But they did *tell* their most loyal followers what they wanted them to know. Over the decades, her war gods' direction had given Ragna the chance to survive during battles, imparted invaluable information on her enemies, and provided the abiding knowledge that her gods had chosen her as one of their favored among all others.

So knowing that one of these monks was following the direction of a war god had Ragna fascinated.

Without thought, she continued to follow until they reached one of the many lakes surrounding the town. She eased around a tree to see who these men were focused on. It was a woman, one she'd never seen. But Ragna did know her. Had heard about her presence as soon as the invaders had entered the first village no more than ten leagues away, where many of the locals were already heading to "safer" towns farther from Forgetown.

This was Annwyl the Bloody, Queen of Dark Plains.

Wearing only chainmail leggings, leather boots, and bindings around her breasts, the despised monarch lay stretched out on a long, wide tree stump. Hands pressed against the wood behind her, arms propping her up, the queen had her eyes closed and lifted her face toward the sun.

There was a small smile on her face and scars on her body, but she seemed quite peaceful.

For, you know, a brutal, murderous dictator.

Ragna's fellow monks watched the queen for a short while before the one who seemed to be in charge, directed by his god's words, stepped past the treeline and out to the shore of the lake.

The foreign royal, oblivious in her privilege, thinking that merely being who she was meant she was automatically safe, didn't even notice another presence. Too busy sunning herself and relaxing without a care in the world. Despite the evil she'd brought with her.

Only home a few hours, Ragna had already heard the rumors of Queen Keeley forming an alliance with this . . . this . . . female. She'd never really understood any of the adults in the Smythe-Farmerson clan, but the queen had to be the most bizarre. She accepted anything that stepped across her path. Demon dogs, undead horses, and bloodthirsty witches. All were welcome!

Ragna couldn't believe, however, that the woman would be so reckless with her family's safety. What was she thinking, to allow this female to stay and, it seemed, become part of her queendom? For all any of them knew, this alliance could be part of some diabolical plan. An alliance first and then a complete conquest. With her dragons, Annwyl the Bloody could take over all these lands in a matter of months. Maybe weeks.

Ragna thought of all the possible plans this female could be plotting when she suddenly heard a . . . campfire? That didn't make any sense, so she looked down and realized that what she heard was the crackling flames in the eyes of one of Queen Keeley's demon dogs. Although now that the beast was standing next to her, she remembered it was actually a demon *wolf*, which only made it more horrifying.

It stood next to Ragna but didn't do anything. It was definitely the specific one that spent most of its time around the queen. So it was strange that it was here with Ragna, yet Queen Keeley was nowhere in sight.

Looking up at Ragna, it acted as if waiting for her to do something.

It turned its gaze toward the monks of the other order. They now all stood outside the forest they'd been hiding in, and still that female had yet to notice.

The wolf looked back at Ragna. And that's when she realized it expected *her* to do something! But do what? And to help which side? She had no idea. Sneering at the thought of doing anything, she again focused on her fellow monks and waited. Until the leader took one step and the wolf suddenly barked.

It was just one bark, but the female opened her eyes and looked in Ragna's direction, which was odd, because she had a battalion of war monks right in front of her. A battalion she still had *not* noticed.

Ragna stepped into view of the female and leaned against the tree beside her. She folded her arms under her breasts as the two gazed at each other until—unable to take another moment of the female's obliviousness—she pointed in the direction of the monks.

The female didn't look, though. She didn't turn her gaze away from Ragna's. She simply smiled. Proving she'd known the monks had been there the whole time.

The demon wolf whimpered and abruptly bolted away. *Away* from the Mad Queen of Garbhán Isle. As if it didn't want to witness whatever was going to happen next.

Gemma was in the middle of explaining to her sister that she was an idiot for meeting with the Mad Queen without informing anyone when something fifty feet away or so charged past them.

"Was that your demon dog?" Kir asked.

"Wolf. It's a demon wolf."

"The demon part of that doesn't bother you at all, does it?" Shona asked.

Before Keeley could go into one of her long-winded explanations about how animals weren't inherently evil, the demon wolf came charging back and wrapped its massive maw around Keeley's upper arm, then began to pull.

"Is he trying to tear your arm off?" Katla demanded, drawing her sword.

Keeley didn't answer, allowing the dog to drag her away.

"What the hell was that?" her cohort questioned.

Gemma wasn't sure. That had definitely been strange. Her sister's wolf dogs didn't panic . . . At least, not until they'd come face-to-face with the Mad Queen.

Looking in the direction of the lake, Gemma muttered, "Uh-oh."

"What's wrong?" Kir asked.

"Where's Ragna? Have you seen her since she was spying on us earlier?"

Then the cohorts all said together, "Uh-oh."

\* \* \*

She came up so fast from the stump that there was a moment of hesitation from the monks and a bit of surprise from Ragna. Was Annwyl the Bloody, the most feared monarch in the world, running away? Was she afraid? Ragna only asked because once the female was on her feet, she immediately ran toward a tree behind her. The leader of the monks ordered an assault and the brothers charged forward. But as they neared her, the female reached down and grabbed a long-handled weapon off the ground. Ragna knew immediately it was the work of one of the Smythe women. A double-headed axe that fit comfortably in the female's hand.

Once she had her weapon, the monarch didn't wait for the brothers to reach her. The mad bitch, instead, charged *them*. Ran right toward the monks and, when she was about ten feet from the first, leaped up, the long-handled weapon tight in her hands, and spun in midair. When she came down, she slashed the weapon across her target, hitting him in the shoulder. The power of her swing brought the blade down and through the brother's neck, chest, and out his hip in one clean move.

As the Mad Queen landed, the tip of the blade slammed into the ground. Beside her landed pieces of the monk she'd just struck.

He hadn't even had time to scream before she'd cut him down.

The other monks hesitated, but the one who had his god in his head ran forward, swinging his sword.

The Mad Queen used the long handle of her weapon to block his, then pushed him back.

That was enough for the other monks. As one, they came screaming at the queen. Again, she didn't run. She simply braced her legs apart, tightened her hands on her steel, and used her long-handled weapon to batter them back and slash those who got too close.

Watching the woman slash and hit, slash and shove with such speed and power was something Ragna would never forget. She knew she herself was one of the best warriors in her order. She'd proven it on the battlefield again and again, and the war gods had blessed her in return. Eventually, her order had blessed her as well with her own army. Not simply because of her skills on the battlefield but because of her ability to recognize that skill in others.

And the Mad Queen had mighty skills.

It was hard to believe Annwyl the Bloody was actually a queen. A soldier? Sure. A sword for hire? Absolutely. But a queen who also had to manage the harvesting of grain and the payment of taxes and the laws of her land? No one who could fight like this should be able to do anything other than fight, eat, and sleep. Just like Ragna.

This, however . . . This was a true war queen. Not Queen Keeley with her sensitive soul. Not Queen Beatrix with her cruel ways and unwillingness to get her own hands dirty. Not even the Old King, who let other men fight all his battles.

Annwyl the Bloody could have screamed once and every dragon within a ten-mile range—and there were many around at the moment—would have heeded her call. They would have come to rescue her. With one breath, a single dragon could have easily ended this fight.

But that wasn't what this queen wanted. An easy way out. No. Instead, like a prey-driven dog that constantly chases barn cats, this queen was in it for the fight.

She split a skull in half before back-kicking a monk coming up behind her. She beheaded another, then rammed the end of her weapon into a different monk's throat, turning and finishing him off with a blow from the double-axe head that went deep into his chest. Yanking the weapon out, she ducked before a sword could cut her throat, but brought her own weapon up and into the groin of the sword holder, splitting him from cock to chin with one brutal move.

"Gods!" Ragna heard, seconds before Brother Gemma attempted to dart past her.

Ragna yanked the woman back by her cowl and held her. "I wouldn't, if I were you," she warned Gemma and her cohorts.

"You've just been standing here?" Shona demanded. "Doing nothing?"

"You never get between a dog and its bone," Ragna replied.

Angry, Gemma snarled, "What the fuck is that supposed to—"

Stunned, her fellow monk stopped speaking as what appeared to be a lung slid down her face, leaving a trail of blood behind, and flopped uselessly to the ground.

They all stared at the human organ lying at their feet for a few seconds, and by the time they returned their gaze to the battle . . . it was over. And Annwyl the Bloody, Queen of Garbhán Isle, stood among the dismembered remains of all those war monks.

People in these lands feared war monks the way most feared the plague. Because Ragna's brethren, in very small numbers, could easily sweep in and decimate an entire village or town and be back at the monastery before dinner, leaving nothing but misery and despair in their wake. And it was well documented that war monks who took on vows of celibacy and silence were the most vicious of combatants. How could they not be? They didn't have sex and couldn't speak!

Ragna knew this order, too. Knew their skill and history of destruction. Knew what they had done to entire covens of powerful witches and small towns that worshipped what her brothers considered pagan gods.

And yet . . .

Queen Annwyl stood among what remained of those monks, soaked in the blood of her enemies. She panted a bit, but Ragna had no doubt that if there had been more monks to fight, she could have kept going. Not simply because she had such massive energy but because she had such massive rage. Even now, the queen was working hard to calm herself down. Closing her eyes and forcing herself to take in deeper and longer breaths.

Once she was calm, she crouched by the lake and proceeded to wash the blood from her face and arms. Then she retrieved her chainmail shirt, pulling it on, and strapped two swords to her back. She returned to the water and quickly rinsed the blood and gore off her double-headed axe before walking away from the evidence of her wrath without even a backward glance.

Gemma yanked herself away from Ragna's grip on her cowl and raised her hands in a placating manner.

"Queen Annwyl, I am—"

The queen held up her right hand and shook her head. "I know," she said.

But what she knew, Ragna had no idea, and, she guessed, neither did Gemma.

Queen Annwyl stepped between Ragna and Gemma, heading back toward the tower. But before Ragna could offer to accompany the royal, the woman's fist was colliding with Ragna's face. A crack-ing sound filled Ragna's ears and she felt her bottom jaw jerk from its place, leaving her unable to move it or speak.

With her hands around her mouth and chin, Ragna looked up to see the queen lean toward her.

"Thanks for all your help, ya twat," she sneered before walk-ing off.

Kir moved close and leaned in toward Ragna.

"Is it bad?" he asked her with true kindness.

Ragna gave a small nod that hurt as if the gods themselves were tearing at her face.

"Should we get you to a healer?"

Another small nod.

"Do you care that she almost took your jaw off?" Shona asked Ragna. "Or are you so enamored of that crazed female that you don't really mind what she does at this point?"

Not wanting to move her head any more because the pain was so intense and unable to speak at all, Ragna simply raised a brow, and that seemed to make her message clear.

"You are a very disturbed person," Gemma said, walking away. "So very fucking disturbed."

# CHAPTER 15

The pain in her ribs forced them to stop when the suns were still high in the sky; Ainsley was unable to take another second of it.

She dismounted from the horse and ended up resting her arms on the saddle, trying her best to breathe.

"We can go back," Gruff said near her ear before shifting back to his human form.

"No. I can do this."

"Screaming in pain with every step your horse takes?"

"If that's what's necessary . . . *yes*."

"Here." Sarff shoved the jar of ointment she'd used earlier into Ainsley's hand. "Keep this. Put it on every hour for at least the next couple of days."

All the centaurs now stood on two legs. Every time they stopped for breaks, they would shift to human to avoid any nosey travelers on the road. When they traveled somewhere as a group, though, the centaurs appeared as a herd of horses galloping beside three human riders.

"We still have five days to go," Gruff needlessly reminded them.

"She'll be fine."

"But that ointment will become ineffective after the first day if you use it that often."

Gripping the jar tight, Ainsley pushed herself away from the horse and faced the two centaurs.

"I can do this." She took a painful step away. "Now if you'll excuse me, I'd like to scream in pain alone for a few minutes."

* * *

"We should go back," Gruff repeated to Sarff and his sister.

"She'll have your balls in a ditch if you suggest that again," Briallen promised him.

He knew that, but he couldn't stand the thought of Ainsley suffering the way she had been for the last hour or so.

"At least let's stay here until tomorrow," he pushed. "Give her a bit more time to heal from her injury."

"There's a town not more than three leagues from here," Sheva offered. "We can find an inn, stay the night."

"I don't think we should travel through towns," Briallen argued. "It's like announcing our presence to the universe."

"I doubt anyone would know who we are," Sheva said.

"A monk, a nun, and a very small combat unit of Amichai warriors...? You don't think *someone* would notice that?" Briallen motioned to the woods on either side of the road they'd been traveling. "We should find a place to stay, near water."

"Ainsley won't like stopping so early," Sheva warned. "Maybe we should—"

"Friends."

Gruff frowned at the softly stated word from Sister Hilda, but when he turned to face her, he saw them. They were dressed as travelers, just as Gruff and his party were. But if one looked a little deeper, it became clear these men were anything but common travelers. Heavy fur capes barely covered swords, axes, spears, and shields. There were only thirty men in front of them, but Gruff would guess they were thirty of Beatrix's strongest fighters; with more lying in wait somewhere.

Lying in wait or stalking through the forest searching for their true target.

He only had a moment to think, *Where's Ainsley?* before those thirty men were attacking Gruff and his party. Racing at them full speed, their weapons unsheathed and their shields at the ready.

Deciding he had to get to Ainsley, Gruff turned to run in the direction she'd gone, but arrows struck him hard. Two in his human leg and one in the upper arm. The force pushed him several steps to the side, but the sight of the wooden shafts sticking out of his body made Gruff a bit ... angry.

\* \* \*

Ainsley stopped by a large tree and started to unscrew the top of the ointment. She knew she didn't have any broken ribs, but the mere bruising didn't make riding a horse or, you know, *breathing* any easier. Every time the horse's hooves hit the ground, she felt it. Every time she took a deep breath—gods!—did she feel it! But she was determined to see this through, no matter the pain.

She knew there was a town nearby and perhaps there she could get another ointment from a healer that would numb the area enough so she could ride for the next few days. Not even a few days really, just a couple. This wasn't the first time she'd had bruised ribs; it was simply the only time she'd had to ride for long miles with bruised ribs.

But she refused to go home now and prove her sisters right. Prove she wasn't up to much more than staying in trees and shooting off her arrows to protect their flank. Or, even worse . . . keeping watch. She could already hear her sisters' arguments. "You like being up high! That's why you climb those trees, right? You can keep lookout for any danger that our many soldiers don't already see!"

Rolling her eyes at the thought, Ainsley dipped two fingers into the ointment. But the sound of steel clashing against steel made her stop and turn her exhausted body toward the sounds of battle just seconds before a hand slapped hard over her face and an arm went around her waist, yanking her off the ground.

The ancient rage of Gruff's ancestors began to course through his blood and, when he looked up to see that human men had blocked his immediate path to the forest—to Ainsley—that ancient rage exploded out of him, sending him into a full shift. To his battle form.

Black antlers sprouted from the top of Gruff's head and four from his back, sliding through the holes perfectly placed in his chainmail shirt. His fingers turned into black claws, and three-inch fangs sprouted from his gums. Those of his party that shared the Torn Moon Clan bloodline also shifted into their battle forms. The men fighting them, though, did not stop attacking. They merely switched to their spears so they didn't have to get close to the centaurs and end up as meat hanging off their racks.

Their calm at the sight of the centaurs told him these men knew exactly who they'd be fighting despite the many humans that lived near the Amichai Mountain range and who dressed just the same as Gruff and his kin.

He knew then he truly had to get to Ainsley. Or at least one of them did. But they were badly outnumbered; all of them were fighting more than one of the human males.

Deciding he had to be the one to get to the royal, Gruff faced the men blocking his path. He snorted and growled in warning and, wisely, the men backed up, but they didn't run.

By contrast, the three horses Ainsley and her friends had been riding, ran off in panic. Not that Gruff blamed them. Even unholy horses knew when things were bad.

While staring directly at the males, Gruff reached over to his right arm, grabbed the arrow shaft embedded there, and yanked it free. He dropped it, then leaned down to his leg and, still looking at the soldiers, took hold of the shafts and pulled.

While he was holding the blood-covered arrows, someone slammed into Gruff's unmoving back. Unwilling to look away from his enemies, he scented the air to be sure it was not one of his travel party, then swung his arm back. The body dropped, the two arrows sticking out of the soldier's throat.

Gruff unsheathed his sword, then yanked free the mace he had strapped to his back. Holding one in each hand, he leaned forward and slammed his front hoof down. The hard ground beneath him cracked, and Gruff unleashed a roar that frightened the birds deep in the woods and sent the animals scattering for miles.

And yet . . . the human men did not run.

The unopened jar of ointment fell from her fingers and Ainsley began kicking and screaming, desperate to remove the hand pushing into her wounded side.

Another set of hands grabbed her legs, trying to hold her firmly as they attempted to carry her off. Normally, she'd go limp—this was not the first time that men had attempted to carry her off. Once, swords-for-hire that had visited her mother's forge had caught a glimpse of Ainsley and decided it would be good to have what they termed a "traveling companion." They'd grabbed her just outside of her old village and Ainsley had gone limp, letting them carry her like a sack of potatoes, believing that she was no more than a weak little girl. It allowed her time to think and avoided being beaten into unconsciousness. When they'd neared their horses, she'd started to retch, pretending she was going to projectile vomit everywhere. When they'd paused to get a better look at her, she'd freed one of her arms and grabbed the small knife she kept sheathed at her side. She slashed a leg and a face before making a run for it. The men had been right behind her but they hadn't slipped from the village unseen. Keeley had spotted them following Ainsley; she'd come to protect her younger sister . . . and she hadn't come alone. The demon wolves had been with her that day and they'd set upon the men in seconds while Keeley ordered Ainsley to *"Run!"* Which she'd done without question, not even bothering to look back. She hadn't needed to. Not with all that male screaming.

This time, though, going limp wouldn't be possible because of the pain. By all the gods everywhere, the pain!

Unable to stand another second of it, Ainsley yanked her legs in toward her body. The man holding her wouldn't let go, so he was dragged close by the move, allowing Ainsley to kick him in the chest. After years of climbing trees—or climbing anything, really—Ainsley had very strong legs. That double-legged kick sent the man reeling back.

He still held her, though, ending up yanking her from his comrade's hold.

Ainsley's upper back hit the ground first. She kept her head elevated so it didn't slam into the hard earth. The man holding her legs also fell to the ground, finally releasing her.

The other man was trying to grab her again but the mere thought of a hand pressing against her bruised side had Ainsley rolling backward into a crouched position.

Operating on muscle memory alone, Ainsley had the bow off her back and in her hands. She nocked an arrow and shot, hitting one of the men in the chest. He stumbled back, but the other one was already coming for her. She nocked two more arrows and hit that man in the chest and throat.

He went down, but two more men materialized from the surrounding forest. Ainsley nocked more arrows and kept firing, but she wished she knew how to fight with something other than a bow, because she was running out of arrows.

And the men just kept coming.

Gruff swung the mace he had in one hand to the left, smashing in the head of some human male. Swung it to the right and caved in another human male's chest. He then brought the axe he had in his other hand down on a still-breathing human at his feet.

Another human male leaped off a nearby boulder, bringing his long sword down in a wide arc toward Gruff's head.

Jerking to the side, Gruff avoided a killing blow, but the weapon did manage to shear off a couple of points from his rack. The damaged antlers would grow back fully in a few days, but it still pissed him off.

As the man's body came down near him, Gruff lowered his head and rammed it forward. His antlers tore through the man and, roaring, Gruff lifted his prize into the air.

The human man screamed in pain and terror, but Gruff ignored all that. Instead, he shook his head from side to side; the points destroying bone and flesh with each violent move. By the time Gruff had shaken the man off, he was dead and Gruff's rack was drenched in blood and gore.

No one else immediately attacked, so he turned to see how the others fared. He barely glanced at his sister and those of his clan. They were happily decimating the remaining humans as they'd been trained to do since they were foals.

His main concerns were the nun and the monk, but one look told him they were just fine. The war monk was busy dragging her blade down the spine of some hysterical human male and the battle nun had separated her steel walking stick into two pieces. One side for battering, the other to stab and slash with a nasty pointed end.

Gruff heard a war cry and, after dropping his mace, he lifted his arm and caught the man who'd been charging at him with his axe raised. Taking solid hold, Gruff slammed the man against the ground three times until the axe fell from his numb fingers. He then lifted the man again and held tight as he stormed into the forest to get to Ainsley.

* * *

Ainsley reached back once more to grab the last two arrows from her quiver. But just as she touched the smooth wood with the tips of her fingers, a blade pressed against her throat. It dug in deep enough so she could feel blood begin to ease down her neck, but not deep enough to end her life.

"Let the bow go," a man told her.

She did, dropping the weapon from her hand.

"That's a good girl. Now stand up and face me. Slowly."

Ainsley turned until she could look at the man pointing a sword at her.

"Greetings, Princess. Now I'm going to explain to you what we're going to—"

Ainsley jumped. She'd heard nothing. Saw nothing coming until Lord Paladin galloped by and yanked the now-screaming man off his feet by his arm.

Shocked, she watched him slam the man to the ground, flip him up in the air, catch him, and slam him against the ground again.

Someone stepped in next to her and she glanced over, relieved to see it was Gruff. He held the bloody handle of his axe in his left hand and a man struggling to breathe in his right.

"Friend of yours?" she asked, focusing again on what Lord Paladin was doing.

"Figured we'd keep one alive to get answers."

Lord Paladin had the man who'd threatened Ainsley on the ground now and was slamming his right front leg into his chest. Over and over.

"The answers? What answers do you need that we don't already know? They were sent here. To grab one of us. One of Keeley's siblings."

"How do you know that?"

"Because it's what I'd do if I were a hateful, unholy monster from the farthest corners of some hell pit. Or if I were Beatrix."

Lord Paladin picked up what was now a corpse and swung it to the side, but Ainsley still heard screaming. It wasn't coming from the man held by Gruff. Nor the corpse being tossed around by Paladin. So where was that coming . . . ? Oh.

Lord Paladin's brother came charging in with a man held in his maw, fangs digging into his chest and abdomen. The black horse ran by, then came charging by the other way, then ran back again. Like a puppy playing with its bone.

The horse brothers' sister was more elegant. She trotted in proudly with her prize, a man's leg being held between the fangs on the right side of her muzzle. She trotted like a general's horse during a parade, bringing her knees up high and moving back and forth in front of Paladin.

But all that showing off didn't last long. Both siblings got bored and began to slam their victims to the ground or toss them into the air. Just what their brother had done only moments before.

While the two siblings did that, Lord Paladin walked over to Ainsley and spit out at her feet part of a corpse.

"Awww, look," Gruff said. "He brought you a gift."

"How nice. No one has ever brought me a torso before."

"There's some leg left."

Ainsley closed her eyes and fought the urge to shudder. She had a feeling Lord Paladin would take that as an insult. Instead, she finally looked at him and said, "Thank you."

Head held high, he returned to his sister and brother. All three took hold of the last of their victims that was still alive. Paladin's brother caught the leg. His sister, an arm. And Paladin took hold of the head. Then, in unison, they began pulling in opposite directions until the body was torn apart.

"That was fun to watch," she said, unable to hide her sarcasm.

"You should be pleased. He's protective of you."

"If you say so."

"He didn't drag you around like a toddler with its least favorite stuffed bear, did he?"

Gruff had a point, and she turned to face the centaur to tell him as much, but she couldn't do anything but gawk.

Frowning, Gruff asked, "What are you staring at?"

"You're magnificent," she whispered.

"What? Huh?" He glanced down at himself. "Oh." Cleared his throat. "I forgot I was in my battle form."

"But I've seen Quinn and Caid in their battle forms. They don't look like . . . this."

"Different clans. Not all centaurs look alike."

"I know, it's just . . . are you taller?"

Not merely taller than Caid and Quinn but taller than he was in his everyday centaur form.

That wasn't all, though.

Gruff also had those gorgeous twenty-point antlers on his head, and simple spiked ones coming out of his back. Dissuading anyone from attacking from behind, she assumed. His fangs were a good inch longer than what she'd seen on other centaurs in their battle form and he had claws now rather than fingers. Even his hooves were different. They had long hair covering them.

"Stop staring at me," he finally ordered.

"Okay."

"You didn't stop."

*"I can't!"*

Gruff didn't know what to do. When he was in his battle form, no one except members of his own clan had ever looked at him with anything but horror and revulsion. Something he was quite used to and didn't care about.

But the way Princess Ainsley was looking at him . . .

"Stop!" he ordered again.

"Sorry!"

She finally glanced away, but then he heard her quietly ask, "Can I touch your antlers?"

"No!"

"Pleasssssse?"

*"No!"*

"Oy!" he heard his sister call out from a few feet away, and Gruff had never felt so relieved.

With a tilt of the antlers on her head, Briallen pointed at the man Gruff had forgotten he was still holding.

"You going to question him or just carry him around for the next few hours?"

Gruff shifted back to his natural form, ignoring the whine of disappointment the royal next to him let out, and followed his sister back to the others. "Come on," he ordered.

Ainsley followed, and he ignored her muttered, "You could have at least let me touch one." But when she followed that up with,

"Fine. I'll just ask your sister," Gruff stopped short and faced her again.

She gazed up at him with wide eyes, and for a long minute neither spoke. Then, finally, she said, "All right. I won't bother your sister."

He grunted and waited.

Finally, she rolled her eyes and added, "I won't bother your sister or anyone in your clan about their antlers."

He gave another grunt and stalked off, ignoring the sad little sigh she gave before quietly following.

Hilda was the one who did the questioning. Not because she threatened or harmed the prisoner. But because she became the very vision of a pious nun. Arms folded and tucked into the long arms of her black robes. Her voice calm, soothing. Her tone pleading. Her eyes mostly downcast unless she felt he was not telling the truth. And when that happened, she gazed at him with such directness that he would suddenly unleash a torrent of truth.

For Ainsley, it was fascinating to watch the hold religion and the fear of the gods had on people.

When Hilda would give her that same look, she simply snorted and walked away.

Of course, the things the man told them didn't exactly surprise her. As she'd guessed, they were Beatrix's soldiers. They'd been sent to grab one of the younger children, but when they saw Ainsley heading out in the middle of the night with a small travel party, their commander had decided it would be just as good to take her rather than attempt to infiltrate the tower and make off with a screaming child they weren't allowed to hurt.

While the others seemed a little shocked and very disgusted by the extremes Beatrix would employ to get what she wanted, Ainsley wasn't shocked at all. How could she be? The bitch had been trying to kill Ainsley since before she was even born, although she didn't think anyone else knew about that. And she'd only guessed because her mother talked about how "clumsy" she'd been when pregnant with Ainsley. A clumsiness she'd never experienced before or after. A clumsiness she'd only seemed to experience when five-year-old Beatrix was in the room.

"Remember that, luv?" their mother would say to Beatrix when relating one of those stories to the rest of them. Beatrix would never reply.

So, no. Ainsley wasn't shocked by any of this.

At least until the soldier admitted who their commander had been.

"Commander Beaton?" Ainsley repeated after the soldier had said the name.

"I thought he was in Duke Jansbatten's territory," Sheva noted. "Neutral territory."

But now Ainsley realized it was a lie told by Beatrix's people to whatever spies were running around the countryside. She was not only aware of them, she was manipulating them so she could distract her family from her true goals. The first: grabbing one of her siblings so she could gain control of Keeley. It was all about control for Beatrix. That's what power was to her.

"Wait," Briallen said. "One of those blokes was Commander Beaton, right?"

The soldier nodded.

"Which one is he?" she barked. "Which one? Is he here?"

Briallen wanted to know because, Ainsley assumed, if he'd escaped, they should go after him. At least to stop him from updating Beatrix on this latest battle. But, with great fear, the soldier slowly adjusted his gaze toward a spot about twenty feet away. The group turned in the same direction and saw Lord Paladin and his siblings standing there. Hanging from his sister's mouth was a head. The same head Paladin had ripped off. Apparently, they'd been playing with it and it had ended up with Sheva's mare.

She seemed quite happy with it, too.

"Huh," Ainsley said, because she had nothing else to say.

"Weren't we supposed to bring him back alive?" Briallen asked.

That was true, but, in all honesty, Ainsley didn't really care. The man wasn't even where he was supposed to be.

"Does this mean we can go back?" Sarff asked.

"In a rush?" Briallen teased.

Ainsley wasn't interested in Sarff's reply until the old bitch poked her bruised side.

"*Owwwwww! Demon female!*" Ainsley bellowed.

"She needs a good poultice and rest," Sarff explained, ignoring Ainsley, who moved around to the other side of Gruff, hoping he'd keep the mad bitch from her. "Better to do that back at the tower than out here. Besides . . . we already have his head."

"And if we leave now," Sheva added, "we'll be back home by morning. We won't have to explain anything to your sisters."

Ainsley nodded. "That works."

There were shrugs of agreement from the others, while Hilda pressed her hand against the soldier's forehead. As she softly prayed over him, the soldier began sobbing. Embarrassed for the man— was the crying *truly* necessary?—Ainsley began to turn away, but not before she saw a quick flash of steel.

She, along with everyone else, gawked while the soldier's blood drained from his slashed throat and Hilda briefly paused to wipe the blade off on her black robes.

"What did you do?" Ainsley demanded, shocked.

"What *did* you do, mad nun!" Even Sheva was shocked! And Sheva was never shocked.

Hilda calmly looked over the group before replying, "We weren't going to keep him alive, were we?"

"We weren't?" Ainsley asked.

"Ainsley, we couldn't let him go. He would go back and tell Beatrix everything. And we couldn't take him with us, because then your sisters would know what you'd been up to. So I took care of it."

"But . . . you were just praying over him."

"I was granting him forgiveness. So he could die in peace."

"Before you slit his throat?"

"What did you want me to do? Stab him in the chest?" Hilda glanced off. "I guess I could have stabbed him in the chest."

"That's not what I meant!"

# CHAPTER 16

The main hall was silent as they all sat at the big dining table. Keeley, Laila, Caid, and Quinn sat on one side and Annwyl, Morfyd, Fearghus, and Gwenvael sat on the other. Briec had been banished to a chair against the wall behind Annwyl because, according to Gwenvael, he was "being a right prat."

It had to be about thirty minutes that they'd all sat there, not speaking, the dragons glaring down the table at them. Not Annwyl, though. She read a book Gemma's father had given her.

"You'll love it," he'd told her the day before when she was still covered with the blood of the monks that had attacked her. "It's full of adventure! And romance! My wife hates it, but it's one of my favorites."

She'd been silently reading it ever since. For once the Mad Queen didn't look insane. She didn't look angry. She seemed completely calm and rational. Maybe it was the reading. Or maybe a good battle always settled her down. A way for her to work out what the elders of Gemma's order called, "inner demons." They hadn't meant actual demons, of course, but who knew what Annwyl the Bloody's emotional problems were?

Gemma wondered how much longer the silence was going to continue when Annwyl suddenly laughed at what she was reading. It was a small, innocent sound, but it seemed to unleash something in Prince Fearghus. He slammed his fist down on the table, nearly buckling it, and making everyone jump but Annwyl.

"*I trusted you with my mate and your people tried to kill her?*" he demanded, voice booming through the room.

"It wasn't *our* people," Gemma immediately insisted.

"So says the woman dressed as a monk."

"I am a monk, but that was a different order."

"Except for Annwyl, I haven't found much difference between you humans and the lowest of jungle animals. The ones I used to feed strips of to the falcons and hawks that helped me learn to fly."

Morfyd at least had the decency to cringe at her brother's statement, which allowed Gemma to ignore it and instead clarify, "That particular brotherhood had an issue with the idea of an alliance between our two queendoms."

"You give so much power to these"—scowling, he coldly looked over Gemma before focusing on a mostly silent Keeley—"priests."

"As Gemma already pointed out, that was an order of *monks*," Quinn unhelpfully interjected.

"*Who cares?*" the dragon bellowed.

Quinn pointed at the dragon across the table. "Don't yell at me, because I'll come right over there and shit in your lap."

The dragon made the gesture back to Quinn and replied, "Don't point at me or I'll shift right here and *take this whole fucking tower down!*"

"All right, that is *enough!*" Morfyd barked as she got to her feet. "We are not here for all this arguing. We're here to discuss what happens next between our two queendoms."

"I say we let their cunty sister wipe this entire place from the map."

"No one asked you, Briec!"

Annwyl finally lifted her head from her book, a confused look on her face, and asked Briec, "And when did you ever start caring about *me?*"

"I don't care about you."

*"Then why the fuck are you saying anything?"*

*"Don't bark at me, little dog, or I'll finish what those weak, pathetic monks started!"*

"*Enough!*" Morfyd abruptly stopped, pressed her hands to her chest, closed her eyes, and took in several large, soothing breaths.

After several seconds of silence, the royal She-dragon began again. Calmly. "I know we are all under a lot of stress. And nothing is worse than when people follow their own orders during such a delicate time and during such sensitive negotiations. But that was then—"

"Literally yesterday," Fearghus muttered.

"—and this is now and shut up, Fearghus."

"Annwyl and I have been discussing an alliance—" Keeley began.

"You want us to trust you now?" Fearghus demanded. "After what *just* happened? *Literally yesterday?*" He snorted. "And they say Annwyl's mad."

"She is mad."

"Shut up, Briec!"

"Although I don't like the way he's expressing it, Fearghus has a point." Morfyd sat in her chair and said to Keeley, "How are we supposed to trust you or believe for a second that you can protect these lands when you don't even have control of the religious factions you're protecting?"

"Right under your fucking noses." Fearghus jerked his head to the side as a chalice of morning wine sailed by his head. "Do not throw things at me, Morfyd!"

"Then shut up and let me handle this."

"The religious factions, as you call them, are only acting this way because they believe your queen to be evil and opposed to their gods," Laila explained.

"Annwyl is insane. Not evil."

Annwyl looked away from her book again, her face briefly twisted in confusion. "Uh . . . thank you?"

Morfyd gave a warm smile. "You're welcome."

"Hasn't she been to one of the hells?" Quinn asked.

"She's been to more than one, but it wasn't her fault, and she wasn't dead at the time. She was simply dragged there to stop her from joining a battle against our enemy at the end of a very long war."

"Didn't she come back alive and unscathed?"

"Mostly unscathed. Mostly. There were some injuries."

Laila looked at Queen Annwyl. "The demon kings and rulers of the many hells just let you come back?"

"No," the foreign royal answered amiably. "I had to fight my way out. Killed a demon king... I think he was a demon king. Or maybe he was a demon duke. Anyway, I killed him and quite a few of his soldiers. Oh! And there were a few demon bounty hunters I had to cut down, but," she added with a happy smile as if she were retelling a charming tale of romance, "like your Queen Keeley, I made friends with most of the demon animals."

"Really?" Quinn said, glancing at Keeley's legs. "Then why are Keeley's demon wolves hiding under the table by her feet? Willing, it seems, to sacrifice themselves protecting her from *dragons* but completely terrified of *you*. That seems... odd."

"Demon wolves? Demon wolves?" she repeated, seemingly attempting to remember. Then she bent over a bit and looked under the table. Gemma heard a lone whimper from the beasts but nothing else.

"Oh!" Annwyl sat up straight again, "*Those* demon wolves. Well, you see, in many of the hells, those wolves are used for hunting, and so they were sent out to find me. And..." she paused a moment and winced. "Um... I did have to decimate a few of them. Or a lot, but I *was* fighting for my life and freedom, so... you know. And the wolves have a collective memory. Meaning they are born with the experiences of all the past and current wolves in their many bloodlines. So I'm sure your little pack there knows exactly what I, um... did. But only because I had to!" she quickly added.

"Was that *supposed* to make us feel better?" Quinn gently asked. "Because I'm not sure."

"It didn't?"

"Not even a little."

There was a snort, and the beautiful gold dragon stood, hand over his mouth to hold in the laughter. He started to walk away from the table.

"Gwenvael, *sit down!*" his sister ordered.

He did, but he was forced to cover his face with both hands. They could still see his shoulders shaking, though.

"At least Annwyl does what she says she's going to do," Briec suddenly announced. "When she says she's going to protect people, that's exactly what she does. Unfortunately, at the moment, none of *you* can say the same."

The rest of the dragons all gawked at him. Even Annwyl turned around in her chair to stare.

Finally, he demanded, "What? I'm right!"

"Prince Briec *is* right." Keeley shook her head. "Once it was decided that you were staying for a bit, Annwyl, I should have called a meeting of all the religious factions and explained the situation to them. I should have had all of them make a vow of no aggression toward you and your dragons, at least for the length of time you will be in my territories. I didn't do that, and I'm sorry."

Now the dragons and Annwyl were all gawking at Keeley. When they continued to stare for what felt like an unhealthy amount of time, she asked, "Yes?"

Morfyd pushed white hair behind her ear. "Did you just admit to making a mistake and then accept responsibility for that mistake? In front of everyone?"

*Shit.*

"Yes."

"Did our mother ever do that?" Morfyd asked her brothers.

"No," Fearghus replied. "Not even once."

Gwenvael tapped the table. "Do you remember that human friend I had when I was much younger?"

"The one who took you on tours of brothels?" Morfyd flatly asked.

"That's the one! Mum accidentally burned him once. Never apologized or took any responsibility. She did heal him, of course, but I think an 'I'm sorry' would have also been nice. Especially because his hair just never grew back."

"Not to sound too hopeful," Keeley said, positive she didn't want to hear any more about dragons "accidentally" burning people, "but there has to be a way we can make this work. A way to solidify an alliance between us that we can all trust."

"You humans seem to use forced marriages for that sort of

thing," Prince Briec suggested. "That always seems quite effective for you people."

Keeley felt her sister get tense next to her, but she quickly slapped her hand on Gemma's chainmail-covered knee and squeezed, so she didn't do anything stupid. Yet.

"Forced marriages are effective," Keeley said, parsing her words carefully and still squeezing her sister's knee. "But I'm not a fan of forcing people to marry for any reason. Especially because it never seems to work out for the *females* in the relationship."

Fearghus nodded. "She has a point."

"We can talk to Uncle Bram," Morfyd suggested.

"He's already mated to Aunt Ghleanna," Fearghus noted.

"Yeah, won't she get pissed if we marry him off to someone here?" Gwenvael asked.

"And no one wants to make her mad," Briec noted. "She hits really hard."

"And whoever marries Bram won't last another night once Ghleanna finds out," Gwenvael added.

Morfyd briefly covered her face with her hands before dragging her fingers through her thick mane. Then she looked at each of her brothers and announced, "You're all idiots."

"Well, that's unkind." Gwenvael pouted and it was gods-damn adorable! "Why don't you love us anymore?"

Morfyd raised a forefinger at her brother but didn't answer his ridiculous question. Because Keeley knew if she didn't love her brothers, Morfyd would have killed them by now.

Forcing a smile, Morfyd explained to Keeley, "Our uncle Bram has handled all of my mother's alliances and truces with other dragon nations. He's here to assist Annwyl, and I'm sure he'll have some ideas we can use. Would you like to speak with him? Maybe he'll be able to arrange something we can all live with."

"Do your brothers have to come?" Gemma wondered out loud.

"No, but"—Morfyd let out a long, pained sigh—"they probably will anyway."

"Gwenvael's right," Fearghus told his sister. "You *have* stopped loving us."

"Shut *up*."

\* \* \*

"So you're arranging murders now?"

"No," Unnvar attempted to explain to his great-uncle Bram. "I told them to bring him back alive. Didn't I?"

"They attacked us," Ainsley argued. "What did you want us to do?"

"Keep the commander alive. How hard was that?"

"We didn't kill him. The horses did!"

Var frowned. "He was trampled?"

Princess Ainsley cringed while she figured out how to answer. "Not trampled . . . no. Uh . . ."

"The horses tore him apart," the monk interjected.

"What horses?"

"The horses the undead Kriegszorn birthed just before we left. They were gifts to us. Right?" she asked, glancing at the travel party for confirmation.

When they all nodded in agreement, Var turned back to Bram.

"I see now some miscalculations were made, Uncle."

"We did learn something, though," Ainsley said. "Beatrix knows about the spies. She gave them false information so we wouldn't learn that Commander Beaton was coming here to kidnap one of my siblings."

"Do you think they know who our people are?" Var asked his great-uncle.

"They probably put the information out to everyone, assuming someone would send it back here."

"We wouldn't have known if it hadn't been for you, Var," Ainsley admitted. "We don't really have spies."

Startled, Var asked, "You don't have a network of spies?"

"We have gossip. Does that work?"

"Not really."

"Not everyone is as prepared as your mother, Var," Bram said with a little smile.

"Of course not. My mother's perfect."

"Anyway," Bram went on, "your sister, Princess Ainsley, is a very new royal. I wouldn't expect her or your family to have a spy network. Dragons, however, have had powerful monarchies for many millenniums and we've been protecting our own all that time.

I'm honestly just glad you were able to protect the children. Although it does tell me a lot about your sister."

The tent flap was pulled back and Var's father walked in. He smiled at the sight of Var and unnecessarily cheered, "Son!"

"No," Var said.

"But—"

"No."

"Can't I even—"

"No."

"Fine." Gwenvael smiled at Bram. "Hello, Uncle."

"Gwenvael."

"And the lovely Princess Ainsley with her religious friends! Although you all do look a little . . . battered."

"Thank you."

"No, no. I mean, you're still stunning, Princess, but has something happened?" Before the princess could answer, Gwenvael glared at Var. "What did you do?"

"Something my mother would rightfully approve of."

"That does *not* make me feel better in any way, Son."

"What were you thinking, Var?"

"I made rational decisions based on the information I had available to me at the time."

Ainsley watched, fascinated, as the two beautiful men—who were not men—faced each other. They both had that gorgeous golden hair, but Unnvar's was much shorter, barely reaching his shoulders, while his father's stretched down his back.

Unnvar was also a good two to three inches shorter than Gwenvael and his uncles, meaning he was only six and a half feet tall.

And then, of course, there were the spectacles. Those round pieces of glass in front of steel-gray eyes that must have come from his mother because Gwenvael's eyes were a warm gold like his hair and his vision seemed perfect. Those spectacles should have made such a large male look ridiculous, but no. They made Unnvar somehow more handsome.

In fact, the dragons were so handsome that, with the help of Sarff's ointment applied a few hours ago, she barely noticed the dull pain in her ribs. Although Sarff had warned Ainsley that she should get one of Sarff's poultices on the bruised area and get some rest in bed "before the screaming starts," which sounded very ominous.

Glancing over at her friends, Ainsley saw that Sheva was dreamily gawking at the two males as well, but Hilda wasn't remotely interested. That was typical. She didn't seem interested in any man and interested even less in any woman. She was one of the few people that Ainsley would say was truly comfortable with her own company.

Of course, many would probably say the same about Ainsley, but even she needed to come down from her tree and spend some time with her family and friends. Before she got fed up with them and fled back to one of her trees.

"All right, all right. Everyone calm down." Var's great-uncle Bram—a dragon who was also extremely attractive in his human form with his silver hair streaked with a few white stripes—stepped away from the table. "There's no reason to be upset about any of this."

"You don't blindly send royals off to fight against unknown enemies," Gwenvael argued.

"That's not what I did."

"That's *exactly* what you did. And how would your aunt Annwyl explain to Queen Keeley if something had happened to her sister? But you never think about that, do you?"

"Are you this hysterical—"

"I am *not* hysterical."

"—because my mother will always love me more than she'll ever love you?"

Bram jumped between the two males before Gwenvael the Handsome could get his hands around his son's throat. The older dragon did his best to push Gwenvael back while Var passively stared. But based on all the books and scrolls lining the walls of his tent and covering the big wooden table he'd been sitting at, Bram was more of a reader than a fighter and he was struggling a bit to get control over Gwenvael.

"I understand that," Var went on, "but there's no reason to take it out on your only son. I promise never to turn her against you."

Ainsley scrambled across the room with her friends, helping

Bram to push a now livid Gwenvael out of the tent and away from his smug son.

"I'd set him on fire," Gwenvael raged, "if the bastard burned!"

"That's your son," Bram chastised.

"It was his mother's choice to keep him."

"Maybe that explains why he's closer to *her*," Hilda guessed.

"But you have lovely daughters who adore you," Bram soothed. "And know how beautiful you are."

"I *am* beautiful, and everyone loves me. Including that boy's mother!"

"You know he probably said those things just to distract you from what he doesn't want to discuss," Ainsley volunteered.

Gwenvael abruptly stopped struggling and looked down at her. "You think?"

She shrugged. "It's what I do to get Gemma to back off. Of course, I don't have to worry about her *setting me on fire*. But I think you get the idea."

He rolled his eyes. "Like his mother, he doesn't burn. Dagmar's gift involved my dragonwitch mother's magicks and the boy was born that way, but they're both perfectly safe around me."

"We also don't burn people who simply irritate us," Bram clarified.

"I'm not sure about Briec—"

The older silver dragon slapped his hand over his nephew's face. "He's joking. Now, Gwenvael, what do you want?" When Gwenvael frowned behind Bram's hand, he added, "You came to see me? Remember?"

The gold dragon said something, but none of them understood because of his uncle's hand, which Bram quickly moved away.

"I said, the queens want to talk to you. I think they'd like to start negotiating an alliance between their two queendoms."

Bram blinked in surprise. "Fearghus agreed to this? Even after . . ."

"Yes. Even after the attack on Annwyl."

Now it was Ainsley's turn to be surprised. As soon as they'd returned to town, she'd sent Gruff and his team off to take a break, get something to eat. Necessary because she knew Gruff wouldn't be happy about her going into the dragons' camp so she could track down Var. Although, to be quite honest, the dragons, whether in their human form or otherwise, were extremely nice to her and her friends.

"Who attacked Annwyl?" she asked.

"Monks," Bram replied. "The Order of Blood and Stone."

Sheva simply shook her head, appearing a bit embarrassed. Hilda had no reaction whatsoever, but Ainsley exploded.

*"These fucking religious fanatics!"*

"Don't blame *us*," Hilda said.

"We're not all fanatics," Sheva briefly argued before looking at Hilda and adding, "I mean . . . you are. But the rest of us usually aren't."

"What happened?" Ainsley asked Bram. "Is Annwyl all right?"

The two dragons stared at her until Gwenvael stated, "You like Annwyl."

"Yes. Why?"

"No reason. Just . . . fascinated."

"Right," Hilda said. "We're all so fascinating. But I think the bigger issue is whether there can be an alliance after Brother Gemma failed to protect Annwyl from an attack of bloodthirsty and sexually deprived monks."

"I'll see what I can do," Bram said. "I need to get my bag."

The older dragon returned to his tent and Ainsley said to Gwenvael, "I know you're mad at Var, but we did stop Commander Beaton and his men from taking one of my younger siblings. That means more to me than anything right now."

"I understand that. But I'm not sure your sister would want an alliance with Annwyl if Beatrix had sent your head back to Keeley in a *box*."

Ainsley didn't know how to respond to that, but she didn't have to because Sheva snorted a laugh. When Ainsley glared at her, the monk raised her hands and said, "Sorry. Sorry."

"I know," Ainsley said to Gwenvael, "that my sisters have you convinced I'm a pathetic mess—"

"They've never said *that*."

"—but I can handle myself in a fight. And I plan to keep helping to protect my sister's queendom whether she wants me to or not. So, in the future, information like that—which Keeley, Gemma, and Laila will only argue about how to handle, although they would insist on calling it debating—should come to *me*. Because if you leave it up to my sisters, we'll lose valuable time, and we just can't afford that right now. Understood?"

Gwenvael nodded, a small smile turning up the corners of his mouth. "Understood, Princess Ainsley."

"Don't call me princess. It sounds stupid."

"Because you live in a tree?"

"I don't live in a tree," she snapped back. "Stop listening to everything my sisters tell you. And stop laughing at me!"

Lord Bram rushed out of his tent, a travel bag hanging off his shoulder, several thick tomes in his hands.

"Come on, boy!" he yelled back at the tent. A few seconds later, Var followed his great-uncle out. He carried even more books.

Gwenvael waited until his son was next to him, then he suddenly lunged toward Var as if about to attack, while screaming, "*I love you so much, Son!*"

Var jerked so hard away from his father that he lost his footing and fell; all those books scattered around him.

Laughing—and how could *any* being be so beautiful and so troublesome all at the same time?—Gwenvael nodded at Ainsley before taking his time heading back to the tower.

# CHAPTER 17

Tadesse of the High Plains pressed his hand against the blood-covered ground and opened his mind. He could only watch for a few seconds. Only a few seconds of the screams and the fire and the murder.

He snatched his hand back and shook his head, a weak attempt to get rid of the ugliness he'd just witnessed.

"I know," Abbess Hurik said before holding her hand out to him so she could help him up. "I saw, too."

The Abbess Butcher released his hand and closed her eyes. Neither of them were able to shut out the brutality they'd seen.

"The king's soldiers?" Balla, leader of the vestal virgins, asked.

"Don't you mean the queen's? The king is as afraid of her as the lowest, gods-fearing peasant, and his soldiers know that."

The Abbess was right, of course. King Marius hated his queen, and to get away from her, he traveled constantly with his soldiers, tormenting the people of his own lands.

Tadesse looked around at what was left of the small town, which was barely anything.

No. This wasn't the work of the king and his men. They did ride into villages, slaughter the innocent, and abscond with a few of the prettier girls, but there were always survivors. Those who told the tale of Marius the Wielder of Hate to other villagers. He wanted everyone to fear him since his wife clearly didn't.

But this . . .

Tadesse hadn't thought this mission would be so hard. When

the bickering between the religious factions had become too much for him and his recent travel party to tolerate, Brother Gemma had asked for a favor. While she sent her monk cohorts out to meet with the remaining religious orders to make sure they were safe after the recent slaughter by Cyrus the Honored and his cult, she'd asked her former travel party to search the countryside closer to Beatrix's territories. She was especially interested to know if Beatrix was encroaching farther into Queen Keeley's lands.

They'd all assumed that, in time, they would find something to report back to Gemma, but not this. Never this.

The destruction of an entire village that was on Queen Keeley's territories. Without survivors, it would take time for the information to get back to the queen and Gemma. That was not acceptable.

"There are no children."

Tadesse turned toward the Blood Warlock who stepped from the wreckage of a home. He hadn't traveled with them, but Ludolf of the Eastern Shores tended to show up unannounced in his all-red robes that hid him from head to toe. None of them had seen his face. None of them wanted to.

"What did you say?" Balla asked.

"I said there are no children. Among the remains. You will find no children."

The vestal virgin closed her eyes and turned away.

"She's taken the children."

"They're easier to turn into slaves than adults who put up a fight," Tadesse's sorcerer brother, Faraji of the Low Mountains, explained.

"This is going to upset Queen Keeley, and Brother Gemma will want blood," battle witch Ima said.

"She'll want to try to kill Beatrix again. Even if that means hunting her down in the queen's very palace."

Tadesse knew his brother was right. "We'll need to handle this . . . delicately."

"Vicar Ferdinand?" As a truce vicar, Ferdinand was trained to deliver difficult information to those of very high rank.

"He's by his horse crying," Father Léandre, a war priest, replied with obvious disgust. "He's very upset by all this."

"Don't be hard on him," Hurik chastised. As a nun, she was one of the few who could get through to the war priests. "He's not battle hardened like the rest of us. He's a peacekeeper."

"So are we."

Hurik smirked. "But he works with words, Léandre. Not steel and magicks."

"Speaking of which," Ima noted, "do you smell it?"

Tadesse did. "Magicks. Lingering in the dirt and burned homes."

Ima nodded. "A god's magicks. It seems Queen Beatrix no longer fights this war alone."

So many suggestions brought up and dismissed. For many reasons.

Bram the Merciful understood. It was hard to create an alliance with someone you knew so little about.

And although Bram was a big believer in knowledge, he also knew that sometimes one must trust one's instincts. His instincts told him Queen Keeley was exactly what she showed herself to be: a blacksmith who'd stumbled into being a queen. He found himself feeling safe with her and with the centaurs that surrounded her. He was less comfortable with Brother Gemma, but he didn't see her as an out-of-control religious hysteric.

Her love of the war gods was strong, but not as strong as her love for her family.

Besides, he knew from past experience that rulers like Beatrix were never good for anyone. Not anyone. Not the people in the villages or the centaurs in the Amichai Mountains, the dwarves *under* the Amichai Mountains, or the animals in the forests or the birds in the trees. Absolutely no one fared well when someone like Beatrix ruled. And once she was done destroying these lands, she would turn her attention to the territories of Queens Rhiannon and Annwyl.

He knew, in his bones, that this alliance was the most important thing he would ever work on. He needed to make it happen.

Which was why, when his nephew Briec suggested the centaurs give Queen Rhiannon—Briec's *mother*—part of the Amichai Mountains, and he wanted the centaurs to allow him to "push out" the dwarves that lived under those mountains because, "We need caves. Cozy, warm caves. But don't worry," he'd promised, "we'll be nice." Bram didn't reach across the table and slap the rude bastard as he'd been wanting to do ever since Briec had been hatched.

He loved all the *many* nephews and nieces that he'd acquired by becoming the mate of Ghleanna the Decimator, favored sister of Queen Rhiannon's mate, Bercelak the Great—or as Bram and many others called him, Bercelak the Unpleasant—but most of them were a lot to take. The Cadwaladr Clan—Ghleanna's kin—loved nothing more than a good battle that allowed them to slaughter as many beings as possible. Involving them in any truce or alliance building was well-nigh impossible. Still, Rhiannon's rank as queen made her own offspring...royal. The reality was, even with all their pomp and royal rudeness, Rhiannon's offspring were Cadwaladrs at heart. Meaning that only sweet Morfyd and fun-loving Keita had always seen the majority of humans as anything but beings to eat, kill, or fuck. And although that general philosophy had changed amongst most of the Cadwaladrs since Annwyl had become mate to Fearghus, the witch Talaith had become mate to Briec, and Dagmar Reinholdt had become mate to Gwenvael, there was still a long way to go before any of Rhiannon's sons would understand that just because they were dragons and royal born, that did not mean everyone else was a meaningless pest to be batted out of the way when they were annoyed.

"I have a suggestion," a voice stated from a chair across the room.

It had been silent since Bram had successfully shoved Briec's proposition away like a chicken pecking at one of his talons. It had helped that Annwyl had laughed outright when Briec made the ridiculous suggestion and Keeley had joined her. The queens had unknowingly prevented a brand-new war between dragons and centaurs, and he would be forever grateful.

"What's that, dear Isadora?" he asked, motioning her to come over to the table.

"I've done some research," she began, and immediately her two eldest sisters glanced at each other and rolled their eyes, causing the girl to stutter to a stop.

"Go on," he said to her, nodding.

He knew Isadora's sisters meant no harm, but older siblings had no idea how crushing their snorts of derisive laughter or eye rolls could be to their younger kin just trying to step out of their usual roles. Bram had been impressed by Isadora ever since she'd organized not only where the royal dragons would sleep, but the quick build of the dragon camp, the dragons' access to domesticated cattle and sheep herds for their meals without angering the local farmers; several fresh water sources; as well as big, strong horses so the dragons in human form could travel to nearby towns as long as they promised not to terrorize the villagers by shifting back into dragon.

Instead of replying to Bram, Isadora came to the table and placed a book in front of him. She quickly flipped it open to a specific page, pointing at a section of laws used by past Old Kings.

After reading, he grinned and looked at Isadora. "Nicely done, Your Royal Highness."

"This is a very old tradition," the older silver dragon explained, "and has been quite effective. Queen Rhiannon has done it herself with the Eastland dragons."

"Done what?" Keeley asked.

"How to describe it," Bram said, tapping his chin. He was definitely an "older" dragon, but it was hard to tell that when he was in his human form. Despite the streaks of white throughout his silver hair, his human face appeared astoundingly young. And yet he was the uncle of the royal dragons and great-uncle to Unnvar Reinholdt. "It's what one might call an exchange program."

"An exchange program?"

"Yes. How it works is that you would send one of the royal family to stay with Queen Annwyl at her court, and we would send one of our royal family to stay at yours."

Keeley had only a moment to think, *Oh, fuck no!* before she and Quinn had to grab Gemma; the centaur held her sword arm so she couldn't pull her weapon. Together, they dragged her across the main hall toward one of the back doors.

Caid was already following, and Laila was practicing the etiquette her mother had drilled into her since she'd been a foal.

"If you'll excuse us a brief moment, Your Majesty. Lord Bram. We'll be right back."

It wasn't easy, but with Quinn's help, Keeley was able to force her sister into the war room. The rest of the centaurs followed them inside, and Laila closed the door.

While Caid blocked the entrance with his big—and, at the moment, human—body, Keeley finally let her sister go.

Gemma had her sword out and pointed right at Keeley.

"*You*," she growled with such intensity that Keeley almost took a step back, "are ready to sell off our siblings *like chattel?*"

Keeley cringed at that ending bellow, knowing the dragons and Annwyl could hear it, but she refused to show her sister any weakness. This was all too important.

"I hadn't said anything yet," she pointed out.

"Exactly!" Gemma began pacing, her sword swinging as she gestured wildly. "They offered to steal the children, and you said *nothing!*"

"I'm just going to take that," Quinn said, grabbing hold of the sword hilt. There was a struggle over it, but he finally yanked it from Gemma's grasp and let out a relieved breath.

"They weren't suggesting they'd steal the children, Gemma."

"And you three!" She now pointed her finger at the centaurs. "You also said nothing!"

"You didn't exactly give us time to say anything," Quinn reminded her.

Ignoring her partner, Gemma again focused on Keeley. "You and Beatrix, exactly the same!"

Keeley started to launch herself at her sister, but Caid caught her around the waist and lifted her off the ground.

"Both of you need to calm down," Laila chastised. "This isn't helping anything."

"You're only saying that because you have no children to give," Gemma reminded the centaur royals. "Unlike *my* parents."

"This kind of royal exchange has been used by other nations for alliances since the beginning of time. It only fell out of favor because one of the Old Kings couldn't be trusted."

"And how do you know we can trust *them*, Laila?"

"Because we don't have any choice but to do so, Gemma."

\* \* \*

When Ainsley had to stop again to catch her breath, Caid was sure she'd never make it back to the tower. And they were only about twenty feet away.

"There's no way your sisters won't notice you're in so much pain," Sheva said, standing in front of Ainsley so no one would see that she was leaning against a building, her hand pressed against her wounded side.

"I can do this," Ainsley insisted. Something she kept insisting.

"You should just tell them," Hilda said, her hand on Ainsley's shoulder. "You have to tell them about Beaton anyway."

"I'm not telling them about Beaton."

"Ainsley—"

"I'll deal with it when I'm back on my feet. Until then, I want you guys to keep an eye out for my siblings. Protect them so I can figure out my next steps."

"I loathe children," Hilda announced with a loud, pain-filled sigh.

"What kind of nun are you?" Gruff finally had to ask.

"An honest one."

"Just go." Ainsley attempted to push her friends but ended up only waving them away.

When they were gone, Gruff began to follow, assuming Ainsley had meant him, too, but she grabbed his arm with her free hand.

"Not you."

"If you need me to carry you inside, your sisters will definitely know something is going on."

"I don't need you to carry me, and I have a plan to distract them."

"Another fight with Gemma?"

"I'm not really up to that."

She took a tentative step away from the wall and forced herself to lower her hand from her wounded side.

"Ainsley—"

"I know. Trust me. You just have to get me back to my room."

"Maybe you should recuperate in the woods."

"I'll never make it up a tree, and anything I do on the ground might be reported back to Gemma by those fucking monks. The only place I'm safe right now is in my room."

She took a few more steps and nodded. "Let's do this."

She moved so slowly, it took a long time just to get to the two short steps in front of the open tower doors. But once there, Ainsley cracked her neck and, with a surprising amount of elegance, walked through the doorway as if nothing was wrong.

Gruff walked right by her side as human, knowing he'd have to get her up the stairs without all the clatter that hooves could cause.

The dragons were at the big dining table having a hushed conversation with Princess Isadora; Ainsley's sisters didn't seem to be anywhere in sight.

*Excellent*, he thought before it all blew apart in seconds.

"And where the holy fuck have you been?"

Brother Gemma, Queen Keeley, and the royal centaurs appeared from a door at the back of the main hall. And while the other royals appeared subdued, Brother Gemma was clearly in a mood about something. And she was about to start taking it out on poor Ainsley.

"It's none of your business," Ainsley replied, stopping in her tracks. Gruff assumed she couldn't argue and keep walking due to the pain she was currently experiencing.

However, the monk marched right up to Ainsley and stood in front of her, inches from her younger sister's face.

"Really?" Brother Gemma snapped. "None of *my* business? That makes me think you were doing something."

"I *was* doing something."

"Leave her alone, Gemma," Queen Keeley ordered. "We have more important things to—"

"No. I want to know what our sister was *doing* that she can't tell us about."

"I didn't say I can't tell you," Ainsley practically snarled back. "I don't *want* to tell you. There's a difference."

"Now I *need* to know what you've been up to," the monk pushed.

"Gemma!" That actually came from Princess Laila, who seemed as frustrated as the queen. "We have no time for this."

"We'll make time." The monk gave a very unfriendly smile. "So . . . what were you up to, little sister?"

"You want to know?"

"Yes. I want to know."

Ainsley shrugged before announcing, "Gruff and I have been fucking for the last few days."

Now everyone in the room was looking at them. The centaur royals. Queen Keeley. The dragons. Princess Morfyd spit out some wine she'd just sipped, and the gold dragon got up from his chair, sat on the table and turned, legs comfortably folded, his elbows resting on his knees. He placed his chin on his raised fists and, grinning, avidly watched everything unfolding before him.

As for Gruff, he didn't know what to say or how to say it. What could he say? The woman had just tossed him in front of an out-of-control chariot. And she'd done it with no remorse. Couldn't she at least have given him a little warning?

Even worse . . . absolutely the *worst* thing about all of it? Hearing her say they were "fucking" had nearly turned him into a giant puddle at her feet. He had to think of several horrible things in succession just to stop his cock from rising to the occasion. Because there would be no hiding *that*.

"Wh . . . uh . . . what?" Gemma stuttered out.

"Yeah. We're fucking. We left town for a bit so your nosey, sycophantic monks wouldn't immediately report back to you what your younger sister was up to, but yes. We've been fucking. It was amazing. Is there anything else?"

"A few details wouldn't hurt! *Owww!* Morfyd!" the gold dragon whined after his sister reached across the table and yanked at his fancy gold locks. "Not the hair, demoness! Never the hair!"

Brother Gemma, however, didn't seem to have any words. None. For anyone. So, with another shrug, Ainsley again started for the stairs leading to the second floor and her room. She grabbed Gruff's hand since he didn't automatically move with her, and he let her take him away. Probably a good thing. The way Princess Laila's two idiot royal brothers—the dark-haired one and the light-haired one—were glowering at him, he knew it could only end badly if he simply stood around . . . glowering back.

Ainsley almost stumbled on the third step, so Gruff got right behind her and placed his hands on her hips to keep her moving up. He did it to assist her, but he knew how it must look to those watching from below.

In silence, they somehow made it to the second floor and down the hall to Ainsley's room. Once inside, she lunged for her bed and stretched out on her mattress. In obvious pain, she lifted her shirt and pressed both hands to her wound. Tears eased out from under her eyelids, and Gruff immediately dismissed the way she'd just made him even more of a target for the royal idiot brothers by lying about how close they were and rushed to her side.

He dug into his travel bag and pulled out the small sack holding the strip of material covered in one of Sarff's poultices.

Gruff dropped the bag at the side of the bed and took a few seconds to gently push Ainsley onto her side. He lifted her shirt just enough to get a good look at her wound, and it took a lot not to gasp in shock. He'd known the area would be bruised, but this was worse than he'd expected or ever really seen on anyone. He didn't know if the bone was actually fractured or if it just looked that bad because she'd been kicked by one of Kriegszorn's demon foals.

He trusted Sarff, though. She'd have known if the bones had been damaged and would have insisted on wrapping Ainsley's entire upper chest. Instead, she'd stated the poultice would not only help with the healing but also numb the pain for the next twenty-four hours so that Ainsley could get some much-needed sleep.

Carefully he unwrapped the poultice and laid it against Ainsley's side. She gritted her teeth and let out a very hard grunt, but she didn't stop him. He made sure the red, black, and purple bruise was covered completely before putting another piece of linen on top. He didn't want to tie it off, as Sarff had suggested, because he knew how much that would hurt the royal. So he simply told her, "Try to sleep on your side."

She nodded but didn't say anything else. Before he knew it, she was asleep. He started for the door to let her sleep in peace, but she suddenly rolled onto her back.

Returning to her bed, he gently pushed her back to her side and adjusted the poultice. He tried to leave again after that, but once more she started to roll onto her back.

Gruff moved Ainsley back to her side and stood there with one hand on her shoulder, holding her in place and wondering how he was going to stay like this for the next twenty-four hours.

\* \* \*

"She's lying."

"How do you know?" Keeley demanded when Gemma said those words. "And why do you care? Ainsley's not a child."

"We can kill him for you if you want," Quinn offered. "That's not a problem."

Keeley glared at her mate's brother. "Go away."

"You're going to let that low-level savage taint your sister like this?"

"*Enough!*" she snapped, and Laila pushed both her brothers away.

"She's lying," Gemma insisted again. "There's no reason for Quinn or anyone to hurt Gruffyn, because he's not fucking her."

"Why does it matter whether she was or was not fucking him?"

"Because if she wasn't off fucking Gruffyn—"

"Please stop saying that about your little sister!" Quinn begged.

"—she was up to something else. Something stupid. We need to find out what."

"Gemmaaaaa," Keeley whined as her sister marched away. She looked at Laila.

"She's really avoiding all this, isn't she?" Laila asked, glancing over at the table of dragons avidly watching the family drama unfold.

"She really is."

Laila nodded. "Come on. Before this turns into a big, unnecessary thing."

They rushed up the stairs after Gemma and had just reached her as she opened the door to Ainsley's room without even knocking.

But whatever Gemma was about to start yelling at her sister died on her lips when they found Ainsley and Gruffyn asleep on her bed. Not just asleep, though. Ainsley was on her side and the centaur was snuggled in tight, right behind her. They were both fully dressed, and there seemed to have been nothing untoward happening before they'd drifted off, but still . . .

Gruffyn had his hand resting on Ainsley's raised hip, and her hand was over his. It was a very intimate position to be in with anyone. Very loving and very protective. Even Gemma saw it, because she kept silent and didn't try to wake Ainsley up just so she could yell at her.

"Still think she's lying?" Keeley whispered.

They would never know whether Gemma had been about to reply, because the monk suddenly used her body to shove them all out of the room and swiftly slam the door closed.

In a small circle they all stood, eyes wide. For a long moment, they were too stunned to say anything until Keeley asked, "What the fuck was that?"

"I think that was her bird," Gemma said.

"Why was its head so big? I mean, that was a big head, right? I wasn't imagining that giant head?"

"I'm more disturbed that it could already fly," Laila noted. "Despite the size of its head and how small its wings were, and the fact that it's only a few days old, it still managed to fly across the room and threaten us . . . somehow."

"Told you she should have killed that bird," Keeley complained before pushing past her sister and heading for the stairs. "We're going to find that thing eating the children one day."

# CHAPTER 18

"Now that we've got all the big issues worked out, there's one last thing." Bram the Merciful—a name Keeley truly did appreciate in the one who would be writing the alliance they would have with Annwyl—looked around the table. "Which royals do we want to send—"

"I like Endolyn," Annwyl the Bloody announced with a warm smile.

That smile faded when everyone from Keeley's side screamed, "*No!*"

"It was just a suggestion," the foreign queen mumbled.

Keeley was confident her sister would be safe in Dark Plains, but that wasn't what she feared. She just didn't want her baby sister coming home one day in the future with the name Endolyn the Bloody as her moniker. Keeley only had a few short years to do her best to steer the youngest girl of the family onto the right path, and she wasn't going to risk another Beatrix.

Forcing a smile in the hope that Queen Annwyl wouldn't take their response personally, Keeley began, "How about—"

"I'll go."

Keeley was so surprised that she didn't even think about making a grab for Gemma, but Quinn did, lifting her monk sister off her feet and holding her while her legs kept moving as if she was running.

"I'll go," Isadora said again.

"But—"

"Who else are you going to send?" she asked, looking only at Keeley. Smart, since Gemma was still trying to fight her way out of Quinn's arms. "Duncan? *Ainsley?*" She snorted. "I think she's too busy fucking Gruff."

Prince Gwenvael laughed, and Gemma finally got Quinn to release her. Much to her credit, though, she didn't jump over the table to tackle Isadora to the ground. Keeley knew that was a lot for her.

"You're not going anywhere," Gemma told their sister.

"I am."

Gemma took a step forward to get into a really hearty argument, but Keeley raised her hand to keep her silent and asked Isadora, "Are you sure?"

Isadora studied her sisters for a moment before she admitted, "I love you all. But I have to get out of here."

At their sister's words, Gemma immediately calmed down. "What? Why?"

Isadora lifted her arms from her sides and immediately dropped them before announcing, "I don't want to be a farmer."

Gemma gasped at that.

"I don't want to be a blacksmith."

Now Keeley gasped. "How could you say such a thing?"

"Because it's true. I want to see the world, Keeley. Meet different people. Experience life. But what I don't want is to be a babysitter for the next twenty years. Mum and Da will just have to raise their children on their own."

Gemma nodded. "I understand how you feel."

"I don't!" Keeley snapped. "How could you not want to help raise our siblings? I love raising our siblings!"

"I *have* helped raise our siblings. And now I'm done. And you love it because you've always had a job. You've been working at Mum's forge since birth, and you only babysit when you're actually *home*. With the children. Even Duncan never babysits, because he's always dealing with the cattle and the pigs and making sure everything is harvested on time. I need to find my own path."

"I think if this is what Isadora wants, we should let her go."

Mouth open, Keeley faced Gemma. "Seriously?"

"What?"

"You practically put Ainsley in a headlock because you hadn't seen her in the last few hours—"

"She was gone for at least a *whole* day!"

"—but you're just ready to ship off our eighteen-year-old sister with fire-breathing dragons and their lunatic queen?"

Cringing a little, Keeley looked down the table at Annwyl. "No offense."

The foreign queen shrugged. "You're not wrong."

"The reason Gemma is so hysterical about Ainsley—" Isadora began.

"I am *not* hysterical about Ainsley!"

"—is because she helped raise her, but she didn't help raise me. She went off to monk-land before she had a real chance—"

"I did not go to *monk*-land. There is no such place as monk-land!"

"—to get to know me as a child. And those first few years I was always strapped to Mum in the forge. But Gemma simply refuses to see Ainsley as anything but the child she left behind."

"I didn't leave you lot behind."

"Actually," Keeley reminded her, "you did."

"It's probably her guilt about deserting the family," Isadora whispered . . . loudly.

"It *is* her guilt. You're right!"

"She is *not* right." Gemma pointed at Isadora. "And where are you going?"

"To get packed."

"You know," Queen Annwyl said, also motioning to Isadora, "I find this one a little bossy. Are you *sure* I can't get Endolyn?"

"*No!*" Keeley and her sisters screamed simultaneously.

"Is it me you're worried about? Or Endolyn?"

"Honestly?" Keeley asked the foreign royal. "It's both."

Annwyl nodded. "That is completely fair."

Bram watched the young royal start to head toward the stairs until Princess Laila called Princess Isadora back and told Bram, "I think you're forgetting something."

It was possible. Bram forgot lots of things, because he had so much on his mind. Drove his mate crazy because she remembered *everything*. But there were so many more interesting and important things to keep track of than where he may have moved her armor or how he may have misplaced her favorite sword. Again.

"Forgetting something?"

"It's an exchange?" the centaur princess pushed. "Remember?"

"Oh! Yes. Of course. I'm sorry."

He looked at Annwyl, and Princess Laila suggested to her, "Perhaps one of *your* precious children, Queen Annwyl?"

There was a pause before Annwyl, Bram's niece and nephews, and even Unnvar—infamous for his lack of humor—exploded into laughter.

Bram raised a finger, attempting to quickly explain what Queen Annwyl's laughter actually meant, but she managed to do it first.

"Sorry, sorry," Annwyl said, working hard to control her mirth. "It's just . . . trust me when I say you do *not* want my children here. Ever. I mean . . . they might visit. And," she added, shaking her finger, "you will definitely want them in any battles you may have in the future. But just living here with you . . . either one of them . . . I'd strongly suggest no. And gods! Not both together. For your own good."

Straightening her back a bit with her brows furrowed, Princess Laila slowly replied, "Alllllll right, then."

"What about Rhian?" Annwyl suggested to her mate and his siblings.

Briec stood up from what Bram had started to call the dragon's banishment chair and told the Queen of Dark Plains, "You are *not* sending *my* perfect and precious daughter to live in this hellhole amongst these barbarians."

"Now you know why we put you in that chair," Morfyd said to her brother before telling Queen Keeley, "And I love my beautiful niece to death, but she can be . . . moody."

"All my siblings are moody," Keeley commented.

"Can they open up the ground we're standing on so it swallows this tower and all the people within?"

"Uh . . . no."

"Exactly."

"The boy will stay."

It took a second to grasp what Gwenvael was saying to every-one in the room. But Bram figured it out around the same time as Var did.

*"You vindictive motherfuc—"*

"I don't know," Bram quickly cut in so that his great nephew didn't finish that insult, "if you've thought this through, Gwen-vael."

"Oh, I have. And it's perfect. And the boy would love to do it!"

"No, I would *not!*"

Morfyd leaned in and desperately warned her brother, "Dagmar will eat your soul."

Gwenvael sat up in his chair. "Look, it's like our dear Ainsley said—"

"I'm Isadora."

"No one cares, dear," Gwenvael replied without even looking at the poor girl. "As I was saying, like Queen Keeley's older sister Isadora said about herself—"

"I'm younger."

"—it's time for my son to see the world. To see what else is out there. To find out what his true path is."

"I know what my true path is. It's to work with Uncle Bram."

"Which you will still do, because I'm sure Bram will be coming and going from this region for a very long time. And you'll be here to work with him while we have dear, sweet Endolyn safe at home in Dark Plains."

"Again . . . I'm Isadora, and I'm not the oldest."

"And again, dear, no one cares."

"My mother will never let this happen."

Gemma watched the gold dragon briefly look around the room before telling his son, "Huh. I don't see her here."

"You can't order me around, Father. You can't tell me what to do. I'm an adult."

"An adult that's been assigned to *my* legion. I'm your com-manding officer. You, *boy*, wear the crest of Queen Rhiannon. You fight in her army. And that means you report to *me*. And your or-ders are that you're to stay here and be a—"

"Hostage?"

"A goodwill ambassador! What excellent training for you! Just like your Uncle Bram."

Unnvar slammed his hands down on the wooden table, muscles bulging under his chainmail shirt as he leaned toward the dragon that had fathered him. Gray eyes glaring, the young prince growled out, "One day, when you least expect it, I will have my revenge, and you . . . you will know true suffering."

The gold dragon gave a warm smile. "I love you, too, Son."

The roar the young man let out rattled the windows . . . and the building. Not making Gemma feel any better about having Unnvar Reinholdt stay with her family, but she knew he was probably their best option. The dragons only seemed concerned about Unnvar's mother. Who, as Gwenvael had pointed out, was not in their territories. Whereas, when it came to Annwyl's offspring, everyone seemed concerned about . . . well . . . Annwyl's offspring.

No. In the end, Gwenvael's son was their best and safest option. Even if he did absolutely detest the idea.

Whether she liked it or not. And, quite honestly, Gemma didn't like it. She didn't like any of it.

Unnvar stormed out of the hall through the front doors, and Bram stood. "I'll talk to him."

"Do whatever you want," the gold dragon told his uncle. "But the boy is staying."

"Of course." Bram turned away to follow his great-nephew, but he stopped long enough to add, "You, however, will be the one to tell your mate."

"I can handle Dagmar Reinholdt," the gold dragon said with a smug snort. "She adores me."

His siblings stared blankly at him until Queen Annwyl asked in disbelief, "Are you fucking serious?"

That's when all of Gwenvael the Handsome's siblings burst out laughing . . . and they couldn't seem to stop.

# CHAPTER 19

Ainsley woke up when the light of the morning suns streamed through her window and hit her bed, and she immediately noticed two things: her wounded side no longer throbbed in endless, unbearable pain; and someone's arms were wrapped around her.

Easing her eyes open, she quickly recognized the tattoo on Gruff's shoulder and relaxed. She'd slept so hard that upon wakening, she wasn't sure where she was or how she'd gotten there.

No matter how comfortable she felt with her nose buried in Gruff's chest, she needed to get up and face the day. She didn't mind, though. The fact that the pain was gone made getting up kind of enjoyable. The only problem . . . ? Gruff didn't seem to be in the mood to let her go.

In fact, the more she tried to pull away, the tighter his arms wrapped around her.

She should have felt smothered, but she didn't. She actually felt very cozy and safe. It also didn't help that Gruff growled when he slept. Not in an angry way, but a low growl that came from the back of his throat and sort of rolled across her skin. Kind of like the way the old barn cat purred when she had him on her lap. This, however, was definitely not a purr. It was a growl. A very comforting growl.

Realizing her thoughts were ridiculous, Ainsley tried again to get away from Gruff, but his arms tightened a little bit more, and she simply gave up the fight. She was just too gods-damn comfortable! So comfortable she almost fell back asleep. But just as she started to slip away, the bedroom door flew open.

Ainsley immediately heard her mother's voice, so she wasn't worried, but before she had a chance to ask her what was wrong or tell her to calm down, Gruff quickly rolled across the bed to the other side with Ainsley still held against him. When he dropped his feet to the floor and stood, he held her high up against his body with one hand, while holding his axe in the other.

Reaching over, she grabbed the hand holding the weapon. The last thing Ainsley needed was for Gruff to throw that axe and take off her mother's head.

She knew when he grunted and his grip on her hip relaxed that he finally understood they weren't in danger of anything but witnessing the rare sight of Emma Smythe, mother of ten thousand children or so, being hysterical.

"You need to come quick!" her mother was babbling. "Right now!"

"Mum," Ainsley said, keeping her voice steady, "just calm down and tell me what's wrong."

"Your sister is planning to leave our home with that woman!"

At the moment, there was only one "that woman" in her mother's life—Queen Annwyl. It didn't make sense, though. As someone who became dangerously unstable at even the mention of the word "slavery," the Mad Queen seemed unlikely to drag anyone anywhere in chains.

But trying to tell her mother that would only set her off, so Ainsley went a different route.

"There's nothing to worry about, Mum. Gemma won't let Keeley run off with Annwyl. And if Gemma's the one leaving . . ." Ainsley shrugged. "Okay."

"Stop it! You love your sister!"

"Okay." She wasn't in the mood to argue the point.

"And I'm not talking about Keeley or Gemma. It's Isadora. You need to talk to her."

"Talk to Annwyl?"

"No. You need to talk to Isadora."

"I thought she was busy being dragged off in chains."

Her mother glared at her. "Why do you have to be so difficult?"

"Not being difficult. Trying to understand what the hells you're talking about."

"Your baby sister. She's leaving."

"In chains?"

"Forget the chains!"

"You brought them up!"

"Forget them. Just go talk to your sister and tell her she can't leave . . . no. Wait. Don't talk to your sister."

"Okay."

"Talk to your sisters."

Gruff let out a long sigh, and Ainsley had to fight hard not to laugh. Few people saw this side of Emma Smythe, and it was not easy for the uninitiated to tolerate the full insanity of it all.

Ainsley, however, almost enjoyed it. Her mother never acted like this when actual murderous threats were coming their way.

"My sisters?"

"Yes."

"Which ones?"

"Keeley and Gemma, of course!"

"Not Endolyn?"

"Stop that! Just go talk to them!"

"Why do I need to talk to Gemma and Keeley?"

"I think they're the ones making her go. They're not giving her a choice. They're just shoving my baby out the door!"

"Mum, you need to make up your mind. Is Isadora being forced to go—in chains—"

"Forget the chains!"

"—or does she *want* to go?"

"They're using her as a hostage, Ainsley!" her mother cried, tears now streaming down her face. "My baby . . . dragged off in chains . . . to that horrible place!"

"I thought you said to forget the chains."

"Dammit, Ainsley!"

Ainsley finally let out a sigh. Her mother wasn't making any sense. It would be better to talk to Isadora on her own to find out what was going on.

Ainsley patted Gruff on the shoulder, gesturing for him to let her down. He pulled one arm away, but she was still a few feet away from the ground. She briefly thought he had his other arm around her—and didn't want to let her go—but then she saw the axe in his other hand.

He was no longer holding her.

That's when she became aware that she was wrapped around the centaur's human body like a snake. A big, ridiculous snake.

Unable to meet his gaze, she released her grip on him and dropped to the ground. Ainsley immediately felt the loss of his heat against her body, but she didn't mention that. It was more embarrassment than she could possibly handle.

"I'll go talk to Isadora," she promised her mother.

"Are you sure you shouldn't talk to Keeley and Gemma first?"

"Yes. I'm sure. Keeley will only dismiss me, and Gemma and I will fight. I'm not in the mood to fight."

Ainsley walked around the bed, but her mother stopped her before she reached the door.

"Is that a new headboard?" she asked, pointing.

Ainsley looked at her bed and wondered why she hadn't noticed the change before.

"That is my bird," she announced. And it *was* her bird. It had grown a lot since she'd briefly left home. The body was still small, but it was already bigger than that of most birds. Its head, however, was enormous. It was a very big head with a gargantuan beak attached. Long and wide, the beak appeared terrifying because it was so thick and hard, with a bent spike at the very end of the upper mandible that closed perfectly over the lower mandible. It was like something from one's nightmares, and yet . . . Ainsley found the damn thing kind of adorable.

"Herbert," Ainsley said.

"What?"

"That's his name. Herbert." She leaned in the bird's direction. "Are you my sweet Herbert?" she cooed.

Herbert stretched out his barely there wings, tipped his giant head back, opened his ridiculously sized beak . . . then closed it again. Six or seven times, in rapid succession, which made a loud, staccato call because of the way the top and bottom mandibles clapped together.

When the noise stopped, Ainsley, her mother, and even Gruff simply stood there. Staring at the bird. They'd all heard the call before, at night, coming from the swamps. But they'd never seen it actually made or understood how disturbing it might be to witness in person.

Deciding not to think about how much bigger this bird would grow or worry about whether it would continue to sit on her headboard when it was giant, Ainsley simply walked from the room and went in search of Isadora.

Gruff couldn't believe Ainsley had just left him and her mother alone with this freakish bird, but he felt he had to get her mother out alive.

He grunted at the Queen Mother, afraid to actually speak words around the bird, and gestured toward the door. With her gaze locked on it, the royal moved slowly across the room. With slow, seconds-long blinks, the bird's massive head turned as it watched the woman back away.

With the axe still in his hand, Gruff also backed his way toward the door. Once the Queen Mother was in the hall, the thing slowly turned its head and its yellow eyes locked on him. It watched him but made no sound and, thankfully, made no moves. Gruff didn't know if it was the axe that warned it off or if it just wasn't in the mood to be aggressive.

Slowly, moving inch by precious inch, the axe held in front of him in case the creature suddenly dove for his face, Gruff made his way to the exit. Once in the hall, he—again slowly—leaned in to grab the knob and close the door.

Once the thing was secured in the room, both Gruff and the Queen Mother let out long, relieved sighs, and rested their backs against the wall.

"She named that thing . . . Herbert?" the stunned woman asked, turning her head to look at him. "*Herbert?*"

"Are you going to keep whining?" Isadora asked.

She pulled her travel bag out from under her bed and found one of Keeley's demon wolf puppies singeing the inside of it with those damn eyes of flame.

"Come here, you," she murmured, not even sure how it had gotten into the bag ... or into her room. Now that the pups were older, they were everywhere in the tower. In things. Under things. Setting little fires when their eyes brushed against paper or dry wood.

She lifted the puppy up and held it out. "Want to hold it?"

"No. I do not want to hold it. And just admit you've ruined my life."

"I did not ruin your life. Your own *father* ruined your life. Take this up with him."

The golden man-dragon sat up and explained, "That would require talking to him. I don't want to talk to him."

"Then I can't help you." She dropped the puppy onto Unnvar's lap so she didn't have to hold it anymore. Unlike her sisters, she could take or leave canines. They really did nothing for her one way or the other, but she appreciated that they were a good source of protection. If she could train bears to protect her family and not maul them, she would, because they were bigger and meaner and her family could use that kind of security even more, but that didn't mean she thought bears were any better than dogs or barn cats or horses. Animals only mattered to Isadora if they were useful to her. Unlike her sisters, she didn't need to have an animal sleep with her in bed. She especially didn't plan to take that love of animals to the very strange conclusion of involving herself with a being that was half man and half ... whatever, as Gemma and Keeley had.

Not that she begrudged her sisters the love they'd found. It was something Keeley deserved, and probably what Gemma deserved as well. Although Isadora didn't know Gemma that well. She'd been away from their family for years, devoting her life to war gods. Since she'd been back, she seemed to care only about keeping Keeley safe, killing Beatrix, and making Ainsley's life an absolute nightmare of annoyance.

Isadora didn't know how Ainsley put up with any of it. Then again, she'd never learned to climb trees as her sister had, which had given Ainsley a much-needed respite from all the family noise.

So much family noise.

"Why does your sister have dogs with flames for eyes?" the foreign royal asked.

"She likes all animals. That's the best I can explain. But if you need more information, you can ask her yourself while you stay here."

Shoving the puppy toward her, he warned, "You will not replace me."

"No one is trying to replace you. Except maybe your father. Come!" Isadora called out when she heard the knock at her bedroom door.

"You busy?" Ainsley asked, eyeing Unnvar sitting comfortably on Isadora's bed. The pair had become somewhat friendly while Isadora had worked with him and his great-uncle Bram when she was assisting Queen Annwyl and the royal dragons.

Yet Isadora didn't think Unnvar was comfortable with her because they'd worked together. Rather, she strongly believed he could sit or stretch out anywhere he liked because he was Unnvar Reinholdt, Firstborn son of Dagmar Reinholdt, prince royal of the House of Gwalchmai fab Gwyar, and his mother's absolute favorite.

She knew this particular title because that's how he introduced himself to absolutely everyone. Even the mason dwarves, who could not care less.

"No. I'm not busy. And Unnvar is leaving. Aren't you, Unnvar?"

"You can just call me Var, and this isn't over." He stood up and held the puppy out to her.

"What do you want me to do with that?"

"Well, it's not mine."

"It's more yours right now than it's mine. Because I'm leaving and you aren't. So start getting used to all of Keeley's pets."

He growled at her, and black smoke snaked from his nostrils. Disturbing, but Isadora assumed she would have to get used to it if she was going to live with dragons now.

The royal stomped out, slamming the door behind him.

"Was that . . . smoke?" Ainsley asked.

"Let's not discuss. I don't want to start obsessing over what I can't control."

Her sister walked around the bed and sat down in the spot Var had just abandoned.

"Mum's hysterical," she said.

Isadora always appreciated how Ainsley just got to it. She didn't hesitate or stumble or delay. She simply said what she meant.

"I'm sure she is."

"Are you doing this because you want to or because you think you're protecting Keeley?"

"I protected Keeley by managing the needs and wants of giant fire-breathing dragons, which kept *them* from eating her subjects. I've done my job. Besides, she has Gemma. She has you. How did it go, anyway?"

"How did what go?"

"While Da and I lie to Keeley and Gemma as much as we deem necessary, we don't lie to each other. And we only occasionally lie to Mum. I know where you've been. I thought you'd be gone longer."

"Commander Beaton wasn't where the spy said he was. He was actually right here . . . Beatrix sent him to snatch one of the brats."

Shocked, Isadora sat back on her heels. "That cunt."

"I know."

"I hope Gemma does kill her one day."

"We can dream."

"Give her time. Our monk sister is cranky but patient." Isadora opened her travel bag and was glad to see that the demon puppy's eyes had only done minor burn damage to the inside. "And I'm leaving because I don't know how to climb trees."

"I'll miss you."

"I'm not dying, Ains."

"No, but you *are* going halfway around the world."

"I'm almost positive Annwyl's queendom is not halfway around the world. More like a few thousand leagues."

"It's over the Amichai Mountains. After that . . . there's nothing. Just empty darkness and death."

"Completely incorrect, but it doesn't matter, and stop looking at me like I'm abandoning you the way Gemma did."

"Have you joined a cult that worships gods that haven't really helped anyone ever?"

"No."

"Then you haven't abandoned me."

Isadora straightened and then sat beside Ainsley on the bed.

"Look," she began, "I'm not just going off to live with dragons and a mad queen because I'm bored and tired of Endolyn hitting me with her hammer."

"I don't know why Keeley gave her that fucking thing."

"I'm going there to learn whatever I can to help Keeley and Gemma."

"What do you think you can learn?" Ainsley questioned. "Wait . . . can they teach you to breathe fire?"

Isadora put her hand on Ainsley's shoulder. "Sometimes you make me sad. No, they can't teach me to breathe fire. But what you and Gemma and Mum, for that matter, don't realize is that Annwyl the Bloody, the Mad Queen of Garbhán Isle, rules an empire. And she has for a very long time. And although the myth about her is that she's a destructive murderer roaming the countryside killing women and eating babies, we both know that's not her. Instead, she's found a way to . . ."

"Create her own dynasty."

"A dynasty with dragons, but still. I want that for us. For the Smythe-Farmerson clan. To have our own dynasty."

"Because you're hungry for power?"

"Because the only way we can ensure our survival is to wipe Beatrix and her armies from this world. If we don't, she'll never stop coming for us."

Ainsley nodded in silent agreement. Isadora knew better than any of them how dangerous their older sister would always be to everyone, but especially their family. Since Isadora had learned to crawl, she'd known that Beatrix hated them. Their father. Their mother. All their siblings. She even hated Keeley, who did nothing but happily protect her.

"But, Ains, I need you to do something too while I'm getting all that valuable knowledge."

"And what's that?"

"I need you to keep working with Prince Unnvar."

"Working with him? I'm not working with him."

"You just worked with the man . . . dragon . . . person. Whatever he is. He told you about Beaton—"

"Incorrect information."

"—and you and your centaur friends drew them away—"

"Not on purpose."

"—and wiped them out."

"We did do that."

"Work with him. He has access to information we don't have."

"But it was incorrect information."

"Only partially. Beaton's destination was wrong. But he was someone who needed to go. Someone close to Beatrix. She's surrounded herself with powerful sycophants who will do anything for her. You need to get rid of as many of them as possible."

Ainsley stared at Isadora, and Isadora stared back until Ainsley finally asked, "Are you suggesting I should go across the countryside looking for Beatrix's closest allies and then murdering them?"

Isadora shrugged. "Yes."

"You don't think that's a strange thing to ask your sister to do?"

"No."

Frowning, Ainsley asked, "Should I be worried about you?"

"Are you asking me if I'm like Beatrix?"

"Sort of."

"Well . . . I haven't once tried to drown Endolyn, and she keeps hitting me with a hammer."

"Beatrix *so* would have tried to drown her by now."

"All I'm trying to do," Isadora assured her sister, "is slow Beatrix down until *we* are ready."

Ainsley slid her arm around Isadora's shoulders and pulled her in until their foreheads touched. "I'll take care of it. You just keep yourself safe."

She had to give a little chuckle at that request. "Oh, Sister, that I *always* do."

# CHAPTER 20

There were few in this world who dared ask Beatrix to go anywhere. They always came to her. No matter their station in life. No matter who they thought they were or how close to the Old King they once claimed to be, everyone came to Beatrix. But Ivan was different. He never feared requesting her presence. He never demanded, but she did wonder if he might someday. He treated everyone else in the world as pests. A simple cleric who was now the right-hand of a queen could definitely become full of himself, but from what Beatrix had heard, Ivan had always been like this, from his days as a cleric to a monk to an angry priest. He no longer had an official title. No religious order would willingly claim him. And yet power came off him in waves. Beatrix could practically smell it.

Without knocking, Beatrix entered Ivan's chamber and walked in just in time to see his new assistant, Maisie, dragging a body across the floor. When Beatrix entered, she stopped, dark eyes wide.

"Uhhhh . . ."

"Is that one of my soldiers?" Beatrix couldn't say she knew *all* her soldiers. She had so many, and there were many in the lower ranks she had never met. But she easily recognized the uniform.

"It is. I needed to test out one of my . . ." She blinked. "Tonics."

Beatrix glanced at the body again. "Success or failure?"

"Failure."

"But he's dead."

"Yes. But I have many . . . tonics . . . that cause death. Mostly quiet, sudden deaths. I was looking for a more painful, bloody, agonizing death."

"For?"

That horrid face hardened. "Sometimes, Your Majesty, one needs to make a point."

Beatrix nodded, agreeing completely. "Where is your master?"

Maisie frowned, and Beatrix realized the title bothered her, but she didn't complain. Although it was clear that was what she really wanted to do.

"He's in his altar room, Your Majesty. Would you like me to—"

"I know the way."

Beatrix walked to the back of the room, lifting her dress a bit so she could easily step over the soldier's body. She went up the stairs and opened the wooden door, going into the room.

"My Queen," Ivan greeted her as he came out of the darkness. The space was mostly dark except for the altar Ivan had built in the middle of the room. It was a good-sized thing made of black marble that caused others to scream when they first saw it. But not Beatrix. All she saw was a slab of rock, dried blood, and some gold tools that Ivan used for his rituals.

It wasn't Ivan and his black altar that had her attention this morning. It was the dark space about twenty feet from her that seemed filled with slithering, moving things.

When Ivan noticed her focus, he said, "My Queen, I'd like to introduce you to my chosen god."

Something in that slithering, skittering dark space adjusted itself and a voice in her head said, "Hello, sweet Beatrix. I am Athanagild."

Morfyd went in search of Annwyl the Bloody. The queen had gone off on her own at least an hour before and her guards had no idea where she was. Normally, Morfyd would be annoyed by that, but she knew her sister-by-mating. Knew her, some days, better than she knew herself. And Annwyl tended to just wander away. Not to taunt or tease her mate or put everyone in a panic but because she just wasn't thinking. At least she wasn't thinking about that. She wasn't thinking that, as the Queen of Dark Plains, she was in more danger than anyone around her. No, Annwyl was thinking about bigger, loftier things. Like how to rule and who she could trust and how she could, one day, hand off a sturdy, powerful queendom to her offspring.

But it was a pain in the ass when she disappeared. The guards watching her right now were not her usual human soldiers, hand-picked by Annwyl and Morfyd's human mate Brastias, Commander General of Annwyl's army.

Those men knew their queen so well, they could inform Morfyd, at any time of day or night, where Annwyl was and when she would be back. Not because Annwyl told them anything but because they just seemed to know. They understood her thoroughly and had made her protection their lives. Because, unlike most royals, Annwyl was as loyal to her soldiers as they were to her. She not only knew every man or woman's name but also knew their families, where they lived when they weren't working, who their parents were, and how much gold or silver they earned. She also made sure that her army leaders made her soldiers' families their top priority. She didn't want any of them suffering because their fathers or mothers were off fighting for her.

The only flaw with Annwyl's personal guards was that they were human and wingless, which meant it was the Cadwaladrs who currently protected Annwyl in these foreign lands they'd flown into. Not a problem, really. Morfyd's kin had come to love Annwyl as if she'd been born into the clan. But knowing all her moods and wanderings wasn't really of interest to members of a war clan. So if she hadn't been dragged out kicking and screaming when she disappeared, all Morfyd received from her kin about Annwyl's current location were shrugs.

Frustrated after nearly half an hour of searching, Morfyd stopped in the middle of the busy market stalls, closed her eyes, lifted her nose, and sniffed. She sniffed the air around her, mentally identifying each smell. She soon located all her brothers, Queen Keeley, Queen Keeley's fanatic sister, and their forge-loving mother. It took nothing to find the queen's father, as well, since he seemed to be working with the pigs and cows in their pens.

But then, just as she was about to give up—she might love bacon but the smell of pigs in their pens were more than she could tolerate on a good day—Morfyd caught a whiff of Annwyl's scent. She moved forward, stopping briefly when she literally crashed into the brother and sister centaurs that followed one of the younger royals around.

"Sorry, luv," the female offered, moving around Morfyd and continuing on. The male merely grunted, barely glancing at her, and followed his sister.

"Barbarians," she muttered to herself before tracking Annwyl's scent again and going after her.

Finding Annwyl talking to herself in the middle of the woods wasn't unusual. Sadly, the human royal had become known as the Mad Queen for a reason, and her habit of having long conversations with those no one else could see was a big part of it.

So finding Annwyl talking out loud in the middle of the woods . . . not strange. Finding Annwyl talking to Morfyd's *mother* . . . that was just infuriating!

"*Mum?*"

The ruling Dragon Queen of all the territories between the Amichai Mountains and the coast of the Seas of Agony and Sorrow smiled at her eldest daughter. "Hello, my sweet Morfyd. It brings me such great joy to see you well and—"

"Stuff the horse shit, Mum. What are you doing here?"

Ivan watched with avid curiosity as the two most important beings in his life met for the first time. Athanagild had been his guide since he'd found himself trapped in a monastery with boring old monks. They were more than happy to live their lives just as they were. The same boring routines, day after day. The same calls to their god, night after night. They weren't war monks, like the queen's loathed sister. They were simply monks, but among them, they had vast knowledge and magicks at their fingertips. Yet they did nothing with any of it but, according to their Abbot, "Keep the balance amongst those who exist in our world."

A decidedly noble but terribly boring way to function.

Ivan had felt so trapped, so miserable. He thought he'd never get out. Then Athanagild had come to him. Had offered Ivan a way out and into something much more interesting.

Of course, like any god, Athanagild had demanded a sacrifice.

Most of his brethren would have offered something of themselves. There were brothers who walked around the halls of the monastery missing an eye, part of an ear, perhaps some fingers. Ivan, however, wasn't sure if he'd need those things later in life. Why harm himself? It seemed to him that he should remain as fit as possible?

So he'd given his god the most important thing he could think of . . . the Abbot. And the other brothers. He was in charge of the dinner wine one night and simply slipped in some herbs to put most of the Order to sleep. Once they were snoring away, he'd disemboweled each and every one of them. The only one he didn't drug was the Abbot. Ivan had decided he should be alive and awake for everything. When he couldn't stop Ivan, he ran. But there was nowhere to go. Their mountain fortress stood alone in the snowy wasteland surrounding them. Ivan only had to follow the Abbot's footsteps until he tracked his mentor down. After a brief struggle, he stripped the man naked, tied him to a large, barren tree, and took his time removing the Abbot's skin.

When he was done, the Abbot still wasn't dead, which was perfect. It allowed Ivan to take the man's life in honor of Athanagild.

The ritual complete, Ivan took the skinless body back to the monastery and burned everything to the ground. He then made his way back to civilization in nothing but his fur boots and cowl, a nearly empty travel bag strung across his shoulders.

He was alone in the winter wilderness for weeks, but he survived. Not because he was so skilled in finding animals to kill or finding homes where there was food. He only survived because Athanagild allowed him to live. The god protected him all the way until he found a town. When Ivan walked through the gate of that town, he heard jingling in the bottom of his travel bag. It was a few coins that allowed him to buy new clothes and some food at a pub. When the proprietor asked him who he was, Ivan replied, "I am Ivan . . . the mystic."

He'd shed his mantle of pious monk and suffering for his god. Athanagild had made him suffer enough, but only to learn the level of his devotion. And, after twenty years of loyalty, the god had delivered Ivan a royal he could respect and stand behind with pride.

He'd delivered Queen Beatrix. And she'd proven herself to be absolutely horrifying. She cared about no one. Feared no one. Was able to control men three times her size without raising a sword or hiding behind her personal guard.

Her only weakness was her family, but she recognized that. Hated that. And was doing everything she could to destroy them.

Ivan admired such determination. Such viciousness. Not because he was inherently cruel. He wasn't. But he loved the unpredictability of Her Majesty. No one knew what she was going to do or when she was going to do it. Not even the gods.

"I'm so happy to meet you, Beatrix," Athanagild said when Her Majesty did not reply to his first greeting.

"It's Queen Beatrix," she said, boldly correcting him.

The easiest thing in the world was to earn a god's wrath. And yet the queen barreled on with no concern.

Ivan adored her for that.

"Is this why you summoned me here, Ivan?" she asked, not even peering into the dark space where the god dwelled. Not out of fear. She didn't fear looking into the abyss. She just didn't feel like it. "To talk to one of your gods? I have much work to do, and you waste my time with—"

"I can offer you power, *Queen* Beatrix," Athanagild interrupted.

Her Majesty rolled her eyes and finally focused on the area where the god crawled and pulsated. "Do you really think you're the only god that has made that offer to me?" And she sounded so deliciously bored by the entire discussion. "The only one that has come to me in the dark of night or in the suns' bright morning and made a case for why I should choose one or the other? Do you really think that this is the first time I've talked to a god? The first time one of you has promised me things? 'We can make you beautiful,' they say, which is just insulting. I already know what I look like. I don't need a reminder." She began to pace in front of that squirming darkness, talking to the god like a tradesman attempting to hawk his wares. "Or they promise, 'I can give you power.' Or my personal favorite, 'I can destroy your family for you.' As if I'd want that blood on anyone else's hands but my own. 'And all you have to do,' they tell me, 'is make the world worship me.'"

She stopped pacing and faced the darkness. "But I already have power, and I expect to get much more. And not being beautiful means it's easier to get men to listen to my words rather than obsessing over sticking their cocks in my cunt. And I've already explained what my family means to me . . . so what could you possibly bring to the table that would make me bother with you? Because, honestly, if I want the world to worship anyone . . . it's me."

With a smirk, Queen Beatrix turned away from that dark space and started toward the door. That's when Athanagild casually called out, "The Dragon Queen is at your sister's tower."

Queen Beatrix froze. "You mean the Mad Queen of Garbhán Isle."

"No. I do not. I mean Queen Rhiannon of the Dark Plains dragons. If it's war you want with those lands . . . it's *she* you need to kill."

Her Majesty slowly turned around again. "King Marius sent a battalion to the tower, and the dragons there—"

"One dragon."

"What?"

"There were many dragons there. But only one dragon wiped out your precious battalion. With fire."

"And you want me to take on the Dragon *Queen*?"

"Dragons have their own gods. And they are strongly protected by them. I can't touch her, but your people can. You just need to understand her weaknesses."

"Excuse me, my god," Ivan softly interjected, "but Queen Rhiannon is not only the Dragon Queen . . . she's a dragonwitch. She can come and go from far distant lands without much thought or effort. By the time our people reach—"

"Do not worry so about that, Ivan. As for you, my dear, sweet Beatrix . . . *Queen* Beatrix, you see what I can provide you, yes?"

"Information."

"The Dragon Queen has just arrived. By the time you would have received the information from anyone else, she'd have been long gone. You see," the god said, the slithering and skittering sounds growing louder as he inched closer to the edge of darkness, "I am not a god that has to play by anyone's rules. For I am a demon god of hell and my currency is information that only I can provide."

"And what do you want for this information? You want all to worship you? To fall before you in supplication?"

Athanagild released a low chuckle. "No, my dear Beatrix, I don't need worship. I don't need supplication."

Finally, Athanagild leaned out of the darkness, and while even Ivan had to look away from the horror, Beatrix did not. She kept her gaze right on the demon god before her.

"What I want from you, dear Beatrix, is one thing. Souls. Send me souls, and I'll help you get anything you want. But first . . . we start with that dragon bitch queen."

"I don't appreciate your tone," Rhiannon told her eldest daughter.

"Well, you will appreciate it even less when I tell you that it's completely unacceptable that you're here!"

"Don't yell at me! I'm still your mother!"

"That was not my choice!"

Trying a different approach, Rhiannon said, "Is it so wrong that I wanted to come here and have a chat with my fellow queen and daughter-by-mating. You know how much our dear Annwyl means to me."

Morfyd and Annwyl looked at each other and laughed. Which Rhiannon didn't appreciate.

"You are such a liar," Annwyl said before picking up one of her swords and taking a few swings.

"Tell me," Morfyd implored, "that you at least flew here."

"Why would I do that?" When it was so easy to create a mystical doorway and walk through, why would Rhiannon waste her precious time and energy *flying* thousands of leagues away from the safety of her home?

"Because when you open mystical doorways, it drains the world of energy. Things die."

"Nothing important."

"Mum!"

"Do the humans ever appreciate how well you protect them?"

"I appreciate it," Annwyl said, now practicing her daily sword drills, her sleeveless chainmail shirt tossed to the ground so that she only fought in her leather leggings, boots, and breast bindings.

"No one asked you, dear," Rhiannon snapped.

"Why are you here, Mum? Really."

"I wanted to know what was going on."

"Why didn't you just contact me?" Any dragon could contact blood relations from thousands of miles away, with no more than a thought simply by opening their mind.

"Because I knew you wouldn't tell me everything. And Annwyl is always so forthcoming."

"Mum, you are a dragon witch."

"I am. And I'm superb."

"Which means you can contact nearly anyone, anywhere, whenever you want from the safety of your throne. You didn't need to come here. But you did."

"Of course you can, dear. But neither of us care." Rhiannon smiled at her daughter. "I came here to ensure, with my own eyes, all was well with my family."

"Unnvar."

"Pardon?"

"You came here to make sure everything was well with *Unnvar*. He contacted you and told you what was happening. Now you want to come here and rescue him. But he doesn't need you to rescue him, and he doesn't need you babying him." Morfyd shook her head. "I can't believe it, but Gwenvael was right . . . for once. That boy does need to get away from all his mother*s*."

"What are you saying?"

"You spoil him."

"I do not!"

"You spoil him like you used to spoil Gwenvael. The only difference is, Unnvar is not Gwenvael. He's not trying to crawl back into his egg. Nor is he trying to fuck every female within a three-thousand-league radius. Var is smart, mean, and dangerous. Just like his mother. And he needs to find out what he can do on his own. So go home before he sees you."

"You just want the boy to be your spy here! Among these barbarians!" Rhiannon shook her head. Shocked at the mere thought. "How could you? Your own nephew and you use him like that?"

"What are you talking about? You made Gwenvael and Keita part of a network of your personal spies. You put your own *children* in danger!" Morfyd looked her up and down. "How do you live with yourself, Mother?"

Rhiannon shrugged and answered very honestly. "Quite easily. I find myself delightful . . . and extremely helpful!"

"But you're not, Mum. You're not delightful and helpful. You're dangerous and selfish."

"And I'm the mother who loves you." She paused a moment before adding, "Not as much as I love my baby Éibhear, but all mothers have a favorite."

"No, they don't. And if they do, *they don't tell anyone!*"

"I never tell Talwyn that her twin brother is my favorite," Annwyl announced, moving past them while continuing to do her drills. "Until she tells me that she loves her father more than me, and then I tell her I love everyone more than her. Even my enemies." She stopped, sword lifted above her head with both hands, each muscle in her body bulging. "Then she calls me a horrible mother. I call her my ungrateful bitch daughter who nearly killed me. And then we have a fistfight."

Her statement made, Annwyl moved off, continuing her drills. Morfyd looked at Rhiannon, lips pursed, and told the Dragon Queen, "She's *still* a better mother than you. Now go home."

"Fine! But you and Bram make sure my precious grandson is safe and protected. Understand?"

"I don't remember you ever worrying this much about Annwyl's twins."

"They're off-putting. I love them both, but they're off-putting."

"What about Briec's girl?"

"You know I love my Rhianwen . . . but the crying. So. Much. Crying. She's like you," Rhiannon accused her daughter. "She just cares too much."

Morfyd dragged her hands through her hair. "Just go, Mum."

"Remember what I told you," Rhiannon said before turning toward the forest, raising her hand, and opening a . . . wait.

She raised her hand again and opened a . . .

Huh.

"What's wrong?"

"Nothing. Nothing." Rhiannon raised her hand again and . . .

Lowering her arm, Rhiannon faced her wide-eyed daughter. "I think I'm trapped."

Morfyd gave a long, drawn-out sigh. So dramatic, that one. "Why?"

"Because someone's locked all the doors."

"Not even you could do that."

"I know."

"So someone very powerful has trapped you here."

"I'm assuming."

"That can't be good."

"It's probably not."

Rhiannon's daughter narrowed her eyes. "Does Daddy even know you're here?"

"I was only planning to be gone a few minutes, so I never bothered to—"

"*Mother!*"

"Well, if you're just going to get hysterical about everything . . ."

# CHAPTER 21

Starving, Gruff went to the tradeswoman who sold roasted chickens. He was surprised when he ended up on a line of others waiting to get the same thing. Based on size alone, he realized they were all dragons. He would normally be annoyed at having to wait, but he was grateful they were eating chickens and not anything else he'd get angry about. Like horses . . . or his sister.

"Hello, centaur!" the tradeswoman greeted. "How many today?"

He held up four fingers. Then changed his mind and added one more. She pulled out a sack and placed five paper-wrapped chickens inside. Then she added a sixth because this was not the first time he'd purchased chicken from her.

"Good thing you didn't come yesterday. I ran out so quickly, but this time I made sure I had much more to feed these"—she eyed the dragons walking by her stall—"people."

Gruff paid and took his food with a nod, stopping long enough to pull a chicken out and take a bite out of the breast meat before he started walking. There were many centaur tribes that only ate fruits and vegetables, but they also didn't have fangs. Gruff had fangs. No self-respecting centaur, however, ate grass or hay. That was just an insult.

He was into his second chicken, pausing at a stall selling weapons to look over the wares, when he heard his sister's voice. And she sounded pissed.

Gruff didn't bolt over there to rescue her; he meandered. Why? Because his sister didn't need to be rescued. She didn't need his protection. She never had. According to their mother, "she dropped out my womb swinging and trying to stand."

Unlike Gruff, who landed on the ground with a grunt and immediately went back to sleep. "Something I have *literally* never seen before," the midwife had told his parents. When one of his uncles attempted to wake him, Gruff slapped him, and from that day on would growl anytime he came near. Gruff's father still called it "My son's first grudge!"

By the time Gruff was standing behind Briallen, however, he wished he'd bolted. Because she now had a finger pointed directly in Princess Leila's face and was nearly screaming, "If my brother wants to fuck the queen mother and she's up for it, then that's what he'll do! If he wants to fuck the queen's father and he's up for it, then that's what he'll do! *My brother will fuck anyone who wants to be fucked by him, and neither you nor your brothers have one damn say in it, Your Royal Highness!*" Briallen took a breath and calmly asked, "Anything else we should discuss, Princess Laila?"

Eyes wide, the princess shook her head, but did not speak. Gruff didn't blame her. He knew, even when one was royal born, there were times one should not speak. Especially when those times involved his sister. Like now.

"Excellent." He stood beside Briallen now and watched her force a smile to her lips. "Now, if you'll excuse us . . . ?"

The princess gestured with her hand, and his sister walked off.

Disturbed by the expression on the royal's face, Gruff opened his mouth to say something—anything, really—that might soothe her nerves, but—

*"Gruff!"*

With a nod, Gruff followed his sister until she stopped behind a large granary. She had her back to him and her hand resting on the wall of the building. She was so upset with him, her shoulders were shaking and she was bent over at the waist.

"I'm sorry, Briallen. I just couldn't . . ." Gruff frowned. "Are you laughing?"

Briallen finally faced him, and tears streamed down her face.

*"You let that mad cow tell everyone that you two are fucking?"*

"It's not funny."

"No, it's not. It's *hilarious!*"

\* \* \*

"I just don't think Isadora should go alone," Ainsley explained to Sheva and Hilda. "I need the two of you to go with her."

"Why don't *you* go with your sister?" Sheva sat down on a boulder by the largest lake within ten leagues of the town and pulled out her sword to sharpen it. This body of water was usually busier late in the day or early in the morning. But right now it was perfect because no one was around. Just what Ainsley wanted. A little privacy to speak with her friends.

"Keeley will never allow that, and Isadora asked me to stay and work with Prince Unnvar."

"You're taking direction from your eighteen-year-old sister now?"

"When she's the smartest one in the family who isn't trying to actively kill us all . . . yes."

Sheva nodded. "Excellent point."

"I need my sister protected by people I trust and who I know will only care about protecting *her*. I've got Gruff and his tribe to back me up here."

Sheva immediately started laughing. "I still can't believe you told everyone you two are—"

"That's Gemma's fault!"

Still laughing, "You're going to get him killed!"

"My sisters would never—"

"Not them, idiot! Their mates! Those two centaurs already hate Gruffyn, and you keep shoving the poor bastard right into their sights! It's like you want him dead."

"I do not!"

"We need to stay here with you, Ainsley. The gods have willed it."

Ainsley looked at Hilda. In her full habit, she sat cross-legged on a large boulder, gazing off across the placid lake, her hands clasped in prayer.

"What?" she asked her friend.

"The gods have willed this. The three of us are meant to be together at this time. It would be wrong to ignore our gods' will."

"Really?" Ainsley flatly asked. "The gods have *nothing* better to do than to give you messages about our tiny group?"

"They're trying to help. You should be grateful."

"Grateful? It was the gods that allowed Beatrix to be born. The gods that allowed her to take over the Old King's lands. The gods that allow her to continue to live. If they wanted to really help, at the very least, they would just kill Beatrix. And yet they don't."

"I will not explain the thinking of gods—"

"Because you can't."

"—I can only tell you that I hear their words and I will follow them. So wherever you are, Princess Ainsley, Sheva and I must be there with you."

"She's right," Sheva said. "We have to do what our gods order us to do."

Ainsley briefly closed her eyes. "Do you and Hilda even worship the same gods, Sheva?"

"It doesn't matter. We're united on this." Sheva clasped her hands in prayer, mimicking Hilda. "For our gods and because I don't want to go to Dark Plains with your sister."

"Bitch."

"Ainsley," Hilda said, "let me show you our gods' power. Let me show you what they can do."

Golden light surrounded the nun and in a few seconds her body, still in that cross-legged position, began to rise. Only a few feet above the boulder, but she remained there, hovering over the earth with the help of an unseen power.

"Your gods' powers are mighty!" Sheva shouted, arms lifted high in the air.

Disgusted, Ainsley closed the space between her and Hilda and, with less strength than she needed to lift up a full-grown sheep, she shoved the nun by her shoulder, sending her head over ass nearly fifty feet before Hilda hit a tree and landed in a habit-covered heap at the base of the trunk.

"Now that you're done showing off, Sister . . ." Ainsley looked back and forth between her two startled friends. "Are you two fanatic heifers going to help me or not?"

"*No!*" they both barked at the same time.

Briallen speared her hands through her hair but she continued laughing. "How many times are you going to let Ainsley Smythe drag you into her insanity?"

"You weren't there. Her sisters were glaring down at her; she had to distract them. And I *was* there."

He thought his sister was about to laugh even harder, but she abruptly stopped and just stared at him. A move that disturbed him deeply.

"What?" he asked, taking a step back.

"You really like her . . . don't you?"

"Well, she's a nice human girl, isn't she? Friendly. Why wouldn't anyone like her, and why are you staring at me like that?"

"Because you're pathetic. If you like her, then make a move."

"A move?"

"You know . . . nudge her, bite her shoulder or ass, smell her body until she pisses on the ground. Then mount her."

Gruff gawked at his sister. He didn't even have a grunt. He had nothing. He could only stare at her with his mouth slightly open.

"What?" she asked. "It worked for Georgie of the Red Tree Clan. We had a lovely time."

"I *never* want you to tell me that again. Ever. As long as our souls are present on this planet and beyond."

"We should give her a proper title."

Gemma looked up from the extensive amount of parchment that Lord Bram had given her and Keeley to look over and sign during some kind of ritual. Gemma didn't trust that word "ritual." Was there witchcraft involved? She studied the silver-haired dragon in his human form. He was, in a word, gorgeous. But he also seemed a little . . . a little . . . goofy? He kept forgetting things. And a few times he'd walked into doors or walls because he was busy reading whatever he had in his hand. He was always reading, this dragon. Always.

The document sitting on top of the pile in front of Gemma was an agreement between the two queendoms. Proof of their alliance to be signed by both queens. It included the "wardship" of Isadora and Unnvar. A very nice way of saying "hostage," as far as Gemma was concerned. But the whole thing was going through no matter how she felt. She just wanted to make sure these papers had nothing tricky in them. Nothing that would turn out to include a forced marriage between her baby sister and some old dragon or a slavery clause of some kind. Keeley thought she was being paranoid, but Gemma *had* to be paranoid because Keeley never was.

Like their father, Keeley wanted to trust everyone. Now, it was true, their father actually *did* trust everyone until he was proven wrong, and—thankfully—Keeley was not that naïve. But if someone was family or a friend, she tended to trust them implicitly. A problem when one had a murderous sister or was trying to make an alliance with someone dubbed the Mad Queen.

"Pardon?"

"Princess Isadora," Lord Bram reiterated. "She needs a proper title."

"I thought being a princess was a proper title."

"It is. But in order to avoid any . . . issues with Annwyl's battle lord—and Var's mother—Dagmar Reinholdt, and the temporary removal of her son from her care, we need to call Isadora something more than just the title of princess."

"He's not a child."

"Oh, I know! I just . . . know Dagmar. Adore her like the suns, but . . . I know Dagmar."

"I see." Confused, Gemma asked, "Soooo . . . you want us to make Isadora queen?"

Bram gazed at Gemma for at least a minute before he said, "No, my lady. I . . . we can't . . . no." He took a breath. "Uh . . . there is a title that we have in Dark Plains, not used in the last century or so, that we can use here as well."

"Which is?"

"Princess Royal."

"What's that?"

"A princess royal is a title that, in the past, has often been used by the eldest daughter of a male monarch so that she feels less slighted when the younger son becomes king upon his father's death."

"Oh! The Old King's eldest sister had that title. Grizelde, I think her name was. Grizelde, Princess Royal."

"Right. Because that kingdom does not allow ruling queens. So when the eldest offspring is a woman, the oldest son still becomes king. And, if the king likes his sister, he might give her the princess royal title."

"But then how did Beatrix become—"

"On parchment, your sister is merely the wife of a ruling king. A queen consort. But in reality . . ."

"She's a ruling queen."

"A dangerously smart ruling queen. When I first heard about her, I never expected her to move so quickly. It's as if she'd been planning it—"

"Since birth," Gemma assured the peacemaker. "My sister does nothing without a plan."

"And what do you think her ultimate plan is?" he asked.

"Everything." Gemma shrugged. "She wants absolutely everything."

"Our commanders will never allow it."

"Mother Superior isn't really a commander," Hilda clarified Sheva's statement. "But she is clearly waiting for a moment when she can rein me in like a horse." She glanced at Ainsley and added, "No offense to your future nieces and nephews."

"None taken . . . ? I think."

"If you want us to go with your sister, we'll have to convince the commanders that they thought of it. Not us."

"You're leaving?"

Briallen trotted out of the woods with Gruff behind her.

"I was actually—" Ainsley responded.

"You can't go!"

Ainsley frowned. "Why not?"

"Uh . . ." Briallen stopped in front of her. "Why not?"

"Yes. Why can't I leave?"

"Because . . . um . . . I'll miss you! Yes! That's it. *I'll* miss you!"

Ainsley glanced at Sheva, but she could only shrug her shoulders.

"Ohhhh-kayyyyy. But I want Isadora protected by someone who will only think of *her*. Not the politics. Not any other royal. Just Isadora."

"It's not going to happen," Sheva cut in.

Ainsley threw her arms out. "What the fuck?"

"No, no. I don't mean you can't find someone who will only

think of her. I mean that *we*"—she motioned between herself and Hilda—"won't think only of her."

"Why not?"

"Because *I*," Hilda replied, her hands once again clasped in prayer as she gazed across the lake, "will only think of my gods."

"Yeah," Sheva tossed in. "Me too."

"Shut up, Sheva."

"If you're really worried about your sister," Briallen offered, "I know the perfect choice among the centaurs."

Gruff moved up so he stood next to his sister. "Who?" he demanded.

"The twins."

The look on Gruff's face worried Ainsley. Because he didn't look annoyed or disgusted . . . two of his most common expressions. Instead, he appeared . . . horrified. She'd never seen the centaur horrified before.

"Laila told me centaurs can't have twins. That it was impossible."

"Not impossible," Gruff explained. "Just very, *very* rare. You're lucky to see a set once every three generations. And we are *not* requesting the twins for this."

"They're perfect."

"What's wrong with them?" Hilda asked.

"Everything."

"Nothing!" Gruff's sister quickly corrected. "The twins are two of the best warriors we've ever fought with."

"But?"

"But—"

"There's no but!" Briallen cut off her brother. "They're perfect. You'll love them! And you can stay here with us forever. I mean . . . you know what I mean. Right, Gruff?" The centaur grunted. "See? It'll be perfect!"

"I just want to ensure that my sister will be safe. Nothing else matters to me."

"Of course, my lady—"

"Brother. Or Brother Gemma. The only one who uses a royal title with me is Quinn and that's just to irritate me."

Bram finally asked the question he'd been dying to ask since he'd arrived. "Shouldn't you be . . . *Sister* Gemma?"

"I'm not a nun."

"No, but . . . um . . . okay." Bram cleared his throat and continued. "And I completely understand your concerns about your sister's safety, but with these agreements . . ."

Bram paused. His niece stood in the back of the main hall, motioning to him. Rather urgently. He just didn't understand why.

The monk quickly noticed that she no longer had his attention and looked over her shoulder. Morfyd quickly changed from frantically motioning to him to waving at them both and attempting to smile. It was a sad, failed attempt and that simply confused Bram more.

"Is everything all right?" Brother Gemma asked.

"Uh . . ."

Glaring in a way that reminded Bram of Morfyd's mother, his niece mouthed, *Get. Over. Here. Now!*

Aye. Just like her mother.

"I'll be right back . . . um . . . Brother."

Bram stood and started to walk forward, which was stupid, because the table was in his way. So, after banging his leg, he rubbed the slightly wounded area, went *around* the table and across the hall until he reached Morfyd. She immediately grabbed his arm and yanked him through the doorway, then led him to a room and shoved him inside.

That's where he saw his three nephews-by-mating: Fearghus, Briec, and Gwenvael. For once, there was no joking from Gwenvael. No boredom from Briec. No growling from Fearghus. Instead, they appeared quite concerned about—

"Rhiannon?" Bram asked once he saw the queen of their people standing a few feet away from her powerful sons.

"Hello, old friend." She gave an adorable shrug before adding, "Oops."

Bram closed his eyes. "Oh, for the love of the suns, Rhiannon, what have you done now?"

# CHAPTER 22

"Are you all right?" Gruff shifted to his human form so he could lean his back against a nearby tree.

"I'm fine," he complained to Ainsley while the nun meditated and the monk sharpened her sword, "but my sister has gone insane."

"Oh, good. You noticed. I was worried I'd have to be the one to tell you."

Gruff could see that she was teasing, and he appreciated it.

He grunted and she laughed, turning to look out over the lake. "So these twins—"

"You'll see."

"Are they . . . bad?"

"No."

"If they go . . . will my sister be safer?"

He let out a long sigh. "Yes."

"But you're still worried."

Gruff didn't know how to answer that. The twins were not easily described, and he wasn't exactly known for his way with words. "You'll see," he said again.

"Okay."

It dawned on Gruff that Ainsley trusted him so much, she was taking him at his word.

"But if you want more info—"

"I'll see soon enough, knowing your sister. She's not one to waste time." She smiled. "But thanks."

"For what?"

"Everything."

Overwhelmed, Gruff started to look away until he noticed that the body of water behind Sheva and Hilda was moving, abruptly beginning to lower as if it was being sucked out of the lake. Black horns slowly appeared, shortly followed by scales and, as the water kept going lower and lower, the body of a black dragon.

Water rushed off the beast as it ascended from the lake, and Sheva and Hilda scrambled to their feet, quickly backing away until they reached Gruff and Ainsley. They all had their weapons drawn and ready, but Gruff honestly wasn't sure if any of it would make a difference. Not when the dragon finally stood to its full height and gazed down at them.

"Hello, tiny humans."

Fearghus watched, fascinated, as his mother massaged his uncle's shoulders and attempted to convince a brilliant dragon that everything was absolutely fine. Just fine!

"I am," Bram said, the tips of his fingers slowly rubbing his temples, "doing my best to save as many lives as I can. And you, Rhiannon, seem to be doing everything to—"

"Fuck that up?"

"Thank you, Briec."

"I am not doing any such thing!" Rhiannon lied, glaring at her three sons over poor Bram's head. "I was merely spending some much-needed time with our Annwyl."

"She is *not* my Annwyl," Briec reminded them.

"Our father," Fearghus let them all know, "is going to realize you're gone, Mother, and destroy the world to get you back."

"This is not my fault!"

"How is this *not* your fault?" Morfyd demanded.

"It just isn't. And I've been trying to contact your father, but—"

"None of us can contact anyone," Briec said.

"Like my beautiful daughter." Fearghus stared at his mother. "And I haven't been able to contact the boy for his daily berating."

"Ahhh," Gwenvael sighed out. "A father's love."

"Shut up."

Morfyd pointed at their mother. "You need to fix this."

Rhiannon cleared her throat and reluctantly admitted, "I'm not sure I can."

"How is that possible?" Briec wanted to know. "You're the dragonwitch of Dark Plains. Your power is—"

"Not perfect." She gave a small shrug, hands still on Uncle Bram's shoulders. Something, Fearghus knew, his father would not like one bit. "There are weaknesses."

"What weaknesses?"

"There are a few who could manage to outdo my skills. For instance, a—"

"Wizard?"

"God."

Morfyd slammed her hands on the table she stood behind. "*You pissed off a god?*"

"Who?" Briec asked.

"Well . . . that's a long list."

Bram sighed. Long and loud. Fearghus angrily dropped back into his chair and folded his arms over his chest before looking away from their mother. Briec buried his face in his hands. Morfyd let out a short, aggravated scream between clenched teeth. And Gwenvael . . . ? Gwenvael let out a loud laugh.

"Everyone says I'm the worst in this family," Gwenvael announced, still laughing. "But it's *you*, Mum!" He laughed louder. "*It's you!*"

A dragoness. The thing that came out of the water was a dragoness.

Gruff didn't know if that made him feel better or worse about the current situation.

It leaned in a bit and studied them for a moment before announcing, "You're one of the royal family, aren't you?" she asked, moving her snout a little closer to a now visibly shaking Ainsley. "You look like the other two. The queen and the fanatic." She glanced at the nun and monk. "No offense."

"Offense greatly taken," Hilda replied.

"I'm fine," Sheva added.

The She-dragon smiled. At least Gruff hoped it was a smile. All those fangs glinting at him because the two suns hit them at just the right angle were, to say the least, disturbing.

"I am Ghleanna the Decimator," the dragoness told them. "General of the Twenty-Eighth and Thirty-Second Legions in the Dragon Queen's Armies."

Ainsley cleared her throat. "I'm, uh . . ." She looked at Gruff, eyes confused by what he was guessing was dragonfear. "Who am I?"

"You're Ainsley," he told her.

"Oh! Yes." She nodded and smiled at the She-dragon. "Right. I'm Ainsley."

"Is that it? Is there not more to your name?"

"I'm Ainsley Smythe? Maybe."

"Do you not know?"

"At the moment, I really don't."

Hilda let out a loud sigh before introducing them all . . . in a way that only Hilda would think was appropriate. "This, hells-beast, is *Princess* Ainsley. Brother Sheva of the Order of Righteous Valor. Gruffyn of the Torn Moon Clan. And I am Sister Hilda."

"The sassy nun!" the She-dragon cheered.

Hilda, her hand gripping her long, steel staff, began to stalk forward, but Sheva yanked her back by the hood of the black fur cape she wore over her habit.

"And you are part of the royal family, yes?" the She-dragon asked, looking at Ainsley.

"I am?" She shook her head. "Right. I am. Sorry. You're just so . . ." She gestured toward the She-dragon. "Giant. And I'm so . . . not."

Somehow, that grin grew wider. "Then I will attempt to ease your worry."

Flames exploded around the She-dragon, despite all that water; but in just a few seconds, the flames died down and left a woman where the dragon had stood. But even in her human form, the She-dragon was massive. As tall as Gruff and nearly as wide—at least her shoulders were—without an ounce of fat on her. There were scars, although not as many as the Mad Queen sported. But the prominent scars she had were in places that suggested she should have been dead a dozen times over.

Naked, she strode toward them. "I have concerns," she said as she came closer.

"About me?" Ainsley asked. "Because I can . . . I can . . ."

"Whimper in fear?" Sheva asked.

"Shut up."

"About my nephew."

"Your nephew?"

"Unnvar."

"*You're* part of the royal family?" And Gruff really wished Hilda would at least attempt to hide her disdain for the dragons. Perhaps her gods would protect her, but then again . . . gods were tricky. And unpredictable. And sometimes just mean.

But the She-dragon didn't seem to be bothered by the nun's tone. In fact, it seemed to amuse her more than anything.

"My brother is the Dragon Queen's consort, but I'm not a royal. I am a Cadwaladr. We're a war clan. Raised on battle and blood from hatching. Royal dragons call us the pit dogs of the queen."

"You seem proud of that."

She moved to stand before Hilda and Sheva. "Because I am, sassy nun."

"Stop calling me sassy nun."

"Stop talking down to me."

"I'll do my best."

"Could you put some clothes on?" Sheva asked. "Nothing personal, but your tits are just . . . right *there*. And they're huge."

"Thank you!" She walked over to a pile of chainmail and armor. Gruff guessed that the She-dragon had gone into the water human. Now she slipped into her human-sized gear while talking to them over her shoulder.

"I've heard they'll be leaving my great-nephew Var here," she said as she got dressed.

"That's true," Ainsley replied.

"Will he be safe with your kin?"

"Shouldn't I be asking if my sister Isadora will be safe with *your* people? She's human. Your nephew isn't."

She shrugged, pulling on a cotton shirt before reaching for the chainmail one. "He's half-human. And most of Annwyl's advisors are human. Your sister will be fine."

"Var is still half-dragon. How vulnerable can he be?"

The general put on a chainmail shirt.

"My Bram adores that boy. He'd worry about him whether he was all dragon or all human. And I won't leave the boy here if he's not truly safe among your kin."

"Your Bram?" Hilda asked.

"Bram the Merciful is my mate. And my brother is Gwenvael's father. So the boy is my great-nephew. And although Var is everything the Cadwaladrs are not, he's favored by the entire clan."

"My sister never breaks her word." Ainsley put her bow on her back. "She has pledged to protect Var and she will."

"If you say—"

"And just so we understand each other," Ainsley continued, suddenly emboldened by a perceived slight to the family she continually argued with, "my sister would never harm the innocent."

General Ghleanna snorted a harsh laugh. "Not even Annwyl makes such a boast."

"Because she *does* harm the innocent?" Sheva asked.

The She-dragon slowly faced them, the breastplate of her armor held in her hand, the crest of the Dragon Queen stamped on the front and back. It shone bright in the suns-light, proving she kept it clean and in pristine condition when not in the middle of battle. A true soldier, despite her high rank.

"How many wars have any of you been in?" the dragoness asked.

When none of them answered, she smirked. "So, no wars."

"We've been in battles," Hilda replied. "And Gruffyn was born into a warrior clan."

"Is that true, centaur?"

He grunted and, when he said nothing else, she looked at Ainsley, who said, "He is."

"Then perhaps you do understand. At least a little. Because for warrior clans, war and death and battle is in our very blood. And the one thing I can tell all of you, so you truly understand what you're getting into, is that innocents *always* die during war. That's why kings and queens have clans like ours."

* * *

"You have to start home now. Ghleanna and her legion can travel with you."

Briec nodded. "I agree, Mother. You're going to have to head back now."

"It's going to take you a few days to get home as it is. But you might be able to meet Daddy before he reaches the Amichai Mountain."

"Someone has stranded you here for a reason, Mum," Gwenvael said. "We need to get you out."

Rhiannon looked over her offspring. Only her youngest daughter Keita was missing. Safely away with her mate and sons in the Northlands.

She adored her family. All of them. They were all strong, smart, and beautiful. And they understood her so well.

With a warm smile, Rhiannon informed her precious offspring, "I am not going anywhere."

They all let out sounds of exasperation.

"Why do you torture us?" Briec asked.

"If you stay," Fearghus noted, "the angry dragon that you have chosen as your mate for life and cursed us with as a father is going to come here and wipe the earth clean of everything until he finds you. Is that what you want?"

"It's not what I don't want."

"Mum!"

"Morfyd, I'm joking."

"It's not funny."

Gwenvael shrugged. "It's a little funny."

"Look, my mate has about a thousand relatives among the armies here," Rhiannon said. "Send some of them to several locations on the Amichai Mountains to see if they can intercept Bercelak before he does any major damage to anyone."

"What if our cousins miss him?"

Rhiannon frowned at Morfyd's question. "Do you really think that the Cadwaladrs will miss several *legions* of dragons flying across the Amichai Mountains?"

"Mum, the Amichai Mountain Range stretches across several *continents*."

"It does?"

"Yes. It's huge!"

"And our cousins can easily miss him and your legions, especially now that blood relatives have been blocked from communicating," Fearghus finished.

"Oh, well then . . . yes. Your father will destroy everyone."

Morfyd pointed an accusing finger and snarled through clenched teeth, "It's like you are *trying* to make me insane."

"I'm not really trying," Rhiannon admitted. "It's just too bloody easy."

With a snarl, Morfyd came across the table at her mother, but Rhiannon's dear sons caught the little cow before she could get to her and pushed her back into a chair.

"Mum," Briec said, pushing his hair off his face, "while all this is going on, what will *you* be doing?"

"I don't know yet," Rhiannon replied earnestly. "But I'm eager to find out."

"Clans like yours?" Hilda repeated back. "To do the nasty work of killing innocents for royals?" she asked.

"You sneer delightfully, fanatic, but you don't need a war clan for that. Kings and queens have soldiers for hire if they just want to destroy the innocent. But a ruler has a war clan like the Cadwaladrs to make sure every bastard royal that thinks they can rule anything will truly have to decide if they want to make that one move against a king or queen that will bring *us* down on their heads. Because when we do come, when our clans are unleashed on those who didn't make better choices . . . they already know what we bring."

She finished putting greaves on over her leather boots. The Dragon Queen's crest was also stamped on those.

"It's not just our war clans, though," the general continued. "The only job a royal has is to protect their people. If there are enemies who are putting them in danger, who are harming them, then those royals call on us. But before it gets that bad, smart royals—and, sadly, there are not a lot of those—always have peacemakers at work to avoid the potential horrors of all-out war. And the peacemakers need to be protected. Peacemakers like me Bram."

"And Prince Unnvar," Ainsley said.

"And Prince Unnvar." She chuckled. "Keep forgetting that boy is a princeling."

"He doesn't look like a royal to you?" Sheva asked, her weapons now put away; her body was loose and relaxed now that the She-dragon was in human form.

"He looks much like his father. So, aye. He *looks* like a royal. But he's got his mother's eyes . . . and her brains. Over the centuries, I've found those with that kind of intelligence are rarely princes and sometimes are far more dangerous than any well-seasoned soldier with a sword. But, luckily for us, the pair of 'em want nothing more than peace and calm."

Now fully dressed in her armor, appearing powerful and intimidating—but not as powerful and intimidating as she had while completely naked—she folded muscular arms over her breast plate. "Will my great-nephew find peace and calm among your kin, Princess Ainsley? Because despite everything . . . the boy needs his peace and calm."

"Huh. Let's think on that." Ainsley rubbed her chin. "My parents have more children than I care to count, all living in one place . . . except for Beatrix, of course. My mother's voice is always at a level that suggests she's working right next to her forge even when she's not. All the children fight, of course, but my older sisters and I fight even more. Constantly, really, like three wet cats in a bag. My sister, the queen, insists on taking in animals that have stumbled out of one of the hells, while my other sister, the monk, has a half-dead horse she rides into battle. I just took in a baby bird that nearly poisoned me to death." She held up her hand with the partially missing forefinger. "And yet I am keeping it as a pet despite its terrifying caw and absolutely giant head, all because I think it's cute."

"In other words . . . no peace or calm for my Var."

"None," Ainsley promised. "None at all. But I can teach him to climb trees."

# CHAPTER 23

Ainsley had just stepped into the main hall when Briallen caught her by the wrist and dragged her across the room.

"Where are we going?" She was hungry and didn't want to miss her mother's boar ribs. She'd discovered that one had to be quick if one wanted to get any food before the dragons. They didn't seem to believe in sharing.

"Ainsley, say hello to the twins."

The pair of female centaurs were in their human form, strong arms crossed over their chests, and were no taller than Ainsley was. One had dark blue eyes. The other had dark brown. Like many centaurs, their hair matched their hides; which, in this case, meant white hair with splotches of black throughout. Hair they kept in thick braids that stretched down their backs to just above their hips. They stared at Ainsley with the same cold expressions. They were heavily armed despite being at what was supposed to be a friendly feast. They didn't speak, even after being introduced to Ainsley. Not even the grunt that everyone else got from a taciturn Gruff.

They were like angry mirror images of each other, and if it wasn't for their eyes, Ainsley would never be able to tell them apart.

"The twins will be protecting Isadora," Briallen explained. "And she couldn't be in safer hands. So, you have no worries."

Sarff called out to Gruff's sister, and she looked over her shoulder to see what was wanted of her. It was then, with Briallen's head turned, that one twin slammed her elbow into the other's side. So the other twin swung a fist, and there was the sound of bone cracking in a cheek when that fist made contact.

"I'll be right there," Briallen called back before facing the twins again. "So, are we good?" she asked, unaware of the sudden explosion of violence since the cheek hadn't begun to swell yet.

The twins looked at Briallen, heads cocking to the side at the same time.

"Oh. Right." She smiled at Ainsley. "Their younger brother is still in training under them, so he'll be going as well. But it will be good for him."

"Younger brother?"

Briallen's gaze did a quick search of the room before spotting the centaur she was looking for. She put two fingers into her mouth and blew; based on the glares she got from the dragons, they did not appreciate the shrill whistle.

A tall, young centaur cut through the crowd toward them in his human form. He held a plate of boar ribs in one hand and another plate of pork ribs—already half-eaten—in the other.

"Did they put the food out?" Ainsley demanded.

"No," he replied, already much more talkative than his siblings. "I went to the kitchen and they gave me some." When Ainsley frowned in annoyance, he added, "Don't blame them. I asked very nicely. Maybe even begged a little."

He did greatly resemble the twins despite his ability to smile, though his hair was dark gray with white streaks, worn in one thick braid that reached past his shoulders. And his eyes . . . well, he had one blue eye and one dark brown one. It reminded her of the Farmersons' barn cat. It had different-colored eyes too. In fact, if one looked at the centaur from a certain angle, the blue eye almost appeared to be missing. The color was just such a light blue, it bordered on white.

"Soooo," Ainsley said, already dreading this interaction, "do any of you have names?"

The centaur eating his ribs frowned. "Of course we have names. Why?"

She lifted her brows and waited a few seconds . . . he eventually caught up.

"Oh! Right. Well, I'm Úlfur, but everyone calls me Úlf. And

these two terrifying specimens are my sisters. Agrona," he said, motioning to the blue-eyed twin. "And Naia. The miraculous twins. Centaurs don't usually have twins, you know. But here you go. And there is a myth about triplets, but who knows how true that is. I mean, of course it's possible. Anything is possible. But I truly doubt it. You're human so you've never seen a centaur birth, but they are an event, I can tell you. But then, every birth is an event, don't you—"

*"By the gods, stop talking!"*

Ainsley briefly closed her eyes. She hadn't meant to snap like that. But he...he wouldn't stop talking! It wasn't that he talked fast. He really didn't. He simply didn't stop. He just kept going with barely a breath at any point.

Instead of anger, though, the centaur chuckled. "Funny, your younger sister said the same thing."

"You've met Isadora?"

"Yeah," he said with another laugh. "I have."

Gruffyn rubbed his eyes with one hand; Ainsley's annoyed bark was still ringing in his ears. It felt like his entire body was cringing. He knew that if the twins were chosen to travel with Isadora and the dragons, that meant one or all of their brothers would have to go with them. The twins were the oldest of that family's siblings, and it was the twins who trained each and every brother that had followed.

He wouldn't say that Úlf was the worst of that particular family, but he was definitely the most annoying. To be in a room with Úlf and all his siblings was like being trapped in an overpopulated chicken coop. Nothing but constant noise, except for the twins. The twins said nothing. Not even to each other. Of course...they were sisters, not friends, which they made clear every moment they possibly could.

What did amuse Gruff and his sister—what had *always* amused them—was the fact that Úlf, his brothers, and the twins were all part of the Scarred Earth Clan. They were, in fact, first cousins to Princess Laila and her idiot brothers on their mother's side. It was kind of the Ruling Mare's shame, really. That one of her brothers had bred such an unruly lot of steeds and mares annoyed their queen more than she would admit out loud. It annoyed her sons and daughter, too, which was why he was surprised Princess Laila had agreed to send the twins—and, in turn, Úlf—into dragon territory.

Gruff knew he and his clan should be the ones making this trip with Isadora, but Briallen could be obsessive, and she'd made up her mind that he belonged at Ainsley's side because she was convinced that he was in . . .

He couldn't even say it! Because it was ridiculous!

"He wouldn't stop talking."

Gruff blinked, realizing that Ainsley was now standing in front of him.

He grunted in response.

"And he was already eating the ribs!" she softly accused. "That's unacceptable!"

She really loved her mother's boar ribs.

Ainsley grabbed two tankards of ale from a tray as a servant went by, and shoved one in Gruff's hand.

"I'm guessing we're going to need this," she muttered before attempting to take a sip, which was immediately interrupted by her sister Gemma.

"And how are our lovebirds this beautiful evening?" the monk asked, causing Gruff to choke on his beer.

Ainsley glared at her sister over the rim of her tankard, but she kept drinking. Even while using her free hand to slap poor Gruff on his back so he didn't choke to death on her father's best ale.

After finishing half the tankard, Ainsley let out a long, "Aaaaah!" and smiled.

"So good," she said, refusing to look away from her sister's intense, fanatic gaze. "And we are doing *great*. You? Everything okay? Any war gods stop by and tell you they appreciate *all* your hard work?"

Gemma's grin faded and her eyes narrowed. Ainsley braced herself.

"Where did those three horses come from in Kriegszorn's stable?"

"Maybe she made friends."

"Kriegszorn has no friends. No horse will go near her unless in the midst of battle."

"Random horses show up and you just assume they're mine?"

"Are they yours?"

"Yes."

Gemma shut her eyes in frustration, and Gruff took the brief respite to bump Ainsley with his hip. That desperate move made Ainsley laugh, but she caught it quick and bit her lip to stop it from leaking out. Still, Gemma knew something was up when she opened her eyes again and found the pair of them looking very guilty.

Gemma suddenly pointed a finger at Ainsley and said, "I know you're up to something, Ainsley Smythe. And I *will* find out what you've been doing."

"You mean besides fucking Gruff?"

The entire hall fell silent, and Gruff didn't even have to look to know that they had everyone's attention.

But before he could drag Ainsley away and the light-haired idiot brother could pull his monk to a far corner to calm her down, a voice boomed from the back of the hall, "Hello, all! I'm so excited to meet everyone!"

All the attention turned to the tall female who'd just entered the hall. She wore a simple pale blue shift and her thick white hair reached her ankles in loose curls. Her blue eyes were bright, and immense power emanated from her in waves that Gruff knew only he and Sarff could see.

For a moment, he thought she was Morfyd until he saw the gray streaks among the white hair. She also stood differently from her daughter. As if she knew the world belonged to her.

"Hello," the queen's father said, walking over to the queen of the dragons. "I am Archie Farmerson."

"I am Rhiannon of the House of Gwalchmai fab Gwyar."

Oblivious, Ainsley's father smiled. "What a name you have, my lady! I adore it! Here. Let me introduce you to my family."

He held his arm out for her and the Dragon Queen looked at it, then at Farmerson's face. Gruff didn't realize he was holding his breath until the She-dragon grinned and took the man's arm. Together they walked across the room until they reached a wide-eyed Queen Keeley. The Dragon Queen was not supposed to be in these lands. In fact, it was said she never left her court. Ever. But here she was. Thousands of miles away from her home.

How had she got here? Had she been here all along? Or . . .

Had she opened a doorway and simply stepped through?

Gruff looked for Sarff but he didn't immediately see her. He knew, though, that she'd felt what he had just a few hours before. They'd both felt it, but they hadn't realized what it had meant. Because neither of them could create mystical doorways and simply walk through. Sarff was powerful, but she wasn't *that* powerful. And Gruff was sure he'd never be that powerful. He wasn't even sure he wanted to be. Walking through doorways made of air and the power of the gods sounded . . . uncomfortable. Especially when he could get anywhere he wanted on his four legs. It might take longer, but he didn't have to worry about the cost of it to himself and the world around him.

"So, you are Queen Keeley?" the Dragon Queen asked the royal. But before her fellow queen could respond . . .

"Why are you here?" Brother Gemma asked . . . or demanded, depending on how you heard her tone. "You are not supposed to be here. We were told we'd never see you."

Without any emotional reaction, the foreign royal leaned back a bit so that Lord Bram could inform her, "This is Brother Gemma of the Order of Righteous Valor, sister to Queen Keeley *and* Queen Beatrix."

"Ahhh, yes! The religious fanatic. How wonderful to meet you. You're much smaller than I imagined, though. I'm surprised your human god didn't give you a tad more height."

When Brother Gemma only gawked, the Dragon Queen added, "You are just so tiny and adorable, I want to put you in one of my travel bags and carry you back to my home! Make you a pet."

That's when Ainsley leaned over and quietly announced to him, "I love that She-dragon more than the suns."

Couldn't she stay? Forever? Ainsley asked for so little and received even less. But she would give up everything if this She-dragon could stay and torment her sister until the end of all times! If for no other reason than for once Gemma had nothing to say. True, she could threaten. She could pull her sword. She could call on her gods. But absolutely none of that would affect the queen of all Dark Plains dragons! Like a gnat landing on a wolf's nose. Just something to swat off. What made it worse was that, on the surface, everything the foreign royal said was nice. "Nice" like someone purposely tripping you but then being the one to help you up.

And, Ainsley guessed, this royal had been playing that nice game for centuries.

"I do love your palace," Queen Rhiannon told Queen Keeley. "It's just so . . . cozy!"

"Don't you live in a cave?" Gemma asked.

"Actually, I live in a mountain. The largest mountain in Dark Plains. But over the years, I've had many humans to my palatial home. Some were guests." She smiled down at Gemma. "Some, of course, were dinner."

"*Mum!*" Morfyd barked, horrified.

"We don't do that anymore, though," the foreign royal went on while impressively ignoring her panicked daughter. "Not since my dear Annwyl joined the royal family."

Queen Annwyl seemed unbothered by all of this. She sat at the head of the dining table, her feet up on the wood, and ate a bright red apple. When Rhiannon pointed her out, the Mad Queen simply waved her half-eaten fruit before returning to the book Ainsley now realized was in the royal's lap.

"And, you know, I'm glad we've outlawed it in most cases—"

"Most?" Keeley asked.

"—all the crying and screaming and begging . . . it does not help with digestion."

Ainsley could easily see that Gemma had had enough by the expression on her face. "You come here and *brag* about eating humans?" she snarled.

Without moving her head, the dragonwitch shifted her gaze to Gemma and softly asked, "Do you monks still burn witches?"

"Only when necessary."

"Okay!" a brave Lord Bram said, pushing his way between the pair. "How about we all sit down and have a lovely, *friendly* dinner? Eh? Wouldn't that be nice?"

Ainsley, determined to get her damn ribs for dinner, headed toward the table to find a seat, but Gruff slipped his hand into hers and tugged her toward the open front doors.

She followed, quickly realizing the thought of Gruff suddenly pulling her off somewhere alone didn't make her uncomfortable. In fact . . . she was almost excited to see what he had planned. Where was he taking her? What was he up to? She doubted anyone in her family would notice she was gone, but the thought of being a little naughty for once—

"I need you to find and kill Lord Broadwils and his men immediately."

Ainsley couldn't express her disappointment at realizing Gruff had only taken her to meet with Var outside the tower. She was reminded of the time when her father told her she was going to get a "very nice present I think you'll love," and the next day he brought home a book. A book! Who was she? Keeley? Or, even worse, Beatrix? Those two liked to read. Ainsley had been hoping for a new bow.

She had the same feeling of disappointment now. Even worse, she couldn't get up the energy to hide it.

"Who? Who the fuck is Lord Broadwils, and why should I miss my mum's boar ribs for him?"

"Slave trader, given his titles by Beatrix. He's been seen on Queen Keeley's territories with a battle unit, and that's not a good thing."

"I strongly agree . . . but boar ribs . . . ?"

"Yes, yes. I know." Var shoved a cloth bag in her hands and pushed her away from the tower.

"You know? How do you know?"

"Isadora told me you have an obsession with your mother's pedestrian cooking."

"It's not pedestrian." She held up the bag. "And what is this?"

"Your mother's boar ribs. I had the kitchen wrap me up some for your journey."

Ainsley stopped walking and faced the young royal. "So I'm just killing people for you now? Is that it?"

"When they're men sent into your sister's territories by that evil cow, I made the assumption it would be important enough for you to—"

"Yes, yes, yes! All right! Fine!"

She started walking again, noticing that although silent, Gruff kept pace with her while Var continued talking.

"I've already rounded up the monk, nun, and your sister, Gruffyn. They'll be meeting you with the horses outside the gate walls and already have your weapons and travel gear. Brother Sheva has the general location, a map, and supplies."

"Did you get the information right this time?" she couldn't help but ask, feeling annoyed. About everything!

"As much as I can. But there's every chance that Beatrix has sent more than just Lord Broadwils to finish the deed."

Ainsley stopped again and, after a brief moment, she faced the dragon-human royal.

"I know," he said before she could get out a word. "I have several of my dragon kin scouring the lands closest to these walls to ensure no small or large armies get within spitting distance of your family. But if they only send a man or two to grab one of the children . . ." He let out a breath. "I think we may need to bring one or both of your sisters into all this."

"You could try, but with your grandmother here—"

"Wait. What? Gran-gran's here?"

Unable to help herself, Ainsley gawked at the normally stalwart royal. Even Gruff was surprised, raising both eyebrows.

Var cleared his throat and briefly looked away. When he had composed himself, his voice back to its normal, low octave, he asked, "My grandmother's here?"

"She is. And making Gemma's life a misery. Something I was hoping to enjoy until the end of my days. Although I think she's also making your uncle Bram's life a bit of a misery too."

"Oh, bloody reason, she's going to undo everything."

"Probably. Eating humans has already been discussed."

Var closed his eyes, placed his fingertips against his temples, and proceeded to rub in small circles.

"I swear," he sighed out, "this family."

Ainsley reached up and put a comforting hand on his shoulder. "I say with all honesty, Unnvar . . . I get it."

# CHAPTER 24

"Come, Keeley. Annwyl. Let's go for a walk."

Morfyd stood. "You're going for a walk? Now?"

"Why wouldn't I?" Rhiannon asked her daughter.

"It's about to rain, Mum," Fearghus pointed out, glancing up at the ceiling when a loud clap of thunder shook the walls. "Sounds like a bad storm."

"I think three mighty queens can handle a little rain."

"We are discussing very important things, Mother."

"What else is there to discuss? They know how I got here. Why I came. I understand what a venomous cunt their other sister is. I've promised I will no longer call the monk a murderous fanatic—"

"A promise you quickly broke . . . several times," Briec muttered.

"And I have grudgingly agreed to allow my most-beloved grandson to be left behind like some half-eaten carcass you're done feasting on. What more could you possibly want from me?"

"To take this seriously."

"I take everything seriously."

All her children threw up their hands and rolled their eyes, but it was Gwenvael who said with a laugh, "Oh, Mum, even *I* don't have the balls to lie on that grand a scale."

"We have to figure out what to do next," Morfyd insisted. "And who has trapped you here."

"I'm not trapped, Morfyd. I can walk away. I just can't"—she flitted her hands in the air—"you know. But instead of telling me what *I* should do—especially when you know how much I hate anyone telling me what to do—you should find out *how* to unlock that door. So I can go home and get to your father before the slaughter begins."

"*Slaughter?*" the monk barked, face angry. "You never mentioned a slaughter!"

"Don't get hysterical." Rhiannon gave a noncommittal shrug. "I'm sure we'll get to my Bercelak before he destroys too many villages or . . . people."

They'd left town before the suns went down, Briallen leading the way since she'd studied the map they'd been given before Ainsley and Gruff arrived.

Var had given a lot of details about the location and a few bits of information on Lord Broadwils. But the number of men he might have with him seemed more a guess, and Gruff was extremely worried about leaving Ainsley's family behind. Of course, the Farmersons weren't exactly alone. They were surrounded by his fellow centaurs, soldiers, and a vast number of dragons. But that didn't change the fact that if anything happened to her siblings or parents, Ainsley would never forgive herself.

And Gruff would never forgive himself if she was made to feel that way.

Still . . . they rode on.

Even when the weather turned bad. First there was thunder and some lightning. And, not long after, a torrent of rain.

Gruff didn't worry about that either. They were on a main road and would ride out of the storm soon enough.

At least that's what he thought. At first.

"*Mother!*" her daughter practically screamed. Rhiannon had no idea why Morfyd was so angry. Rhiannon was only being honest because her daughter always got so bitchy when she lied. Why wouldn't she make up her mind?

Laughing, Gwenvael said, "Talking about our father slaughtering anyone is not helpful, Mum. And you're hearing that from *me*, which should definitely tell you something."

Finally fed up, Rhiannon swiped her hands through the air and loudly announced, "That's it! I am done with this conversation."

"But—"

"Morfyd, do what you do best and research how we can open a doorway to get me home."

"How? I don't have my books here. No proper library."

"There are covens living in this town and in the valley. I'm sure the monk knows exactly where they are in case she needs to set any of them aflame."

"At least this time she didn't call you a venomous fanatic," Gwenvael said to the human royal with a wink.

"Talk to our fellow witches. Find out what they know. I'm sure they'll help."

Var rested his hands on the big dining table, now cleared of all the plates and platters and chalices. "It's still not a good idea for you to go walking around alone, Grandmother."

"But I won't be alone! I'll have dear Annwyl and Queen Keeley with me."

"Providing the perfect opportunity to kidnap three queens," Gemma pointed out.

"My powers aren't gone, Monk. And I think Annwyl and Keeley are both brawny enough to take on any army that comes to your doors."

"We have dragon patrols scouring the lands within three leagues in all directions," Var announced. "I've also put all of your guards on alert, Queen Keeley; and all of your siblings are being held in a safe location with both your parents, your cousin Keran, and a hefty cadre of well-armed centaurs."

"Wait!" both Queen Keeley and the monk said together. Then, after eyeing each other, the monk asked, "Is my father's brother with the children?"

Var smirked. "Isadora made it very clear your Uncle Archie was to be put somewhere else. Not only for his safety but for the children's. Don't worry. We have control of the situation. But considering that so much effort has been put into keeping my grandmother here, one can only assume that our enemies care less about your siblings and more about getting to *her*."

"I am not that easy to kill, Var."

"It may not be about killing you, Gran. It could be, as Brother

Gemma has already suggested, about holding you captive. Using you to control Grandfather and Aunt Annwyl's human armies."

Rhiannon couldn't help but snort. "Your grandfather never negotiates. With anyone. And neither do I. Let Beatrix take me. I'll burn her and whatever human god she's become friends with to the fucking ground. Now, if you'll excuse us . . . we queens would like to stretch our legs before the storm starts."

She gestured to the open front doors and Annwyl immediately got up, tossing her book to Fearghus. Keeley, however, looked to her sister and the centaurs before she finally got up and followed Annwyl.

Their small group walked out into the night. The courtyard had been completely cleared of everything but soldiers and guards. Even the demon dogs seemed to be on patrol somewhere. Although Rhiannon could see why the human queen enjoyed having them around. They were very cute. Then again, she'd only caught a brief glimpse of them here and there because they kept running away anytime Annwyl entered the room, which Rhiannon secretly found very humorous.

None of them spoke as they walked to the walls surrounding the town and stopped just inside the gates. Gazing out over the land, Rhiannon tried again to contact Bercelak. Though she'd attempted to give the human royals the best-case scenario, she knew as well as any of her children what her mate would do when he discovered her missing. She would guess that by now, he'd already called all his generals and troops to meet him near the peak of Destruction's End Mountain. There he would order everyone to head across their land to the Amichai Mountains, destroying absolutely anything that got in their way.

And what dragons believed was someone "getting in their way" varied. Often depending on their mood. A stolen queen and Bercelak's rage would bring nothing but a very bad mood among her subjects.

Still, there was no reason to upset all these humans. Yet.

Var, who was always on top of everything, had already sent out Cadwaladr troops to take several routes back to Dark Plains in the hope that at least one of the groups would come in direct contact with her mate. Her brilliant grandson had also kept Ghleanna and her legion behind to protect Queen Keeley and her kin. Normally, she would not allow that because she strongly felt these humans should be able to fight their own battles. But she did feel a little responsible about some of this situation. She hadn't been asked to come to these lands, but she had, and now here they all were.

Besides, it felt nice to be the helpful one for once. And she was being helpful. Quite helpful!

"So where would you like to go?" the human queen asked when the silence seemed to stretch on too long. "Anything you'd like to see?"

Here? She hadn't seen a town this small and pathetic in generations. But Rhiannon wasn't about to say that. She knew it would just piss off her daughter, who would hear about it from big-mouth Annwyl. So, instead, Rhiannon replied, "I thought we'd just walk around the outside walls for a bit. Discuss future plans. That sort of thing."

"That's fine." The big-shouldered royal glanced at Rhiannon. "I do have a question, though."

"Yes?"

"You said you told us why you came here in the first place. But you really didn't."

"Didn't I?"

"Queen Rhiannon, I have twelve siblings. One of them pure evil. I know when someone is not telling me something. It's how I keep my other siblings from setting the tower on fire or getting trampled by my father's pigs."

She debated how honest to be but decided to simply speak the truth.

"We're not immortal," Queen Rhiannon began. "Dragons. We are bigger, smarter, and much more impressive than you, but we're not immortal."

"I understand."

"And because we're not immortal, I need to know I'm entrusting the life of my subjects and, more importantly, my kin to humans I can trust. Because of the centuries I've been alive, I have not met many humans I can trust. Annwyl's one."

"Thank you."

"And my daughter's mate, Brastias, is another. And that's mostly it. If we were simply building a truce, not trusting you would be fine, because I would always be on my guard. And as soon as there was the slightest sign of betrayal, I would have no problem destroying everyone and everything you love. But you and I and Annwyl will not have a truce. Because we haven't been fighting. We will have an alliance. And I need to know I can trust those I have an alliance with. Especially when we'll be leaving my precious, precious grandson behind."

"You do know you have other grandchildren, right?" Annwyl asked. "Including *my* son. Who is perfect in every way."

"Talan raises the dead, Annwyl."

"And he's perfect at it."

Rhiannon twisted her lips. "It's disgusting. Toying with the dead."

"He doesn't toy with them. And considering you used to eat humans—"

"They weren't dead until I bit down on them. It was fresh blood that burst into my mouth like ripe fruit. Not congealed carcass meat. We're not vultures, Annwyl."

"I'm sorry," Queen Keeley finally interrupted. "Can we *not* have this conversation? Both of you are making me panic about the safety of my family *and* making me nauseated."

"Keeley is right. Let's just go for that walk and enjoy this beautiful evening!" Rhiannon blinked and looked up at the sky. "Huh."

Annwyl looked up too. "What?"

"It is a beautiful night, isn't it?"

"So?"

"So, there was thunder two minutes ago. If a storm is about to happen . . ."

The trio glanced at each other, then, together, stepped away from the gate and set off down the well-worn path. But they'd taken just a few steps before there was another crack of thunder. They stopped and looked up again.

"Such a clear sky," Rhiannon said.

"That's really bothering you," Annwyl noted.

"It is."

"Why?"

"Because, my friends, this isn't natural. And when things aren't natural . . . that worries me."

"But you never worry, Rhiannon," Annwyl reminded her. "You worry others."

"Which should tell you, dearest Annwyl, exactly how concerning this situation is."

The storm turned so nasty and strong that it started to take down trees. When a big, ancient tree suddenly crashed to the ground, Ainsley barely had time to steer Paladin out of the way before they were both crushed under it.

She panicked for a moment, because Gruff had been by her side since they'd left the tower. But she immediately felt relief when he pressed himself against her; his horse body pushing Paladin back.

"*Go!*" she screamed out to the others. There was a town nearby, and they could get inside somewhere safe. "*We'll find you!*"

The combination of wind and rain made it impossible for Ainsley to be sure her friends had gotten away. Not when it nearly knocked her off Paladin's back. Instead of waiting for that to happen, she dismounted and grabbed his reins. Walking was harder, but a little safer considering she could barely see. If she kept riding, there was every chance she could hit a tree branch or send Paladin into a gopher hole.

But once she was on solid, if muddy, ground, Paladin started to trot off while Ainsley still held the reins. She had a feeling he was going somewhere specific, so she ran to keep up, confident Gruff was still by her side.

When she saw that Paladin was leading her to a cave in the side of a big hill—a cave she never would have seen because it was hidden behind big, old trees with lots of leaves—she nearly cried in relief.

Once inside, Ainsley let Paladin's reins go and attempted to push her hair out of her eyes while she called out for Gruff.

"I'm right here," he told her, pressing his hand against her back. "You all right?"

"Yes. I'm fine." She just couldn't see. Between the hair and the debris swirling around in the storm, her eyes were burning. It was also incredibly dark in this cave.

A soft flame suddenly appeared, floating in the air and providing a bit of light around Ainsley and Gruff.

"That won't last long," Gruff said. "We need to find dry wood so we can set up a normal pitfire."

Smiling, Ainsley pointed at the flying flame and asked, "You did this?"

Gruff shrugged but kept his focus on the ground as he searched for kindling. "It's an easy enough trick."

"I can't do it."

As she searched the ground along with Gruff, picking up anything that looked like it would burn, Ainsley heard a roar. One so powerful it felt as if the cave walls shook from the force of it.

She dropped the wood in her arms, nocked an arrow in her bow, and aimed into the darkness. Gruff stood by her now, his axe unleashed.

She heard Paladin's hooves against the cave floor, but there was something else charging. Something coming after him as they barreled toward her and Gruff. But just when she was about to let her arrow fly, Ainsley realized that what was coming toward her was not her horse . . . it was a huge black bear. Something she would normally take hours stalking before bringing it down while safely high in a tree. But this time, the bear was running right at her. No tree for her to escape to.

But Ainsley didn't have to escape. Instead, she simply stepped out of the way. Because the bear wasn't attacking her and Gruff. It was running away. From Paladin.

Her horse chased the bear past them and out into the frightening storm.

"Was that bear missing an eye?" Gruff asked.

It had been. An open socket had splattered fresh blood everywhere as the animal sped by.

A few seconds later, Paladin returned. He trotted past them and went deeper into the cave. With the storm still raging and water splashing into the opening, Ainsley and Gruff followed her horse deeper inside.

Gruff motioned to the flying light and it followed the horse, lighting their way.

In time, they found a decent spot in another cavern. No more bears or anything else that might kill them except Paladin. Once they found more wood, lit a non-magickal fire, and spread out their fur bedding, Paladin wandered from the cavern. Ainsley was more than happy to let the horse search out anything else that might be a danger and scare the hells out of it. With Paladin on watch, both she and Gruff could actually get some sleep.

"You think everyone will be all right?" Ainsley asked, her arms around her body while she jumped from foot to foot in order to get warm.

"My sister won't let anything happen to anyone and . . . what are you doing?"

"I'm freezing."

"Then take your—"

When Gruff abruptly stopped speaking, Ainsley looked around, expecting to see some other danger in the cavern with them.

"What were you about to say?" she asked when she found nothing but the pair of them.

Gruff shook his head. "Nothing."

Ainsley was sure she didn't believe that.

Queen Keeley squinted off to the left. "What is that?" she asked.

Rhiannon turned to look and replied, "That, my dear, is a tornado."

"I've heard of those."

"You don't get them here normally?"

"No. Why?"

"Then that's a problem."

"They don't want you to leave, Rhiannon," Annwyl guessed. "They're having that storm trap you here."

Thunder boomed again, followed by lightning strikes.

"They're coming for me," Rhiannon said.

"Another one." Keeley pointed to the south and a second tornado swirling toward them.

"Get back inside the tower," Rhiannon ordered.

"I'm not leaving without you."

"Don't be so dramatic, Annwyl." Rhiannon gently pushed Annwyl's hand off her elbow. "I have no intention of walking into my death today. But I can't do what I need to do as long as you two are standing around me with all that fear oozing from your pores. It's distracting. Now go."

Once the other two walked away, Rhiannon closed her eyes and let out a long, cleansing breath. She explored around her. Feeling the dirt. Looking for clues. Scenting the air. She didn't do this with her hands but with her magicks.

Strange. The storm did not have the feel of any magicks she knew. Not dragon. Not human. Not even elven or dwarf. Yet, it was somehow familiar. And empty. This storm was empty.

Not that it wasn't dangerous. It was, in fact, quite dangerous. It had lightning, and lightning for fire dragons is not only painful but deadly if a dragon is hit enough times. Even her. Tornados were also bad for dragons. Powerful enough to make their wings useless and toss them around the way baby dragons could toss around humans.

She didn't understand. Even gods gave off energy. A taste of those they ruled. Whether human or dragon or anything else. And yet she could not get a fix on . . .

Rhiannon opened her eyes and saw them standing about twenty feet away from her. Those eyes of flame watching her. Var had told her that these animals were terrified of Annwyl. Their kind had met her when she'd been dragged to one of the hells and, because they could pass on previous knowledge to each new pup, all of them avoided Rhiannon's daughter-by-mating. It was rumored among the many covens that the Mad Queen of Garbhán Isle had done so much damage in those pits of misery that the rulers had put protections on every entry. They refused to have her back.

Not that Rhiannon in any way blamed them.

But Annwyl wasn't the only one with a rather unfortunate reputation among hells' pits. When a young dragoness, Rhiannon's powers had been constricted by her own mother. It was the easiest way to keep control over her. To keep her daughter from reaching her full potential. At least that had been her mother's plan. She'd been worried that Rhiannon would try to take her throne, which Rhiannon never would have done if her bitch mother hadn't pissed her off. But once all those bound magicks were unleashed inside Rhiannon, she'd done a little . . . how should she put it? Testing. At the time, she didn't feel right testing on fellow witches, either dragon or human. So she'd pulled a few demons from the pits and had done what she had to do on them. Didn't really think it was a big deal. Now she realized she might have been underestimating hells' resentment toward their own being used for experimentation.

As the wind picked up and the tornados became bigger, guards and townspeople charged by her into the safety of the tower. She waited until the majority had passed before shifting into her dragon form. She looked down at the demon wolves. They had not run because they didn't fear her. Not like they did Annwyl anyway.

"You'd better get inside," she told them. "This storm won't care where you're from or who your loyalty is to. And neither will I."

Another flash of lightning and the wolves were gone. Not that one had to do with the other but, still, it was entertaining.

Sitting back on her haunches, Rhiannon lifted her claws and drew energy from the land around her. Doors might be shut to her, but not the skills that had been given to her by her own gods.

Writing runes in the air, Rhiannon unleashed a powerful shield that would protect the entire town from the damages of the storm. A storm not naturally made. Unfortunately, though, this shield would not stop soldiers from entering to kidnap human children or attempt to take her.

If someone did come for her, she'd have to find a way to stop them without destroying the tower where all those human children were hiding. That would definitely be unfortunate. She'd hate to do that.

No. Really. She would!

# CHAPTER 25

"Were you going to tell me to take off my clothes?"
"No," Gruff lied.

"So you're going to let me freeze to death?"

"Yes."

Ainsley frowned. "Are you okay?"

"I'm fine. Why?"

"I don't know. You just seem very okay with me freezing to death. That's unusual for . . . anyone."

Gruff didn't know what to say. He was confused and frustrated and . . .

He didn't know!

"Just . . . take care of it. I'll be in the next cavern."

"Wait," she said before he could walk out. "You're going to stand in a dark cavern while I get warm?"

"Is that a problem for you?" he snapped.

"It's weird. Even for you, it's really weird." She waved her hand around. "Forget it. I'll just go in the other cavern and get naked. So you're not affronted by my hideousness."

"*What?*"

"Why else are you trying to escape the room? I've seen my sister naked around her warrior monks, and none of them ever have to run away from the sight of her many scars. I can only assume that I'm some kind of disgusting thing you don't want to look at."

"You're being ridiculous!"

"*I'm* being ridiculous? You're the one trying to run away from the sight of all my horrid scars!"

"You don't have any scars!"

"I do too!" She pointed at a silver mark under her chin. "Like this one."

"Didn't Endelyon give you that when she threw her old hammer at you? The wooden one? It had a little edge that nicked you, right?"

"Look at that! You know the whole story."

"You *told* me the whole story! You said it was why she has a steel hammer now. More bruises but fewer scars."

"So I just sit around, telling you random stories about my family?"

"Yes. You do it all the . . . why are we yelling about any of this?"

"Because you find me repulsive! And that hurts my feelings!"

"*I do not find you*—" Gruff stopped. He had to stop. This was ridiculous!

He pressed the palms of his hands to his eyes. "I don't find you repulsive," he finally admitted. "That's the problem."

"How's that a problem?"

"Because we're alone—except for your bear-killing horse—and if we take off our clothes, we'll be naked. In a fire-lit cavern." She just gazed at him. Completely oblivious.

Perhaps, then, she had no interest in him. Fair enough. Painful, but fair enough. Gruff would simply have to live with that knowledge. Forever. Until he died. Alone and unloved.

"You're right," he finally said. "This is silly. Let's just get warm."

"Fine."

Ainsley went to the other side of the fire and began to strip off her clothes and chainmail.

To give her a modicum of privacy, he turned his back, shifted to human, and reached for his chainmail shirt. That was when he heard her growl, "You won't even *look* at me?"

"*What?*" he demanded, turning back around to face her again.

"I'm leaving," she announced, suddenly looking like the spoiled princess she swore she wasn't.

"And where are you going?"

"Anywhere!" She walked out of the cavern, only to return five seconds later. "It's very dark out there."

"I know."

"Can you teach me that ball of light thing?"

"I don't know. Do you have years of training and magicks from your ancestors to allow you to learn it properly?"

"You are being such an asshole!"

"And you're being a royal!"

She gasped. "How dare you say such a thing to me!"

"You called me an asshole!"

"*Because you're being an asshole!*" She stalked around the pit-fire toward him. "Just because you have no interest in me doesn't mean you need to make it so gods-damn obvious!"

"No interest? You are so oblivious! Just like every damn royal I've ever known!"

"*What are you talking about?*"

"All I want is *you! But you're too blind to see it!*"

Scowling, Ainsley reared back, and Gruff felt like the ultimate fool.

Until she abruptly hurtled toward him and threw herself against his body. Surprised by the attack, Gruff stumbled into the wall behind him, grunting when his back slammed against the hard stone.

He thought she was trying to take him down so she could punch him. But she leaned back a little and asked, "Why didn't you say that before, you *asshole?*"

Gruff glowered at her; arms tight around Ainsley's waist so she didn't fall to the ground.

"I didn't say anything," he growled at her, "because you are a princess, and I lost my right to be ruling stallion seven thousand years ago."

"What does that have to do with anything?"

"Everything!"

"You're an idiot!"

"You're spoiled!"

Deciding she couldn't stand hearing how spoiled she was anymore, Ainsley kissed him.

She wasn't sure why she thought that would change anything. Or what she thought it would do at all. She was glad she did it, though. Because Gruff immediately kissed her back and, to be quite honest, it was the best thing that had happened to her in a long time.

A kiss that managed to do what nothing else had in a very long time. Stop her from worrying, obsessing, about *everything*. For once, she could simply focus on the one thing she hadn't thought much about lately. Her own pleasure. And that kiss was all about pleasure. Gruff's tongue pushed her lips open and took over her mouth while she dug her fingers into his hair and gripped his scalp. She tightened her arms and legs around him and prayed he wouldn't change his mind. She didn't want him to change his mind. She didn't want him to start thinking about bigger, more important things than what was going on at this moment.

Ainsley decided distraction would be her best bet. So she drew back just enough to pull off her chainmail shirt, followed by the protective cotton shirt underneath, and then the bindings. When done, she kissed Gruff again, but this time making sure her bare chest was pressing against him. Then she realized he was still wearing his chainmail shirt. He couldn't feel her chest at all. How would it distract him if he couldn't feel it?

That answer came when one of Gruff's big hands wrapped around her breast and squeezed. She let out a surprised little squeak, which must have startled Gruff because she felt his hand start to move away. She quickly grabbed it with her own and pushed it back. Since she was busy using her tongue to play with his, she squeezed his hand and hoped he would get the message.

He did, and her legs tightened around his waist because she wanted to either close them or put something between them.

She needed to get her leggings off, but she didn't want to stop touching him. Thankfully she was wearing chainmail leggings made by her mother. Emma Smythe had been convinced her daughter's thighs would be getting bigger the more she continued to climb trees and ride horses, so she'd made them, according to her mother, "a little more roomy." At first, Ainsley had been insulted. She loved her big meaty thighs and was positive her mother was trying to say something that would just make her mad.

Now, however, she realized a side benefit to her roomy chain-mail leggings.

She kicked off her boots, reached down with her right hand to untie the belt that kept her leggings up, then raised her leg and easily pushed the legging down so that it hung off her other leg. Now she grabbed the cotton cloth that covered her sex and tore it off.

"What are you doing?" he asked against her mouth, the sound of his panting between each word making her even crazier.

So crazy, she could barely get out a "Sorry," before she grabbed his chainmail kilt and attempted to drag it up. She knew there was nothing between a centaur and his kilt. "I think we just need to get this first one out of the way."

Gruff pulled back a bit and gazed into her eyes. "Are you sure?"

Ainsley, by this point, was too overwhelmed to do anything but growl in response to his stupid question. Of course, she was sure! Why did he bother her with such horse shit?

Gruff's hands reached down and caught hold of her ass. He turned and Ainsley found herself pressed up against the cave wall. Gruff lowered his head and sucked one of her nipples into his mouth.

She cried out, her fingers returning to his scalp while he kept them pinned there. She was so distracted, she didn't even notice that his hands had left her. Now, his body pinned her to the wall. That's when she heard the soft metallic clang of his kilt as his hands lifted the chainmail up, exposing his cock. She still couldn't see it, though. Didn't think about it too much either until Gruff lowered her a bit and the next thing she knew, that cock was inside her.

He pushed it in roughly because his hands were trying to regrip her hips.

And what could Ainsley say? She loved it. Loved how his cock entered her. It was massive, too; hurting a little when it reached its limit. But the pleasure outweighed the pain.

She reached for his shoulders and gripped them, fingernails digging in as soon as Gruff's hips began to thrust in and out.

He took her at her word. That this was what she wanted. And it was. She simply held on and let him do what he wanted, not because she had no choice—she did—she knew if she wanted him to stop, all she had to do was say it—but because she trusted him so much. He would never hurt her. Not unless she liked it. The way she liked it now.

She really liked it.

He did, too, she guessed, by the way his groaning got louder with each thrust. And the way his hands on her ass got so tight, she knew his fingers would leave some bruises. She didn't care. Especially when he began sucking on her other breast.

Ainsley threw her head back and let out a loud yelp, unable to help herself. She raised her bare leg higher, so it comfortably rested on Gruff's hip and again held his head pressed against her breast.

He was still groaning, but now he was doing it against her breast. The low rumble shot through her nipple and spread across her body, shooting out as if something was about to explode inside her. Her toes curled and Ainsley could no longer make any sound but a harsh gasp with each thrust of Gruff's cock and each suck of his mouth.

It almost hurt, what happened next. That explosion she'd been anticipating finally detonated deep inside her. It took her by surprise. Not only the force of it but the fact it happened at all when she usually needed fingers pressed against her clit and moving in a certain way to get her to that point. But other than the occasional grazing of his groin against hers, her clit was left pretty much alone, and yet . . . she felt that explosion right through her clit as if it was being forcefully touched to get her where she needed to go.

Apparently, though, all she needed tonight was a big cock and Gruffyn of the Torn Moon Clan making her feel like nothing else in the world mattered but her.

She screamed out as her entire body tightened around him, and even if he'd wanted to stop, he couldn't. He came hard, burying his cock deep inside her so that she tightened on him like a vise.

They held on to each other as the waves kept coming, both of them gasping and groaning until they were completely drained.

Gruff dropped his head against her neck and panted, waiting for his brain to clear and his knees to stop shaking. He didn't want to drop her at this point. That would not be attractive to any woman. So he just let them lean against the wall until he felt he had his strength back enough to carry her to the fur bedding they'd set out earlier.

He could have let her go once he'd gotten them down on the floor, on their sides, facing each other. But he didn't. He also didn't pull his cock out of her. It was extremely happy to be right where it was. And when Ainsley didn't pull away either, he assumed she was also comfortable.

They didn't say anything for quite a while because they both knew they didn't need to. One of the things he'd always enjoyed about Ainsley was her ability to not talk if there was nothing to be said. She knew how to sit in comfortable silence without worrying.

She also knew how to make his cock hard again. By kissing his neck and nipping his ear and along his jaw.

Within minutes, she pushed him to his back and shoved his chainmail shirt up his chest, her mouth following. Kissing its way up until she could lick and suck his nipples.

Gruff quickly pulled his shirt off and reached down between them to get rid of the kilt. He kicked off his boots and flipped Ainsley onto her back. He wanted to do one thing before they continued. Something he'd had a late-night dream about a few times that had him waking up sweaty, spent, and lying to himself about who he'd been with in that dream.

On his knees, he grabbed Ainsley under the ass and lifted her hips up until he had only to lean down a bit to reach her pussy. He slid his mouth over her clit and began to suck.

With her arms flung over her head, Ainsley immediately arched her back and tightened her thighs around his head.

Her groaning made him want to stop and bury himself inside her again, but he kept control this time, sucking and, when she began to shake, stopping to lick her pussy inside and out. He could taste himself on her, and that only made him harder. Knowing she'd taken all of him and had loved it.

With her eyes closed, she grabbed her nipples with her fingers and began to tug and squeeze. Her body began to writhe against his hands, so he held her tighter and went ruthlessly to her clit. Sucking and circling with his tongue until Ainsley let out another scream and grabbed his head, keeping him in place as her hips moved back and forth and her head tossed from side to side. She came, but he didn't stop because she didn't let go. So he continued on and watched her come again. Then, a few minutes later and nearly sobbing, she came again. Her entire body clenching from how strong it was for her.

When she collapsed back to the floor, Gruff finally pulled his mouth away and gently stretched her out on the bedding.

He lay down next to her and gave her time to get her breath back. He'd closed his eyes, thinking he might get some sleep while she recovered, but he didn't even have time to snore before her mouth was sucking his cock down her throat.

She kneeled between his legs, ass up in the air, as she swallowed him whole. Relaxed and smiling, she sucked on his cock until Gruff thought he might lose his mind. Then she pulled her mouth away long enough to tell him, "I taste myself on you. I like it."

That's when he really lost his mind. He dug his fingers into her hair and held her in place while he thrust his hips up, fucking her mouth. She should have stopped him. Maybe told him to slow down. But she didn't. She just made it all worse by keeping her lips tight around him, her hands gripping the base, and groaning as if she'd never enjoyed anything more.

Unable to hold back, he just took her. Took her mouth with his entire cock. Going so deep he could feel the back of her throat against the head. And she was right there with him. Never stopping. Never trying to push him back.

Knowing she wanted this as much as he did had him roaring when he finally came in her mouth, holding her in place so that she had to swallow everything he gave her. When he was finally done and he fell back to the bedding, she stared down at him but said nothing. Was she angry? Was she done with him? Did she never want to have him in her bed again because he was so fucking selfish?

He was about to apologize for what he considered rudeness when her tongue eased out of her mouth and swiped the corner where a drop remained.

Then she smiled.

She. Smiled.

\* \* \*

She didn't really know what she'd done, but Gruff abruptly sat up, grabbed her face with both hands, and kissed her so hard, she lost her breath.

Before she knew it, she was on her back and a hard cock—how could it be hard so quickly?—was buried deep inside her. Gruff was on top of her, staring down at her as he pumped his cock inside her over and over.

They'd both already come several times, so this might take a while. But the smile that eased across Gruff's face told her he didn't mind.

Of course . . . neither did she.

# CHAPTER 26

"What are you doing?"

Beatrix looked up into the face of the useless male she'd been forced to marry in order to do what she knew needed to be done. Order brought to an out-of-control world . . . or whatever.

It galled her that someone like her had to lower herself to marry someone like *him*. A weak-willed male who thought no farther than the tip of his diseased penis.

But it was a price she was more than willing to pay in order to get what she knew was rightfully hers.

She leaned back in her chair and gazed up at King Marius. "What am I doing?" she asked. "You'll have to be much more specific than that if you hope for an answer."

"I took my troops to Lord Hatton's lands, prepared to force him into taking my very generous offer—"

*His* generous offer? So pathetic.

"—and there was nothing." He stopped talking, but she had no idea what he expected. For her to gasp? For her to spill information? To care? Because she just didn't care anymore. He'd stopped being useful a long time ago.

"*Nothing!*" he bellowed, slamming his hands down on the desk and leaning toward her so their faces were inches apart. "Hatton's castle, his soldiers, his wife and children, even the peasants who worked his lands. *All gone!*"

"I don't know what you expect me to say to that."

"Was it you?"

"Of course it wasn't me," she replied easily. "It was the soldiers I sent there to kill Hatton, his friends and family, all his serfs, and to wipe the land clean of any evidence of their having once existed. I don't see the problem."

"You don't see what you've . . ."

"What was I supposed to do?" she finally asked. "Let *you* go there? Rape all the women? Possibly the men if you were in the mood? And then burn a few buildings while you pranced around Hatton's castle, telling everyone it was yours now and wanting to see all those weak peasants quake in fear before your army? Quite honestly, I no longer have time for that bullshit."

"You killed his children!"

"And?" she said on a shrug. "What was I supposed to do? Let them live? That's not making a point. Making a point is hanging their lifeless remains outside Lord Bagnold's stronghold and surprise, surprise. He cowers before me now. Just as he should. Just as you all should."

With a snarl, Marius grabbed her throat and squeezed. His expression was filled with intense rage, but Beatrix didn't care. She didn't care if he choked the life from her. She didn't care if he buried a sword in her chest. She didn't care about anything. Too bad for Marius, he refused to learn that about his wife.

"What's that?" Marius suddenly demanded, his gaze no longer focused on her face, but something behind her.

Beatrix removed the now-loosened grip on her throat and returned to the scrolls Ivan had left with her before he'd headed to his rituals and bloodletting back in his rooms. She'd used her husband for all she'd needed; now she was done with him.

"That is my friend. Marius, this is Athanagild. Athanagild, this is Marius."

The big warrior took a step back, away from the slithering and skittering in the darkness behind Beatrix's desk. She had no problem ignoring that sound, but it looked as if the one she'd married had trouble doing the same.

"A *demon* god?" he asked, now slowly backing away. "You've aligned yourself with a demon god?"

"It's not final yet," she explained, checking over some figures for army supplies. "We're seeing how tomorrow goes in my sister's territories. If well, then we may finalize." She looked up, enjoying the sight of the color draining from Marius's face because he was just so afraid. Now he knew how all his victims felt. Some kind of justice, she was sure.

"You know," she said, again leaning back in her chair, "*if* the deal is done, I've promised dear Athanagild here an enormous number of souls for his collection. And"—she gestured to Marius with a wave of her hand—"I feel it would be wise to give him a taste of what might come."

There was a single beat of time, and then her husband was running toward the door. He never reached it. Athanagild slipped and slid through the dark crevices of her chamber and snatched her husband out of sight before Marius could even get his hand on the door handle.

Going back to her missives and numbers, Beatrix smiled a bit at the sound of her husband's screams as his soul was torn apart just a few feet from her desk.

Yes. Definitely. Some kind of justice, somewhere. At least that's what her sister Keeley would probably say.

She could hardly wait for tomorrow. If all went according to plan, she would finally end the one who threatened her most.

# CHAPTER 27

Gemma stood by the gates and gazed out over the land. The storm was so horrifying that everything should have been destroyed. Literally everything. But it wasn't. The birds were back. The trees stood tall and grounded. The boulders and rocks that dotted the territory were in the same places they'd been for hundreds of years. And still covered in moss. And that was down to one reason only . . . Rhiannon, the Dragon Queen of Dark Plains.

She should hate such a beast. With those white wings and fangs and magicks that she tore straight from the earth beneath Gemma's feet. But how could she when she had saved them all.

Even stranger was watching Queen Annwyl play with Endelyon and Little Rexie while the family remained huddled in the main hall. It was decided they would all be safer together, with that storm raging all around them. So it was together they all sat and listened to the nightmarish winds and thunder; watched the lightning strikes through the high windows as each one shook the ground all around them. Queen Annwyl hadn't acted like a royal then, though, sitting on the floor and playing pretend battle with the children well into the night before offering to read them stories until they fell asleep. The Mad Queen hadn't had to do any of that, but she had, more comfortable with Gemma's crazy baby sister and oblivious Rexie than she was with anyone else in the room. Except the dragons, of course. She was clearly comfortable with them. Even Quinn had seemed to find a co-conspirator in the torment of his dark-haired brother: Gwenvael the Handsome, who enjoyed torturing *his* dark-haired brother just as much.

She couldn't shake the feeling, however, that she shouldn't allow their friendship to thrive too much. Not if she hoped for the love of her life to have a long and happy existence with all four of his legs.

Gemma watched the sky turn pink as the two suns began to rise in the distance. Prince Unnvar silently moved up beside her. He was unbelievably quiet for such a big male.

"Your horse has gone missing," he announced.

Gemma and Keeley had checked on the horses first thing, knowing the sounds of the storm would have frightened them, but the stable boys and Gemma's squire had done a very good job of keeping the animals calm during the night.

"Which horse?" she asked. "I have several, depending on what I need."

"The one that drips bits of itself all over your small town."

"Oh. Kriegszorn." She dismissed his concern with a sniff. "That's fine."

"Really? Your undead horse roaming the land doesn't bother you?"

"I trust Kriegszorn more than I trust most people." She glanced at the royal. "Or you. Her loyalty to me will never be in question."

"It didn't take down the fence. How did it get out?"

Gemma wasn't going to answer that.

"Where's your grandmother?" she asked Var instead. "I should thank her for her protection before she says something to piss me off."

"The protection spell she cast was a bit draining. She'll need extra rest."

Gemma nodded, understanding.

"Anything else?" he asked.

"Keeley is in the main hall," Gemma told Var. "And I want her to stay there. I don't want her or anyone else outside the tower walls until the situation with Queen Rhiannon finds some kind of solution."

"I'll find a way to distract her."

Gemma rubbed her eyes. She hadn't slept well at all the previous night with so much on her mind, which meant Quinn hadn't slept either. Now both of them were in a bad mood.

"And your Queen Annwyl?" she asked Var. "Can you find a way to distract her too?"

"She's already out, roaming the lands and looking for a fight."

"By herself?"

"She has Morfyd with her."

"And why is your aunt looking for a fight?"

"Because she hates your evil sister. First the slavery and then Beatrix's attempts to kill her own young siblings—those acts remind her too much of her brother, the dead King Lorcan. So my aunt Annwyl won't relax until that woman's head is on a pike and planted either here or in Dark Plains. I could try to find her, though."

"No, no. I need you here. I'll look for her in a bit myself and nicely urge her to return to the safety of the tower." She scratched her head before announcing to Var, "I have some . . . associates returning to the tower sometime today. I don't want Keeley dealing with them because I don't trust them not to use her."

Var raised a golden brow. "You don't trust your own associates?"

"The creation of those relationships is . . . a very long story. But these people are similar to my three monk cohorts, whom you met yesterday. Only none of the ones arriving today are monks. They're witches, battle priests, assassins—"

"A loving, open-minded group of friends, I'm sure."

She heard his sarcasm but ignored it. "When they arrive, ask them to wait for me in my Order's barracks. Don't let them go into the tower."

"And you can't perform this particular job because . . . ?"

"I must go to a high peak and praise my god under the light of the mighty suns. Then, to honor him, I must search these lands for a proper blood sacrifice, which will hopefully bring peace and joy to all."

"In other words, you're going to scour the lands outside these walls until you hunt down and kill any of Beatrix's soldiers that were foolish enough to come here to kidnap your siblings and put your sister's throne at risk?"

"That's exactly what I mean. But the way I phrased it sounds better coming from a monk."

Gemma rubbed her tired eyes again.

"Anything else I can do to help, Brother? You seem unusually . . . placid."

That was true, and it wasn't just the exhaustion brought on by lack of sleep. But other than taking a quick bath in the cold river, Gemma had no idea what to do about it.

She didn't go into any of that, though. She was just getting to know Prince Unnvar and wasn't ready to take him completely into her confidences yet. So she simply told him, "Once we get past all this craziness, I'm going to want to ensure this won't happen again."

"Once we know what *this* is," Var responded, "I'll be able to prevent it from happening again. Preventing problems is one of my specialties. My mother taught it to me. But you'll need to understand that wise prevention doesn't mean new things won't pop up to make your life and the life of your family hell."

Gemma frowned. "I know that. Why are you telling me so?"

"Dragons tend to believe that once they strike something out of their lives, the problem is gone forever. They are always stunned when something new and also problematic comes along, and they tend to blame those of us who, despite having prevented millions of other disasters from occurring, did our best. They insist on saying we let them down. That we're not as smart as some of us think we are." He blinked. "I can assure you I *am* as smart as I know I am."

"And as humble!"

Ainsley had her head on Gruff's shoulder as the pair of them gazed up at the stone ceiling above their heads. She had one arm stretched across his chest while Gruff's big fingers gently stroked back and forth along the skin of her forearm. Her other hand was currently curled inside his fist. She'd woken up like that and neither of them had bothered to move. She'd say they were too exhausted to do much of anything but, at least for her, she was also just too comfortable.

"Do you think dragons really live in caves?"

"I heard the black-haired one—"

"Fearghus."

"Yes. Him. He told Queen Annwyl he couldn't wait to get back to their cave. So apparently human queens live in caves, too."

"How sad. I'd hate to live here. Even with a fire, it's very damp and depressing. One night is fine but a lifetime? With a fire-breathing dragon as a mate? I can't see it being very enjoyable."

"Maybe they have a hoard of gold in their caves."

"I could be wrong, but I don't think Annwyl cares much for gold."

"Not as much as she cares for blood and steel. No."

They fell silent again for another twenty minutes until Ainsley asked, "Did the storm end?"

"A few hours ago. At least the thunder part. It may still be raining."

"Think it's morning?"

"It's definitely morning."

"We should get up."

"We should."

But they didn't.

Again, they went silent, but it was Gruffyn who broke it this time. "Ainsley?"

"Yes?" When he didn't say anything, she told him, "Don't worry. It's fine."

"All right. Good." Another moment of silence and then, "Wait . . . what's fine?"

"Making this complicated. I have no intention of making this complicated."

"Why would it be complicated?"

"I just don't want you to think it will be."

"Okay. Good."

More silence. Then . . .

"Wait," Gruff said again, "what the fuck are we talking about?"

Ainsley turned her head so she could look into his face. "Us after this. This night."

"Yeah . . . and?"

"Well, I'm just saying there's no pressure."

"Of course there's pressure."

"There is?"

"Once those two idiots find out. I think they've been leaving me alone for the last few days because they thought you were just tormenting Brother Gemma. But once they know it's true . . ."

"Oh."

She felt him shrug under her head. "Ech, I'll let my sister deal with them. She loves making them miserable."

"Okay."

"Okay."

Ainsley relaxed again, but less than a minute later she sat up. "I don't understand what's happening."

"I don't want to get hit in the face," he replied. It was his expression that confused her more than his words. It was so . . . placid. So calm. As if it was an obvious thing to say. But how was it obvious?"

"Why would you get hit in the face?"

"Because once those two idiots find out I'm in love with you and we're not together just to annoy your sister, they're *going to hit me in the face.*"

Startled, Ainsley cleared her throat. "Oh. All right, then."

Gruff sat up but she caught his arm before he could move away. "You're in love with me?"

He gawked at her for a moment before he snapped, "What's it like?"

"What's what like?"

"Being so oblivious! Living in a world where you don't need to know anything that's going on around you. You are *such* a royal!"

"You don't have to be nasty!"

Growling, he stood and grabbed his kilt.

Ainsley started to do the same, but then he was crouching right in front of her, looking her directly in the eye.

"Are you not in love with me?" he demanded.

"Well, when you're snarling the question at me . . ."

"You see . . . this is the problem!"

"Your insanity?"

"No. You keep thinking I'm human. I am *not* human! I'm centaur, which makes me—"

When his words stopped abruptly, she shot back, "You were going to say 'better,' weren't you? Better than we mere humans!"

"At the very least, my kind is better than human males."

"I already know *that*."

He waited a moment before barking, "Then answer me!"

"If you're asking me if I love you, then yes! *But not if you keep yelling at me!*"

"Finally," he huffed.

Gruff stood tall and began picking up the clothes scattered around the cavern. All while muttering to himself. "Simple question and she just can't simply answer it. Always making things difficult."

Rolling her eyes, Ainsley got to her feet. She wished she could take a quick bath, but they had to track down the others and then find—

"Hello, my friends!" Sheva announced as she sauntered into the cavern. "Good night?" she asked, grinning at them. Meaning the evil bitch had been listening to their argument. See? This was why Ainsley stayed in trees. Away from people. Because people were so annoying!

Sheva took a step back into the passage. "Hilda! Come! See our friends safe and healthy!"

"You cow," Ainsley muttered seconds before Hilda entered the chamber and immediately threw her hands in the air.

"Do you really think I want to see *that*?" she asked, gesturing to Gruff's cock, which didn't surprise Ainsley at all. But then she motioned to her and added, "Or *that!*"

"Hey! Not fair," Ainsley complained before reaching for her clothes from Gruff.

"Are you that insecure with human bodies?" Sheva asked.

"I'm not insecure about anything. I just know what I like and what I don't like. And what I don't like is people touching me. And flashing their bits about."

"You walked in on *us*," Gruff reminded her, now dressed, his weapons strapped on.

"It's really Sheva's fault," Ainsley pointed out.

"You're right. It is her fault." Hilda slapped Sheva's shoulder with her steel walking stick.

"Ow!"

"Horrible monk."

"How did you find us?" Gruff asked the monk. "We thought we'd have to search for you."

"My horse," Sheva said. "The mare tracked her brother down quite easily. And we were less than a league away from this place."

"Where did you end up staying? Another cave?"

"We spent the night inside a local town pub with many drunk residents who were also afraid of the storm," Hilda replied. "I did not enjoy myself."

Sheva rolled her eyes at Ainsley as they walked toward the exit from the cavern.

Gruff, now comfortably back in his natural form, looked up at the sky as soon as they'd cleared the cave walls and stepped out into the surrounding forest. The suns had just cleared the tops of the local mountains so it was midmorning. They should get on the road as soon as possible. They still had work to do.

"Gruff!" Briallen called out. She trotted to his side and placed her head on his shoulder. He stroked her hair and let out a breath, relieved to see her alive and well.

Sarff and the rest of his Torn Moon Clan joined them.

"We should get on the road," Ainsley pushed, calling her horse over with a click of her tongue.

"No," Sarff said. "We should all eat first."

"But the storm pushed us back." Ainsley put the strap of her travel bag over her shoulder. "We need to get on the road and—"

"No," Sarff said again. "We should take a much-needed break under this beautiful sky and eat something."

It was the way Sarff said it that made Gruff's ears prick up. She was so calm. Almost pleasant. Not like her at all. She, of course, was not one for hysterics. But she was never pleasant. To anyone!

Ainsley knew something was going on with Sarff, but she had no idea what. And one look at Gruff told her he didn't know what was happening either.

It couldn't hurt, though, to take five minutes to eat before they set off.

The group walked over to a large shady tree and Sarff handed out the dried meat and loaves of bread they'd packed for their trip.

"You look worried," Briallen said to Ainsley before taking a bite of her food. "What is it?"

"Just worried about the children. A few of them are scared of storms. And that one—"

"Wasn't normal," Sarff announced.

"In what way?"

The centaur motioned to Hilda and Sheva. "The virgin and the witch murderer know. Don't ya?"

Sheva shrugged. "I have *no* idea what you're talking about."

And Ainsley believed her. She was, when it came to worship, the absolute *worst* monk.

Hilda, however, said nothing.

"What?" Ainsley pushed when Hilda just stood there.

"When it began to rain," she said, pressing her hand to her chest, closing her eyes, and briefly bowing her head, "my god warned me to get inside where I would be safe."

"Just you?" Ainsley couldn't help asking with a little bit of tone.

"I'm the one who is devoted to him," Hilda snipped back. "But that's why I was pushing us last night. I wanted to get to a town where we could take shelter."

"But we got separated from you." Ainsley looked down, then asked. "So a god was trying to separate us?"

Sarff snorted a laugh, which Ainsley didn't appreciate at all.

"Gods ain't got time for you, gal. I bet the plan was simply to keep that dragonwitch from flying off home. Fire dragons ain't keen on lightning."

"Why would that be necessary?"

"To wait for whatever that evil sister of yours is sending her way."

"Then the question becomes," Sheva guessed, "whether we continue on or go back?"

"Go back for what?" Briallen wanted to know. "What can our squad do that Keeley's soldiers and all those dragons *can't*? Whether it's to protect Queen Rhiannon or Ainsley's sisters and brothers?"

Everyone silently agreed with that. None of them had powers that could compete with an actual dragonwitch. Not even Sarff. And definitely not a nun or monk still in training.

"Then we should move forward?" Sheva asked. "Is that what we're saying?"

Sarff, now busy chewing her food, would only shrug her shoulders, but they all seemed to take it as tacit agreement and went back to their meals.

Ainsley just couldn't get rid of an anxious feeling deep in her gut. She tried pacing the feeling away, but the centaurs kept glancing at her. She was making them nervous the same way she did with the horses at home when she anxiously paced around the stables.

She decided to give them a little space by moving farther away and pacing next to a different tree. She couldn't relax. She was too anxious!

Ainsley suddenly had so many thoughts but none of them made sense, and she didn't understand what was bothering her so intensely.

She shook her head. She was probably just worried about her siblings being caught in the middle of a fight between some god and a dragonwitch.

"What are you doing?" she heard Gruff ask.

"Giving everyone space."

"By sitting in a tree?"

"I'm not sitting in a—"

Ainsley looked down. She was in a tree! She didn't even remember climbing it.

"What is it, Ainsley?" Gruff pushed.

"I'm randomly climbing trees without realizing it. That can't be good."

"It just means something's bothering you. What is it?"

"It's . . . it's . . ." Ainsley swung her arms around. "It's all of this!" she yelled. "It's just another distraction!"

She climbed down the tree and walked back over to the others, with Gruff right behind her.

"All this is just a distraction," she said again.

"To get to Rhiannon? Or maybe Annwyl?" Sheva suggested.

"My sister has gotten where she is by carefully planning each and every step she's ever taken. She doesn't do anything sudden. She doesn't take chances. She examines her actions from every angle."

"So?" Hilda asked.

"So . . . how can she look at every angle when a Dragon Queen comes out of nowhere? I've only met that female once, but I can tell you she's the opposite of my sister. She just does shit. Makes her mind up in a split second and moves forward accordingly. There was no way anyone could know she was coming here or how long she planned to stay, which according to her, wasn't long."

"But if a god's involved . . . doesn't that change everything for Beatrix?"

Ainsley almost said, "Yes. Of course." But she quickly realized she didn't mean that. She didn't mean that at all.

"My sister could give a shit about the gods. They could promise to make her emperor of the entire world tomorrow but..." She shook her head. "No. Beatrix would never go for that."

"Why?"

"Because the gods are fickle. All of them. They give and, just as quickly, they take away. She wouldn't risk all she's gotten because a god promised her... *anything*."

Ainsley realized she was pacing again, but the centaurs didn't seem bothered this time because now they understood she was just working things out.

"No. She wouldn't take an offer from the gods..." A large rabbit hopped by behind Briallen, trying to make it to its home before anyone noticed it was there.

Abruptly, sweat broke out on Ainsley's flesh and her fingers curled into fists that she pressed against her forehead.

"Ainsley?"

"She wouldn't take an offer from the gods," Ainsley told them. "But she would *use* the gods to get what she wants."

"To get what? Your sister's throne? Queen Rhiannon's?" Briallen guessed.

"The children?" Sheva asked.

"You?" Gruff wanted to know.

"No. No, no, no!" She covered her eyes. "I'm such an idiot!"

Of all the people who knew Beatrix—who really *knew* her—Ainsley understood her best. She should have known. She should have known from the very beginning.

"Ainsley?" Gruff asked calmly. "What is it?"

"Beatrix doesn't want Rhiannon," she explained. "Or Annwyl. Or even Keeley. She already has plans for them, and my sister doesn't deviate from her plans." She swung her arms out. "All this is nothing but pig shit! A quagmire for us to crawl through so she can be free to kill the one she hates the most. Hates even more than me because she never saw me as a threat."

"Who are you talking about?"

"Gemma. She's going to kill Gemma."

# CHAPTER 28

Rhiannon turned over in the tiny bed she'd been forced to sleep in. She didn't know how humans did it. Cramming their limbs into these tiny things and living on these lumpy mattresses made of . . . what? Straw? Tree bark? Dead animals?

She didn't know. She just knew she didn't like it. She could be home, cuddled up with her mate; their tails intertwined. Or sleeping on their piles of gold and jewels. But she was here. With these easily irritated humans.

She rolled over and attempted to relax. That's when she heard it. A voice in her head, calling her name. It wasn't anyone who should be able to talk to her that way. None of her offspring were calling her. Her mate, not related by blood, couldn't unless she'd already opened a message-way for him before leaving Dark Plains, which she hadn't because she thought she'd be right back. And any blood relations on her mother's side wouldn't have the balls to contact Rhiannon unless they wanted to be tracked down and wiped out by the Cadwaladrs.

Knowing this was someone who shouldn't be in her head, Rhiannon spit out an ancient spell that sent the voice screaming in pain to the far reaches of dark domains. Satisfied she wouldn't be interrupted again, she went back to sleep, only pouting a little because she missed Bercelak's naughty tail so much.

Var was standing with his uncle Bram a few miles outside of town for a little privacy. With everything so strange at the moment, there were people everywhere. Guards. Soldiers. Townspeople. Tradesmen. They were all lurking around the tower, inside the protection of the walls.

No one knew what was going on, but these humans were surprisingly sensitive. Like the wild horses Var had noticed roaming these lands, they knew something was not right in their already unusual world. But while the wild horses had simply disappeared, the humans drifted to places where they felt they and their families would be safest. Not that Bram blamed them.

He knew how important his own family was to him.

It was all those people, though, that had sent Var and Bram to this quiet little clearing. They needed to discuss important things in private and the tower was too busy; the lakes, rivers, and ponds had too many bathers; and the forests had quite a few hunters searching for game to cook at a pitfire in case they didn't get home that night.

This little clearing, though, was working out very well. They needed to discuss last-minute changes to the agreement between the two queens. Actually, it was now three queens involved in the agreement. Although Isadora would be living with Annwyl the Bloody, it was decided that an agreement with Queen Rhiannon would be a good idea as well. Probably because Brother Gemma wanted more assurances that her sister would be safe around the Dragon Queen after his grandmother had casually discussed those long ago, halcyon days when eating humans was a common thing among his father's kind.

Var adored his grandmother but, as his mother liked to say, "She does not make things easy for any of us."

But that was okay. Rhiannon always made him laugh, and there were few who managed that. Mostly because they weren't very funny.

"Perhaps if we move this paragraph here," Bram suggested, "and then take this section out completely but put in something about—"

"Do you two not hear that?"

Var and Bram looked up to see Aunt Ghleanna stalking toward them in her human form, covered in armor and carrying more weapons than seemed necessary.

"Hear what?" Bram asked. "I don't hear anything. Do you hear anything, Var?"

He didn't, but he'd been totally focused on the alliance agreement.

"You truly are the son he's always wanted," Ghleanna said as she pushed between them and kept going.

"I love all our offspring, Ghleanna. I have no favorites." He glanced at Var and whispered, "You actually are my favorite but that's between us."

"But as a nephew," Var said, in case his aunt had heard.

"Right. Right. As a nephew. My actual offspring are all so . . . great. Despite having no interest in anything but swords and blood. Just like their mum."

"You two should see this," Ghleanna called out, and the pair jogged into the trees, stopping when they reached her.

"What in all hells *is* that?" Bram wanted to know.

"That's Brother Gemma's horse."

"The undead thing I've been hearing about? What's wrong with it?"

Kriegszorn was writhing and struggling in the middle of the trees, but there was no one around her. No one trying to hold her. Nothing on her four legs or body to elicit such a response.

Now he heard the sound Ghleanna had been complaining about. It was actually sounds. One was the panicked and angry wailing of the undead horse. The other was growling.

"Like a wolf."

"What? Var! Wait! Where are you going?"

"To find Annwyl! Ghleanna, get your troops together! Now!"

Ghleanna watched her nephew run off. "Annwyl?" she asked. "Shouldn't he be going to get Rhiannon? Or the tiny monk?"

She looked to her mate to get his opinion, but he was walking toward the horse.

"Bram?"

"I can't let the poor animal suffer. Maybe I can help."

Ghleanna ran over to the stupid, brilliant dragon she loved and grabbed him by the back of his neck.

"Oh, no, you don't, Bram the Silver," she snarled, using the name he'd been given at birth. She pushed him back toward the tower. "Var will deal with the hysterical horse—"

"But the poor animal!"

"—and you will alert Queen Keeley of trouble on her lands and get the offspring to safety."

"I can take care of myself, Ghleanna."

"I know. But I was born to do this."

"Born to do what?"

"Get my army together and stop whatever the hells has our always-calm nephew running off in a panic."

Var wasn't sure where Annwyl might be, but he had an idea, because she was a woman of habits and not as insane as everyone thought.

He went up. Annwyl always took advantage of high ground. Then he went to a small overhanging cliff that wasn't immediately obvious, which was where he located her.

"Ann—"

"Shhhh! Down!"

Var dropped and crawled over to his aunt's side. She was stretched out, belly down, at the very edge of the cliff. He didn't have to lean far to see what she was looking at.

"How many soldiers?" he asked.

"A regiment. So . . . five thousand or so."

"How could they get here without us hearing anything about it?"

"A god sent them."

He glanced at his aunt. "Pardon?"

"It wouldn't be the first time. Beings just literally appearing and killing people."

Var believed her. Because there were no camps. No tents. No sense that any of these thousands of soldiers had marched here over a number of days or even weeks.

"It's a good move," she explained. "Meant to terrify, mostly."

"Is that why you're so calm? Because you're too insane to be terrified?"

"No. I'm calm because I've been through this sort of thing before." She shrugged. "And I'm also not easy to terrify. But I am *not* insane. No matter what your uncle Briec says."

Annwyl suddenly grunted.

"What?" Var asked.

"We do have an issue I find concerning, though."

"Just one?"

She pointed. "Those."

"Oh, for fuck's sake. Giant crossbows?"

"This is why dragons learn to fight as human."

"Who just has giant crossbows lying around?" he wanted to know.

"You'd be amazed. Come on. We need to let your kin know."

"I actually came here to get you," he said as they crawled back from the cliff. "But it can wait until—"

"Get me for what?"

"Brother Gemma's undead horse is trapped in those woods that Uncle Briec almost set on fire with a sneeze."

"I think he's just allergic to those weird flowers by the old trees. And get Brother Gemma to deal with her half-dead horse problems."

"I would, except the animal is trapped by something I can't see."

Annwyl stopped walking and looked back at him. "What?"

"I don't know what has hold of that horse, but I do know it's not good and it's not normal. And it's growling. And when something's growling, Aunt, I come looking for you."

"Something invisible has hold of the monk's half-dead horse and it's growling?"

"Yes."

Annwyl suddenly took off running.

"Get the information about those soldiers and the weapons they possess back to your Aunt Ghleanna!" she yelled at him over her shoulder.

"Are you sure you don't want to deal with the army below first? *They do seem the higher priority.*"

"Don't be overdramatic, Var! It's not an army. It's a regiment. And right now they're the least of our problems."

Never in her life had Ainsley been so relieved to see that dwarf-built tower. Hours on the road and she was near a full-blown panic.

Ignoring the other travelers heading into town, she spurred Lord Paladin on. She yelled for everyone to get out of her way, unwilling to stop for any reason, knowing without checking that Hilda, Sheva, Gruff, and the centaurs were right behind her.

But she was forced to rein in when she saw a line of royal guards in front of those open gates.

Paladin stopped in front of them and Ainsley asked, "Where's Brother Gemma?"

"She went out early this morning, Your Highness," one of the guards replied.

"Do any of you know where she might be right now? It's important."

A soldier stood and moved up next to her. She hadn't even noticed him until he put his hand on her leg. It was the lieutenant.

He smiled at her in that way he had, and she realized how calculated it was. That smile. Because he thought he could get her into bed again—despite the way he'd treated her. Or was it because he was up to something much more sinister?

Squeezing her calf, he asked, "I could help you look if you'd—"

Ainsley pushed the tip of one of her arrows under the lieutenant's chin, ready to tear open a hole that could never be healed. "Are you trying to distract me, sir?"

"Wha—"

She pressed harder, and blood began to slide down the shaft. "If you know where my sister is, now is the time to tell me, or I'll end you like one of Daddy's sick pigs."

He gestured with one hand, afraid to move more than that. "North! I saw her going north nearly an hour ago!"

"Are you lying to me?" she asked coldly.

"No! It was north!"

"It better be." She yanked the arrow away from him and turned her horse, riding north with the others behind her.

Annwyl ran toward the woods, then simply followed the sound of wailing. In minutes, she found the monk's half-dead horse.

Unlike Var, she knew exactly what had hold of the panicking animal. She knew because she could see. She could see lots of things that others couldn't. Especially hells' beasts.

She recognized it too. It wasn't like the other demon wolves that roamed the castle walls. This one was the leader. The breeder. She knew it had delivered puppies recently.

Annwyl liked the puppies. Liked Queen Keeley's favorite and the wolves that traveled with it. But the breeder . . . this one still took orders from its masters, unlike Keeley's favorite, who now lived its life here. Among the humans.

Annwyl stepped behind the tree when the beast looked in her direction. No. This one wasn't like the others. She knew that because the others didn't have tentacles.

Tentacles that it used to drag down Gemma's poor horse. If it wasn't already half-dead, the beast would have killed it by now.

Annwyl slowly brought out her swords and eased around the other side of the tree.

She took one step away and the beast turned toward her, baring an entire mouthful of long fangs in triple rows.

Then it roared at her. A loud, painful roar that made the ground beneath her feet shake and sent piercing pain through her ears.

And, when it was done, it used its tentacles to raise the screaming horse up before slamming her back to the ground.

That's when the screaming started. Not the horse's screams—she was still wailing—but Annwyl's. She started screaming and she couldn't stop. She screamed and she screamed and she kept screaming even as she charged toward the beast, both swords raised.

The tentacles released the horse and turned back into the demon's four legs. Now, focused only on Annwyl, it ran toward her.

Annwyl kept coming until she was a few feet from the thing's giant maw. Using her speed, she leaped up enough to get her booted foot inside the beast's mouth, then mounted its head. She yanked her leg out before it could bite it off and forward rolled down to its neck.

It spun around, attempting to get her off, and then unleashed its tentacles again.

Annwyl slashed at two of the foul things before they could touch her and then rammed one sword into the top of the creature's neck and her second sword into the side.

Still screaming, she pulled the swords one way and then another.

The beast reared up on its hind legs and Annwyl, still screaming and holding on to her swords by their hilts, hung there for a moment with her feet dangling.

More tentacles came toward her from either side, and Annwyl pulled out one of the swords to slash at the closest. Another reached over and grabbed her ankle, yanking her from its back and dropping her to the ground. It spun toward her and let out an angry roar, but Annwyl was still screaming and barely heard it this time.

Instead of coming toward her, it began pulling her close, using the tentacle that had hold of her leg.

Annwyl raised her sword to slash it, but she didn't have a chance.

The half-dead horse was back on its feet and *pissed*.

It barreled at the beast; then both went up on their hind legs. The tentacle yanked Annwyl up along with it, but she was able to slash at it this time and landed back on the ground.

She got to her feet, but stopped when Fearghus landed a few feet away from her, followed by his brothers, all in their dragon form.

"Annwyl! We're under—"

She didn't let him finish, simply continued to scream and jumped on the beast's back to get her other sword.

Once she'd yanked it out and dropped down, the half-dead horse caught the beast by its throat and took it to the ground. The horse held it there and Annwyl finally stopped screaming. Panting hard, she came up to its head and raised her swords.

"I curse you, beast," Annwyl snarled out, her rage taking over. "I curse you to return to the never-ending pits of despair and suffering where you shall spend the *rest of eternity!*"

Annwyl slammed her weapons into the beast's eyes. The move unleashed its feral soul, sending her and the half-dead horse hurtling in opposite directions.

When she landed facedown, Annwyl managed to lift her head in time to see the horse gallop off.

"Annwyl!" Fearghus slid his tail under her hips and helped her to her feet. "Are you all right?"

Waving off his concern, she stumbled around until she located her swords and returned them to their sheaths.

"We're under attack. We have to—"

"Follow that horse."

"What?"

"The horse. Follow it." She grabbed his hair, attempting to use it to climb onto his back. But she was still a little dizzy.

"For fuck's sake," Briec growled, using his tail to toss Annwyl onto her mate's back.

"Oy! Watch it!" she complained.

"I'm taking you back to the tower," Fearghus said.

"Either you follow that fucking horse, Fearghus, or I will *lose my mind!*"

"Too late," Briec muttered.

"Fine." Fearghus unleashed his wings and took to the skies; his brothers following. "But no screaming, woman! That noise is terrifying!"

Ainsley was still riding hard, worried that the idiot guard had lied to her, when Kriegszorn galloped past. She knew the horse was heading to her sister, so she let Paladin follow his mother.

Her horse jumped the giant trunk of fallen tree and that's when she saw Gemma standing near the lake at the base of a waterfall. The monk had her hand to her mouth and was calling out for Kriegszorn.

"There you are!" Gemma cheered when she saw the horse, but her smile faded a second later when she caught sight of Ainsley right behind her.

"And where in all the hells have you been?" her sister demanded, turning so she could point at her accusingly, as she liked to do. That's when the arrows slammed into her. If Gemma hadn't moved in that split second, they would have hit her directly in the chest. Instead, they tore into her shoulder and breast.

Ainsley pulled her shield off Paladin's saddle, and jumped from his back before he could stop. She rolled with the fall and came up standing. Covering herself with her shield, she ran to her sister's side, using the shield in time to block the next volley of arrows.

The centaurs who'd been following her separated and disappeared into nearby trees. Except Gruff and his sister. The siblings came to Ainsley and added their shields to hers, creating a wall they hid behind. But the arrows continued to come, raining down from the top of the waterfall.

"Get out of here, Ains!" Gemma gasped out, her hand reaching for her sister in an attempt to push her away.

"If you think," Ainsley warned, "that I'm going to let you die a martyr, so I have to live with Mum and Da reminding me of that shit for the rest of my days, you, Monk, are sadly mistaken. Now shut up and let me figure out how we're going to get out of this alive."

Gruff signaled to his clan, and they made their way toward the waterfall, using the trees as protection.

He was about to tell Ainsley to drag her sister away while he and Briallen used their shields to continue protecting them, but then Kriegszorn ran in front of their shields. Her right side faced their unseen enemies and arrows slammed into her. But the right side was her dead side. The decaying, sometimes-dripping-fluids side. And those arrows did nothing but dissolve in the fluids or hang limply from her skeleton.

"Go!" he ordered Ainsley.

Hilda and Sheva ran in a crouch until they reached Gemma. Hilda took the monk's outstretched hand while Sheva grabbed her cowl. They began dragging her toward the trees, Ainsley using her shield to block the arrows.

"Behind you!" Briallen yelled out, and Ainsley turned and lifted her shield in time to block the axe blow aimed at her head.

A small band of warriors came out of the trees, and Hilda and Sheva released Gemma and faced this new threat.

"Gruff! Go!" Ainsley ordered.

"I'm not leaving you!"

Another enemy's axe joined the first, both now battering Ainsley's shield. "Stop those arrows or we'll all be dead!"

"She's right!" Briallen yanked Gruff by the back of the neck and pushed him away from the royals, then placed two fingers in her mouth and whistled.

The Torn Moon Clan ran from the safety of the trees and began climbing up the sides of the waterfall, their hooves easily managing the moss-covered rocks.

"Gruff, go!" his sister ordered again. And, with a snarl, he followed his clan up the waterfall.

With her shield in front of her, Ainsley shoved her body forward, and the soldiers attacking her stumbled back. She got to her feet and again slammed her shield at the two men.

Ainsley stepped between them and swung her shield one way and then the other, dropping both men to the ground. Starting with the first soldier, she brought down her steel shield on his head. By the time she landed the third blow, his face was crushed and covered in blood.

She spun around to handle the second soldier, but he was already up and swinging his axe at her again. Ainsley lifted up her shield and, when the weapon made contact, she immediately turned it, bringing the soldier in the same direction. She twisted until she'd forced him to his knees and then brought up the bottom of the shield, hitting him under the chin with such force his head snapped back and she heard his jawbone break.

Ainsley dropped her shield and picked up the axe. She briefly watched as the soldier struggled to drag himself away while using both hands to hold his jaw in place.

Gripping the axe handle in both fists, Ainsley kicked the soldier over onto his back and slammed her foot down on his chest to hold him in place. She hoisted the weapon above her head and swiftly brought it down on his skull. The blade cut past bone and cartilage until finally coming to a halt at the soldier's broken jaw.

Ainsley released the axe and pulled her bow from behind her back. She nocked an arrow and turned to Sheva first. But her friend was in the middle of cutting down two soldiers with her sword. Pivoting to her right, Ainsley aimed her bow again.

Hilda had a soldier by the throat, using her steel walking stick to choke the life from him.

With her friends not needing her, Ainsley now aimed her weapon up at the waterfall. The centaurs had just reached the top. She heard orders shouted and the clash of steel. Human soldiers began falling over the waterfall. Some without heads or cut in half.

Ainsley moved over to a nearby tall tree. She slung her bow over her shoulder and started to climb, but she'd barely gotten five feet off the ground when Sheva called to her.

"Ainsley! Look!"

Gripping the trunk with her legs, Ainsley leaned back and watched as the centaurs began jumping off the top of the waterfall and into the lake below.

Gruff heard it. Felt it. The very air changing. As if it was being sucked out and forced back in, again and again.

He snapped the neck of the soldier in his hand and tugged his battle-axe out of another's belly before he turned his gaze to the skies. Because he now understood what was happening.

Wings. Giant wings were approaching.

"*The water!*" Gruff yelled at his clan. "Now!" On his order, the centaurs ran to the edge of the waterfall, knocking down and sometimes trampling the human soldiers in their way. Once they reached the edge, they shifted to human and dove into the lake.

When Gruff and his sister jumped from the edge of the waterfall and didn't immediately swim back to the surface, Ainsley scrambled back down the tree and over to her sister.

"What are you doing?" Gemma demanded.

"Shut up. Sheva! Hilda!" Ainsley called out before grabbing her sister's arm, ignoring her screams of pain, and dragging her toward the forest. The monk and nun quickly joined her and helped get her sibling behind a wide tree. They huddled together, using their bodies to protect Gemma as best they could.

She knew it wasn't much, especially when those dragon wings came into sight. But then Kriegszorn ran in front of the tree they were behind and, this time, the half-dead horse's offspring joined her.

Seconds later, bright orange dragon fire exploded from above, engulfing the land around them. Ainsley heard screams from the top of the waterfall, but they were quickly silenced. Nothing that wasn't in water or safely out of the line of literal fire was able to survive such an attack.

Except, of course, Kriegszorn and her offspring. They were just fine.

\* \* \*

Laila trotted up to Keeley's side. With dragons waiting to strike on either side of Beatrix's army; Keeley, her own army, and the centaurs moved forward. Laila on her left. Caid and Quinn on her right.

She took her hammer off her back; swung it a few times. She'd kill them all. All these men . . .

"Halt!" she called out, and her generals yelled her command down the line. Her army halted and she glanced at Laila to make sure she wasn't seeing something that wasn't really there. Perhaps she was imagining all this. Perhaps her mind had finally snapped.

But the expression on Laila's face told Keeley she was not imagining anything. What she saw was very real and very horrifying.

It was an army. A very large army. But they weren't human. Instead, she was staring down a regiment of demons.

Demons.

Keeley didn't know how to fight actual demons. Even her demon wolves weren't standing with her. She should have known then that something was very wrong. They were always by her side during battle because they got to eat. But, she guessed, they didn't want to eat their own.

That didn't seem right, though. Because her demon wolves ate everything. They were not finicky.

So then what was stopping them from being here? Even if it was just to watch the carnage.

There seemed to be eight demon commanders at the front of the army. Their armor and colors were different from the others. Moving together, like they were one thing rather than eight separate things, the demons raised their big battle-axes adorned with human skulls and opened their fang-filled maws to unleash the command to attack.

But then dragon wings passed low over them. Keeley was going to call out a warning about the enemy's dragon-ready weapons. But then the wings were gone and something else fell from the sky, landing between Keeley's army and the demons in a tall burst of dirt that briefly hid it. Even the demons waited to see.

As the dirt cleared, Annwyl the Bloody stood tall, a sword in each hand.

The demon ranks immediately reacted to her presence, baring their fangs and roaring in warning. But they kept their lines.

The commanders, however, showed nothing but amusement.

The one on the far right charged first, coming right at Annwyl. A second later, the one in the middle also charged.

She moved so fast, Keeley didn't really see anything until a severed head rolled to a stop several feet away from her. Another head rolled off, but it was still attached to half of the body.

The remaining commanders paused in their attack. And Annwyl glared back at them until, out of the depths of some unknown hell that only Annwyl knew, the foreign queen let out a scream that had the centaurs beside Keeley nervously slamming down their hooves. If they'd been actual horses, they would have run. And she wouldn't have blamed them.

Annwyl suddenly bolted toward enemy lines, screaming the entire way. She started slashing her sword, cutting demons in half and quarters. The commanders fought back, but Keeley didn't know why. Because Annwyl just kept going. She didn't stop. Keeley wasn't sure the woman *could* stop.

In seconds, she'd decimated the entire army command and now turned her attention to the remaining demons.

All Keeley heard was, "Run!" And they were running. All two thousand demon soldiers were running, slipping and jumping into open portals and mystical doorways. They battled each other to get away from the crazed monarch, pushing the slower ones aside or cutting leg tendons so they had time to escape while their cohorts screamed on the ground.

The ones Annwyl reached, she killed. Without question. Without mercy.

She chased them all until they were either dead or gone.

But she was still screaming. Standing in the middle of that now-open battlefield, Annwyl the Bloody continued to scream and scream and scream.

Until Fearghus the Destroyer landed a few yards away and called her name.

"Annwyl. *Annwyl.*"

Panting but silent now, she looked at her mate.

"You forgot," the black dragon said, motioning toward the trees behind which the demon army had stood. "Beatrix's men. They can't open doorways, and it seems no one is opening portals for them."

Annwyl's head snapped forward, her gaze locked on the thick woods where a small squad had been hiding. The plan had probably been for them to report back to Beatrix about the outcome. Or to steal one of Keeley's siblings if they had the chance.

"*Runnnn!*" came a hysterical scream from the woods, and the trees began to move as the small group made a desperate and useless run for it.

Useless, because Annwyl was right behind them. And she was screaming again.

Keeley would have nightmares about that scream. But at least she'd be alive to tell the tale of the crazed warrior queen with the horrible, crazed scream.

Beatrix's men would not be able to say the same.

# CHAPTER 29

Quinn shoved a tankard of very hard ale into his mate's hand, and she gulped down several mouthfuls before Sarff approached her. He took the empty tankard back and handed it to Caid. Then Quinn took Gemma's hand and she nodded at Sarff.

The old witch gripped the arrow shafts sticking out of Gemma's shoulder and breast. But then he saw Morfyd enter the main hall and yelped, "Wait!"

Sarff released her hold and took a step back.

"Princess Morfyd." He nodded at the She-dragon in human form. "You're a healer, yes?"

"I am."

"So am I," Sarff said.

"You cut off Ainsley's finger."

"Not all of it! Show him Ains!"

Ainsley, sitting on a table against the wall with that idiot Gruffyn standing next to her, held up her maimed hand.

"See?" Sarff insisted. "Most of it's still there. Besides, this ain't a big deal. Just need to push the arrows through so the head comes out her back and we break it from there."

"I thought monks liked pain," Ainsley volunteered.

"Shut up!" Gemma barked.

Quinn looked at Morfyd. "Please?"

"Fine!" Sarff snarled. "Hope she doesn't sneeze and set your girl on fire, Quinn of the Scarred Earth Clan."

Morfyd walked over to the big dining table where Gemma was

326 • *G. A. Aiken*

sitting, still holding Quinn's hand. The dragonwitch took a brief moment to wash her hands in the big bowl of water someone had put out.

"Ohhhh, fancy!" Sarff accused. "Washes her hands, does she?"

"You didn't wash your hands before you cut off my finger?"

"Stop your whining! You're alive, ain't ya?"

Morfyd took a cotton cloth from Isadora and dried her hands. She moved in front of Gemma and smiled warmly at her.

"Ready?"

Gemma nodded.

"Okay, on three. One. Two—"

The She-dragon grabbed the arrow shafts and, with no mercy, shoved.

Gemma let out a pain-filled scream between clenched teeth.

"*You evil bitch!*" she accused.

"Did you think I was going to do something different?" the dragonwitch asked.

"Ha!" an exuberant Sarff cheered. "Told you, ya daffy bastard."

"That's *Prince* Daffy Bastard to you, ancient female," Quinn shot back.

Ainsley moved over a bit so Keeley could sit on the table beside her. She looked exhausted and ready for a good sleep, but she knew her sister well enough to know she was waiting for information to come back from her commanders to be sure all her subjects, in town and out, were safe.

Silently, they watched Princess Morfyd use typical healing techniques combined with magicks to stop Gemma's bleeding and begin the healing of the internal damage to her body. Finally, she put Gemma to sleep, laying her carefully back on the table.

"Leave her here for the night. I'll stay with her to make sure there's no fever."

"There won't be," Sarff said. "Nice work, dragon."

"Thank you, centaur."

The front doors, which were closed for once, were pushed open and a blood-drenched Annwyl the Bloody walked into the main hall. Behind her were Prince Fearghus, Prince Gwenvael, Prince Briec, and, for some strange reason, Master General Ragna.

Annwyl poured herself a chalice of fresh water, draining it in one gulp. Seemingly satisfied, she faced them. And smiled.

Which Ainsley just found off-putting.

The foreign royal glanced at Gemma. "How's she doing?"

"She'll survive," Morfyd replied. "Anything I need to worry about with you?"

"No."

Morfyd studied Annwyl. "You're lying."

"I'm fine."

"You're going to get a fever if you don't treat any wounds you may have."

"Let it go already!" Annwyl looked at Keeley, and Ainsley felt her sister tense up beside her. "Good work today, Queen Keeley."

"Thank you, Queen Annwyl. Although I didn't really have to do anything. The"—she cleared her throat—"demons seemed ready to run as soon as you appeared."

"Yeah. I do have a bit of a reputation where they're from."

"You mean one of the hells?"

"That battalion represented more than just one or two of the hells, and I guess they'd all heard about me."

"Uh-huh."

"Rumor is I'm not allowed back into any of the hells, but it wasn't pleasant when I went there, so that doesn't really bother me."

"Good. That's good."

She headed toward the bedrooms on the upper floors. "Let me know if you need anything else."

"Will do!"

Annwyl abruptly spun around and glowered at Ragna, who'd just been standing behind her without saying anything.

"Is there something you want?" Annwyl growled at the monk.

Smiling, Ragna replied, "Just your love and admiration and permission for me to worship you as I do all war gods."

Sheva and Hilda both snorted a laugh, but cut it off when the royal looked at them.

"I'm going to walk away now," Annwyl told Ragna. "I don't want to see you again before I leave. Or I'll show you exactly why those demons were scared of me."

She started up the stairs, covered in the blood of her enemies, having just threatened a war monk—the most feared religious warriors in their territory. And she'd done it with an ease that belied the fact she'd just recently battled thousands of demons and human soldiers. The Mad Queen suddenly noticed that the gentle and kind Morfyd was behind her. The dragonwitch held a small white jar in her hand and when she held it up for Annwyl to see, the mighty queen squealed, "Fuck no!" and ran up the stairs.

Morfyd followed right behind, screaming, "Get back here, you mad cow!"

"Get away from me with that shit, Morfyd!"

"I'm trying to help you!"

"Fuck off!"

They disappeared down a hallway, yelling at each other the entire way.

When she heard one of the bedroom doors slam shut, muffling the arguing, Keeley looked over at Lord Bram. But before she could say anything, he promised, "We'll be leaving in the next day or two."

"Not that there's any rush," Keeley lied.

"Communications have once again opened up between blood relations. I'm sure all is back to normal. At least for us."

"Are you sure?" Keeley felt the need to ask. "I want to make sure Queen Rhiannon is—"

Keeley's next words were cut off as a stretching, yawning Rhiannon appeared at the top of the stairs.

"Morning all!"

"It's almost evening, Mum," one of her sons drily noted.

The dragonwitch queen grinned. "So . . . what have I missed?"

There was no feast that night. One reason was that a healing Gemma was stretched out on the dining table. Seemed tacky to eat with her lying there.

Everyone was also exhausted. Even the dragons, who never really got a chance to fight at all. Instead, everyone ate in their room and waited for the long day to end.

There were no boar ribs, but the queen mother promised them to Ainsley for the next day once she found out she'd saved Gemma's life.

"I told you that you loved your sister!" the blacksmith reminded her daughter. But Ainsley simply rolled her eyes and headed up the stairs, briefly stopping when Isadora shoved the youngest Farmerson-Smythe child into her mother's arms and stomped away.

"I am done babysitting!" she yelled over her shoulder before disappearing into the back of the main hall.

Now Gruff was stretched out on Ainsley's bed with Ainsley cuddled up right next to him. He thought she was asleep until she said, "Where's my bird?"

"Your father put it somewhere safe. I think he was afraid Gemma or Keeley might kill it."

"Still?"

"It's apparently tripled in size. And nearly tore the eyes out of one of the royal guards."

"I need to see him."

"Right now?"

"Fuck no," she muttered, burrowing in closer to his side. "I can see him in the morning. Come," she said when she heard a knock at the door.

Var leaned in. "You all right?" he asked.

"Fine. You?"

"I didn't fight. Ghleanna had me stay with Uncle Bram until it was over."

"Don't get used to that."

"I know. Your sister the war monk is . . . quite determined. I just spent some time with her religious friends. The war priests. The vestal virgins. The battle witches. Something called a truce vicar. On and on."

"And?"

"They've found some disturbing things in Queen Keeley's territories. Something you should look into."

"If you think I'm getting my ass off this bed—"

"Not now. Tomorrow," Var said.

"What?"

"Fine. We'll *discuss* it tomorrow. Is that better?"

"But Lord Broadwils—"

The young royal quickly waved that off. "When the day went . . .

330 • *G. A. Aiken*

as it went . . . I sent Ghleanna and some of my cousins to deal with Lord Broadwils. So don't worry about that."

"Good. Now get out."

And he did. Without complaint or appearing hurt.

"How often does someone tell that boy to get out of a room?" Gruff asked.

Ainsley sat up, leaving Gruff's side cold and lonely.

"After having met his father and uncles, I'm guessing a lot."

To Gruff's delight, Ainsley slipped onto his lap, facing him. She leaned in and smiled.

"Really?" he asked, his cock already hard under his kilt. "You sure you're up for it?"

"It'll help us sleep." She leaned down to give him a kiss, but the next Gruff knew, Ainsley's face was buried against his neck and her body had gone limp.

Chuckling, he wrapped his arms around her and held her tight.

"I love you, crazy royal," he whispered against her ear.

"Love you too," she muttered against his shoulder. Then she was snoring, and Gruff had never been happier.

# EPILOGUE

Bercelak the Great—also called Bercelak the Vengeful, Dragon-warrior Leader, Queen's Champion, Consort to the Dragon Queen, Dragonwarrior Supreme of the Old Guard, and Supreme Commander of the Dragon Queen's Armies—led his army over the expansive Amichai Mountains. His anger kept him moving without thought of his army's need for food or rest. He cared about nothing at this point. Only Rhiannon mattered.

Because those bastards had his queen, and he would do whatever was necessary to get her back and crush anyone who had tried to destroy—

*Bercelak!* rang out in his head.

*Rhiannon?*

*Hello.*

She sounded so casual.

*Where the battle fuck are you?*

*Home.*

Bercelak came to a complete stop, his wings keeping him aloft over the Amichai Mountains.

*What now?*

*Yeah. Sorry. Bram reminded me to contact you right away to let you know, but my mind wandered, and things came up, and—*

*Rhiannon?*

*Yes?*

*Have the chains ready for when I get home.*

*But—*

*Don't want to hear it.*

He cut off the contact by shoving her out of his mind—a skill he'd had to learn so she didn't interrupt him in the middle of battle—and turned in the air to face his army.

"We're heading back!" he announced. "Now!"

"She's fine, isn't she?" one of his sisters demanded.

"I don't want to talk about it."

"We're out here for nothing!"

"We're out here because I ordered it. Now turn around and—"

Bercelak heard the rumble and immediately looked down at the mountain beneath him. Centaurs had been migrating when their army first appeared on the horizon. And at the first sight of them, there were screams and orders for everyone to run. To take shelter.

That turned out to be a good thing. A very good thing. Because the mountain was cracking open in the middle and crumbling. Crumbling like an anthill some human child hit with their foot. It was as if the entire thing was caving in from the bottom up.

"Bercelak?" one of his brothers called out.

"Move!" he yelled. "Go!" He lifted his wings and dove toward the mountains and the screaming, running centaurs. "Get as many as you can to safety! Do whatever you can!"

Bercelak swooped low and used his tail and front claws to scoop up the centaurs and put them on his back or hold them in his arms.

"Hold on!" he ordered, but before he took off again, he saw them. Standing miles away from the mountain, simply watching their handywork.

He saw Beatrix's colors streaming from spears and, once the mountain started to fall apart, the soldiers turned around and headed away. Away from the carnage they'd caused, all in the name of Queen Beatrix. All so she could now invade his mate's territory whenever she felt ready.

An act of war if he'd ever seen one. And Bercelak would make sure that bitch queen Beatrix regretted every gods-damn second of it.